A Ricepaper

Airplane

INTERSECTIONS

Asian and Pacific American
Transcultural Studies

Russell C. Leong
General Editor

University
of Hawai'i
Press
Honolulu

in association
with UCLA
Asian American
Studies Center
Los Angeles

A Ricepaper Airplane

Gary Pak

To Mom and Pop,
and my aunties and uncles
for giving me the seed for this story.

To Merle and the children
for letting me plant the seed,
and watering it during the times I neglected it,
and providing it with sunshine on my cloudy days.

© 1998 *University of Hawai'i Press*
All rights reserved
Printed in the United States of America
03 02 01 00 99 98   5 4 3 2 1

Library of Congress
Cataloging-in-Publication Data

Pak, Gary, 1952–
A ricepaper airplane : a novel / by Gary Pak.
p.   cm. — (Intersections)
ISBN 0–8248–1301–4 (paper : alk. paper)
I. Chinese Americans—Hawaii—Fiction.
I. Title. II. Series: Intersections (Honolulu, Hawaii)
PS3566.A39R53 1998
813'.54—dc21   97–50407
                                           CIP

University of Hawai'i Press books are printed on acid-free
paper and meet the guidelines for permanence and
durability of the Council on Library Resources

Design by Barbara Pope Book Design

*Divergence between dreams and reality
causes no harm if only the person dreaming
believes seriously in his dream. . . .
If there is some connection
between dreams and life
then all is well.*

LENIN

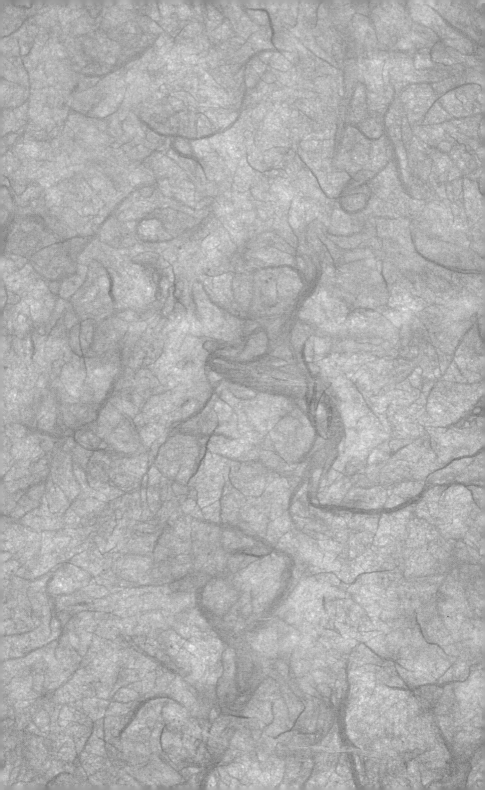

A Journey of Dreams,

to the Land of Tigers

and Revolution

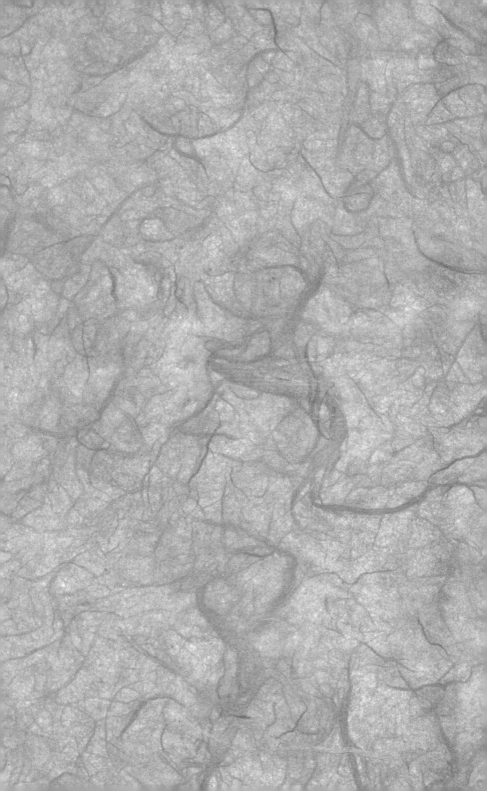

"I dunno, but dis River Street no look like da River Street I used to know."

Uncle Sung Wha is daydreaming again.

Probably he's thinking about River Street in Chinatown, the street that ran alongside the stagnant canal, smelly like a cesspool, which once used to be filled with flashing schools of *āhole-hole* and fat mullet, and juicy crabs. I used to fish and crab there with Uncle a long time ago.

Summer is ending and classes will be starting in a couple of weeks. This morning I called the school and asked my friend Joe Leong, the principal, if it was all right to take a leave of absence, without pay. He told me that it was too late, that I should have thought about it earlier, that three other teachers weren't coming back, and that right now he wasn't sure if he would have enough teachers for the start of school. I asked him again, banking on our long-term friendship, if it were possible to take leave, that it was kind of a family emergency. There was silence on his side of the line. I could hear one of the secretaries tittering in the background. I could tell that he was kind of pissed. I explained that there was a problem in the family, that my uncle, who was like a father to me, was dying, that it was important for me to be with him by his bedside. It was an emergency. "Yeah, all right," he finally let out. Before we hung up, he told me to come to the office to fill out the necessary papers.

For days now, Uncle has been in a semi-conscious state. Sometimes he struggles to open his eyes, calls my name weakly, heaves out a string of words, then falls back to sleep, mumbling to himself. Sometimes he continues on, string after string of words, the start of another journey into the near or far past, or both. Uncle, then, is like a book. Every day with him is like reading—or hearing—another chapter of an adventure story. And it's hard to believe all that I'm hearing. I can't believe that Uncle was all of these things: the revolutionary in China, the Korean patriot, the Communist, the aviator. What else is he? What more is there to tell?

But I look forward to coming to his hospital room and listening to these fantastic stories. At first, the hospital smells of vomit and excrement and disinfectant repulsed me. But now they don't bother me, they don't seem that bad. I've gotten used to the smell. The minute I enter Uncle's room, I forget these bad smells.

"You know, Yong Gil, befo' time, nevah had all dese rundown-kine buildings. All dese building ovah here, all brand new. Fresh paint. Fresh lumber. Fresh smells. *'Ono* da smells, da food. And da faces of da people, all fresh and clean and smooth.

"Dey wen burn down Chinatown long-long time ago 'cause dey think had bubonic plague. Dey think da rats from all da boats wen bring 'em in. Racist assholes, fucking haoles, dey think da *Pākēs* da rats. Dis long-long time befo' you born. Den aftah dat, dey rebuild da town, 'round 'A'ala Park side. All da buildings brand new. Was one nice place go. When you say you going *holoholo* downtown, you *hemo* yo' work clothes, you dress up wit' all yo' nice clothes, da kine Sunday clothes special.

"Me, I had one nice wool black pants, one tailor in China-town wen make 'em fo' me. And I had one nice, long-sleeve silk shirt my Filipino friend give me. Us in dis strike togethah, yeah, him and me—1928? '29?—him and me, brothah-brothah."

He raises a thin arm that is weighted with IV tubes and brings his index and middle fingers together.

"My friend name, José, give dis shirt to me. Dey call *barong tagalog*, or something like dat."

"Yo' papa nevah tol' you what him did, him first come Hawai'i? I tell you, yo' papa one smart-smart man, re-e-eal *aka-mai*, yo' papa. Between him and me, he mo' smart. He tol' me dis story when us live up da homestead. You know, yo' papa one real proud man. Every time him tell me dis story when us drink da pine swipe. Always same-same story."

The bright white light flashes on the wide screen. Then THE News of the World, according to AMERICA, the world according to the U. S. of A. Send all over the world. Make A. Then the cigarette cowboy come in the picture and take the pretty girl pretty haole girl pretty girl pretty girl blonde hair blue blue eyes blue eyes blonde hair blonde bluehair eyes eyes eyesblonde eyes hair hair blonde hairy blue blue blue hairy eyes-eys galloping away to Never-Never-Land or the EXOTIC Hawaiian sunset or someplace anyplace paradise—Yes! Yes! Isn't Hawai'i this paradise our paradise Puritanic Paradises Regained once thought they had lost, now reclaimed—as God given?—take take reclaimed from natives—what do they know?—outstretched brown hands of natives brown on white, those Hollywood people think natives like only touch her white breasts and pink nips and fuck her hairy smelly white cunt, anemic calf's liver, brah, yeah das *the only thing on the minds of those darkies and other shadies, they would dump their own kind to have a touch a scent a lick of white meat,* so they kiss OUR women and give us pictures of theirs to wack off on. Meet THE white. Hollywood.

Haolewood.

Burn the wood.

US fock you.

"Sometimes him he get sad, yo' papa. Sometimes him get all angry, worked up like hell. Da next day him always regret telling me da story. Aftah 'while I used to tell him, no tell me da story, I hear 'em how many times already. But still he tell 'em to me. Him, he no listen. He no take my advise. He jus' like get 'em off his chest, I think.

"Anyway, when yo' papa first come Hawai'i, him work fo' da sugah plantation, Maui. Had one nada Korean man, one old-old man, I dunno why he come here, I think da old man wen *maké* later on. But dis old man, he look at yo' papa and say to him, 'No spend da rest of yo' life digging da field fo' haole man. You smart boy, Eung Whan. Smart-smart boy. Here, me give you dis money me go save. You *hele* Honolulu, go *hele* big city and go study Korean school ovah dere. You go dere go be smart man, no work wit' yo' hands.'

"Da old Korean man was thinking 'bout dis school jus' wen open up, one school jus' fo' Korean immigrants. You know where da state capitol is, da cornah King and . . . and . . . and Punchbowl? Yeah-yeah, Punchbowl Street—you know where dis I stay talking 'bout? Okay, was right ovah dere, right by da cornah, I think da *mauka* kokohead cornah. Someplace 'round dere. Had one church ovah dere, one Korean church, and dey wen build one school right on same piece land. Dey teach English, but mostly dey teach Korean and 'rithmetic, dat kine subjects.

"So dis old man give yo' papa some *kālā*, I dunno how much, but must be big *kālā* dem days. Was fo' yo' papa pay tuition and fo' room and board. So yo' papa catch da barge *hele* Honolulu. So yo' papa had all dis *kālā* in his pocket and come to Honolulu, and nevah in his life he go one big city befo'. I think his *maka*, I think, wen pop open. Him, he see dese big-big buildings, tall-tall buildings, I think dose days Aloha Tower was da biggest, was only ten stories, but still yet da sonavabitch big fo' dose days.

"And den yo' papa tell me he go show, go one movie house, see one motion picture. You gotta remembah, Yong Gil, dose days nobody know what one show was. YouknowwhatImean? You look up one wall and you see dis picture screen, picture moving and flat—ho! You dunno what is what, what expect. Was something else. So yo' papa was so . . . amaze, yeah, das da word . . . he so amaze 'cause he nevah see anything like dis befo'. So instead go school, fo' one whole month all yo' papa go do was go show every day. Every day. I no joke you. Him nevah tell you dis story? Did? Den, youknowwhatImeanden?

"So every day he go show. He spend all da money da old

man give him supposed to be fo' him go school. But latah, da old man find out what yo' papa doing. He send fo' yo' papa *hele* back Maui. Ho! I glad I not dere hear da old man raise hell at yo' papa."

"You remembah In Ja Kang, dat radical lady, da one all da menfolks in da camp used to be scared of?"

Uncle Sung Wha is beginning another story.

"You know, da one her son and you was good-good friends grammah school days? Yo' friend, him da one used to come ovah da house allatime an' I used to take you folks fishing down da *Pākē* man fishpond Waikīkī, waaay befo' all da hotels wen build up ovah dere. You no remembah him?"

I nod my head. But I'm not sure. I glance around the bare hospital room, out the doorway. Everything's a pale porcelain blue or chrome-shiny. A short, plump Filipino nurse, bluesmocked, passes by without looking in, her eyes unfocused like she's on autopilot.

You know, nowadays my mind is not as sharp as it was before.

"His name, Yong Gil, whas his name?" Uncle coughs, his whole body thrown into the cough. He leans over the side of the bed, the side away from me, gasping, then turns toward me and points to the pan on the table across the room. *"Pā kini! Pā kini!"* he barely says, his throat thick with phlegm.

I hurry over, take the bedpan, and give it to Uncle, who spits out a thick bubbly discharge. I feel queasy, my mouth waters in disgust. I look away, but that sight stays in my mind.

Uncle's hand clutching the bed sheet: a wrinkled and thin hand calloused thick blue veins gnarled sea-washed *ogo*

with bamboo rake from wooden pier   planks weatherworn   raised grains of wood   Uncle reaches out   his extended arm   splayed slats of bamboo   then pulls through the sea   to the bottom   the coral the rocks the scurrying crabs   the darting 'o'opu disturbed: ogo lifted from the ocean   can see weight of the water   straining

cords in Uncle's forearms   but the smile: Eh Yong Gil . . . look!
mound of dripping ogo like an untamed mane of a summer's girl
caught in rake's long fangs   lifted and swept across to clear the sky

brown aged spots all over skin bones arm.

I regard my hands, my arms.

Uncle wipes his lips with the border of the bed sheet.

"Ho . . . no mattah how much I try," he grumbles, "no mattah how much I try, no can unclog da lungs." Uncle clears his throat. "But you remembah da boy?" he asks, looking at me with eyes sun-faded hazel.

Must've been a good thirty, maybe forty years, since I last saw In Ja Kang's son. My friend. Cannot remember his name. 1944. We went into the service together. Boot camp was the last time I saw him. Then we got stationed in different places. But what was his name? Forgot . . . been so long. What was his name? Harold? Howard Kang? George? Joseph Kang? James Kang?

James. James Kang. Jimmy Kang.

And he had a beautiful sister. Naomi. Naomi Kang. Pretty-pretty. One year older than us. I used to make excuse go over Jimmy's house, the second to the last house down that row of green plantation worker cottages. Just to be near her. So I could take side-eyed looks at her. I used to say to Jimmy: I no like go my house, my older brother and sister going bother me, make me work, I no like go home right away. If I told him the real reason I wanted to be at his house, now that would've been embarrassing. He would've kidded me to death.

"You listening to me, Yong Gil?"

I nod my head. "Yeah-yeah, his name is Jimmy. Jimmy Kang."

"No-no. Whas his sistah's name? His sistah's name. You know, da one she wen become one college professor."

College professor. Scholarship at the U. When I came back from the service she was already married to one haole she met at the university. Dr. Naomi Wittenburg. Or something like that.

"Naomi," I say. "Naomi Kang."

"Yeah. You get one good memory, Yong Gil."

Every day after school we used to follow her home, Jimmy and me. Her hair was long, black, and braided. Jimmy and I used to sneak up from behind and pull her hair. I used to like the feel of her hair. Tried smelling it once. Smelled like mint and flowers. Can't forget the smell.

"You know, dat wahine, her was one tough fightah," Uncle says.

"Who?"

"In Ja Kang."

Uncle's eyes light up. Something devilish in them eyes.

"You know, I going tell you one secret," he whispers to me. "No tell nobody."

He glances around the room to make sure no one is listening.

The bed next to his has been empty for the past three days. There was an old Japanese man in it. Cancer of the stomach. The doctors told him he could go back home. I saw him the day he left, his face gray and pointless. His daughter came to pick him up; her eyes spoke no words, her cheeks were full but colorless, as if infected by her father's suffering. He said good-bye with a silent nod, his eyes morosely heavy, as if in final agreement to his fate, his daughter's patient tugging persuading him out of the hospital room.

"If me not marry already, me marry her." Uncle shakes his head. "Yeah, me marry her."

"Marry who?"

"In Ja Kang."

I would have married Naomi. Sonovabitch. Used to spy on her when I was at her house. While she was cooking rice or making underpants with rice bags. I knew what she was doing, though I don't think she knew I did. My sister Chung Hee used to make her panties out of empty rice bags, then soaked them in harsh bleach to soften them.

Checking my watch. Twenty-three past ten. A.M. Time to go? Hate coming to hospitals. Disinfectant smell. Dead flat blue color. Oh, it's not that bad, I have to remind myself again. Uncle is bringing me back. Needs the company. Boy, how Uncle aged fast. Look at him. All shriveled up. His body collapsing into the bed. He was so healthy a little while ago. Been that long already? Twenty, thirty years? Sonavabitch. Time coming and going. Fast. He looks terrible, his eyes filmed with *maka piapia*. He doesn't look like the Uncle Sung Wha I knew. The man with the tiger's heart.

"She get hard head, dat wahine. I think maybe her hard head wen make her husband go *maké*-die-dead." Uncle laughs. Then another fit of coughs. He leans over the side and spits into the bedpan. Settles back in bed and wipes his mouth on the bed sheet again, his eyes moistened from the ordeal. "Me marry her if me not marry already," he continues. "She marry one old man. One old-old man, white-white hair and everything. And her only young girl den when she get married. One picture bride. I tol' you dat story?" I tell him, "No."

She had very long black hair, falling like a midnight waterfall down her shoulders. But when she walked, her hair swayed side to side like the carefree tail of a horse. I used to dream of marrying her. I'd buy her anything she wanted, I'd tell myself. She wouldn't have to wear rice-bag panties ever again.

I can see her face. Soft. Round. Eyes a deep brown.

"You see, she was from P'ih-yon. Da women dere, dey get real hard head. Dey talk what in dey minds."

But she got married. To one haole. When I returned home from the war, Chung Hee told me that Naomi won a scholarship to the U. There she met the haole and ended up marrying him. This old fut haole who taught there. I was sad. And angry. More angry than sad. One haole. The second night back home, the night I was told the bad news, me and a friend who was in the service with me—one local Kalihi boy, a Hawaiian named Solomon Kahalewai, we used to call him "Blackie"—went out on the town and got drunk. Blackie lectured me all night: "Eh, Yobo, forget 'bout her. You one handsome Yobo, get so much *kūmū* in

da ocean you gotta fight 'em off wit' yo' *hauna* kimchee breath."
Next day I was already forgetting her. But still the pain.
"Dey own men from da village no like marry dem. Das how
hardhead dem. If da men was looking fo' wife, dey go one nada
village and marry da wahine dere. But funny, you know, when
dey bring da wahine from nada village back to dey own village,
somehow da outside wahine get influence by all da village
wahine. Little while, da wahine from da ada village get all hardhead, too. And sharp mouth. Das why when da Japanees wen
take ovah da village, dey nevah go aftah da menfolks, dey went
aftah da wahines. Dey was da ones doing all da speeches, organizing, rousing up da people.

"And das why dem wahines had to split from da village.
Plenny wen go Japan, plenny mo' wen come Hawai'i. But dey
had to have sponsah fo' bring 'em here, dey no had money. So
plenny was picture brides. In Ja Kang send her picture and her
husband-to-be wen send his picture back Korea. But only thing,
he send one picture of one young man, not his real picture
'cause he know if one wahine see how old fut him, she no come
be his wife. Yo' mama one picture bride, too. She come here,
marry my cousin, yo' papa. Yo' mothah good luck, but. Yo'
papa good-lookin' buggah. Good looks run in da family."
Uncle laughs. "Yo' mama was from P'ih-yon, too. Das why yo'
papa had hard time."

The sun's coming out, but it doesn't know if it wants to
shine in your window or not, Uncle. Mary's flowers by the window. Still fresh from the day before yesterday. I told her Uncle
doesn't like flowers, but she insisted; she never listens to me.
That's my wife for you. That's why the flowers are by the window and not next to him. At least the flowers can see outside.

"Da boy, yo' friend, whas his name again?"

"Jimmy," I say. "Jimmy Kang."

"Yeah-yeah. So what him doing now? Where him stay living?"

"I dunno, Uncle, was long time ago. I never see him since
the war. Was long time ago." I shake my head to make my point.

Look at his eyes. So weak. The last time he coughed his eyes fluttered. Then he stared at the ceiling for too long a moment without moving. Chrissakes, I thought he died. Can't believe how old he got all of a sudden. It seemed like yesterday that he and my older brother and I were hunting for doves up by Kolekole Pass, Kunia homestead. Has it been that long ago?

Grunting, Uncle turns to his side and reaches for a half-filled glass of water on the nightstand. I ask him if he needs help, but he doesn't answer. Hardheaded buggah. Never mind the women of P'ih-yon.

I go over to the other side of the bed and offer him the water. He sits up, takes the tumbler and sips it, then gulps the rest down in one quivering swallow. He gives the empty glass to me, and I set it down on the nightstand next to an old faded photograph of a young Korean woman.

It's a picture of Auntie. *Ajumoni.* Uncle's wife. I never met her. Is she still alive? Very young when they took that picture. And pretty. She was eighteen. Maybe nineteen. Hard to say. Those days they looked more mature. She could've been fourteen or fifteen, who knows. She's holding a small Korean flag. Looks like it would be impossible to wrestle it from her hand. And the serious face of a patriot, ready to lay down her life for the cause: freeing the Motherland. That's what Uncle told me once. "If you think me radical, den you dunno Auntie. You bettah believe it!" And she was from P'ih-yon, too, that hardheaded, outspoken province where my mother was from. And my father. And Uncle.

"You know dat wahine, her one real fightah."

"Who?"

"In Ja. In Ja Kang."

"Oh." I nod my head. I glance at the photograph and give *Ajumoni* an apology with a twitch of my eye.

"Everybody used to be scared her wen she talk. I remembah da old Korean meeting house, King Street. You was too small fo' remembah. Ho! Had one big pow-wow ovah dere, fireworks and everything! Da Kook Min Hur was meeting to figgah out what to do when Syngman Rhee come into town. Dat no good sonavabitch. No good traitah. Ass kissah. Den In Ja Kang stand and start talking her mind. Ho! Da kine fire words coming outta her mouth!

"But dis meeting too had membahs of Tongjihoe, dis rival organization. Dey used to be supportahs of Syngman Rhee. Ass kissahs. Ho! Had big fight dat day. Me, I sitting by da door when dis man Kim come running inside from da street. He go straight fo' In Ja. She nevah see him coming and da buggah grab her hair and start twisting her arm. Ho! Den everybody get into da fight, throwing chairs and books and whatnot, Kook Min Hur membahs fighting Tongjihoe.

"And den, aftah everything quiet down, I see In Ja Kang lying on da ground wit' blood all ovah her head. Da friggin' buggah Kim wen pull out one clump her hair. Friggin' coward. He nevah like stay 'round and face da heat. And all dem ada sonavabitch Tongjihoe membahs, dey take off. All one bunch cowards.

"But you know something? All dis time da wahine, wit' all dis blood running down her head, she nevah say one word or cry or complain. Dat woman one tough wahine, one real tough wahine.

"You know, Yong Gil, if me nevah marry already," Uncle says, "me marry her."

I remember the first time I came to visit him at the hospital. He was so happy to see me. He called me his favorite nephew. I knew he said that to each of my five brothers. Still, I believe him.

His eyes drooping. Deep lines on his gray face like the face of a mountain I know I have seen. Maybe Kumgangsan, those mountains I have seen so well through Papa's and Mama's and Uncle's eyes.

With a weak wave of his hand, Uncle motions me to leave. That story about In Ja Kang must've weakened him. He opens his glassy eyes for a moment, those sun-soaked irises asking me to come back. I nod my head, and he closes his eyes and falls into instant slumber.

It was a few months ago when my oldest sister, whom I had not heard from or seen for three years even though we live only across town from each other, phoned me late in the night, informing me in a voice with less concern than caution that Uncle Sung Wha was in the hospital. The police found him collapsed on the side of the freeway. What he was doing there nobody knew. Uncle has done strange things, some people thinking he's *pupule*. The next night I visited him at the hospital. Later, a doctor told me that he had at the most—if he was lucky—another month to live. Bleeding ulcers. Lung cancer. Shot kidneys. The works. I decided not to teach the summer term and instead spend the time with Uncle.

It isn't pleasant coming to the hospital every day, the smell of disinfectant and death everywhere. But when he starts telling his stories with no end, I am hooked, like an addict. Sometimes I even visit him two times in a day.

When he tells these stories, I begin to live them. It is a bizarre feeling—frightening at times—to be suddenly thousands of miles away, or forty or fifty years in the past. When a story begins, I lose track of myself and time. I don't know how to explain it any clearer: pictures just start to come to my mind, but I can also smell, hear, and feel things. It is a real world.

Sometimes while I sit watching Uncle sleep, I cry quietly. He can't see or hear me, but I turn to hide my face anyway. If he had just listened to Mary and me, perhaps he'd be in better shape, perhaps not in this godforsaken place. I told him how many times to come and live with us! But this hardheaded old man! "I going be all right," he was always saying, even after doctors removed a rotted lung. "No worry 'bout me," he said. "I can take care myself."

And now the cancer got the other.

Every day after Uncle was discharged from his first hospitalization, Mary cooked his dinners, and I'd bring them to his stuffy room in that broken-down, Chinatown rooming house off River Street next to the canal. At least he never protested the home-cooked meals. And when he started hanging out at 'A'ala Park again, I took the food there. He used to watch his friends play their marathon games of checkers. I told my wife to make more food, but I never told her why. She happily complied, thinking that Uncle had developed a robust appetite. But then she found out that she was cooking for Ricardo, Eddie, Pedro, and the rest of Uncle's gang. She blew her stack, but cooled down fast. That's how Mary is. I told her: that's how Uncle. That's how him. What can you do about it? He's always sharing whatever he has with his friends, even if it's nothing.

Uncle's friends made it a habit to delay the last game until I delivered the food.

"We used to go up da mountains go hunting, cut wood, listen to da tigah roaring like thundah inside da pine trees, yo' papa and me. I tell you, Yong Gil, da old country is beautiful. And strange if you no understand it. And full of magic. Da magic everywhere in da countryside."

"What you mean?" I ask.

No answer.

"You know, wen you was small, you wen go visit da old country. I talking what dey call 'North Korea,' da old country. You was small baby dat time. I no think you remembah."

I remember. That old family picture in the album with the black moldy cover. North Korea. The family village.

I'm sitting on *Harabagi*'s lap. Surrounded by our large family, *Harabagi*'s sitting behind a long table stacked with food: *pahm* and *yak sik* on the right; all kinds of *tuk* on the left; persimmons and oranges stacked like pyramids; huge pumpkins at both ends. In the foreground, in front of the table, are drums and horns and cymbals all set for the celebration. And Mama's sitting to the left of *Harabagi;* an old man and an old woman are between her and me. Mama has a long, sad look, as if she feels that she doesn't belong here.

hungry hungry   i grab for the tuk   harabagi *holds me back   he grumbles at me   i look at* omoni   *she is looking at me   she is angry the pumpkin is the biggest I have ever seen*

But she does: her husband is the son of the village chief. And there's the rest of the family: *ajisis, ajumonis,* cousins, and whatnot. There're a few old men with straggly white beards standing in the back, wearing those squarish black caps signifying their status as *yangban,* the venerable learned ones of the village. And behind all this are the dirt walls and straw-thatched roof of the main house. Everyone's bone-thin, with sunken cheeks. But there's all of this food on the table. And nobody's smiling. Nobody wants to smile for the photographer.

man in black   waving his hand harabagi *does not like him   who is this Korean man who dresses like a Japanese? where from this smile that reeks of garlic and fish eggs and betrayal? what of those glass lenses smudged with body oils?*

"So one day, yo' papa oldah brothah—Il Whan his name, I dunno if him still stay living or what, was so long ago—him, he come back from da big city wit' one rifle he go steal from one drunk Japanee soldier. So yo' papa and me we go up da mountains and shoot dis rifle. Dis one real beautiful rifle: blue metal barrel and da stock nice dark oily wood. Nobody dose days in da village know how da rifle work, but we figure out how. We used to hunt fo' deer up in da mountains wit' dis rifle. But den one day, da Japanee soldiers come into our village and dey take everything dey think us can use as weapon. Anything made of metal: hoes, picks, knifes . . . anything. Even *Omoni*'s brass soup bowls. But dose sonavabitches nevah find da rifle cause us hide 'em in one secret place in da mountains.

"Das how come yo' papa and me had to *hele* from our village, 'cause dose damn Japanee troops come bothah us. Later on, both us come Hawai'i."

"Now, I nevah going see dem again."
"What you mean?"
"My wife and children. I dunno what happened to dem, all dese years."

"When you get better, you can take a trip back to Korea."
"No bullshit me. Me no have too long live."
"Don't say that, Uncle."
"No bullshit me."
"Okay, okay. Calm down, before the nurse comes in and checks on the commotion."

"Yong Gil, I like tell you da story 'bout da airplane me go fly back Korea on."
"One airplane?"
"Das right. You hear me right first time. One airplane. Me build one airplane."
"What do you mean? You built an airplane?"
"One ricepaper airplane. Me build dat airplane in yo' papa's shed behind da house you guys living in, da time you folks living Kunia, by Kolekole Pass. Yo' papa get pineapple fields dere, you no remembah? You no remembah da airplane? You born already dat time."

Okay. I remember my older sister Chung Hee telling me about this when we were still on talking terms. She said one time Uncle was trying to construct an airplane out of scrap lumber, bamboo, parts of a broken bicycle. "And newspaper?" I said. "No," she corrected. "Ricepaper."

I'm beginning to remember now. An airplane to fly back to Korea. The time we were living up on the homestead. But I was too small at the time. Can't remember all the details. A ricepaper airplane.

"So, how did you make the airplane?"

"Outta ricepaper. What you t'ink?" He laughs. He coughs.
"Tell me this story."
Uncle smiles. His eyes close. I think he's going to sleep.
I wait.

His eyes finally open. A dry smile parts his purplish lips. His eyes sparkle.

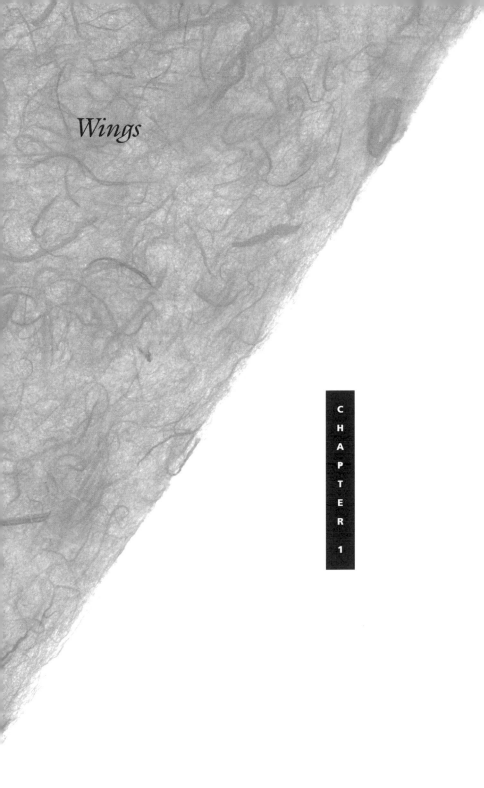

Wings

CHAPTER 1

Waipahu Plantation: February 1928

Kim Sung Wha paused under the noonday sun, straightening his stiff back. Doffing his *pāpale,* he ran a sleeve across his forehead and turned to the sun, swearing at its merciless heat. Then turning toward two mounted *luna*s chatting some twenty yards away. Protection against the striking canecutters.

"I tell you, this is all no good," said Cho, in Korean.

No answer from Sung Wha. He dipped his body back into the work, the gathering of cane. *Hāpai go,* as *he* would say. Others were loading the harvest on wagons.

"Look at all those *luna*s watching over us. Three of them."

"Five."

"Six," said another. "Where's Souza?"

"Who cares about him?"

"We should not have come out."

"We are doomed."

"Anything to get back at those Japanese dogs."

"What about the Filipinos? Are they dogs, too?"

"Yes, for being with the Japanese."

"No."

Sung Wha broke with his silence. "You are wrong. We

should not have come out here. Do you know what we are? We're strike breakers."

"I'm no strike breaker. I work hard too hard for my money."

"You are an idiot."

"Who said that?!"

"Shut up. Or the plantation will slap you with a big penalty."

"Bastards. Bastards of pigs."

"Sung Wha, you better watch yourself. This morning you could have gotten yourself in big trouble."

No answer.

"Sung Wha—"

"We should not be out here."

"Don't tell me that. Then why are you out here yourself?"

"Yo' fathah, Mistah Souza, is coming to check on you, see if you all good boys or not."

Uncle Sung Wha is reminiscing again. And he doesn't even know I'm sitting here next to his hospital bed.

"Bango 576. Where you?"

"Frickin' drunkard *luna*. I know his name. How come him dunno mine?"

"That's you, Sung Wha. What does he want?" Cho's eyes tell Sung Wha that he has answered his own question.

How can we work when the Japanese and Filipino laborers are striking? They're just like us. Or are they? Damn plantation wants to divide us. But if we Koreans went out on strike, would the Japanese support our cause? And why do they have so many lunas watching us? So the strikers don't attack us? Or so we don't run away? Must they force us to work?

"576! 576! Yes—you! 576, you make too much *pilikia*, too much trouble. You make too much *pilikia*, den bumbye you *pau hana* fo' good. You sabby? No sabby?"

The horse is restless. Souza strikes its buttocks with the handle of his black snake.

Sung Wha steps forward, calling, motioning the others to stop work. "Me no *pilikia*. You *pilikia*. Pahm-bye you *pau hana*."

"What you said, you friggin' yellow bastard? 576. I get yo' bango numbah. 576. You no talk *pilau* to me, 576. You no talk back to me. You go back *hanahana* right now, or I cut you down!"

> *Black snake! Black snake!*
> *Eat 'em up cake!*
> *Eat 'em up cake!*

"Boy, 576, you watch out. Mr. Hollander already know you already. You one big troublemaker on hees list. You *pau hana* work ovah heah as far as I concern, you friggin' yellow bastard. You sabby? No sabby? You no-good sonavabitch, stinkin' yellow bastard."

Holding up his machete—sun glistening off the wet blade—Sung Wha takes a few steps toward the *luna*.

Cho: "Don't be stupid, Sung Wha! Look at all the other *luna*s! They have guns!"

Sung Wha lowers the blade, lowers his eyes, lowers the power he's so proud of, that strain of dignity so Kumgangsanesque.

"Dat friggin' *luna*, I wen raise my machete right to his *maka*, dat friggin' *luna*. And in front all dem crappy *luna*s. Yeah, right in front all dem. I tol' dat no-good sonavabitch where to go!"

Coward American, I'll cut you to pieces and leave you all over the field for the mongooses. That's what I'll do.

"You sonavabitch Korean. You da main ringleader, eh? Mr. Hollander know 'bout you. No worry. I going get one full report 'bout you right to him, right on hees desk."

"What dat Souza doing now? Making trouble wit' dose damn Koreans?"

"I dunno. But dat Korean he talkin' to, he one trouble-maker. Make plenny *pilikia*, him."

"Whassamattah wit' dat Korean? He no like *hanahana?*"

"He okay until Souza come chargin' out. Where dat bastard Souza was hiding anyways? Hiding in da cane field, drinking his *'ōkolehao?* Bastard. No good sonavabitch."

"You have to watch out," Cho warned Sung Wha as they followed the others back to work. "The company is singling you out. You heard what Souza said."

"I've faced worse things."

"Be careful. The *luna* means what he says. You know what they did to Lee Chi Ha."

"C'mon, Sung Wha, get back to work, before they hit all of us with big fines."

Back to work, *hāpai ko* today. Another day they might swing machetes into juice-rich stalks that would fall to the ground in a melancholy rhythm, slashing and falling, twang-twang-shuck, bodies wet with sweat in that hot syrupy sauna hot Hawaiian sun sultry sun, calloused hands grasping hardwood handles. The men worked while humming singing a work song their hearts beating in syncopation and mindsinthought living in the past. And brooding: what's the future now?

"Ah! This sun is too cruel—beating my back like lashings from my stepmother!"

"I hope those Japanese dogs lose whatever they're fighting for!"

"We should not work. Japanese, Filipino, Korean . . . we're all the same."

"Japanese are bastard pigs! Don't you know what they're doing to our country?"

"The white bosses are bastard pigs!"

"Come on, Song Juk! Another of your songs!"

Many suns rise.
Many stars in the deep sky.
This cane that I cut
Does not cry but laugh.

Many days of wandering,
But my body stays right here.
I dream of smoky days
Climbing mountains, not hills.

They work and sing while the sun—a swollen ball of fire—falls slowly on the not-so-distant sea. Cane is piled on a wagon, then loaded on flatbed railroad cars. Which take the harvest to the mill to be manufactured into raw sugar and bagasse. Then refined into white sugar.

". . . so dat da haole wahine housewife can make her tea party sweet someplace in da mainland someplace . . . so dat da kid who live down da block can lick his fav'rite lollipop . . . so dat da haole who own da plantation can make plenny mo' *kālā* on top da millions he already get. And he already living in dat big mansion up Nuʻuanu Valley. And he get one nada big house on da North Shore, Mokuleʻia-side, and play polo wit' his stable of horses and wit' his rich friends who own da Big Island of Honolulu. And . . . and him get one big ranch Big Island, he send his kids Punahou School, den later go send dem one high-class East Coast university, you know, da kine Ivy League. And every year, or maybe every ada year, dem dey go take one trip, sail around da world wit' no mo' problems bothering dere minds.

"I tell you, Yong Gil, you heard people say how dey work so hard dey feel like dropping dead. I tell you, das no joke. Actually das what happened to plenny people. Way back dose days, how many people *maké* overworking. Da worker feeling sick so he go see da plantation doctah, but da doctah, him no believe da man sick so him send 'em out back work. How many people dey go work in dis kine condition and den *maké* da next day. Da plantation bosses, dem no give one shit. Dem think us dogs. Dem treat us like dogs. Even da dogs in da houses get mo' better life den us. Dey work us like dogs so da money can keep coming in fo' dem buggahs, no stop. "No forget what I telling you, Yong Gil. Dis is history. Dis is what happen in da past. No forget all dis. Even when I *maké*, you remember what I telling you. No can forget how things was befo'. No make forget, like how da haoles trying make us forget everything what was like befo'. Dey trying brainwash everybody, tell us how us lucky live here, lucky come Hawai'i, lucky live in America, all dat bullshit. Dose buggahs, dem stay changing what really wen happen every time dem write and rewrite one history book. Dem brainwashing everybody, starting wit' da schoolkids. Dem say how being one American is one big honor. Like Thanksgiving turkey and corn bread, and forget da Indians who was da first ones in America in da first place who gave dem all dat food so dem no starve in da first place, and forget dey stole all da land from da same Indians. You know, dat bullshit. Dose Indians, dem should let dem Pilgrims starve.

"Life worth nothin' back den, plantation days. If one man *maké*, eh, can be replace. Das how dem think, dose days, dose sonavabitch haole capitalists. You try go O'ahu Cemetery up Nu'uanu, you go da corner, you know, where yo' wife's mama stay buried. You go check da gravestones dere. Eh, get so many Korean names ovah dere and dey all *maké* so young. All from ovahwork. No mo' good food eat, no mo' medical care. Eh, I tell you, was one crime, you see da workahs all sick, almost dying, and da boss, he tell dem dey no can stay home rest li'dat, gotta go *hanahana* in da field. And was hard work . . . and long hours. And you go da graveyard and you going find plenny young wahine wen *maké* real young. Dey no have medical care, plenny wen *maké* in childbirt'. I tell you, is one real crime what dose fucking haole bosses did.

"And I tell you, yo' eyes going really cry when you see da part of da graveyard where get all da stones and da pictures on da stones of all da *keiki* who wen *maké*. I tell you, I go dere and see dis, I get *hūhū*, so angry, my blood boiling over. Go dere fo’ yo’self. Go look da pictures dese *keiki* on da gravestones. Ho! Dem all so skinny-skinny, like pencils da arms, like dem never get one good meal eat since da day dey born. If dem alive today, would be yo’ age, Yong Gil. Yo’ age. I tell you, Yong Gil, is so sad. You go dere, you going cry-cry-cry. You dunno how much people wen suffer so much dose days jus’ to make dem haoles rich and fat and get da high position dem get yesterday and get today.”

Tired, the men return to the barracks. Day is done, and they trudge over the red dirt road as quickly as their heavy feet can take them. Perhaps they can hear the bugle from Schofield Barracks ending the day, if they use their imaginations:

> *Day is done*
> *Gone is the sun*
> *From the*

And no question about their relationship to this foreign soil: their bond, if not consanguineous, then spiritual. Seven thousand miles away: the land their ancestors worked.

> *a thousand years of springs and full fertile moons*
> *blossoms of persimmon and apple*
> *rice shoots*

Here: the *'āina* they work.

“And twenty or so miles away from da plantation, da haole tourists, dem stay wrapping demselves wit’ big beach towels, dem going shower off da salt water and stay sunburn all over. You can get skin cancer, you know, Yong Gil. But dem, dey like get dark, like get one beautiful suntan. But funny, yeah, dey make prejudice against color people. Shee . . . if like get beautiful suntan like all da Haolewood stars, why dem no come up here and *hanahana* under da sun? Dem going be *pāpaʻa* in no time and good workout, too, if dem come up help *hāpai* go. No?"

Summer sun falls like a drowsy eye closing.

At least there's light to show them the way to the camp barracks. The truck that was supposed to pick them up does not show. Scaly workings of the *luna*, no doubt about that.

"Da *luna*, if I know what him going do to me, I think I cut da buggah up in small pieces right dere and den. And feed him to da mongooses. Yeah, das what I do. Da damn buggah, him not worth da shit he gotta shit. He not worth it. Later on, I hear from da other boys he get fired by da company. Drinking too much on da job, whipping da horses too much. Cruel-cruel buggah, him. Somebody tol' me he wen kill one horse wit' his whip. Dey call da whip da 'black snake,' dose days. But kinda hard kill one horse wit' one black snake. But anyway he wen kill one horse wit' something. Maybe wit' his stink whiskey breath. Heh-heh-heh!

"Da buggah was one mean buggah, but. Dat frickin' *luna*. Den later on him wen go *makē* in one cane fire. Somebody tol' me dis. Da buggah one heavy drinker, too much he drink. And him get plenny *pilikia*. One day, he *moe* in da cane field and early da next morning, dem wen burn da cane and da buggah still sleeping inside. Him come running out screaming. Nobody know him inside. But den, maybe even if dem know, maybe dem still burn da field anyway.

"Nobody like him, das how lousy guy him. Da boss hate his guts, too. Heard da story da boss found him sleeping 'round wit' his wife. Dey say da boss almost kill da bastard. Da wife suppose to be one heavy drinker, too. Funny, you know, how her, she no go fo' da good kine liquor, da kine expensive kine whiskey. Her husband making good money, but. But her like da pineapple swipe. Her like be wit' da natives!

"But anyway, da buggah wen run out da field, fire all over his body. Da buggah nevah live see da next day. Ho! Somebody tell me da buggah wen look real ugly wen he *maké*. Ugly-ugly. Nobody can recognize his face, his face all burn off, all raw, jus' like he wen get like *kalua* pig. Da buggah *maké* all in pain, I hear, screaming and howling. Da buggah wen *maké* wit' no mo' face. Das da worst way fo' die, die wit' no mo' yo' own face. But good fo' him, dat no-good sonavabitch."

By the time they reach the barracks, the sun has disappeared behind the mountains, leaving the sky with swaths of purple and orange. They bathe in a steaming *furo* in the small shed behind the barracks. Their hired cook, a Korean woman, wife of another laborer, has prepared a dinner of rice, kimchee, fried fish, and beef broth. The aroma is possessing and sexual. Sung Wha can think of only comfort and warmth, and the lush softness of the straw mattress and flax blanket he once shared with Hae Soon those cold-cold Manchurian winter nights.

They eat their dinner. Swipe is drunk. Stories are told. Then they sleep.

Late night, the plantation dicks sneak into the sleeping barracks: big, hefty men, well fed on corned beef and potatoes and poi and trained with weights. And they enter the barracks with their breaths on fire from fine-blended whiskey, a gift from the boss. They attack the snoring men indiscriminately, but when one of them finds 576—the man whom they are really after—they grab and throw him on the floor and kick in his stomach, then his head, hurtling Sung Wha out of a dream of dead men wandering in a city of diamond spires. They flood his face with the light of a lantern, then one of them strikes him repeatedly on the side of the head with the handle of a black snake. They drag him out to the back, where they beat him more and knock his head against the rusty, cast-iron charcoal stove still warm from cooking.

The Koreans are aroused out of their nightmare. They kick one goon in the balls, slam one head-on into a supporting wooden post, almost bringing down the roof. They go to the back and send those goons, as well as the other two, running and embarrassed at losing in their own game.

"Dey was after me, but stupid on dey part. Dem need us fo' scabs. Stupid."

When they found Sung Wha in the back, they saw a man babbling nonsense. They knew that the goons were after him, no one else. They carried him back into the barracks. A kerosene lantern was lit and held close to his face. It was a bloody mess they saw. Someone cried that his nose was missing. Another ran out back to look for the nose, returning a few minutes later with his hands open: "I could not find it." But they found it after cleaning the dirt and blood from his face. A bottle of cheap whiskey was brought out from someone's secret hold, and they poured a shot into his system. Coughing, Sung Wha bellied over and spilled out the rest of his dinner.

"No mistake," Cho said, shaking his head. "They were after you, Sung Wha."

"Cowards," Sung Wha gasped. He wiped the blood and saliva and taste of digesting food from his lips.

"Remember what happened to Lee Chi Ha? They killed him, and the killers—those bastards!—they're still free. You better leave tonight, Sung Wha, or your fate will be like Lee Chi Ha's."

They gathered his belongings, wrapped them in a small bundle. They tried to force more whiskey into his collapsed system, but he refused. They collected some money, a total of fifteen dollars and some change, and Cho pressed it into Sung Wha's hand, closing his fingers over it. The money fell through his fingers.

"Come on, Sung Wha. Wake up. The morning has already dawned for you."

Cho stuffed the money into Sung Wha's pants pocket.

Braced by his friends, Sung Wha stood up, his head spinning, a pounding in his ears. Then darkness.

"I dunno how long I was out. Da next thing I remember hearing was my friends' voices calling me. And den I see Hae Soon and our children, and dey crying. Das what shook me up. I got up real fast."

His eyes opened to a circle of worried faces and to a lantern's white light, some faces partly hidden in shadows. He struggled to his feet, called out a name unknown to the men, and stood determinedly for a moment before his knees buckled again. Cho broke his fall. They propped him on the edge of the cot, bending his head forward to bring back consciousness. A rag was pressed to a cut on his head. He pushed away their arms and tried to get up.

"Rest for a while," Cho advised, holding him down. "But leave right after that. They'll be back."

Sung Wha rested for a few minutes, then got up.

They gave him his things. They found his savings tucked in his mattress and added that to the money in the pants pocket. Sung Wha left the barracks. In the bathhouse, he washed his face. Then, with his friends wishing him well, he tumbled into the darkness, holding the bundle tightly against his chest.

In the bundle, which is really Sung Wha's things wrapped in a dirty workshirt, is a picture of his wife with the Yalu River in the background. She is wearing a quiet, skeptical look: what is this box, this machine that claims to draw my picture so exact like no artist can?

And there are also other items: a comb, dirty clothes, a chocolate bar, and several books and pamphlets.

The summer night was cool and breezy. Around him the cane rustled. But every step down that dark road sharpened the pains from his beating. He rested not far from the barracks on the side of the road, rubbing gently the swellings all over his body. Then he scanned the heavens, and his eyes homed into the stellar fires: Dan-gun the Great, the Great Bear, the progenitor of the Korean race; the boat of the Great Helmsman, navigating the rivers of Heaven; and then, unmistakably, the star Hae Soon and he had made a promise on *Was it that long ago? How long? when they were on that road to Manchuria before becoming lovers. The heavens are cruel to me tonight?*

Bouncing headlights appear down the road. He hides behind a bush and a large rock. As the car nears, he hears gruff voices singing American songs, songs he has heard sung with sweet, bird-like voices on that radio in the general store. A beam of light glances off the rock he's behind. He digs deeper into his hole. The car trundles by squeakily, leaving a nauseating trail of alcohol and car exhaust. When he hears the flat singing no more, he comes out and squints his eyes in the direction of the car's red backlights until he can see them no more. He swears, mumbles an apology to Cho and the rest of the gang for putting them through more trouble, then slips into the cane field.

A full moon comes out of the clouds.

He follows the path of a dry irrigation ditch. It will lead him out of the plantation. Once off the plantation, he will go to Wahiawā and stay with a friend for a day or two. Then take the train to Honolulu. This is his only option. Hanging around is asking for trouble, probably getting caught by the goons and hanged from a mango tree. At the very least, beaten up so badly he wouldn't be able to remember his name. He'll take no chances. He'll find work in Honolulu, make enough money to buy boat passage back to Korea. The money he has saved plus what the others gave him is just not enough.

An hour later he stops to rest, sitting on the top of the ditch. Breathing in the heavy, sweet redolence of cane, looking at the sky, he tries to find consolation from the stars, the moon. But he's alone in the midst of this vast field, thousands of miles away from family or friends, his friends on the plantation just as well a thousand million miles away, as far away as the stars.

Stars, you are my friends tonight in the middle of this friendless sea. You're my only friends. Tell me, dear friends, how many times has a man told you this? Once? Twice? Three times . . . in each man's lifetime? Ah . . . growling stomach. Always complaining. Never satisfied. Why do you hunger when you're not supposed to? No . . . it's not your fault. I'm sorry. It's man's greed. Yes? But why force other men to live hungrily?

He has not eaten much that night, and what he ate was forced out of him. But isn't he surrounded by a sea of food? He takes a stalk of cane, bends it—stubborn stalk of cane—twists it back and forth and sideways, finally breaks it at the base. Stripping off the smooth, hard skin, he bites off a piece, crunchy and fibrous marrow. The juice fills his mouth and spills from the corners. And he chews until his tongue is numb from the sweetness. He spits out the pulp and chews more. When he has taken enough juice to settle his stomach, he tosses the stalk into the irrigation ditch. *A slave to its harvest.* He leans back, lowering his head on a clump of dry grass. His eyes roll with the wax and wane of the stars and the moon. The heavens pulse deliberately. And his eyes became smaller, like the fall of the afternoon sun.

Just as he is about to roll over and sleep, he bolts up and pats the ground around him until he touches the fullness of his bundle. He feels for the bulge in his pants pocket, the money. He takes Hae Soon's picture from the bundle, slips it in his shirt pocket, and reties the bundle. Then he lays down his head and closes his eyes.

There is fire and heat, and opaque choking smoke swirling like angry clouds of a storm. Has he died in his sleep and ended up in a white man's hell? He covers his eyes and nose, hacking his guts out, his lungs on fire.

They found me in my sleep and are burning me alive!

He jumps to his feet, then slips—yelling—down to the bottom of the flume. He gets up and runs and trips over a burning stalk. A roof of hot ash collapses on him, the fire penetrating the back of his head, neck, and body like red hot spikes. He scrubs his neck and scalp, desperately clawing the heat out. Head bent, he charges through the smoke and flames and falls out of the hell, landing on bare ground.

He coughs and gasps for air, but he is out of the fire. He gets up, limps across a narrow, unplanted tract, and hides among the young leaves of the next field. The roar and crackle are behind him now, but the fire is still with him, his body burning all over. Deeper in the field, he comes across an irrigation ditch that is rushing with artesian water, and he lowers himself into it, the chill of the water rippling through his body. He stays in the water for a long while until his body becomes numb with cold. Climbing out, he inspects his body. Miraculously, he sees no charred flesh or blisters, only a lot of redness. Teeth chattering, he lowers himself back into the water.

Voices shouting.

Cautiously, he creeps to the edge of the field and looks from behind a cover of long, razor-edged cane leaves. Several field hands are working the fire. A couple of *luna*s are nearby.

"One cane fire. You stupid buggah, I tol' myself. And den I remember dey wen cut off da water supply fo' dat field fo' how many days already. Da cane ready fo' harvest. Dem already dry up da field fo' burn da leaves and *ʻōpala*. And almost dem burn me alive. Dumb buggah, me. I almost kill myself. If I *maké* in dat fire, nobody know it was me. Maybe I *maké* like dat damn *luna*. Wit' no face. Maybe my ash in one sugar cube in somebody's coffee."

He waited it out, lowering himself into the water now and then when the heat came back. He had escaped with his life for the third time in twenty-four hours. Three times. Was this a good omen? He had lost his belongings—Hae Soon's picture! Carefully he took the soggy picture from his shirt pocket, then flattened it on the top of the flume to dry. And he had all of the money. Not a cent was taken by the fire. He unfolded the paper bills and spread them out next to the photograph.

In the late afternoon, when the *luna*s had gone, he left the field and hurried down the main road, making sure that he was close to the cover of cane. Once he was off the plantation, the bosses wouldn't be able to do anything to him. Right?

But don't you remember what happened to Lee Chi Ha? He, too, was off the company's property—wasn't he?—when his friends found him, his head swollen and crusted over with dried blood, his face beaten almost beyond recognition. The plantation bosses didn't want no loud-mouth, radical Korean just off the boat spouting angry diatribes against the ruling plantation order, rousing the rest of those already hardheaded Koreans, turning them into an unmanageable, anarchistic mass. The company had also found out that Lee Chi Ha was wanted by the Japanese government for suspicion of bombing a building in Kwangju, which had killed a government official and the chief of police. When they discovered his background, the company fired him immediately. They gave him no reason for his termination, and in addition they informed the immigration authorities and the Japanese embassy. Lee Chi Ha fled on a tip before the authorities could catch him.

"But da crazy buggah, he keep on coming back fo' mo', yeah, coming back to da camp and talking to all da Koreans . . ."

. . . and firing up the other Koreans with his incendiary speeches. He was stupid for doing so, wasn't he? Hard to believe that a smart man like him would make a mistake like that. He should have known when to stop. But you know those anarchists. They live in such a romantic, spontaneous, dreamlike world. They live day-to-day. They don't seem to fear anything. They live for the moment. And when death comes to an anarchist, it's just an end of a life dedicated to the cause. And that's all. An end to an illustrious, adventurous life with a purpose.

"An end to an illustrious, adventurous life with a purpose?"

But Lee Chi Ha, with his words forged in fire, kept on returning to the camp like a damn fool. He had escaped danger many times, the goons always on him. But finally, one night, after a secret meeting with other Korean patriots at a church, he was the last to leave when . . .

"Da goons wen catch him, kidnap him, dey wen take him to da field and beat him to death. Den dey wen drag his body back to da church and tie him up to da cross and left him hanging dere like one Jesus. Even his head tilted da same way Jesus' head stay tilted in da pictures. But how dey found out 'bout him and his activities and whereabouts where dey can catch him?

"Well, you see, Lee Chi Ha, he kine of sloppy, leaving all kine trails where he was, where he going be. He lucky he nevah get caught earlier den da time he get caught. Dose other times he mo' fast take da bait and run befo' da fisherman can catch him. But dat sonavabitch Chun Chong Buk, he da no-good damn traitor.

"One day, after work, some Koreans see Chun Chong Buk get pull aside by da goons. Dem stay talking stories. Den da next week he no working wit' us no mo'. Den everybody see him wit' one good-looking mule and one nice wagon, and den somebody say Chun going open one store in town. All of us thinking how da hell he get all dat *kālā*. He one field worker jus' like us. So den we figgah out da goons wen give him some *kālā* fo' spy on us, 'specially on Lee Chi Ha.

"After we wen find out what happened to Lee Chi Ha, some of da Koreans wen approach Chun. Da sonavabitch, him deny he wen cause Lee Chi Ha's murder. But everybody know da buggah was lying. So somebody right dere and den stab him right in da heart, befo' da traitor get one chance run away and open up his store. Da buggah, I heard, wen *maké* right on da spot.

"How I know all dis? No ask me how I know. I know da person who kill him, das how I know. But of course, I not going say his name. He still living. Yes, da guy who stab Chun Chong

Buk still alive. And healthy still yet, what I last heard. We all wen make one secret pact no say nothin' 'bout it, and to dis day nobody break silence. You understand, Yong Gil? Maybe wen da buggah is dead, den I can tell his name. But look like I going *maké* first."

The summer sun had reached its noonday height when he reached the Wahiawā Reservoir, and Kim Sung Wha, tired and hungry and shirtless and reddened from fire and sun, rested his sleepy and aching and dried eyes on the cool waters of a dark still lake that . . . slowly fed itself through a complex of rivulets to the mighty Yalu River. And there, kneeling at the shore, he saw Hae Soon, facing the green mirror lake, her back toward him, sloughing her spring clothes that fell like large white feathers, washing her face and secret body parts. And far in the distance, almost completely hidden by clouds that perhaps held some snow, were the mountains. But they wouldn't have to cross those mountains, not right now, and . . . they weren't as beautiful and majestic as Kumgangsan, but he liked all mountains anyway, no matter if they were low and rounded and their tops never dressed in snow; mountains were mountains, and Sung Wha held a dear affinity for all mountains, even though these Hawaiian mountains seemed more like foothills. And Sung Wha began to sing to himself as he looked down the gravelly road that would lead him to Wahiawā town, and he felt the breeze that smelled of eucalyptus and cane, and his eyes remembered the fields of cane that sloped gradually to the sea, their windblown tops moving in rhythmic, wavy patterns; and keeping time with them, he heard . . . drum beats bamboo slats against pigskin spiking damp crisp air, the song of return:

> *Ari-rang, A-ri-rang,*
> *A-ra-ri-yo-o-o.*
> *A-ri-rang ko-gae-rul*
> *No-mo-gan-da.*

The smells of persimmon and pine. A cool spring breeze blowing from the north. Kumgangsan. The breeze messing my hair. Hair tickling my face. Can't scratch. Why did they tie my hands together so tightly? Can't feel with my hands anymore. Damn king, bastard pig of a whore pig. He should be tied up, not me. I shit on you, I'll come back and haunt you, kill you this time. Look at this ugly guard in front of me. Smells as bad as me. But I smell bad, being in prison for all these months. Swimming in the cold river: that's what I want to do right now. So the king wishes to hang me from the executioner's tree? How does this tree look? Tall and black and lets no sunlight through its leaves, they say. One dies without the sun. Let me look at the sky and clouds one last time. Ugh—damn guard! Farts in my face. And without a warning. I'll get back at you. Wait. There. Ha! You think you could get away with that, huh? You low-class beast, bastard son of a pig whore. Smell of persimmons again. Stop. Look at those fallen fruits on the ground. No one will eat them. Let me eat one of them, even if it's overripe, my only wish. Bastard . . . I knew you wouldn't let me. Bastard. That tree near the river. After swimming, Tae Woo and I eating all we want. This guard in front of me smells. I wish he were behind me and the other in front, the one with a baby's face, brown fuzz above his upper lip. How old is he? Fourteen? Fifteen? Hasn't even touched a woman yet. A pale and thin face. A sharp nose. While the smelly guard is ugly, fat, pock marks all over the back of his neck. The ugly one smells like fermented fish and garlic and sour rice wine. And this younger one is trembling. Maybe he's to execute a man for the first time. He'll see life squeezed out of this peasant. Remember this day, boy. This rebel will be dangling at the end of a rope. It's been only a few weeks, maybe even days, since you left your mother's cooking. What are you thinking about? Ha! I hope my death will haunt you. May you be so disgusted with what you'll see that you'll not eat and sleep for days. There's no hope for the smelly one. His mind is too far gone, diseased and rotted from rice wine. His mind is dulled from seeing too many executions. My death will be nothing new to him. But it will be the first time for you, young boy. Get sick, boy. Throw up. Then quit this mindless, barbaric service to the king. Return to your farm. Or fishing boat. And try to figure out for yourself why life is as hard as it is, why peasants who speak up for their rights are executed with their tongues cut out. Maybe you'll start thinking after watching my helpless legs kick. But you'll never hear me cry for help. You are young, your mind is fresh. You have a life ahead of you. Maybe you'll start thinking like how I did when I was your age. Maybe you'll become a rebel like me. Maybe my death will bring you to life. But maybe you'll like your job. Maybe you'll like this power over simple men. Maybe you'll turn out like this smelly product of a pig sty who is so stupid he is wearing his shirt backward. But you think this peasant gives up easily? I'll stop you from becoming an animal like the one we match strides with. My absent tongue flaps. I'll disgust you with the sight of my smelly body swinging. But, a song for you, too, this song I've been composing since my arrest. Listen carefully. I have time to sing it once. Remember the words, the melody . . . ah, the words don't come. At least remember the feeling. If only I had my tongue. I'm one man with one song. But remember: this song is for many, if you let it. I have waited for awhile now this final crossing of the twelve hills. I must slow down going up this trail so I can sing it. Damn stupid, ox-headed guard is pulling me up. If my arms were not tied, I'd knock him down. He wants to get this execution over with so he can cut me down fast and throw my body into some ravine to be eaten slowly by maggots. He has no heart to take my corpse deep into the forest and to bury me where my tiger ancestors lie. Then he'll run down the hill to his favorite inn and spend the evening drinking rice wine and chasing the innkeeper's daughters. But before I forget, the song. . . .

Arirang! Arirang! Arari-yo!
Climbing the hills of Arirang.
There are twelve hills of Arirang.
And now I am climbing the last hill.

Many stars in the deep night.
Many crimes in the life of man.
Arirang! Arirang! Arari-yo!
Climbing the hills of Arirang.

Sung Wha standing at the edge of the muddy reservoir and watching fish leap. Towering eucalyptus trees lining the shore. Lowering his warm body into the crotch between the splayed roots of a tree and looking to the tree's heaventouch. Then eyes drifting earthward. Falling asleep before his eyes touch ground.

A gauzy whiteness, the sky. On my toes, I grab the edge of the table and bob my head to see what is making those hungry smells. Honey ricecakes, piled up like a mountain on a thick white platter. I bob my head again and shoot my arm out, grabbing a handful of soft tuk, *dusted with potato starch, but before I stuff my mouth, a sting on my hand. I jerk my hand back. The* tuk *falls to the ground. A cold grip on my shoulders. My body spins around. My teacher Roh Jung Shik and his sour fish breath. I break free from him and run, but my legs are slow moving, moving so, so very slow. . . . And he has me against the wall of the American church, and I feel the rough whitewashed wall through my shirt, my shoulder bruising and my arms flailing helplessly against a stinging switch that's crisscrossing my face.*

Waking, his arms fighting off the blows. Then the confusion dissipates and the setting tells him where he is, warm cold sweat rolling down his face down his fired body. He touches through his pants. The money is there. Or is it? He empties the pocket and counts. It's all there. *But who's watching me?* His eyes dart between the trees, search the depthless shadows between. "Who's there?!" Jumps up. *The eyes.* "WHO'S THERE?!" Twig snaps. A fish jumps. He bolts through the shadows, bursts past branches raking his sides.

Out on the main road, he catches his breath: he has beat the nightmare in a footrace. *It must have been that strange dream,* he thinks. That feeling of being watched. He shakes off the rising shivers, then watches the sun set behind a hill of trees, the trees for a few surreal moments in a glorious blaze. The sun leaves, as seen through a keyhole, and then the trees reappear: dark still dense. There's a ghostly scar in Sung Wha's eyes.

And where from here? First things first, he tells himself. He'll go to the town and buy some food and a shirt. Then he'll find a place to sleep, anywhere, maybe behind a building or on a hard pew of a church. He studies with tired eyes the road that meanders toward Wahiawā, and sighs. Then he is off.

About a mile down the road he stops. Behind him is the sound of a wagon approaching. It is too dim and too far for Sung Wha to see clearly the driver, but fatigue tells him that the wagon is not a company wagon and that it will give him a ride to town. The wagon draws closer, and the mule nods in a familiar way: doubt ices Sung Wha's mind. He sees himself running into the bush. But a moment of hesitation: *legs, wait . . . must you . . . is it not? . . .*

The driver of the wagon is jarred from his concentration by the apparition rushing toward him. He whoas his mule to a stop. Two small children are in the bed of the wagon. He turns to them and places a protective hand on the head of the child closest to him while ordering both children not to be afraid, but they are not listening, absorbed in their game of "guess hand" using the seeds of the haole koa. Grabbing the crowbar from under his seat, the driver stands, one hand holding hard the reins to control the mule, the other raising the weapon above his head. There's a hard rapping in his heart. There's a breath-grasping panic in his gut. He shouts, "Mean spirit, go away!"

The apparition stops and shouts back.

He is shaking all over. "Who are you?" the driver demands.

He is stunned and baffled: *How does this ghost know my name?* He lowers the weapon, then raises it again. Perhaps the ghost is an unappreciated ancestor. Again his name is pronounced, and again he demands, "Who are you?" And: "What do you want?" But now he lowers the crowbar. *No . . . it cannot be.* "Sung Wha?" *Sung Wha?*

"Yo' papa was so scared, jus' like he was seeing one *ku-sin.* I was laughing and laughing inside. Out of nowhere dis *ku-sin* come running after him!"

Now Eung Whan could see shirtless Sung Wha, red streaks all over his half-naked body, running toward him like a madman. "Sung Wha?"

"It is you! Eung Whan!"

Lowering one unsteady leg at a time, Eung Whan got down from the wagon and shakily removed his straw hat, an uneasy smile cracking the hardened look of doubt. They embraced.

"Sung Wha—what are you doing here? When did you come?"

"Ah! My family! It is so good to see you, Eung Whan, my family!"

"Sung Wha! You no-good leper! You want to give me an early death? How did you get here? Sung Wha, we're in the middle of the wilderness and here you are!"

Sung Wha laughed. "Fourteen months ago I came here. I was trying to find you. Someone told me you were up in the mountains growing pineapples, but nobody knew where exactly. You don't want your family to find you, eh? What's so secretive about your life?"

"And what happened to you? Why is your body all red? What happened to your face? Did you run into a train? And why didn't you try to find me?"

"A long story." Sung Wha shook his head, chiding himself: *you faceless, nameless arse of a pig.* "I was in a cane fire."

"A cane fire?"

"Crazy, yes? I lost everything, except for my life and some money. The plantation bosses were trying to get me for organizing the workers."

"Ha! Same old Sung Wha! The troublemaker!"

Sung Wha noticed the children peeking over the side of the wagon. A huge smile. "Yours?"

Eung Whan nodded. "Say hello to your Uncle Sung Wha," he ordered, and the children did what they were told, though still keeping their faces partly hidden.

"Get in the wagon. You're coming home with me. And put on this." He handed Sung Wha a dirty jacket smelling of sweat and pineapple. "The nights get cold here."

Sung Wha climbed into the front seat, leaning back and ruffling the children's heads. "Handsome children, very handsome." Held their faces in his roughened hands. Discomfort on their faces. "Your daughter looks all over Grandmother. And your son . . . your spitting image!"

A proud smile surfaced on Eung Whan's face. "And you? Are you married? You have children?"

"Yes. Two. A son and . . . I don't know what my second child is."

Eung Whan gave him a puzzled look. "Where are they?"

"With their mother. Somewhere in Manchuria."

"Ah. So, a big sacrifice. But when you make your money, you'll be back with them."

"Yes," he said, nodding emphatically. "Yes. I will return to them."

"So where were you staying? Where did you come from?"

"Those bastards of pig whores at the plantation beat me up, chased me off the plantation. I'm glad to be alive. They're still after me, so I decided to hide in Wahiawā town."

"Still the same hotheaded radical, eh? But you can stay with me. I live up in the hills. They'll never be able to find you there."

Eung Whan slapped the reins on the mule's buttocks, sending the resident fat flies scattering, and the wagon lurched forward.

And they talked, about home and Sung Wha's troubles at the plantation. About the hard work life in Hawai'i. About Eung Whan's dream to go back home with money to buy the land the family had perpetually worked on but was too poor to own. About returning home and fighting the Japanese. The slow, bumpy ride to Wahiawā was a get-reacquainted transition for the cousins, and their laughter became more and more at ease and full and marked with the spontaneity that was the trademark of their lives as youths, that was like the north wind blowing over fields of gold, orange, and sapphire *doragi* and sending the flowers bending in all directions.

When the wagon began trundling over the worn-smooth road outside of Wahiawā, Eung Whan instructed Sung Wha to hide in the wagon bed. And there Sung Wha lay as the wagon passed storefronts lit with kerosene lanterns. And Sung Wha heard pockets of garbled conversation and wagons rolling by and a motor car driven in the opposite direction. And when they were out of the town's lights, Sung Wha sat up and watched the clear night sky with the children. There was a shower of stars, and Sung Wha and children counted the falling stars. Then the wagon rolled off the main road, and a few minutes later they entered a plantation camp.

"I thought you live in the mountains?" Sung Wha asked.

"Yes, but we're going to the moving pictures first."

"The moving pictures?" Sung Wha lowered himself, his eyes roving worriedly from camp house to camp house, searching the darkness between them.

"Don't worry," Eung Whan said in a voice tempered with assurance. "This is the pineapple company. They won't find you here."

"How can you be so sure?"

"Don't worry. Why would they come to a place full of children?"

"What's here?" Sung Wha asked, his eyes still searching uneasily.

"The moving pictures."

"What's 'the moving pictures'?"

"You have never heard of it?" Eung Whan laughed. "Still a country bumpkin. Where have you been? How long did you say you've been in Hawai'i?"

"Not long enough. What is this, 'the moving pictures'?"

"You'll see. Come."

Eung Whan tied the mule to a hitching post alongside three other mules and two horses, and they followed a Japanese husband and wife and their three children into a long, airy garage. A large white sheet was draped across the far opening of the garage. The interior smelled of diesel oil and manure: trucks and carriages were parked on both sides, and in closed stalls several horses were eating their grain, occasionally swishing off the flies with their tails. There were about fifty children and a handful of adults sitting on straw mats on the hardened dirt ground, the children squirming and noisy, and the air heavy and warm with their movement. Several kerosene lanterns lit the interior. One lantern hanging from a post cast the shadows of the children's heads and their shadowplaying on the makeshift screen. Outside, a power generator puttered abrasively. Eung Whan pointed to an area behind the last row, and there they sat.

Behind them, propped on top of a table covered with red calico cloth, was a machine made of glass, spindles, and pulleys. A large spindle of shiny black tape was mounted on the top of the machine. Standing next to the machine was a tall, clean-shaven, bespectacled *paginsaryum*, his head nodding with appreciation as he watched two more children and their father enter and promptly sit. The sleeves of his white shirt were rolled up past his elbows—the left side more than the right—and his dark pants looked several sizes too large.

A man of the Christian god, Sung Wha thought. Look at the way he looks at everyone. We are all his sheep. What new kind of deception, what magical sleight of hand, is he trying now to pull over our children?

The projectionist raised his thin, angular arm and in English asked in a gentle but firm voice for quiet. Then he asked for the lanterns to be extinguished, except for the one next to him, which he dimmed to a flicker. He switched on the machine, and a bright light shot from it and projected a white rectangle on the makeshift screen. There were screams and shrills from the audience. Inverted flashing black digits appeared, followed by English words, then a black-and-white frame of stylishly dressed Caucasians smiling and waving, their eyes darkened by the paleness of their complexions, their eyes focused on some object off to the side.

Exterior. Day. Long shot. Camera pans to the right. An expansive flat field. An American flag waving in a breeze. A crowd of spectators behind a roped area guarded by sturdy policemen with hands clasped behind their backs.

Closeup of a tall white male with a sharp nose and tousled hair, smiling and waving nervously. Next to him stands a white female, also smiling, with one hand holding down her hat to keep it from flying off. They pose for pictures in front of a group of photographers. The man kisses the woman.

Medium shot. The man climbs into the cockpit of an airplane.

POV of pilot. The instrument panel inside the cockpit.

Closeup of pilot sticking his head out of the window, posing for pictures.

Closeup of the words on the side of the airplane: "The Spirit of St. Louis."

Closeup of pilot putting on a helmet and goggles. He waves good-bye, blows a kiss, then closes the window of the cockpit.

Long Shot of the airplane, *Front* view. Waving crowd of people in the background.

Medium Shot of airplane, *POV* of crowd. The airplane's engine is started.

Medium Shot, Front view. The airplane moves away from the crowd.

POV of crowd. The airplane begins a bumpy taxi down the field, becoming smaller and smaller in size. Finally, it lifts off and ascends uncertainly into the sky.

Close shot of the crowd. People looking skyward, shading their eyes. Some are cheering and waving American flags.

Long Shot of airplane, now the size of a tiny bird.

"You like it, the moving pictures?"

"Yes. But this machine that flies like a bird. What do they call it?"

"They call it *paeng-gi*."

"*Paeng-gi*. Yes . . . *paeng-gi*. I . . . have seen it before."

"You like the moving pictures?"

Other images flash on the screen: women marching down a city street with arms linked, some carrying placards; models wearing the fashions of the time, glissading across a stage before flashing cameras; a train of shiny black cars rolling down a factory ramp and onto a street.

But the airplane. Sung Wha has tasted a strange fruit.

Mass demonstrations he's seen, been in, before. And he's seen tall and thinnish, beak-nosed *paginsaryum* women wearing satin robes and fox tails and awkward-looking hats with enormous feathers tucked in. And automobiles he's seen, ridden on. And cowboys on gallantly prancing stallions and cows grazing on a home on the range. And he isn't interested in the Hollywood gunfights: cowboy versus cowboy; cowboy versus Indian, and the cowboy always winning. He has seen enough of death, with real bullets, and it's not like how it is shown on the screen: no guts spilling out of a hole in the body or blood spurting like there's no tomorrow; no screams or primordial wails or swearing; no desperate last-second wills and testaments; no body parts and shards of bone scattered every which way. But then there's dashing Ken Maynard riding off into the western sunset on his sleek steed while cradling-embracing the beautiful heroine with sunburst hair, that helpless one-dimensional character of weeps and oohs and ahhs and helps and flapping fat eyelids, and the like. And by the end of the movie Sung Wha has already made up his mind: this is how he's going back home.

The upside-down digits flash on the screen again, followed by the white luminous frame. The lanterns are lit, and everyone's eyes are sensitive to this sudden blooming of light. A sea of disoriented heads rolls drowsily.

There's no airplane now, or a romantic runway to sunset, or silent laughter. No beautiful *paginsaryum* film queen. No new-world industrialized life portrayed in shades of factory black and cocktail white. This dream world has left now, replaced with a frame of flashing inverted digits, which is quickly vaporized by another frame, this time of white light and the fires of lanterns. Now, only memory holds vaguely the shapes, depth, movement of these dream images; like handprints in wet sand, they are left perhaps to be erased, perhaps to be reshaped, reworked, reinstated through language and dreams. Perhaps this Sung Wha will . . .

Early in the morning a huge metallic cloud of giant locusts rose from the bleak horizon. The buzzing grew horrendously louder and louder, until finally the monstrous shadows and bombs fell on the town, forcing everyone to scatter for cover. Except Sung Wha, who stood trancelike, watching them roar over him while a hell of thunder and fire destroyed everything around him. Until a comrade yanked him under the cover of a half-fallen roof, just in time, before another cloudburst of bullets shredded the ground where he had stood: "Are you crazy, Sung Wha?! What are you doing?!"

He studied the movie projector, an intricate maze of metal and glass and cellulose that created movements of life and yet itself did not live. *Perhaps electricity gives it life? But it has no blood, no flesh, no organs for breathing. It cannot see and feel, it has no eyes or the sense of touch. And yet it can see. And it can feel. How does it work? How can a world exist that is so real and dreamlike at the same time?*

Eung Whan, his coffee-colored face grinning: "You like?"

Sung Wha regarded his cousin's typically Korean face: those high cheek bones, that long nose so characteristic of their tribe. He smiled his answer.

Back toward Wahiawā town they rode with the light of a full moon.

"Have you seen one before?" Sung Wha asked.

"Seen what?"

"That man-made bird."

"The *paeng-gi?* You've never seen one before?" Eung Whan laughed. "And where have you been, Sung Wha?"

"I've seen many," Sung Wha said.

"Oh? Where?" He laughed.

"What is it?"

The sound . . . a dull drone, like a hundred oxen complaining. Sung Wha first noticed them above the horizon of the dusty Manchurian plain. Then the sound. And the noise got louder and louder.

"Quickly! Take cover!"

"What is it?"

"Fool! The Japanese!"

"But the sound—"

"Fool! Do you value your life?"

"Huh?"

"They fly them all the time over the pineapple fields," Eung Whan remarked. Sung Wha's eyes were inward. The wheel slipped in a pothole, jolting Sung Wha back to the now. They were entering the town again; this time it was dark and lifeless. Cold. "From that American military post," Eung Whan said, pointing in the direction with reins in hand.

"Where?" Sung Wha asked.

"The one outside of Wahiawā." Eung Whan nodded his head in the direction behind the wagon. "I forget its name."

"What did it do?"

"What do you mean, 'What did it do?' The *paeng-gi*? It flew like a bird, like how it did in the moving pictures. But it makes more noise than a clan of hungry tigers. Hey, you better get in the back."

Entering Wahiawā. The storefronts were dark and silent. A pack of wild dogs loped across the street ahead of them. One of them stopped in the middle, pointed its narrow snout toward the wagon and sniffed, then trotted away with the rest of pack.

When they were out of the town, Sung Wha climbed back to the front of the wagon. Through a field of ripening pineapple, then a field of tall bending cane, then more pineapple. While the wagon crawled up a narrow trail through thickets of *kiawe* and guava, then a grove of *kukui,* the children slept and the men talked about home, about the family. And Sung Wha, pushing away a low-hanging, thorny *kiawe* branch: "Let me tell you about China. It is unbelievable what is happening there." And Eung Whan: "I don't want to talk about China. I want to know what's happening at home." And Sung Wha: "But if you want to know about home, you must know about China." And Eung Whan: "No, I don't want to know about China. Tell me about Korea. But first, tell me when did you get here. How long have you been working for Del Monte? You know a bastard named Li Yong Sul? That son-of-a-bitch-that-was-born-out-of-his-mother's-arse. I think he worked for Del Monte. That crooked bastard, he owes me money. I loaned him twenty dollars. He said he was bringing in a wife. But I haven't seen him since the time he took my money. That bastard of a dog."

Later, halfway up the winding trail, they fell into silence. The mule continued on without any urging from Eung Whan, and Eung Whan's head began to loll with sleep.

But Sung Wha's eyes were sparkling: *what a wonderful thing, that mechanical bird.* He pictured birds and kites flying, dropping and rising in the wind, and himself among them. Excited with that vision, he slapped the bench of the wagon, forgetting himself and startling Eung Whan.

"What is it?" burst Eung Whan, looking around with alarm.

"If the *paginsaryum* can do it, so can I," Sung Wha declared.

"What? Do what?"

"Build a *paeng-gi*. That's what I'll do. I'll build myself a *paeng-gi* and fly back to Korea."

"I thought you saw a ghost. There're many ghosts here."

"You don't believe me?"

"Believe what?" Eung Whan yawned.

"That I will build an airplane."

"Build an airplane? If you say so, Sung Wha, if you say so." He sighed. "Still the dreamer." The mule began slipping on a steep section of the trail. "Come on. Let's get off before this mule dies of overwork."

The two men pushed the wagon past the difficulty, then got back on when the trail flattened.

"Ah . . . this mule is a good mule," Eung Whan said, slapping it on the buttocks. "Every day she goes up and down this mountain without a complaint."

"How far up is the house?"

"Not too far. A short ways. But this trail makes it long."

Sung Wha began whistling: *Doragi, Doragi, Do-o-ra-gi-i-i* . . .

"Stop-p-p whistling," Eung Whan stammered. "The spirits. I told you. They'll start talking to you."

"What spirits? Ghosts?"

No answer from Eung Whan. He coaxed the mule on.

A few more turns in the trail. At the top, under a large *kukui* tree, a small cottage, its interior lit by a lantern. "It's late and they're burning expensive kerosene," Eung Whan grumbled. Wakening his son: "Yong Joon, take Uncle into the house." Sung Wha and the children got off the wagon, and Eung Whan drove the mule to the back of the house.

Sung Wha entered the house, snores reverberating throughout. Eung Whan came in, motioned Sung Wha to sit down at the kitchen table, then quickly cooked up a meal for Sung Wha, stir-frying a can of oil sardines with chopped watercress, then ladling the stir-fry and its juices on a mound of cold rice. He set out a dish of daikon kimchee.

"You eat like a starving dog," Eung Whan said, watching Sung Wha devour the meal. "When was the last time you ate?" Sung Wha looked up, his mouth filled with food. "This is the best meal I've had in a long time."

"Da best meal ever. Can still taste, smell, da sardine oil and garlic."

Eung Whan smiles: "More rice?" Sung Wha grunts, then waves off the suggestion, patting his stomach gently: *enough, cousin, I am full. You have a growing family to feed.*

Setting the empty dishes to the side, Eung Whan brings out two earthen cups and dips them into a large crock of bubbly pineapple swipe he keeps in a corner, the swipe now ripe for three days and exuding a rich sweet-sour aroma. They toast, then drink the brew. The brew is strong, burns Sung Wha's throat, but it is good, very good, bringing quickly a warmth to his stomach.

"Eh, you rascal Sung Wha . . . tell me about home," Eung Whan says, bending over the crock to refill the cups.

"I no think I ever going feel dat lost feeling again, dat way I wen feel dat cold morning in Korea when yo' papa and me wen split up on dat road da rice farmer wen take us, fo' go our separate ways. Nevah goin' forget."

"Sung Wha, tell me about the spring time. Remember those days when we used to fly our kites up in that field of *doragi*, that field next to the pine forest where Il Whan shot his first deer? I was always a better kite flier than you!"

"It was spring, da spring jus' after we had one real bad winter, and still had plenny snow on da ground, and da trees and plants, dem never wake up yet from sleep . . ."

"You remember Kae Song, Eung Whan? That rascal. He took the charm that Grandmother gave me. But we tangled by the stream one day and I beat him good. But I never got that charm back. He said he lost it, or that's what he claimed. But anyway, I forgave him after the fight. And that was that. I held no grudge. And he had none for me, too."

". . . and when I look up da mountain, da mountain is green, cover wit' pine trees. All through da cold-cold winter da pine trees dem keep da dark green color. And I hear da snow melting, water running down da steep slopes. Den, in da distance, someplace hiding deep-deep in da forest, I hear da tiger, roaring like one sonavabitch. Ho! At first, sound so terrible. Da roar shake me up all inside. I scared, my skin come chickenskin, even though da tiger I know is miles and miles away. But still yet I scared shitless 'cause I think maybe da tiger—I dunno how— but I think maybe da tiger going jump right outta da forest and land right on top of me and eat me all up.

"But den I remember what *Halmuni* tell me one time. She tell us kids all kines of stories in da winter time 'round da fireplace. Yo' papa go sit right next to me when we small kids. *Halmuni,* her one strong wahine from P'ih-yon, no can go bully her around, even *Harabagi* get hard time, no can fight her and win. But *Halmuni* tell us when we small kids—maybe we six or seven years old, maybe smaller den dat, dat time—but anyway she tell us no be 'fraid da tiger. When da tiger growl, she tell us, means he hungry or maybe he happy or sad, you gotta learn which one is which. But he never going attack you, or anybody else in dis village, cause we all da same-same. So we ask her, 'What you mean by "same-same," *Halmuni?*'

"Her sit there real quiet fo' little while, her no say nothing, jus' quiet. Den her smile. 'Us all from same-same family,' she tell us, 'you understand? Das why we one strong people. Nobody can make us do something we no like do.

" 'All da foreigners come here and take our food and money from us. Dem come here and kill us and tell us what to do, how us suppose live. Dey rule over us, do any kine bad things to us.'

"Our *halmuni*, she look us straight in da eye, she say, 'Listen to me and no forget dis. We all tigers. We all come from da tiger family. We tiger people. No matter what go happen to us, we always going survive. Da adas going rule over us maybe fo' little while, dey going try take our land and ada things from us, make us starve. But not forever 'cause us strong and powerful like da tiger and flexible like bamboo. We going endure like da tiger and roar no-end like him make when daytime going to nighttime, roaring up in da forest.'

"So dat morning, when I looking all around me and I hear da tiger, what *Halmuni* tell us back den come back to me. Yeah, I remember what our *halmuni* tell us kids. So dat time, after I hear da tiger and remember what *Halmuni* tell us, right after dat my heart wen . . . wen . . . wen fly.

"I remember how hard fo' me and yo' papa leave each ada, Yong Gil. It was so hard. Yo' papa and me, we was like brothers. But mo', mo' close den dat. Closer dan blood can be. But him and me, we decide mo' better us go our dif'rent ways, mo' safe, him go one way, me go one nada way. Dat way, if one of us get caught by da Japanee soldiers, at least da ada guy get mo' chance survive. You understand what I talking?

"But you know, strange, you know, how yo' papa and me wen bump into each ada in Hawai'i. To dis day, I no can figgah dat one out. I no believe in God or religion li'dat, but maybe somebody, or something, was looking over us. Maybe.

"But dat morning, something funny kine when move inside me, something was talking to me. Da scenery around me was so quiet, da pine trees and everything so still, was so quiet. But something, one voice, was calling me, talking to me. I can still remember dat feeling. Funny kine feeling. All dis quiet beautiful landscape around me, but dey was all talking to me, making me feel dis funny kine but good feeling. I dunno what dey call dis, but it like you have so much respect, so much love fo' all da things growing 'round you, all da things growing from da land. I think das what da young Hawaiians nowadays dey call *aloha 'āina*. You know, da love fo' da land. Love fo' everything living in dey own natural way. Something li'dat. Funny kine feeling, dis feeling dat jus' wen come ovah me right den.

"No one going know dis feeling wen touch me right dere and den, how wen really get inside me. Dis feeling was telling me, 'Eh, you cannot jus' do something any kine way and try expect everything going turn out right. You gotta go out and work hard fo' things happen fo' da good.' YouknowwhatImean, Yong Gil? In ada words, no can jus' sit back on yo' ass and do nothing and think everything good going happen to you, jus' li'dat. You gotta go out dere fo' yo'self and try make da best of things, try make da good things happen. YouknowwhatImean? So anyway, dis feeling wen come inside me and to dis day I cannot just sit still, I gotta keep moving, I gotta be doing something, anything, as long as what I doing is making something good fo' dis world, to make dis world maybe one mo' inch mo' bettah one place to live.

"But you ever know dat yo' papa and me was real-kine rebels? No? He nevah tell you dat? No? Den I tell you, den. Yo' papa and me—ho!—was big-kine troublemakers in da village. Him and me, we get dirty lickings every time 'cause every time we talk back our elders. You know, suppose to show respect fo' da old people. But dey no understand. We respect dem, but sometimes dey wrong, we cannot jus' sit back and let dem be wrong, right? What if dem make wrong mistake and going cost somebody's life? Den what you do? Of course, we try make sure no mistake going take somebody's life, right? But dem no understand, dem no understand dis kine thinking, dem know only dem own kine thinking, if you one young kid you bettah listen and obey yo' elders or else.

"Yo' papa and me, we get good lickings every time we talk back. But I tell you da reason. Was 'cause da wahine of da village, das why. Da way yo' papa's mama and my mama raise us was no let nobody push you 'round. You no push nobody 'round, but den again, you no let nobody push you 'round. And if dey push you 'round, den you push back, but even mo' hard. And you know dose days how da menfolks, dey like order 'round da women, make dem slaves. Das da old-kine style. So naturally da womenfolk going be mo' hardhead. Da mo' da menfolks push dem 'round, da mo' dem going get *huhu* and no listen.

"Anyway, one day me and yo' papa wen go up da mountains wit' dat Japanee gun yo' papa's brother wen take from da drunk soldier. And we wen shoot one deer and was bringing 'em back to da village when we notice strange something going on. From one rock ledge, we look down da village and see all dis horses and soldiers in da village. We know was da Japanees who was in our village. So we hide da deer and da rifle and den we go down. Dey make us stand in one line wit' da rest of da family— our uncles, aunties, cousins, brothers, sisters, parents. Da Japanee soldiers give da order fo' us bring all our farming tools together one big pile—hoes, shovels, knife, any kine iron stuff 'cause dem think anything li'dat us can go use like one weapon 'gainst dem. Dose guys, dey so scared, dey even scared one Korean farmer wit' one hoe! Den dey start using all kine bad kine language 'bout us, you know, dey make fun how we look, da lousy clothes we get, how stink we smell like garlic, dey make da kine real vulgar remarks 'bout da womenfolk, li'dat.

"Eh, yo' papa and me, we was all burning up inside. We no can handle dis. We was all mad inside. I look at yo' papa, and to dis day I still no can forget how fire his eyes was. You know, da kine angry-angry eyes when somebody get real, real *hūhū*. You know Koreans, when dey get *hūhū*, dey face come like stone and dey eyes get *mo'* small and can see da fire flaming real hot. But me too, I was li'dat.

"Den yo' papa start shouting at da Japanee officer, he say, 'You stinking dirty dog!' And den he spit on da officer. Ho! You can see da face of dat officer. His face come red-red, his face

almost melt away, he shaking so much all over he nevah know
what to do. Den he take out his sword.

"Yo' papa, he one brave man . . . maybe sometimes he little
bit jump da gun. But even da Japanee had all dat shiny-shiny
guns and rifles, he *no* scared dem. At first, I scared, but jus' one
second, 'cause right after dat, I start yelling-yelling at dem, too.
Even da officer holding his sharp sword I no scared. Dat kine
time, you no care if dey outnumber you or what going happen
to you. All you know is what you doing is right 'cause you get
deep-deep angry but smart feeling inside, you no care what
going happen to you. Das dangerous feeling wen somebody get
like dis: whoever da buggah is, him no care what going happen
to him as long as him get his revenge or what belong to him.
But dangerous fo' da ada guy.

"But ho! Da Japanee soldiers was real scared now. Dem start
waving all da guns in front of our face, tell us, 'Shut up!' But us,
we no shut up, and den da ada people start shouting, too. Den
somebody grab one rock and throw 'um at dem. Den all of a
sudden da whole village start grabbing da tools. Somebody wen
knock down one soldier, smash his head. Da chief of da police,
his horse wen go wild and run outta da village, and da ada soldiers running, too, dey never even had chance shoot one bullet,
jus' like dem never know how shoot gun. Everybody in da village was feeling good, but little while later, dey all get scared
cause dem know something bad going happen, something bad
going come down on us.

"Dem start talking 'bout how da Japanee governor going
send mo' police and soldiers, how maybe dey going arrest me
and yo' papa, den kill us. So da village chief, him go talk wit' da
rest of da menfolks, dem decide maybe, eh, me and yo' papa
bettah *hele,* run away and hide befo' dey come back. Dem say
dem know da Japanee governor going come down hard, going
get us and take us jail and den kill us. Dem think not going
harm da rest of da village cause dis place make too much rice fo'
dem punish everybody, but going try get us 'cause us da ones

start everything and maybe like make one sample of us in front of everybody.

"So dat night we get ready. We pack some things, some food, we was going leave early da next morning. But befo' we can wake up da next morning, da soldiers was already in da village. Early-early in da morning. We never had time get our things. My sister wen shake me up, 'Get up! Dey here! You bettah go now! Dey shakin' up da village. Yong Soon's house burning!'

"So I took off. I wen get yo' papa first. Den we wen run up da mountains. Da Japanee soldiers, dem seen us and give us hard chase, dem start shooting da rifles—POW! POW! POW! So quick we hide behind da ironwood trees, da pine trees. I remember I can hear bullets flying over my head, zipping all 'round us, hitting da tree trunks. And yo' papa and me, we was moving all 'round behind da trees, ducking our heads, crawling, rolling on da ground, hiding behind big rocks, all kines we was doing.

"But we know da mountains and da soldiers, dem never know shit. So little while later we lose dem. We go deep inside da mountains where da soldiers no can find us, we go deep inside where da mountain tiger stay rule."

On a sheet of stained butcher paper, Sung Wha sketches his plans: chicken-scratches and twisting, ambivalent lines for the airplane he desires. It is not the picture that he has in memory. Frustrated, and angry at the distance between his idea and what he has before him, he crushes the paper into a ball and tosses it to the ground. In two bounces it is out of the shed, the paper dream disappearing. Sung Wha looks out into the growing morning light. He rolls a cigarette, lights and puffs it, and thinks. He grunts.

Why make plans on paper?

He has never drawn plans for his champion fighting kites, so why now for this machine that is really like a very large kite? Why make chicken-scratches that have no connection to dreams?

His eyes look within, and with an imaginary brush he paints the bold orange color of morning across a canvas of blue sky, and with another brush, a fine-pointed one, he draws wavy black lines, the push of wind. And now he must imagine his airplane. How will it look? How large will it be? What color can it be? He searches in the churning darkness of his creating mind. Then two wheels, a bicycle, appear, and now he's sitting on it, and spanning above him is a wing made of paper and bamboo, which shades him from the sun. And can this airplane fly! High on the wind, on the muscled shoulders of this giant wind. Oh! And there are other winds, all pushing and pulling at him. Ah! But this is a lively wind! A lively air! This wing of ricepaper and bamboo cuts cleanly in this lively air, this air of auspicious wind spirits.

His eyes revert back to the morning. His eyes have soared, are moistened from that lifting dream. He flexes his arms, kneads his hard-ridged abdominal muscles. He will need these muscles to be a birdman. He returns to the image of his airplane.

The bamboo must be the best. I must find the best. But I must speak to the spirit that lives inside before I use it.

But where can he find such bamboo?

Wait. That grove in the gulch below Eung Whan's field. There's singing sometimes, late at night or in the early dark chill of morning. A few mornings he has awakened and listened to its reedy melody, then fallen back to sleep.

And there's ricepaper at the Japanese store in Wahiawā.

He unfolds his money and counts it on an empty orange crate. Not enough to purchase a steamship passage back home, but enough for the sheets of ricepaper he needs. But he also needs to give some of the *tuhn* to Eung Whan for his keep. Perhaps he can work off the obligation in his cousin's field.

Tomorrow morning he'll go into town and buy ricepaper from Sakata-san's general store, and in the afternoon he'll hike down into the gulch and search near the patch of watercress for that right bamboo. When he finds the straightest and strongest and most flexible yellow spears, he'll pray to their spirits, then with his sharpened cane knife make the cut close to the roots, leaving enough to let each bamboo's life rise again.

Balancing on his shoulder the shafts of bamboo stripped of branches and leaves, he sings of twelve hills as he slips and climbs up the wet trail leading out of the gulch. He slaps mosquitoes on his arm and neck in rhythm with the song, while the falling sun, like a bright egg yolk, plays hide-and-seek with him among the tree trunks ahead of him.

Tomorrow, with a new sun, he begins work on his airship.

They ate a dinner again of rice, kimchee, and stir-fried watercress and canned sardines—more watercress than fish—this is Eung Whan's favorite recipe, the only dish he knows how to make. When they were finished, the plates were cleared and cleaned, and the children sent off to bed. Eung Whan turned down the kerosene lantern. They went outside to sit on the airy patio. Sung Wha, on his favorite chair—an orange crate reclaimed from Wahiawā's refuse—rolled two cigarettes and gave one to his cousin.

"Tell me about home," Eung Whan began, lighting their cigarettes. He uncovered the crock of swipe—a new batch—and dipped their cups to dripping fullnesses. Eung Whan sipped his cup, then wiped his mouth with the back of his hand. "Come on, stubborn-head ox," Eung Whan grumbled. One sip had already relaxed his tongue. "Tell me about home. About our village. Who is doing what. Who married who."

"We left the village at the same time, you son of a monkey," Sung Wha returned. "You forget already? Your memory is as bad as a mosquito's."

With tilts of their heads, they finished the contents of their cups.

"Did we? Here, have more." Eung Whan filled them to the brim again.

"You forget too easily. You work too hard, Eung Whan. And

you drink too much of this stuff that softens your brain."

"But it's good stuff. *You're* not grumbling. You're enjoying it."

Sung Wha offered a grin, nodding. Then he drank the swipe in one take.

"Tell me about the changes in the village. Did the Japanese dogs go back there again and try to fuck it up?"

"You know Koreans are brave," Sung Wha remarked. "No matter what the Japanese say, Koreans are not going to listen. But we can't stay in our own country! In order to fight the enemy, we have to cross the Yalu and go into Manchuria."

"There you go again! I don't want to hear about China. They stole Manchuria from us."

"The Japanese control Manchuria," Sung Wha corrected.

"But I don't want to hear about China. I want to hear about Korea."

"But you know as much about Korea as I. Remember, we left Korea at the same time. But I can tell you about what's happening in China."

"I want to know about Korea. What are Koreans doing?"

"The Koreans are fighting back, but the Japanese, right now, are stronger. Their soldiers are armed with the best firearms. You know that. Those dogs' asses."

"Dogs' asses."

"But the Chinese are fighting the Japanese, too, and that's good. You have to understand that."

"Ahh! Again China!"

"We must look at China because something is happening there that has never happened in human history."

"Human history? What is this?" grumbled Eung Whan. "What are you talking about? If you must talk, talk to me about Korea. Every day I think about home. When I get back, I'll buy a huge mountain for the village. Our family will be rich."

"If you love Korea and want what's best for her, you must look at China."

"Who cares about China?! I don't want to hear about China. They stole Manchuria. Talk to me about Korea."

"Wait. Listen, you bullhead."

"And you are not one yourself?"

"Koreans are the bravest fighters in China. I was there. I know."

"I know Koreans are brave," Eung Whan said matter-of-factly. "That's no news to me. But why fight in China for the Chinese? Why fight and die like fools for the same people who took our land from us?"

"You must have a brain of a chicken. Japan controls Manchuria, not China."

"Why are you talking about all of this nonsense? Who cares about China? Who cares about Japan? I don't want to hear about China. I want to hear about Korea."

"You bullhead, stubborn arse of a water buffalo. You have to know what's going on in China in order to understand the future of Korea."

"But why? I don't care about what's happening in China."

"Why? I just told you why. Because what happens in China is also good for us Koreans. In China, they're fighting against the Japanese imperialist, the same enemy of ours. There's a popular revolution going on there. The farmers are rebelling against the landlords in the countryside."

"Bah! And what's this . . . 'imperialist'? What's that? Don't make up words."

"Give me more of that stuff."

"Eung Whan, in our country the king and the rest of the *yangban* are not for the people."

"So what is new? You think you're a smart guy talking to a fool?"

"And in Japan," Sung Wha continued, "their *yangban* is more powerful, and therefore more dangerous. That's what imperialism is. A ruling class that is more powerful than another country's ruling class. Our *yangban* might fight with us against the enemy, but they'll fight only so that they'll get back what they lost to the Japanese *yangban*, so they can rule again over us."

"So what's all this got to do with China?"

"This has a lot to do with China."

"Ahhh . . . wait." Belching, Eung Whan took the cups and refilled them.

"They say that when you pass gas, you're alive," Sung Wha said. He took a drink, then wiped his mouth again with the back of his hand. "Great heroes are made from the books written by the *yangban*," he continued. "But in China, the entire population of farmers and working people are the heroes. They are the new makers of history."

"Yo' papa . . . he so hardhead. One-track mind."

Papa . . . he so badly wanted to go back home. He only intended to stay here in Hawai'i and work for a little while, to make enough money for his growing family and the family back in Korea. We were all going to move back to the old country. But the war came. Ended the dream.

But before the war, he did go back to Korea, two times that I can remember, each time to get ready for the move back. The first time he bought land with the money he had made and saved working the land in Hawai'i. He bought a huge mountain and several rice paddies, so that the family in Korea wouldn't suffer anymore. He must've stayed for a whole month. Then he returned to Hawai'i, bringing back with him huge oak barrels filled with food. Dried clams. Dried black mushrooms, the mushrooms as big as the span of my hand. Dried abalone, the biggest I've ever seen. He gave us kids each a few clams and an abalone to eat. Mama kept some of the food for the family, but the rest she and Papa sold down in the camp to make a little extra money.

Papa was a real entrepreneur. He had his own pineapple field, leasing the land from the company and selling what he produced from the field back to them. Then the Depression hit. Wiped him out. But if it wasn't for Mama, Papa would have sunk earlier, with his heavy drinking. Actually, when you think about it, it was Mama who was the entrepreneur. She kept Papa's business floating. Until the Depression came. There was nothing she or Papa could do about it.

But I remember the clams. They were so *'ono*. And the abalone. Was a treat when Papa gave us kids the clams and abalone. I used to chew and chew the clams until it was like paste. The abalone, too.

The second time he went to Korea Papa took along two sewing machines. I remember one was a Singer and the other a White. That was so that the family back in the village could learn to make a good livelihood. He was trying to get the family on their feet financially. It was this visit, I think, when he got real sick, when he almost died in Korea.

A few years after he came back from this second trip the war broke out. And that was that.

"Koreans in Hawai'i need to learn how to become soldiers so that when we return, we can fight for the Motherland."

Can you imagine how outraged Papa was? Getting off the boat and the first person he sees is a Japanese official, demanding his passport and other papers. And asking him all kinds of nosy questions: "Where are you going?" "Who is your family?" "What are their names?" "Where do they live?" "How long are you staying?" "How much money did you bring?" What right did he have asking him all those questions? I bet you, Papa wanted to break his nose!

And they searched his luggage. Maybe they thought he was smuggling in guns and ammunition, or, worse yet, Communist literature. And then next to the official was this other lowlife, a Korean, the interpreter for the official, probably a *yangban*. Uncle Sung Wha told me once that the Japanese never learned the Korean language because they thought their race was genetically too superior to learn a low-class language like Korean. So they used their Korean flunkies to interpret Korean for them. I know Papa must've been all worked up inside, burning mad, not only because he was in his own country and getting asked all these stupid questions, which really was nobody's business to ask, and seeing how the Japanese were running the entire show in Korea, but more so because here was this no-good Yobo right in front of him, right next to the Japanese official, helping the enemy.

". . . and learn to read and write and study."

"Where did you learn to read and write and talk like this?" Eung Whan grunts, finishing the rest of his brew. "Back in the village, you were stupid, like the rest of us. Remember that lousy schoolteacher who used to beat us every day instead of teach us? He used to think himself too high to be teaching stupid farmers' children. That bastard. And you know how to speak and read Japanese, too?"

"A little."

"A little is a lot, for a farmer's son. You were always smart, Sung Wha. But again, why should we study and learn all of this? Sounds foolish to me."

Papa almost never made it back from his second trip. He got sick over there, so sick that they thought for sure he was going to *maké*. They even made him a coffin out of pine. And they found him a grave site. They had the hole dug out, all ready.

Mama got a letter from Korea saying how sick Papa was. Or was it a telegram? Quickly Mama went down to the watering hole where all the cows drank their water, where we used to get our water, too, and there she cut bunches and bunches of watercress, which she set out in the sun to dry. The watercress grew wild there, like weeds. Then she collected a large handful of small pebbles from the stream down in the gully, and with the dried watercress she wrapped them all up in a package and shipped it to Papa's village in Korea.

I don't know how long it took for the package to get there. You know, those days, steamboats carried the mail and that took a long time. And then when it reached Korea they must've used horseback to get the package from the seaport to Papa's village. I'm not sure if they had trains back then. Anyway, it took a long-long time for the package to reach Papa's village.

But finally the package got there, and miraculously Papa was still alive. So they boiled and boiled the watercress and the pebbles in a pot, making a broth, then gave this broth to Papa. And pretty soon Papa got better, he got stronger. Pretty soon he was strong enough to come back home.

That was Papa's last trip back home. He was supposed to go back another time when his grandfather was really sick, ready to die. But he was too busy with the pineapples, it was just about harvest time, and so Mama went instead. Mama was pregnant at the time and I went along, too, because I was a baby then, about two years old, though I don't remember much about the trip.

Mama told us about that long boat ride and how sick she was the entire time. How she couldn't eat the greasy food. It was lucky that she had brought along some dried fish and dried watercress, but that didn't last too long. And that long trip overland to the village. When she arrived at the village, of course there was this sad spirit everywhere because Papa's grandfather had died a day or two before. But Mama said there was something else bothering her, something she couldn't explain. She thought it was her pregnancy making her feel so sickly, feel funny, though later she realized it was something else.

This funny feeling grew stronger at the grave site. When the service was finished, she turned to leave when this feeling almost overwhelmed her. It was as if something in the grave was pulling her in. She became very frightened. She never escaped this feeling during the rest of her pregnancy. She believed that was why months later the baby, a boy, was stillborn.

A few years after her return from that trip, the Communists closed up the borders. At least that's what we were told. The family couldn't go back and visit after that.

"We have to turn ourselves into an army of tigers. We Koreans have to toughen our bodies, strengthen our minds. We have to think like tigers, be strong as tigers, become tigers. The Japanese army cannot fight an army of tigers. Tigers are too large and powerful for them. Tigers are invisible in the forest. And tigers never lose a fight. But we have to fight the *yangban*, too. They're just as bad and cruel as the Japanese, perhaps even worse, for they hide themselves better than the field mice in a forest. Do you understand what I'm saying, cousin?"

"How come your tone of voice is so strange all of a sudden?" Eung Whan asks. He shakes his head, then turns to refill his cup.

Papa took some *tuhn* with him, some hard-earned cash he had saved working on the plantation. And with that *tuhn* he bought the family in the village some *tung*, some land, a big piece of land that included a huge mountain. You see, the family in the old country was very poor, dirt-dirt poor. They never owned their own land, always paying rent to a landlord. But when Papa went back, he bought the family some land, freed the family from the greedy landlord. The money he took isn't much in today's money, but back then it was big money, and he bought a huge piece of land with it. Land was cheap. Everything was cheap in those days.

Papa used to describe the land to us, how it stretched from the sea, where fat abalone covered the rocks by the shore, to all the way up to the snowcap of the mountain! In fact, I think, he even bought the other side of the mountain. Land was cheap. But even how cheap it was, it was still big money for poor people.

Papa used to tell us how it was so beautiful up in the mountain. There were big-big pine trees and so many waterfalls you couldn't count them, the mist from the high falls creeping into the forest like an army of giant ghosts. The water of the streams was cold and clean, so clean that you could drink it and feel it cleanse your insides.

But now, I don't know if the family still owns the land. After the Communists took over, I think they took the land, too. Sometimes I think about that, about all that beautiful land that Papa's and Mama's hard-earned cash had bought, taken away.

"The revolutionaries in Korea, the Communists, are promising farmers land after the revolution. In fact, they're even parceling out the land right now. What land they've liberated from the bloodsucking landlords they're turning over to the farmers. The upper class! All they care about is their own position and wealth. They take the rice and millet we produce by our hard work for payment to work their land!"

"So what else is new?" Eung Whan belched. He smiled, sig nifying how good this latest batch of swipe had turned out.

"All the upper class wants to do is collect rent and taxes from us. All they're interested in is counting money—*our* money."

"But it's their land," Eung Whan said. "If it's their land, they have the right to collect rent and taxes. That's why we must work here and save our money. Then we can go back and buy our own land. Then we can become landlords."

"I don't understand you. At one time you talked so boldly against the landlords. And then the next time I hear you talking like a pig's arse."

"You bastard of a bitch."

"You don't understand. They need us, but we don't need them."

"Who needs who? What are you talking about?"

"The *yangban*. They need us, but we don't need them. We work their land. We make their land valuable. If it wasn't for us, their land would be idle, worthless."

"I don't understand where you get these crazy ideas from, Sung Wha. And anyway, even if you could change it, the upper class is too strong."

"Bah! The king is a weak-minded idiot. Look what he did to our country, giving it away to the Japanese imperialists!"

"That's true. But I still think it's impossible to do anything about it."

"Listen to this. The upper class stores *our* rice in *their* big warehouses, and when winter comes and everyone is hungry, they bring this rice out and sell it back to us at a high price. Farmers can't even afford to buy the rice they themselves grew in the first place! This is criminal!"

Eung Whan smiled, his cheeks flushed contentedly. "You're right. That's not right. This makes sense. This I understand. Sung Wha, where have you learned all of these ideas? But here . . . have some more of this good swipe."

"Listen to this. More and more every winter people are starving to death or killing themselves. It's a harsh life for Korean farmers and their families."

"Yes. So what is new about that?"

"My eyes have seen mothers throwing their babies into icy streams, and then themselves. It's horrible. It's criminal. It shouldn't be like this. I tell you, Eung Whan, you and me, as well as everyone else, know this is madness. I used to ask myself many times why it's like this, and I could never answer myself. But now I understand it all." Sung Wha paused to drink the swipe. "The Communists are promising everyone land," he continued. And they're keeping their promises."

"When I saw you the last time, I was very sad," Eung Whan said, his eyes moistened by the memory. The light from the kerosene lantern had dimmed. "Remember? We parted, I went south to find a way to Hawai'i, and you journeyed to the north. And you haven't told me fully what happened to you." He set aside his empty cup, enough brew for the night. "I have never felt as lost as I did then. I didn't know where I was going. It seemed like all of my attachments to the world—our family and friends, the village—had all been cut off. I was free, but I didn't like this freedom. When eldest brother Il Whan came back with that rifle and told us of the high living in the city, I wanted to go immediately and see the world, right then and there.

"But all of that changed that morning we parted. The last night we were together at that rice farmer's house I cried before sleeping. I was ashamed. I couldn't help it, but the tears just came out. I couldn't help it. I felt like a lost child." Eung Whan yawned and rubbed his eyes. "Let's go to sleep. It's late. And tomorrow is another long workday."

"And tomorrow I'll start building my airplane."

"You foolish dreamer."

"I have to get back to my wife and children."

"But why did you leave your family in the first place?"

Kim Sung Wha passes through the backside of the plantation camp, behind the mud-stained shanties and outhouses and the community bathhouse. He hears the sing-song voices of children playing nearby. A baby cries. Behind the company garage of trucks and tractors, that makeshift weekend camp cinema, he stumbles upon a cockfight. He sees the backs of squatting and swaggering men, tobacco smoke rising in disturbed tresses. Two heads turn, two Korean men standing at the side aloof from the rest. Sung Wha is vaguely acquainted with them; they once worked for the sugar plantation he worked on, but they were fired for unknown reasons. Sung Wha surprises himself by remembering their names. They're not thought of highly by their fellow Koreans: one was caught loving another man's wife, the other known for his overpriced opium.

The two men regard each other for a moment, with a whispered word or two. Opportunity. Then, smiling, they break from the fringes of the crowd and approach Sung Wha.

"Sung Wha, how have you been?" says one, the short, wiry one with a scar on his right cheek. "Where have you been? I heard the bad news about your firing. So what are you doing now?"

"Come, good friend, and join in the fun and moneymaking," says the other, a little taller and wider and with an oval

69

reddish face covered with pock marks. "Persimmonface," the other Koreans call him. His face always a bright red, never tanning to a brown.

Sung Wha shakes his head. He is not a gambler; he knows he'll lose everything if he is to bet. He touches the slight bulge of his pants pocket, money for supplies to build his ricepaper airplane, his way back home, Korea. Persimmonface has an eye on Sung Wha's hand.

"Sung Wha," Persimmonface says, "we can give you a good tip. You see that Filipino with the cock back there, ready to fight the next match? That cock is the best fighter in the camp. That cock is undefeatable. A sure win. You can double your money in a minute. You can make a lot of money for so little work on that cock right there, if you take our advice."

Sung Wha shakes his head, thinking: *no, I don't gamble. Gambling is for fools, misfits, and bums, like them. I'm no gambler.*

"Sung Wha, you can make a lot of money, in a snap," says Scarface.

"Yes . . . a lot of money," says Persimmonface.

"No," Sung Wha says. "I don't know how to gamble. I have more important things to do than gamble."

Scarface laughs. "This Sung Wha is a real joker!"

"Oh, come on, Sung Wha," says Persimmonface. "Gambling is clean fun, especially when you have the inside tip on the next match." He winks an eye.

"But you don't have to be a gambler," says Scarface. "That cock is a sure shot. You know what a sure shot is, Sung Wha? It means you have practically won already. You can start counting all the money you have already won. Think about it. Money in your hand. Easy money." Scarface holds up a fat wad of money for Sung Wha to see.

Sung Wha's eyes widen. He touches his pocket, his hands sweat. He shakes his head.

"This is money I won in only half an hour," Scarface says. He spreads the soiled bills fanlike. It is the most money Sung Wha has ever seen.

Sung Wha shakes his head again and walks away from them, but Persimmonface runs him down and puts a hand on his shoulder, stopping him. Scarface catches up with them.

"Sung Wha, it takes no great skill to win money," Persimmonface remarks. "Just a little smarts. And you have a lot up there. I know. And besides, we're giving you unmistakable advice."

"Yes," Scarface says, huffing and nodding.

Sung Wha shakes his head. "No."

"But you must be quick in taking it," Scarface advises. He draws a deep breath. He points back at the crowd. "The cock is fighting next. This match is already over. They're getting set for the next one. And look, Myung"—coughing—"Duk, at that other cock they're bringing out. My! How bad that cock looks! Look at how its head droops. And it hasn't even fought yet!"—coughing—"And look at how its feathers . . . are all ruffled. It surely will lose. It's no match for the other cock. They should stop this fight. I feel sorry for that cock. But it'll make a good stew . . . for its owner tonight. Ha ha—" coughing.

"Think of all that money you'll make, Sung Wha," Persimmonface says. "Enough to live like a *yangban* for a year. Think of it."

If he wins, he'll have enough to pay passage to Korea on a steamship. Maybe not quite enough. But perhaps he can make up the remainder by working on Eung Whan's plot of pineapples. Or perhaps his cousin could loan him the few needed dollars. Then, in no time, he'll be back, united with his family.

But if he loses, he loses everything; he won't even have money to buy materials for the airplane. There's too much to lose.

Scarface talks with his hands: "Come on, Sung Wha. You're a winner already. It's a guarantee."

Sung Wha shakes his head. He turns to move on, but Persimmonface has a hand on his shoulder again. "Look," he says. He waves a ten-dollar bill in front of Sung Wha's face. "To show you my confidence in this cock, I'll give you some of my own money to add to your cash. Just give me back the ten dollars after you collect your winner's take and we'll call it even."

Sung Wha's hands sweat more. With the fifty-three dollars in his pocket plus the ten dollars from Myung Duk, he could win sixty-three dollars. Plus his fifty-three, that adds to one hundred and sixteen dollars. Would that be enough for his passage home? Perhaps it would take care of most of it. For a moment he thinks about his wife and two children struggling in a cold winter somewhere in Manchuria.

He takes the ten from Myung Duk. With the money from his pocket, he enters his bet in the circle.

The two hand-held cocks face each other, beak-to-beak, their coiling necks dodging each other's jabs. Then they are thrown together. Mad fluttering of feathers. Long blades affixed to their legs slice the air, missing. On the ground they prance after each other, like boxers, like feathered gladiators, then up they fly, the death knives lifted and missing again. One, two more times. Then Sung Wha's cock is down, a sliver of bright steel in its breast. Blood spurts from its wound to the ground, forming purple stains. The other cock struts proudly around the fallen one, spreads its wings in triumph, then attacks again. In and out. The dying cock is grabbed by a wing and raised high above the loud men, its head lolling, its eyes half-closed, death coming fast.

Sung Wha is crestfallen. He sees only the dirt under his feet. He cannot believe what has happened.

Myung Duk, out of a mean kindness from his cold-cold heart, gives him minor consolation by telling him to forget about the ten dollars. Sung Wha is speechless; he cannot utter a word; he turns and shuffles away, his feet heavy and numb. A thought flashes through his mind: *but why is Myung Duk so happy?*

Mo Kee runs after Sung Wha, pats him on the back. Sung Wha turns and catches Mo Kee, forcing back a smile. "That is too bad, Sung Wha," he says. "Maybe next time your luck will change."

Sung Wha brushes away Scarface's hand. He draws a deep, painful breath.

"Here, take this. Go into the town and have some drinks on us."

On us?

Sung Wha takes the money, one dollar. Maybe he will use the money to get drunk; there's nothing else to do, that's not enough money to buy ricepaper with anyway. He'll buy a bottle of cheap wine and get drunk. He doesn't say a word. He waves Mo Kee away and walks on. Behind him, a roar of cheers rises as the winners divide the money. Mostly it's Sung Wha's money, Sung Wha's passage money to Korea, his dream money going up in tobacco smoke.

An hour later, while wandering in the darkening side streets of Wahiawā town, he comes upon a small group of Filipino cane workers sitting around a large crock, dipping cups and drinking. Sung Wha knows it's pineapple swipe they are drinking. Hoping that they might sell him some of the stuff, he approaches them with the dollar bill out. One worker, sucking on a fat, wet stub of a cigar, waves off the offer and shakes his head: no we aren't selling the swipe, the swipe is for us to drink and enjoy. But he motions Sung Wha into their circle, holding up his empty cup. Come and sip a few, he seems to say. Sung Wha's parched tongue probes a parched mouth; lips chapped, he smiles, sure, thank you, *mahalo,* why not. He sits among his new friends and his new friends offer him sip after sip, and Sung Wha becomes mellow in no time. In broken English and in pidgin they exchange their thoughts; there is a lot in common, everyone being workers on the plantations owned by the haoles, everyone pining for a return trip home with money to live like a king, but: no, that's wrong, Sung Wha argues, wondering if his Filipino comrades can understand his words, you must go back to your homeland and fight against the rich who're controlling your country. And they, in their Mix-Mix and Ilocano: rich, you say? Yes-yes, we want to be rich men when we get home, rich like a provincial governor, masters of our own haciendas; if we save enough money we can become banana barons or the chief of the coconuts. But then one of them: you need a lot of money to do all of that, fool! How can we make money when none of us has a job? And another: aiii, don't remind me of our misfortune. And another: we must stand firm and persevere in this strike, it is in the interest of everyone. And the other: but what's wrong with just dreaming? Must you interfere with my dream making? I don't bother you, so let me do what I please. And Sung Wha: yes, I agree with you, it's bad what's happening in your country as well as mine, but it's something that can be corrected through struggle. And later one of the Filipino workers brings out a small battered guitar and the singing commences: songs of lost love, of unrequited love, of love eternal, of fleeting love under the light of the moon. Their faces are enamored of the music and singing, their eyes moistening in a seasoned melancholy: how long more, boys, until we can go home, smell those mouth-watering good smells of our food, feel our bodies swelter under that hot but friendly Filipino sun? How long, boys, how long, until our eyes can rest on beautiful Filipino women in their flowing sarongs and with the bright sunlight shimmering off their black-black hair held together in buns?

They finish all that swipe. Sung Wha stands up shakily, gesturing his words: I come back. They read his arms and hands and fingers clearly, and nod their heads. Sung Wha goes to the nearest store and purchases the largest bottle of the cheapest wine. He returns and they polish off all that wine in no time, that warm red wine sweet and mellow and syrupy, no comparison to the firewater they have just drunk. And that purchase leaves Sung Wha with a thin dime in his pocket.

Sung Wha leaves them soon after, friendships and brotherhood seamed together securely. They bid him farewell; come back again, they say. Sung Wha cannot decipher Ilocano, but he understands what his new friends are saying.

He reels down the deserted main road with hands in pockets, fingering the coin. Then, in frustration, thinking of the bad luck he had at the chicken fight, he flings the coin into the street. They cheated him, those two lousy Koreans; deep inside he knows he is right. After all, who in his right mind would loan ten dollars to a mere acquaintance? They probably knew that the cock was diseased. Or old. It couldn't even lift its feathers, the way it fought. He kicks the dirt.

His eyes catch sight of a gleaming black sedan parked outside a bar; tonight the bar is quiet, the ill-lit doorway speaks of no business. Sung Wha cannot see the driver; he is either too drunk or it is too dark, but the orange glow of the cab dome is appealing to his eyes. Sung Wha staggers toward the cab; maybe he'll take the taxi home, at least as close to home as possible. Why not. But wait . . . the money. He backtracks in search of the dime and luckily, by the light of the moon, discovers the dull glimmer of the coin. He picks it up and goes to the taxi, and now the cab's domelight is off. Sung Wha looks in the cab at the worried face of the young Filipino driver: you know, no can trust these Yobos, they get drunk, they dunno what they doing, bumbye they hit me in the head and steal my money.

"You . . . okay?" Sung Wha asks.

"No-no, phrend," the driver says anxiously. "Me *pau hana* today."

"You takey me home, den."

"No-no." The driver shakes his head with finality, waving off the potential fare. "Me *pau hana. Pau.*"

Sung Wha offers him the dime. "Nuff *kālā?*" The drivers crutinizes him. "Nuff? No nuff?"

The driver sighs, his eyes vexed. "Twenty-phive cents," he says, "den I take you."

Sung Wha fishes in his empty pockets, then offers an honest look of despair. "No mo *kālā*. Ten cents no nuff?"

The driver studies the anguish on Sung Wha's face, regards the dismal entrance of the bar, then nods his head regretfully. "Okay, den. We go," he says, taking the coin from Sung Wha and motioning him in. The driver starts the engine.

A happy Sung Wha gets into the front seat. He admires the shine of the car's interior. "Nice-nice," he says, pointing to the dashboard.

The driver offers a weak smile. "Where you go?" he asks.

"Ko camp. Camp. Pineapple." Sung Wha points in the direction he wants to go. "Pineapple camp."

The car slowly accelerates down the street. They pass the last squat wooden building of the town and head toward the plantation camp, some six miles down the dark road.

"Kim Sung Wha." Sung Wha offers his hand. They shake.

"Eddie Miguel."

"Me ko . . . eh . . . Korea. Me fly *paeng-gi*." Sung Wha spreads his arms out, almost poking the driver in the eye, flapping his arms like a bird. *"Paeng-gi."*

Miguel shakes his head. "Whas dis?"

"Paeng-gi. Paeng-gi."

"Whas dis . . . *paeng-gi?*"

"Ko zoom-zoom!"

"Paeng-gi? Zoom-zoom?"

Sung Wha nods. *"Paeng-gi."*

"Paeng-gi? Zoom-zoom? Oh! Eh-p'ane. *Ehhh*-p'ane." Miguel's eyes glitter with understanding. He makes circles with a finger, prop-like. "Zoom-zoom-zoom. Yeah-yeah?"

"Yeah-yeah." Sung Wha nods his head with satisfaction. "Eh-p'ane." Sung Wha sighs. "Me fly eh-p'ane ko Korea."

Miguel laughs nervously. "You good joke, you."

Sung Wha shakes his head.

The driver gives Sung Wha a skeptical look. "How you can? You mo' akamai den haole boy? No can do. How you fly eh-p'ane? *Where* yo' eh-p'ane?"

"No. Me fly. Like . . . like . . . " Sung Wha spreads his arms again and flaps.

The driver laughs. "You funny man, you. Whas yo' name again? You too much drink, I t'ink."

Sung Wha joins him in light laughter. Then: "No. Me no joke."

Miguel stops laughing and regards Sung Wha with earnest. "You no joke? You smaht man, den. If can. Smaht-smaht man." He holds back an urge to laugh.

"Me fly. Same-same bird."

"Same-same bird? Den you no joke, den?"

"Me no joke. Why you say?"

Miguel rolls his shoulders. "Me no *sabe*." He pauses, sorting out his thoughts. "Dis kine, no suppose to t'ink 'bout."

"Why you say?"

"Me no know. No suppose to t'ink 'bout. You *sabe?* You makey dream . . . good-good. But no can do, dis dream." Miguel shakes his head. "Only dream, but no can do."

"Haole man can. Me can. You can."

Miguel chuckles agreeably, but with reservation. "You hard-head, eh, you Yobo!"

"Me can fly. Me makey eh-p'ane," Sung Wha says in drunken defiance. "Me ko Korea."

"Okay, den, mistah. How you makey yo' eh-p'ane?"

A finger to his temple: it's all in the head, the figures, the facts, the pictures. "Me ko Korea," Sung Wha says mistily, his eyes drifting out the side of the car into the darkness: he sees thick, dark clouds, and that's all he sees. He doesn't see his air-plane flying. Just those dark clouds coming closer, surrounding him, absorbing him.

The men are silent until they reach the camp. Miguel stops in the middle of a dark dirt road. Sung Wha thanks the driver, then opens the door.

Sung Wha feels a tap on his shoulder as he's getting out. He turns around. Miguel offers the dime back to him. "You take," Miguel says. "You go makey yo' eh-p'ane."

Sung Wha shakes his head emphatically. But Miguel is persistent; he grabs Sung Wha's wrist and presses the coin into his closed fist. Sung Wha tosses the coin on Miguel's lap. The coin slips between Miguel's legs, dropping to the irretrievable darkness of the floor. Miguel shakes his head. He searches for the coin, muttering: you hardhead Yobo, you hardhead you. . . .

Before Sung Wha can get completely out of the car, Miguel slips something into Sung Wha's back pants pocket. Then he drives off before Sung Wha can close the door. The cab stops about five yards away. Miguel leans over to the passenger side to shut the door, then sticks his head out the window and says, "Fo' yo' eh-p'ane, mistah. Go fly Korea. *Mabuhay!*"

The taxi leaves Sung Wha breathing a cloud of dust.

The dime. He doesn't want that dime back. Too much bad luck. Now he has brought the bad luck home. Fretfully, he sinks his hand into the back pocket; he is thinking of throwing the dime in the dirt, but maybe someone will pick it up and get its bad luck. Sung Wha doesn't want that to happen.

He finds not a dime but a folded piece of paper. He opens it. It is paper money. Studying it closely under the light of the moon, he reads a "5" in one corner. Five dollars. It is a big gift from a struggling taxi driver. How long did it take Eddie Miguel to earn this? One week of work? Two? He cannot believe a total stranger has given him this. Earlier, he was robbed of his money. And now this.

As Sung Wha treks up the trail on the slopes above the plantation camp to his cousin's homestead, tears fall from his eyes. He is thinking of all the good people he has met since arriving in Hawai'i, forget about all those bad eggs. Then he dreams of home. Korea. And of his marvelous ricepaper airplane, flying in a clear blue sky.

I turn away from Uncle. I cannot stand the sight of a man crying. Uncle is an old man. Maybe now he's regretting some of the things he did in his life. Maybe he's thinking that life hasn't turned out the way he thought it should have, or that all the hardships he suffered, after all, weren't necessary. Though he has never complained about it, I know Uncle led a hard life. Maybe now he's getting bitter about it all. Maybe he's thinking that he brought all of those hardships on himself, and because of that, life's golden opportunities have never fallen on his lap, like how they have on others.

But Uncle's not like this, right, feeling sorry for himself?
But I am embarrassed watching Uncle cry like this. I wish
he'd stop crying. A man who cries fails to hide his emotions and
therefore is not a man. Didn't Uncle tell me this? A man should
never show his sorrows. He's supposed to hide his feelings, hurt
or otherwise. Be a man. A man is supposed to be strong, not
weak, and not cry like a lost child in front of others. And here's
Uncle, my always tough-talking uncle . . . here he is crying like
a child.

Yong Gil, you got no respect for your uncle, thinking that
way about him. C'mon, you ungrateful person, you . . . be
ashamed of yourself.

He doesn't make a sound, not even a whimper, when he
cries. And now his tears have stopped. His crying is perhaps like
a brief but soothing warm summer rain. Uncle is a strong man.
This must be a freak of nature . . . his crying. He's feeling lousy
tonight. He told me when I first came in that he feels the pain
now, entering and leaving his body, then entering again, like a
dull knife going in and out and in. He still refuses the pain-
killers, but I think in a little while he's going to soften. From the
pain. He's going to start welcoming those easy shots of mor-
phine; he'll begin listening to the doctors' orders and not to his
willpower. Maybe that's why he argues less now when they
come on their rounds. He's breaking down. How can I sit here
and watch this once strong, outspoken, fearless man break
down? It's not natural. It's unjust. Why does this cancer have to
be so dehumanizing, sneaking into a healthy body and slowly—
no, quickly—destroy everything living?

Shit. Now I'm crying.

July 1928

Humming a tune of return, Kim Sung Wha hitched the mule to
the wooden post outside the general store. He glanced down
the dusty main street of Wahiawā town, a passing warm rain

turning the red dirt of the street to the color of fresh blood *when rains come hard mud splashes on sides of flat-green buildings staining them red, when men walk on this dirt trouser cuffs turn red, all day working in fields this red dirt gets in clothes hair eyes enters the pores of skin.* He taps the butt of the old animal in time with his song and steps up to the store.

Sitting on a bench next to the entrance, Persimmonface and Scarface—yeah, those two no-good lousy Koreans from the camp games—stop in the middle of a dried-up story. They watch Sung Wha tramp up the steps unaware of their presence. Persimmonface runs a finger across a wet forehead, then touches the front of his sweat-brimmed hat and tips it back to the notch of his hairline. Hatless, Scarface rubs his whiskered chin, his tired eyes now glinting. They whisper. Sung Wha sees them when he reaches the top of the steps; Persimmonface's and Scarface's eyes hesitate when they see him see them. His walk rhythm shaken, Sung Wha shrinks back, then moves forward toward the door, his footfall now noticeably soft.

"Long time no see, Sung Wha!" greets Scarface. "My! You're looking good."

A sullen Sung Wha looks beyond their touchy, grabby eyes.

"You have a nice-looking mule there," comments Scarface.

Sung Wha sneers, walks past them. He'd pound their heads in if he thought it would be worth it.

"We haven't seen you at the camp games for a long time," says Persimmonface. "So what have you been doing?"

Sung Wha stops at the entrance, turning to them. "At least I'm not robbing people of their hard-earned cash."

Persimmonface erupts from his seat and takes an angry step forward, a redness bursting onto his cheeks. Scarface grabs him by the shirt, pulling him back, saying, "But Sung Wha, what we do is provide a necessary service for the plantation workers. They don't have to come if they don't want to. But if any Korean loses money, at least the money circulates among Koreans and not anyone else. They will eventually win it back some other day. Right?" He grins at his cohort, who spats out an unpleasant word. "You see, Sung Wha, people are not forced to come. It's their own choice if they want a chance at winning big money. It was just not your lucky day, that unfortunate day. You will have a good day. It's due to you."

"I did not lose. You stole my money."

"Ah—Sung Wha! It's not good to be a poor loser."

Sung Wha lunges at them and strikes Scarface on the face. Persimmonface wraps Sung Wha in a headlock, and all three wrestle against the wooden railing, then tumble down the steps and into the street. People in the store poke their heads out the doorway to see what the racket is about. Then a plantation *luna,* a heavyset Portuguese, runs into the street and pulls them apart.

"Cut da fightin'! Cut it out!" the *luna* shouts, drawing more attention to himself than the grapplers. "You guys *pupule* or what? Cut it out befo' I call da cops!"

The two gamblers disperse quickly. Sung Wha dusts off his clothes and regards the *luna* with narrow, distrusting eyes.

"You heard what I said? You get hard time hearing or what?" The *luna* shakes his head.

Thinking that the *luna* has said something derogatory to him in English, Sung Wha says, "Shit you." He swears in Korean, too. Then, turning his back on the *luna,* he unhitches the mule and leads it down the street.

His ribs are sore. That fall down the steps. With each footfall he feels the sharp pain.

Be strong like bamboo. Bend in the wind.

The blur of the bamboo switch coming down on his hand. The pain sharp, stinging. He bites his tongue. The taste of blood. The cruel switch of the teacher comes down another half dozen times. Tears burst forth, but there is no wailing. The biting of the tongue. The taste of blood. Chun and his power rule. Those flat, accusing black eyes distanced by a pince-nez. Dressed in the dark clothes of foreigners. "Why did you do this? Not telling, huh? Well, then, you will after this." Eyes wincing. A numbness. Warm swellings.

"But my body like one bamboo. Strong and hard. And flexible. I no can feel da pain, no can feel 'em. Da pain not here. No mo' pain. My body like one strong pole bamboo. Can survive one terrific monsoon season, da wind blowing heavy on it, bending 'em to da ground."

August 1928

He parks the wagon in the middle of the town next to a garbage bin. The biting smell of rotting food rises in the still summer heat. With an iron rod, he pokes into the heap of rubbish, looking for anything he can use for his airship. He pushes aside empty wooden crates, broken brown bottles, newspapers, and maggot-covered food. He hooks a twisted, rusted front wheel of a bicycle and pulls it partly out of the bin.

What can he use this for? For what part of the airplane?

He envisions himself at the seat of the bicycle, pedaling, his airplane taking the wind and flying, though he cannot see how the bicycle is connected to the airplane. But it is certainly too valuable to leave in the garbage. There must be some use for it.

He yanks it out of the bin and stands it on its flattened tires. He examines the rust-caked chain. He sits on the hard seat. Then, balancing for a moment, he tries the stubborn pedals and the chain breaks off the ungiving sprocket.

Perhaps he can power the airplane with this pedaling action, somehow connecting the bicycle to a propeller like the propeller that powered the airplane in the moving pictures. He cannot see the connecting mechanical details of the idea, but again he sees himself flying above thick whorls of clouds and blue skies and a blinding morning sun above him. He is pedaling his flying machine above the clouds.

He loads the bicycle on the wagon, then returns to the bin. "You friggin' dumb Yobo! Dere you go again. Das all what you good fo' anyway, picking up everybody else's '*opala!*"

The voice of the *luna*, Souza. Sung Wha turns around.

On the landing of the next building, the *luna* stands tall and proud, his hairy, thin arms folded over a shoulderless body. He grins, showing a set of bad teeth. "Eh, Yobo . . . you heard what I said? You deaf ear or what?"

Eyes meet eyes, though Sung Wha lowers his. He waves the *luna* off with the poker, a flag of surrender. He doesn't want any trouble, not now. He turns his back to the *luna*.

The *luna* jumps down from the landing, balling his hands into fists and moving his arms in a John Sullivan-esque manner. "What, Yobo! You threatening me wit' yo' iron bar or what?! Hah?! What?—you like me bus' yo' ass fo' good?!"

Sung Wha stops and waves the poker again at him: *no, you damn stupid fool. I don't want to fight. I have too many important things to do than fight with you. Don't bother me.*

Souza crouches low, moving sideways, his fists stabbing the air with uppercuts.

". . . like one ugly, long-legged hairy crab."

"You friggin' Yobo! You one dirty fighter too, eh? What—you cannot go one-on-one wit' me? You gotta pick up one iron bar?! Eh—you sca'd me? Come on! I take you on!"

The *luna* swung wildly at the Korean. Sung Wha threw the poker down and charged. The two tangled, punching each other's back and sides, kicking and grappling, grunting, finally falling and rolling in the dirt with their shirts bunched up. Souza wrestled his way up and jabbed Sung Wha's head twice before being knocked down with a kick to the back of his head. They rolled side-to-side on the ground, their arms locked together, neither able to get in any punishing blows. After an exhausting minute or two of stalemate, they were broken apart by a shopkeeper and a couple of plantation workers passing by.

Blood flowed from a gash on Sung Wha's forehead; Souza's nose was bloodied. They were breathing hard, their eyes showing exhaustion and frustration.

"I going get you—you friggin' Yobo! You watch out! You bettah watch yo' ass—Yobo—I going right now—tell da company where you stay! You watch out! I going get you deported outta Hawai'i!"

Sung Wha surged after the *luna* but was held back. The *luna* climbed the landing, then scampered down the street, craning his long neck back and swearing.

"You nevah seen in yo' life how one scared bastard can run so fast."

Sung Wha sloughed the dust from his clothes and straightened himself. A button was missing from his shirt. He got on the creaky wagon and drove off, turning down a side road and stopping the mule in front of a church converted from a plantation workers' barrack, newly whitewashed and signified by a solitary wooden cross nailed to the front peak of the corrugated iron roof. He didn't know why he had stopped the wagon; he had never stopped in front of this church before, though he had passed it many, many times. There was never a necessity for him to stop at any opium den. He never believed in any of those Korean gods or the work of shamans, so why believe in a white man's god? Perhaps it was something about the fresh whiteness of the building in contrast to the redness of the rest of Wahiawā that stopped him. It was a sinister feeling he felt, this building standing out from the rest with its color of death. His eyes deliberated on the cross. The setting sun came out fully from behind a cloud, and it gave the cross and the side of the building a vibrant, golden tinge. The sun also showed him a water spigot on the side, partly hidden by weeds.

Water is water, at a Korean's house or white man's. And I am thirsty.

He got off the wagon, tied the mule to the picket fence, and went to the faucet, where he washed his hands and face, then quenched his thirst. Backing away and wiping his face with a sleeve, he looked up at the cross and saw an image that paralyzed him.

Lee Chi Ha was hanging there, his head in a deathly tilt, flies buzzing around and in an open mouth.

Sung Wha squeezed his eyes tightly, beads of water dripping down his cheeks.

I forbid you to see this. I forbid it. I forbid it.

He broke away from the vision and turned to the sun, opening his eyes to its blinding light.

Leave me.

He returned to the cross, his sight now blotched with a large blind spot. A voice called out, startling him: "You are welcome to enter the house of God."

Standing at the church's entrance was a tall, thin figure in black. Sung Wha rubbed his eyes, and his sight cleared enough to see a young bespectacled Korean looking at him curiously. He had a frail face, his protruding cheek bones and small, fragile chin giving it a top-heavy look. He motioned Sung Wha to enter.

"Who are you?"

"Let me introduce myself. I am the new minister of the church. Please. You are welcome to come in for fellowship with our Lord."

Sung Wha shook his head. "I don't have a lord," he said, "and I don't believe in religion."

The minister smiled. "Then, may I ask, what do you believe in, sir? Are you, then, a Buddhist?"

Sung Wha shook his head.

"Then of what religion are you, if I may so kindly intrude?"

"Nothing."

The minister's smile faded. "Come now. Everyone must believe in some sort of faith."

Sung Wha regarded the minister's words sourly. "I don't believe in nonsense, in lies." He paused, checking on the mule and wagon. "But I believe in man."

"Then you are at the right place. The church believes in the salvation of man. Jesus Christ died for our sins. Please come in. You're very welcome in the house of our Savior."

"No, thank you. I just came here for your water."

"Please, help yourself."

Sung Wha thanked the minister and started back to the wagon.

"Can I offer you," the minister called out, "some rice cakes and tea?"

The rice cakes were delicious and filling. Sung Wha had not eaten for the entire day. *The house of God is a farce,* he thought, *but it fills one's stomach.*

"And what province are you from?" the minister asked. He poured more hot tea into Sung Wha's cup.

"P'ih-yon."

The minister nodded as if he were familiar with the area. "My mother's family is from there. The Choe family?"

We are distant cousins. At first we are strangers and now we are family.

"My name is Chang Il-buk. I have just been assigned to this church. When I was a small child, I left Korea with my parents to come to America. Since then, I have never been back to Korea. It is wonderful to see many Koreans living here. I studied the word of God at an American university. This is my first charge. But please tell me about Korea. Has it changed much these past years? I gather it has."

"The Japanese still control Korea. The Japanese have conquered our land. They are nothing but dogs."

"Not all Japanese are as what you harshly describe. At my theology school, I met a fellow from Japan who thought it was sinful what the Japanese imperial government is doing in Korea."

"Not all Japanese are the same. You are right. But most of them are. Look at the Japanese here. Do you think for a moment they are concerned with what is happening to Koreans? Never. But they will support anything that will benefit Japan. Koreans and Japanese will never get along. Friends of mine who were here before me said that when Japan annexed Korea, Koreans in the fields broke their hoe handles and attacked the Japanese field workers."

"But wasn't that Koreans attacking Japanese?"

"Yes . . . but no. They brought that attack on themselves when Japan annexed Korea."

"But these Japanese here, are they not innocent of the crimes of their government?"

"What kind of Korean are you? If you're Japanese, you're Japanese. Why do you sit here and defend the Japanese for the atrocities they commit against the Korean people?"

"I'm not defending the Japanese government. But it seems to me that the blame of such a crime should not be put on innocent people. I'm against what the emperor of Japan and his government are doing in Korea. The Japanese army should not be in Korea at all. Korea should be for Koreans. But we must not be blinded by simple prejudices. God loves everyone. That is all I'm saying. But tell me more about the homeland. At times I crave any news from the country of my birth. Has it changed much? Do the streams still flow with icy clear water? Are the springs still accompanied by the beautiful songs of birds? Is the snow as white as clouds and do they feel like clouds?"

"Dis *moksa* . . . first time I thought he one agent fo' da Japanee gov'ment. Cannot trust anybody talking like dat dose days. You nevah hear one Korean talk li'dat. But throw me off, even da traitors no talk like that. But da way he asking me questions, I look at him and think to myself, 'No, dis guy get too honest one face. He probably *is* one man of God.'"

"What brought you here to Hawai'i, Mr. Kim?"

"I came here to escape the Japanese. I am a wanted man in Korea. The Japanese are looking for me and want to hang me from a tree."

A worried look wavered on the face of the minister. "May I be so bold as to ask what kind of crime did you commit, Mr. Kim?"

Sung Wha studied the minister's sensitive, querying face.

All religious people seem so honest and trustworthy, yet this is the danger, when you let these types of people influence your mind with their ideas of salvation and heaven and hell.

"My only crime is that of being a revolutionary who wants to see my homeland free from the Japanese invaders. And I don't believe that your god, or any other god for that matter, can ever free the Motherland. I believe in truth. I believe in revolution. Revolution is the only way Korea can free itself from the tyranny of imperialism and its own ruling class."

"What is this word you use, 'imperialism'?"

"The Japanese want to kill me because I have spoken and acted against their imperialist designs for our country. I'm a fighter for the people, the Korean people, and they don't like this one bit. They fear my kind. Those bastards of dogs!

"We'll free Korea one day and that day is coming soon. In fact, in China, a giant revolution is happening. It'll spread to Korea. Then gone will be the bastard upper class who steals every grain of rice we harvest. And gone will be the dog-fucking Japanese army. We'll be free. We'll build Korea into a powerful, democratic country."

"You speak . . . with much force, much power," the minister says. His face is tentative. "But I am sad that you do not embrace our Father in heaven and our Lord and Savior Jesus Christ. If you truly want to free the soul, you must embrace Him. But your words interest me. Tell me more about your experiences. I, too, believe that Korea must be free, but only through the kingdom of God will it achieve such full glory. When we Koreans free ourselves within, when we let the Lord into our hearts to give us spiritual direction and strength, only then can Koreans experience true freedom. We must fill ourselves with the love of God and Jesus Christ and for the brotherhood of all mankind."

"Your god is worse than a bastard dog's."

"Ho! You should see his face when I told him dat, Yong Gil. Da *moksa*, he almost *huli* on da floor. His face wen turn from white to pink to one green color. I seen him breathing hard, having one hard time. I know he all angry inside, but shit, I no like listen to his bullshit. I hear it all already. But right aftah dat, jus' as I was getting up to go, he pour me one nada cup tea, he bring out some mo' rice cakes, he tell me sit down, Mr. Kim, we disagree wit' each ada, but I like listen what you get say 'bout Korea, 'bout China.

"I almost flip. Wen throw me off. Here dis *moksa*, dis man of god, sitting right 'cross dis table front of me wit' his thick-thick eyeglasses and he telling me he like hear some mo' my story, all da things I did. No can believe what I was hearing.

"So I drink one sip tea. I sit back. Den I tell him my story."

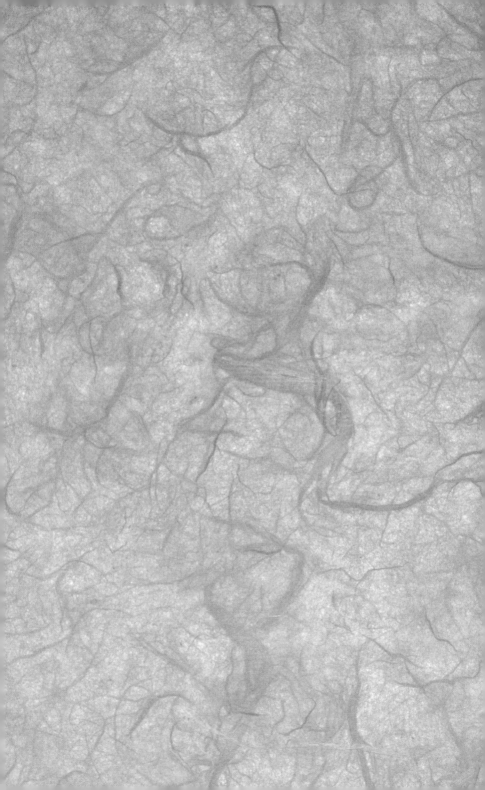

The Tiger of

Kumgangsan

and Other

Stories

We travel south along gentle running brook, our feet numb from morning cold. Old snow still clings to banks, and broken-off bits drift down with lethargic whorl of water. But it is beautiful, this time of year: birds awakening, quarreling, and singing spring songs; green buds pushing out like barnacles on bare branches; the fecund odors of a reviving earth rising in wild, clean air of country. We follow brook's persuasion for *li* and *li*. We are silent, we of simple hearts. No words of sadness and regret we carry, only the feel of aimless, empty hearts. Behind us is our village, the only world we know, and our bodies race to an uncertainty. We are being chased: our heads they're after. We know that. And what can we do? "We are men!" We laugh. We can call ourselves men? Our faces smooth like ripe persimmons. What's up for grabs in this world? We reach and grab at the empty air! But hunger. Oh, yes, hunger. We have not eaten for days. Missing stomachs, ours. What is it like to be not hungry? We only have that scant relief from the brook, biting cold it is. And as we drink, our mouths water for steaming bowls of rice or millet. We passed a hamlet yesterday oozing with the warm aromas of rice cooking that turned our heads and stomachs, and yet we went on, hungrier and weaker from the temptation. But we went on.

Once I almost broke our silence. I was ready to run off to a farmer's shack and beg for a bowl of rice. But Eung Whan held me back. He is the strong one, the brave one. He said we can go without food for another day, we must get out of the area, the Japanese are looking for us, once we are out of the province then we can stop for some food and rest, if we stop now we are dead. I told him, how can we run when we don't have the energy to do so? He didn't answer my question but showed me a few coins he had taken before our flight from the village. On one side of a coin was the ugly, monocled profile of the Japanese emperor, and on the other, a chrysanthemum.

Instead of eating we sleep. It is hard to sleep at nights with the cold ground our bed and the cold air our blanket. Sometimes we cover ourselves with straw, but still the cold creeps in with us. We have to keep on moving even in our sleep: rolling this way, rolling that way to keep warm. And we can never stay in one place long, maybe for three or four hours at the most, afraid that our snores may attract the enemy.

But what gives these dreary times meaning are the talks Eung Whan and I have. We talk about where we are going or what we are going to do. Should we head north toward Manchuria where all patriotic Koreans are going? My cousin says that the Korean army, led by the famous General Li, is broken up in various small units and has gone there to reorganize and train in guerrilla warfare. "We Koreans are fleet like the swiftest deer," said General Li, according to my cousin, when the Korean army was crossing the Yalu. "We'll endure like the old turtle, and when we return, we'll be as strong and brave as the Great Tiger of Kumgangsan. We'll rid the Motherland of the Japanese pests once and for all." (How my cousin knows General Li's exact words is a mystery to me.)

Or we can go south and try to find work. But the conditions there are just as bad if not worse, I said. Our cousin Chung Juk went there and returned a few months ago. He said it was very bad there, very bad, people starving and freezing to death, and selling their young children into slavery, their daughters to houses of dishonor.

Or perhaps we could go to Miguk, Eung Whan said. I heard from my brother that the *paginsarym* are hiring *hanguksarym* to work overseas. There is much opportunity there, he said, and I have heard stories of people going to Miguk and working for a short time and in that short time saving a mountain of money, enough to be rich for the rest of their lives. We can return to the village and free the family from work for the rest of our lives.

We lie on the cold ground, shivering, gazing at the stars and the moon, wondering what it would be like to be rich and not worry about money, food, and the planting of rice. We could buy clothes made of silk and wear covered shoes, handle the finest farming tools, and eat polished rice and meat for every meal.

"You understand, Yong Gil, people dose days was poor, dirt poor. No can go market and jus' go buy any kine food, li'dat. People work hard fo' dey money, and all people eat dose days was jus' rice: rice and soup fo' *ah-chim,* ball rice fo' *chom-sim,* rice and kimchee and little bit fish fo' *jhun-yuk,* maybe once a month some *ko-ghee.*"

"Would you like more tea, Mr. Kim? And tell me, what did you and your cousin decide to do? I suppose you decided to come to Hawai'i. But what of your cousin?"

We rested under a huge willow tree. It looked strange and fearful, like a fantastic sea monster with long swaying tentacles. I felt a paralyzing fear for a while, thinking that it was keeping us captive for its next meal. But the thought passed; we were too cold and tired to be afraid of something supernatural.

"Dose days, we believe in *ku-sin.* You know what dat is, eh? But dat time, I think us, we was mo' 'fraid being caught and hanged by da living, by da Japanee soldiers, dan by some ugly-kine ghosts."

Eung Whan said he would take the first watch, that he would wake me when it was my turn, but in a short while I heard him snoring. I fought the urge to sleep; someone had to keep watch, especially with my cousin snoring so loudly, like a groaning pregnant cow. But I couldn't stop my body's desire for sleep; I fell numbly, like a rock plummeting through clouds.

I dreamt that I was alone, high up on a barren mountain trail of Kumgangsan. I had never been in those mountains and I don't know how I knew in that dream that I was in Kumgangsan. But there I was, alone and very cold. I was admiring the giant pine trees and the magnificent frozen waterfalls and the snow-covered mountain peaks that looked like twisted, glistening spires.

Suddenly, a tiger roared in the forest behind me. I must have leaped a *li* into the air for now I was atop a tall tree, frantically grabbing for a branch to hold, snow crumbling through my fingers. Finally my hands found a handle, and I grabbed on desperately. I peeked below. A giant tiger stood on its hind legs, its front claws digging into the trunk of the tree, tearing off bark. The tiger's eyes were emerald fires, and they bored into me. Steam flared from its nostrils like a dragon. My body shook hard and uncontrollably.

The tiger laughed and bellowed in a dark, human voice, "You're a fool to be afraid of me! Only fools are fearful of tigers, and therefore I will eat you because I love to eat fools!" The tiger laughed again. So thunderous was its laughter that an avalanche was started on a nearby mountain; I could hear its distant, groaning rumble. But the tiger's laughter also disturbed the snow on the tree, which fell and covered the tiger completely.

Now the tiger can't harm me, I thought . . . but too hastily.

A terrible jolt went up the tree and left me hanging from the tip of a bending branch. The tiger had burst through the snow and now was climbing toward me. I pulled myself up the branch and reached for a higher one, but all I grasped was thin air.

The tiger was getting closer and closer, snarling and flashing its famous fangs, thick cords of steam funneling from its nostrils.

Then a funny thing happened.

When the tiger was but a couple of branches below me, I swatted the air between us with my bare hand in a desperate gesture to scare it. That was when I discovered that my hands were not hands, that my arms were not arms, and that my legs were not legs. Well, I did have hands, arms, and legs, but not of the human kind. My hands were not hands but paws now. And I was covered all over with thick yellow fur.

I was shocked, perhaps horrified. I could not understand what had happened to me. I forgot myself and slipped down the branch; only my claws digging deep in the bark at the last moment prevented a long fall. With his head tilted and an odd glint in his eyes, the tiger regarded me as if in awe of my transformation.

Another thing happened to me.

A fever surged through my body, shaking it with tremendous hot and cold spells, rocking me convulsively, almost causing me to fall off the tree again. But it went away, quickly and with no residual effect save a blinking of my eyes.

Now, I glare at the tiger, challenging his darkening eyes. Taking a deep breath of the icy air, I roar so loudly—I surprise myself so that I nearly laugh in the middle of my burst—that the trees around us shake, and another avalanche is set off. My thunder streaks to the deepest reaches of the forest and rebounds back, an echo darker than the original and weighted with the dense air of its travel. But the tiger laughs so hard that he himself nearly falls off the tree.

I watch him with alarm. But I discard that concern the way one sloughs off a snowflake from a shoulder. My eyes turn to the pale, purplish sky and they roll with laughter. And when my laughter becomes frivolous trickles that warmly shudder through my body, I look below. The tiger has disappeared.

"So, Uncle Sung Wha, what it means . . . your dream?"

Uncle's eyes were fixed to the ceiling all the time he was telling me the story. I have never seen a giant wild tiger or the mysterious mountains of Kumgangsan that Uncle always talks about. But, then again, I am experiencing these things for the first time, through Uncle: I see the barren color of snow; I feel its blinding cold; I hear the wind running wild over the tops of distant pine.

"I dunno," Uncle said dryly. "Me, I jus' remembah da dreams. I dunno what means, da dreams. My *halmuni*—yo' great-grandmother, yo' *kum-halmuni*—she know how talk what da meaning of dreams. Maybe she say to me I jus' trying be one tiger, 'cause da tiger suppose to be in my blood, in all our family blood. Das all.

"Yong Gil, no talk to me what my dream mean. Me no *sabe* dis kine. I no care what da stuff means, or what it not means. And I too tired talk anymo'."

"My grandfather often told me stories about woodsmen in the Diamond Mountains who were half-tigers. The folklore of Korea is full of these remarkable, fantastic tales. I am quite amused by your stories, Mr. Kim. You are an excellent storyteller. Are you sure I cannot get you more hot tea? How about more rice cakes? Good. I'll be right back."

I was awakened suddenly. Eung Whan was shaking me all over. In the bright light of the full moon, I could see *him* shaking all over, as if a *ku-sin* had passed through us. Fragments of whispered words fell from his mouth like broken teeth from an ancient soothsayer. Why do you howl like that in your sleep? he stammered. I'm a tiger, I told him. Crazy! he told me. You'll bring the Japanese soldiers on us! People from all around can hear you! I told him I was sorry. He let me go, turned away, his back toward me. We were silent for a while. Then I asked him, as we frequently asked each other in the morning, did you also dream? He shook his head, then nodded, then changed his mind again. What is this? I asked. Did you dream or not? He said that he must have dreamt, everyone dreams at night, but that he had forgotten what his dream was about. But I knew he wasn't telling me the truth; I knew he didn't forget. It was that turning of his head, that shying away from the question that told me so. And the faltering of his voice. He didn't want to tell me about his dream. How could he forget a dream so quickly, so easily, unless he wanted to forget? But by wanting so, a dream would cling more tenaciously to a fold in one's mind. And, besides, we had just gotten up, the darkness of night still tightly hedging around us: there is something about darkness that makes dreams linger, even while eyes are open. The darkness becomes—how can I say it?—an extension of the mind? But my cousin didn't want to tell me about his dream, this particular dream. Why, I don't know. We were always telling each other our dreams and experiences; why this time he held back still escapes me.

There must have been a good reason. We never hid anything from each other. We were closer than the closest brothers. Our blood was thicker than blood. But that night, he hid this dream from me, and I remember feeling a sense of betrayal, as if a sacred pact between us had been violated. Of course, that dream was his property only, but still I was angered and confused at his decision to leave it at that. I remember thinking that something evil was happening to us, some powerful, unexplainable force was changing us, dividing us, making us aware of the differences in each other.

Later, however, I realized—embarrassingly—that Eung Whan had kept secret his terrible vision perhaps to protect me from its destructive power. Perhaps he had dreamed of my death at the hands of the Japanese, my body bloodied and bullet-riddled and hanging from a dark, damp tree. Or perhaps he had seen my teeth fall out or birds flying upside down in dawn's light. He knew how I tried to read everything in a dream. Whatever it was, the portent must have shaken him badly; the dream must have shown him my death, violent and unfulfilled.

This I know: if it had been a dream of his own tragic death, he would have told me right away. My cousin is the bravest person I have ever known. He has never feared his own death. But if it was the death of someone he loves, he would hide it.

I remember another time, long ago when we were children, when he tried to keep a dream from me. But because of my stubbornness, he finally released this vision.

I play alongside *Halmuni*. She bends into the stream. She is washing our clothes. She cries, "Aigoo!" She chases away the ache in her back with the pounding of a fist. She says, *"Ah-pah!"* She calls for me to help her. She lifts the basket of clothes. She steps over a wet rock. She slips and falls on her face. Clothes are scattered everywhere. The rock she has fallen on has knocked out her front teeth. Blood is everywhere. Blood is all over the rock, all over the clothes. Blood flows down the stream. Clothes float away down the stream. Blood flows down the stream. Blood is all over the clothes. *Halmuni* has no teeth. She has no teeth.

"One month later, the coldest winter from Kumgangsan that I have ever experienced came down to our village. Our grandmother died that winter while gathering firewood in the forest."

All these years I have often wondered the exact nature of his dream that cold, full-moon night, and if what he had dreamed had come true. Maybe he didn't dream of my death. Maybe it was about something else. Still, his refusal to divulge his dream has bothered me at times.

Since becoming a revolutionary, I have studied the science of men's relationships to other men and nature, and of the armed struggle, and I have rid myself of any remnants of feudal beliefs, like the falsities professed by shamans and the like. Are not all religions built on superstition, lies, and half-truths, and perpetuated by the ignorance of the masses who are kept this way purposely by the ruling class? Are not these ideas ridiculous and, more important, oppressive?

But I must admit this: this cousin of mine, he is as hard as granite, as strong as the thickest mountain bamboo. And yet inside, he is so human, so sensitive to the ways of the four winds. Indeed, he is very soft inside, like a bamboo shoot. And yet so hard.

"We must be out of the province," Eung Whan said. He was leaning into the crook of a dark tree. The full moon shone through the budding branches, and the surface of a speaking brook glimmered with the moon's soft, cold light.

"How do you know?" Sung Wha asked.

Eung Whan took in the moon for a while, then said, "The air . . . it feels different."

Sung Wha rubbed his shrunken stomach. "Let's go to a farmer's hut and beg for a bowl of rice."

"You're always thinking about your stomach, Sung Wha. You live for your stomach, not your heart. And don't you know that people are starving all around us?" Then: "But I'm hungry, too."

"How much money did you say you have?"

"A few coins, no more."

"Enough for a meal at an inn?"

"No."

Sung Wha sighed disconsolately. Bending over the brook, he drank the icy water that numbed but did not satisfy his hunger. He turned to Eung Whan. "And where are we going? Do you have any idea where we're going?"

Eung Whan shook his head and said flatly, "Do you?"

Sung Wha sat on a flat rock and looked over the brook, his eyes sullen and tearing from hunger. "We can't return home, at least for a while. So where do we go from here?"

A long silence separated them.

Finally, Eung Whan: "We could go south. Maybe we can sign up for the boat to America. They say they are hiring men. And they say they pay well."

"I don't want to go to America. I want to stay here."

"Me, too. But where can we go? What can we do?"

"We could go to Manchuria. That's where all Korean patriots are going. That's what you said we should do. That's where General Li is. We could join him."

Eung Whan scratched his head. "But where in Manchuria? Manchuria is a big land."

"We could ask for directions."

"From whom?"

Silence again.

"I guess it wouldn't hurt if we ask around," Eung Whan said. "People around here might know. But we better be careful who we talk to. We don't know who is or isn't a spy for the Japanese. You know, Koreans are telling on Koreans. Not a lot of them are like this, but there're a few here and there." Eung Whan regarded the moon again. "But maybe it is also better," he said, drawing out his last word, "if we did not stay together. The Japanese are looking for two peasant youth."

Another silence. Then, Sung Wha: "Yes . . . I think you're right. So what should we do?"

"We could go our separate ways. One of us goes to America, and the other goes to Manchuria. If one is caught by the Japanese, then at least the other still has a chance."

"You don't think we have a better chance together?"

"No."

Bowing his head, Sung Wha: "But how do we choose who'll go where?"

"We'll throw fingers."

Eyes lowered, Sung Wha nodded in agreement. Each hid one hand behind his back. They decided that whoever won was to head north and the other would go south. Sung Wha called for odd fingers. On the count of three, each showed his hand. Sung Wha showed one finger; Eung Whan, two.

"It's decided," Eung Whan said, a sadness and relief in his voice. "In the morning, we'll go our own ways. But now let's find some food."

"Yes."

They followed a tributary of the brook that led them to a farm. "This water will lead us to a farmer's hospitality," Eung Whan said. "I have a good feeling."

"But it was one sad time when we decide who was going where. I dunno how long we was dere, feeling sad and quiet under dat cold-cold moon, but was one long time. But aftah dat we jus' had to do what we had to do. So we wen follow dis irrigation ditch through one dark, woody area, plenny trees and all kine bushes. Den all of a sudden da trees wen disappear and dis big rice paddy open up right in front of us. And I remembah da moon was big and swollen, kinda lopsided like one egg, and its reflection was fat in da rice paddy. So we walked around da paddy and found dis farmer's house. We was lucky, da farmer was home, he was one nice guy, but when he first saw us he give us one strange look. But what you going think if out of da blue moon two dirty buggahs come right outta yo' rice paddy and stay standing in front of you, asking you fo' food?

"Anyway dis man—I forget his name, but going come back to me, I know I going remembah him, how can I forget da man who wen feed and treat us good?—anyway dis farmer, he was inside his shack sitting on da floor, his legs folded, and he was smoking one pipe, you know da kine lo-o-ong kine pipe you see da old Korean men dey stay smoke in da pictures. His wife was inside, too, right next to him, and dey look like dey jus' wen *pau* eat. He was smoking his pipe, so we jus' go right by da door-way and ask him if can have something fo' eat. First he ask us where we from. So we tell him our village. And to dis day, I cannot forget da look on his face and da exact words he tell us when we tol' him all dis. I cannot forget his words. Can nevah forget."

"So how come it took you so long to get here?" the rice farmer demanded. "We've been expecting both of you for the past three nights. My wife has been preparing more food than we can eat in expectation of your coming. We thought for sure that the Japanese must have captured you.

"Clean your feet on the mat over there. And come inside. Sit down over here. You boys must be hungry. Soon Ja, go and get these young men something to eat, that rice soup you made tonight, and bring some of that salted fish we got from the market yesterday."

Sung Wha sipped his tea and said, "My cousin and I were so surprised. The farmer even knew what our names were! My heart was storming! I thought for sure the Japanese police were hiding in his house, ready to pounce on us."

"Please continue," the *moksa* said impatiently. "So what happened?"

"I thought the rice farmer was an informer, the way he knew our names, the fact that he said he was waiting for us. But one look at my cousin calmed me. My cousin has the ability to judge one's character fast and accurately. I studied my cousin's face—my eyes were round like pumpkins—and I could tell that he had a genuine trust for the farmer. So I felt a little better, though I couldn't help but still feel guarded. And as we sat down on the warm *ondul* floor, what disarmed me was the ever-so-gratifying warm smell of steamed rice. Ah! It smelled so good!

"The farmer said not a word. He just sat there cross-legged with his body leaning to one side, then to the other, and with an inquiring, tired grin on his face. He was puffing the pipe from the corner of his mouth. That's the way he watched us while we ate. I still can remember his pose. A couple of times I looked up from my bowl, and he always had that same grin on his face.

"Later, after we finished eating, he told us that by word of mouth the whole countryside had learned about the rebellion in our village. Our names were passed on through the underground, alerting farmers many *li* around of our flight. He said that people in neighboring villages were prepared to help us in any way."

"That is remarkable. I never knew we Koreans had such an extensive network as that."

"Not really. It wasn't that complex. Just ordinary country

people helping other country people. Koreans helping fellow Koreans. That's all."

"Hmm. But it's still remarkable."

"We all hate the Japanese. It's simple as that."

"That is true. Tell me, Mr. Kim, were there other rebellions of that nature?"

"I really don't know, but I'm sure of it. You must know that it's the very nature of Koreans to speak their minds. That, I know. And this I know, too: whenever Koreans rebelled against the Japanese occupation forces, they were put down brutally. I heard that in one village the Japanese soldiers, to make their point and to further humiliate the Korean people, forced every male to line up in the village square. Then the Japanese commander had one ear cut off each of them. A pile of ears was made in the middle of the village for everyone to see. And the atrocities the Japanese soldiers did to our women!"

"I have heard much of the soldiers' crimes, especially their violations of Korean women. But I have not seen this. What I understand is only through word of mouth, from the mouths of Koreans and Japanese sympathizers."

"Listen, you don't have to witness this to understand that it's the nature of mindless soldiers to do all this dirty work for an imperialist government. Listen, I'll tell you another story. Though our women have been vilified, raped, and murdered, they don't just sit back and do nothing about it. It's not their nature. Many of the best and most courageous fighters in the revolution are women."

"What is this 'revolution' you are talking about?"

"Let me tell you this story. I personally did not see it happen, but my source is truthful. My cousin Yong Wha does not lie. Let me tell you his story."

"Listen, cousin, I have seen this with my very eyes, though at the time my eyes were blurred with the heavy tears of a turtle. My eyes have often told me lies before, but this . . . no. I could not believe what I saw. It is a disgrace! It is an outrage! It is criminal! My blood boils in rage! I cannot sleep without witnessing this over and over again in my dreams. I am tortured and haunted the rest of my life! Maybe when I tell you what happened, some small peace of mind will come to me.

"But there is one thing that I can tell you surely. Never in my entire life have I felt so proud to be a Korean! Though I cry unwillingly and incessantly whenever I think about this, this is what holds me together: the unquestionable bravery and courage of this young peasant girl.

"Cousin, let me sit quietly for a moment. I must weep for her . . . before I tell you her name. Let me sip more this forgetting rice wine. I think you know her, at least her family, but let me lessen my grief, for a little while. . . .

"There, I feel a little better. This wine helps with the mending.

"I went into the village to sell our vegetables. It was a hot day at the market, even our ox was complaining, hotter than most summer days, but it was an ordinary day, nothing odd or special about it. Well, that's how the day started. I was thirsty for a drink, and I remember telling myself that if I had a good day at the market, I didn't think the family would mind if I had a sip or two of rice wine at the inn.

"It was busy and noisy, and I had placed the cart where I usually do, right next to that loudmouth Moon. Even though I cannot stand him, he brings flocks of people around him with his irritating, high-pitched voice, and some of his customers always spill over to my station. Anyway, like I said, it was a normal day, when suddenly people began shrieking, panicking, dispersing in fear. Booths were overturned. Some of my vegetables toppled off my cart and were stepped on and destroyed. There was so much commotion: people screaming, babies crying, horses neighing, dogs barking. Cousin, I thought perhaps a starved tiger of Kumgangsan had come down and was terrorizing the people. But when some of the crowd cleared, I saw what monster it really was.

"The Japanese magistrate and his soldiers had entered the

village on their horses and were beating on anyone in their path. Those insensitive, cruel dogs! Dogs of a bitch of a dozen lovers! They divided the crowd in half and began heaving insult upon insult on us: 'You Koreans are filthy pigs!' 'You Koreans are so stupid, that is why we Japanese have to come here and conquer you and teach you how to live like human beings!' 'Garlic stinkers!' Everyone was silent, our eyes wild but brimming with angry, helpless tears. No one uttered a word, much less took in a breath, we were all deathly afraid of the guns the soldiers held high over our heads and those long, shiny sabers that swung on the magistrate's and the officer's sides.

"Then a young girl—you know her, her name is Chung Min Ja, her family is the Chung family from the next village over—all of a sudden burst out in the open holding high the Korean flag. We all shuddered; we knew the possible danger to her. Chung Min Ja waved the flag above her head undauntedly, she began to shout slogans against the Japanese rule of Korea, she began to sing our anthem. The magistrate's face turned red, his lips pouting like a grunting pig's. The officer commanded his sergeant to clear the crowd and arrest her. The sergeant went up to Chung Min Ja and ordered her to throw down the flag. But she kept waving the flag and singing. We were all tense. I know some of us, maybe all of us, wanted to move in and help her, join her, but how great were our fears.

"The sergeant pointed his rifle at her and ordered her again to stop. But Chung Min Ja did not heed his order. The sergeant's face showed his terror and frustration. He looked at the officer, who looked toward the magistrate, who nodded his head. The officer got off his horse and strutted toward Chung Min Ja, drawing his sword to the disbelief of the crowd. He raised his sword above his head. There were screams and wails. Several women fainted. The officer came down with the sword and severed Chung Min Ja's arm.

"No! I can't go on!

"But courageous Chung Min Ja! She screamed in pain, but with her other arm she grabbed the fallen flag and raised it up.

Then the crowd began attacking the soldiers. There were gunshots and everything went crazy.

"Something inside of me died with her. My life will never be the same. Everyone in the crowd, too. She was so brave.

"But never have I felt so proud. Never have I felt so much pain. I cannot fear death now. I cannot."

"I've seen blood too, Uncle. And death. I was in the war. And we were fighting for democracy, for the free world. The Japanese was our enemy, too, and so were the Italians and Germans. They were Fascists, all of them, believing in their racial superiority. And that's why the Japanese treated the Korean people so badly. If the Germans were in the Orient instead, the Germans would have done the same, that I know.

"I was part of the American forces. We were defending the world against fascism and Communism. If it wasn't for the American forces, these crazy things would still be going on in Korea. And the rest of the world. That I'm sure of, very sure of."

"You know, all my life, yeah, I fight against something—anything—dat is wrong. Sometimes my thinking and actions go far to da extreme, sometimes too far. I know dat. And I know sometimes you think, dat Uncle, sometimes he think and act kine of *pupule*. But I going tell you something, Yong Gil, and I like you listen real close. No get fool by how something look on da outside, you understand? Me, I here talking all dis kine bad things 'bout da Japanee, li'dat.

"But I tell you something: I come Hawai'i, I meet plenny Japanee, and dey no all think da same-same like da kine Japanee who make plenny *pilikia* in Korea, da kine I fight against, da kine yo' papa, too, he fight against. Dey get good and bad in ev'ry kine race, youknowwhatImean? Look at Korea right now, or any place else in da world fo' dat mattah. You go try look at any country right now. Same-same. Still get da kine rulers ovah everybody. You see? Jus' like in Korea. Dere, get dis Korean as one dictator. One Korean. Everybody think, eh, at least one

Korean ruling Korea and not somebody else, right? Youknow-whatImean?

"But I going tell you something. No mattah if one Korean ruling Korea, or one Japanee, or one haole, or one Filipino. No mattah. What mattah is da buggah is ruling. You no see? And even if da buggah's face is same-same like everybody else's face, eh, you gotta look mo' hard behind da scene, behind da ugly-ugly mask. Mo' hard you gotta look. You *sabe*? You no *sabe*?

"You go try look who behind da scene in Korea or any place else. I tell you who. Is Americans, das who, da American imperialists, da kine guys you wen go fight fo' like one damn stupid fool. If you *maké*, you *maké* fo' dem, fo' dem guys' dictators and all dey bullshit. YouknowwhatImean? Das all it is, da plain truth of da mattah and simple as dat. You see? No . . . you no see. Ho! You real hardhead Yobo!"

"My name is Choe," the farmer said. He overturned the miniature bowl of his pipe on a stone in the hearth and tapped it empty of ash, then refilled it with tobacco. "Yes, we've been waiting for you two or three days now," he said, puffing. "Word came to us that there was a rebellion in your village, that you two were the instigators and had escaped. We thought you might pass through here. They said that you might be moving southward, and my farm is directly in that path."

The youths were quiet, their eyes clouded with fatigue and suspicion.

The farmer laughed. "You think I'm an agent, do you? Ha! Ha! Don't worry. I'm not an agent for the Japanese. You are safe in my house. My wife and I will provide you with food and a safe place to sleep, until your next move. Are your stomachs filled? Don't be ashamed to ask for more. This is a prosperous farmer's house."

His wife hushed him.

They told the couple that they were satisfied, thanking them.

"But tell me," the farmer said, surrounded by his tobacco smoke, "what are your plans?"

They hesitated, looking at each other for reassurance but finding none. But Eung Whan trusted his instincts and told the couple what he and Sung Wha had talked about, that Sung Wha was to go north and join the patriotic forces in Manchuria, and he was to head south, perhaps to Pusan, to try to get on a boat to America.

"You're not going back to your village?" the farmer's wife charged.

Eyes lowered to the straw-covered floor: no, we can't, but where do we go from here? What can we do? Why do you say this to us?

"You say that one of you wants to go to America?" the farmer asked. "Who's going where?"

Eung Whan told the farmer and his wife of their decision.

"But why go to America?" the woman drilled. "Young people are needed here to fight the Japanese."

"It's their choice, Soon Ja."

"It's better if we went our separate ways," explained Sung Wha. "Then if one of us gets caught, the other is still free. Then only one of us will suffer. And if Eung Whan goes to America, he'll be able to make a lot of money. They say that there is a lot of money to be made there. Then, when he makes his money, he can return to our village and buy many rifles and bullets."

"Suffer?" the farmer's wife burst. "Aren't we all suffering enough?"

"You think that money and guns are going to make a big difference?" the farmer asked.

"This is where young men are needed, not in America!"

"Soon Ja . . ."

The farmer's wife gathered the dishes and left them, disappointment hardening her face.

"Excuse my wife," the farmer muttered, pipe in mouth. "She is very opinionated, which is good, you understand. Our two sons were fighters. Our two sons . . . they were murdered by the Japanese." The farmer paused, as if to bring a picture of their faces to his mind. "Our daughter left to join the movement, too. She's somewhere in Manchuria . . . training. We've not heard from her in a year. That's why my wife feels so compelled to express her opinion. She worries that everyone is leaving, you understand, and that no one will remain in Korea to fight the Japanese."

Choe saw that the two young men were tired, their eyes heavy and droopy. Talking politics was making them sleepy. Taking in a long, last drag, he extinguished the pipe, emptying the ash once again in the hearth. He set the pipe to the side and studied their faces. *Barely men,* he thought. *Not even men, boys still attached to their mothers and yet thrown out to the winds of the world.*

"You have a long day tomorrow," the farmer said. "You must be on your way before the sun rises. Sleep on that there"— pointing to several straw mats—"and I'll wake you before the rooster laments of his loss."

Obediently, they curled their bodies under the mats. Sleep came quickly.

They dreamt, though in the morning all would be forgotten.

Shortly after their fall to sleep, they began talking to each other in that garbled language of dream; perhaps two minds had become one, perhaps two minds were dreaming the same dream. They might have dreamt of playing in the stream behind their village: in the middle of some hot summer day, they'd sneak away from work on the family's millet fields and run off to the stream, stripping themselves of their farmers' clothes and swimming in the frigid mountain waters that shriveled their testicles the way sun dries fruit; and later, they would race through fields of yellow *doragi,* their bodies sweltering under a skin of sweat and pollen; and climbing a shady hill, they'd lie on that large, flat blue rock near the odorous fringes of the great pine forest that rose high into the deep purplish mountains, that rock that overlooked the stream and their village and the fields, that rock that talked to them at times of stars and clouds and sun;

and no one could see them on it, and they'd crawl to the edge and peep down at the members of their family and the other villagers, tiny specks toiling under the hot sun in those yellow-green fields of grain not-yet-ready-to-harvest, and they'd laugh to themselves defiantly but stop quickly and turn over on their backs and bathe in the languishing liquid sun and listen to the wind and let the drifting clouds behind the highest treetops make their eyes heavy and crossed, the clouds like soft white breakers on a beach. Or they might have dreamed about the times when in early spring the northern winds brought the scent of tiger to the village, arousing the village children from their wintry hibernation: out from dusty corners of their crowded dwellings would come kites flashing with colors of earth's spirits, and aggressive declarations would ring in the air: *I will be the champion of the wind and sky!*

Or they might have dreamt of that incident that marked their first trip to the big city: Eung Whan's father had taken the boys with him to buy metal hoes and other farming equipment, and for the first time the boys saw people wearing silk clothes and cobbler-made leather shoes, and they watched the well-to-do children playing in the compound of that beautiful house surrounded by white clay walls; curiously they had poked their heads through the oval entrance to the courtyard, and when the *yangban*'s children noticed them, Eung Whan and Sung Wha were pounced on mercilessly with insults and mocking laughter by these rich brats in soiled silk garments: look at the filthy country bumpkins! And look! They don't even have shoes! And look at their clothes made of burlap sack! Eung Whan and Sung Wha never knew what good city manners were: they ran into the compound and gave those spoiled brats all a good beating. But the master of the house, a porcelain figurine of a government official with sparse black threads for a beard, stormed out of the house after hearing this commotion, his flowing silk robe dragging over the ground and a scroll tumbling through his long, refined fingers. You offspring of beggar bastard dogs! he cried.

How dare you enter my household and strike my children! His fine robe weighing down his arms, the master swung out awkwardly, missing the boys' bobbing heads. Quickly they retreated behind Eung Whan's bewildered father, who had come running into the compound. The master began denouncing Eung Whan's father and his progeny. Eung Whan's father said not a word, his face hanging to the ground, an immeasurable humiliation on a face hardened by wind, rain, and sun. Gripping the arms of the boys, he turned away from the squawking master and dragged them back into the street. Around a corner, Eung Whan's father leveled his bamboo walking stick on the boys' bodies, their cries of mercy compelling him more to strike them with an unrequited vengeance, their tears blinding them from seeing the knotted ones dripping from Eung Whan's father's eyes.

That night while deep in their dreams, a metamorphosis took place.

An icy cloud descended from the heavens. On it was Dan-gun, the Great Bear and father of the Korean race and nation; and beside him was Giant Tiger; and on the other side was Wise Deer; and in front of Dan-gun was Ageless Turtle; and they were stolid and motionless as the cloud descended slowly through the thin, cold air, finally lighting on the farmer's rice paddy. The moon swelled and dimmed, and from it a silvery mist burst forth and swirled over Dan-gun and friends, spreading fine snow over them. They were motionless for a long while, the snow making them glow dully under the moon. And when the mist dissipated, they floated off the cloud, one by one— Turtle, Tiger, Deer, and finally Dan-gun —to the farmer's hut. Entering the dwelling, they formed a circle around the two sleeping boys and in turn gave each a gift: from Tiger, raw lashing power; from Deer, fleetness; from Turtle, endurance and perseverance; and from Dan-gun, generation. And when the bestowing of gifts was complete, Dan-gun and companions quietly left that cacophonous mix of grinds and snores, grunts and farts, and fractured words and murmurings from dreams rising and falling; they climbed back on their cloud. The cloud rose slowly, wavering now and then from changes in the wind affected by the leaving of night and the coming of morning, then merged with the darkness and the light of moon and stars.

And thus, Eung Whan and Sung Wha became men during that cold autumn night.

When Sung Wha's eyes opened to the dark morning, he saw people falling from the sky. He bolted up and fought with arms that were holding him down, his outburst bouncing off the blue clay walls of the farmhouse.

Eung Whan cuffed Sung Wha's mouth. "Quiet! Do you want people to wake up?! Do you want people to know we're here?!"

Choe was lighting a small fire in the hearth. Rubbing his hands over it, he looked back and forth between the fire and the young men.

"Where—?"

"Have you lost your mind?" Eung Whan chided.

Sung Wha shook his head. Cold perspiration lathered his face. He wiped it off with his hand. "A bad dream . . . a bad dream."

"What?"

"They were falling."

"Who were falling?"

"Nothing."

"Enough of your dreams," the farmer said, slapping his hands together and standing. "Dawn is a rooster's crow away. You had better get on your feet and start on your journey. My wife prepared some food for both of you. Go outside to the barrel of water and wash yourselves. Then eat, quickly. We must leave fast."

Outside, a full moon in a still sky. Chilly morning. A pig gurgling in sleep. Drowsy purring of hens.

"Who telling you dis story?"

Returning, they found the farmer wrapped in his straw coat, ready to leave. "We don't have time to sit here and eat," he said, giving each a ball of rice. "Let's move. Who is going north and who is going south?" They answered him. "Come, then. Let's go."

They followed the farmer out into the back, through a field of barley, then through a thick bush: the lulling scent of persimmon and mint. Later, emerging from clinging vines, their bodies warm and rosy, they arrived at the main road.

"Listen to me carefully," Choe said, breathing vigorously. "This road will take both of you where you want to go. This direction is south"—pointing. "After you have gone about a hundred *li* down this road, you'll come across an inn. Ask there where you can find the middle school. At the school you'll find Mr. Li Nam Sul. Li Nam Sul. Remember that name. He's the master of the school, my eldest son's former teacher. Find him, tell him what you told me, and he'll help you. Remember now, Li Nam Sul. The road south will eventually take you to Seoul. From there you'll have to find your own way to Pusan. Many boats there, and be careful which one you choose. And for you," turning to Sung Wha and pointing in the opposite direction, "this road will lead you to Kumgangsan."

"When he said dat name, my body start shaking inside. Kumgangsan. Kumgangsan. Is like somebody coming up to you and saying, 'Eh, Jesus Christ like meet you at da corner of . . .'"

"When you get by the foot of the mountains, you'll find an old inn. The innkeeper's name is Lim Tong Il. Ask for him. Explain yourself in secret. He has probably heard of you and your cousin and will help you. Remember his name: Lim Tong Il." The farmer scanned the road, then studied their faces for a last time. "Good luck," he said.

Then the parting. Hearts thumping. Embracing. Wouldn't it be better if we stayed together? Eyes moistening. Tears held back. At the end of the next rice season, on the night of the new moon, we'll meet on that flat blue rock. Wouldn't it be better if we stayed together? Go. You must be on your way. Kumgangsan. Pusan. Remember the rock. Go. Wouldn't it be better if we stayed together? Go.

"I no think yo' papa wen keep his promise. I know I nevah. I no could. I think dat time I up in Manchuria, was in training. Yeah, I made it up to Manchuria, I was learning how shoot rifle and making my body tough. You know, we fill our knapsack full wit' rocks and den go climb da mountains. We go up and down da mountains, up and down, our legs come hard like rock. You nevah did dat, eh, Yong Gil, when you in da army? I tell you, we train really hard, real hard, and all we eat was rice and sometimes fish we catch in da rivah, and vegetables da peasants give us. Dey think what we doing was right.

"But lotta times I think 'bout yo' papa, my cousin, and I know he think 'bout me too. I know dat. I think I feel 'em most dat night befo' I go *moe*, da night of da day we suppose to meet each ada at dat blue flat rock. YouknowwhatImean? Couple times in yo' lifetime you get dis strange, funny feeling dat somebody thinking 'bout you da same time you stay thinking 'bout him. I was thinking 'bout yo' papa and I know he was thinking 'bout me, right at dat same moment. I know, I wen feel 'em. No joke. Dis funny kine feeling, real funny kine. But was dere, dat feeling. Dat night, when I was sleeping on da hard dirt ground under da cold-cold Manchuria sky, thinking like dat and feeling dis way, I jus' start crying. To myself."

In the darkness, farmers were already wading ankle-deep in the muddy waters of the rice paddies. The moon had disappeared, and shortly after the sky began to lighten with the touch of the rising sun. Then the sun burst into the cloudless sky and rose fast and hot, and Sung Wha began to feel its burn on his back. Rice paddies, cutting wedgelike geometric patterns into the hilly land, spread endlessly all around him.

And now there was no concealing darkness, and Sung Wha skirted close to the roadside, relying on pockets of woods here and there just in case he needed to hide. The farmer had told them that Eung Whan had more of a chance running into the soldiers, that the Japanese occupation army rarely marched into the countryside because of rumors of mindless peasants who fought with only hoes and picks. But still Sung Wha's anxiety grew. Now and then, he stopped and looked back: gunshots? Are they on my trail? Where can I go to hide? Into the bush? Up the hills? Run into that paddy and hide in the farmhouse? Would that farmer let me hide? Would he let me pretend to work back-bent with him planting rice?

Later, as the sun became hotter, hunger diverted him temporarily from fear. He sat on a smooth boulder on the side of the road, a farmer's chair perhaps, and opened the straw bag Choe's wife had given him. But he noticed totems of grotesque faces glaring at him, those manifestations of a nearby family's spiritual guardians, and he moved on to another boulder down the road away from their fierce stares.

Inside the bag were two rice balls. He took one and devoured it in three bites. Better if he saved the other for later. But a salivating mouth told him otherwise. His hunger now satisfied, he needed water. As he was surrounded by rice paddies, a stream must be nearby. He discarded the bag and went into the brush to search. And deeper toward the scent of running water.

Then: a trotting horse. A march of tired feet.

Thirst leaves him. Rushing back to the road. Stopping. *Don't go out.* Marching feet. Dragging feet. Clopping of a horse. Bending branch. Branch snapping back. His heart stopping. *Did they hear? See? Still. Keep still.*

He barks a command, that scurried-voiced house dog, and the movement of men and horse stops. Horse whinnies. Stoic and decorous, he dismounts and struts to the side of the road, gripping the handle of his sword. He looks back, frowning, and scans the column of soldiers. Yelping another command, he then high-steps through the tall grass and pushes into the thick brush. Once cloaked by the foliage, desperation is forced to his face, and he fights the vines that entangle his saber. He senses that the waiting soldiers are holding back laughter and trading knowing looks, and this angers him. But what can you do when the body begs for purging? Finally he breaks free from the vines and hurries through branches and leaves to a small clearing where he can do his business. He drops his pants, whining about the sword that always is in his way.

Don't breathe. Still.

Grunting and farting, shitting in the countryside. Korean rice returning to Korean land.

He will see me if I move. Still. Don't move. Don't breathe.

When the sounds of horse and men were gone from his ears, he came out of hiding and peered down the road. His thirst was forgotten. And his heart still fluttered from the scare. Wasn't that a close call with death? Now, what was he going to do? It was not safe to travel on the main road anymore. But how was he to travel? Burrow a tunnel? Fly like a bird? Perhaps he could zig-zag between rice paddies, but there were no trees or brush to hide behind. He still would have to follow the road, and now he must proceed more cautiously.

He pressed on. From behind a bend in the road, he spied on the soldiers ahead. They were marching through a vast complex of paddies toward a blue hill. When they disappeared over the top, he continued on, feeling now the coming cold of night.

"Nevah been so hungry in my life. Fo' days and days jus' trudging down da road, all da time thinkin' if I going get caught or what. My stomach wen disappear after a while. All I ate was drink water. But I remembah after couple days, jus' like I wen wake up. My legs getting lighter, not so much heavy. And j'like one magnet pulling me. Dis strong feeling coming and taking me, cannot explain. I jus' feel 'em right den. Was like something pulling me down da road. No can forget da feeling. Like magnet. No can forget. Funny kine feeling."

Night was deep when Sung Wha reached Tiger's Inn. It was three days since his encounter with the soldiers, and being cautious had slowed his progress. A northern wind from Kumgangsan now rushed over the land, roaring through the tall pine and blowing away the high clouds from the sky. He stopped at the inn's dark double doors, his numb hands tucked under his armpits. Shivering, he opened one of the doors and entered.

A single oil lamp dimly lit the interior. Warm, thick smells of garlic, fried fish, and steamed rice rubbed against him. Tables were pushed against the whitewashed walls, and off to the side a snoring guest was bundled up in straw mats. From a bright back room appeared a tall man with rice bowl and chopsticks in hand, his silhouette filling the doorway. "Yes? Can I help you?" A deep voice. Chewing.

Sung Wha can't talk. He's too tired, the wind and night having drained him of words and thoughts.

"Can I help you?" the man repeats. He raises the bowl to his face and shovels in rice with the chopsticks.

Finally: "I'm looking for Lim Tong Il."

The man swallows his food, clears his throat, takes a step toward the lantern, and turns it up a couple of notches. Scrutinizes Sung Wha. "I am Lim Tong Il. And who are you?"

Peasant youth identifies himself: family name, village, father's name. His black eyes stare back at the innkeeper's; they don't back down.

Doesn't this peasant boy know the protocol?

Bare remnants of straw shoes. Dirty bluish feet. And smells bad.

"I'm Lim Tong Il," he repeats. "What's your business with me?"

"Mr. Choe the rice farmer instructed me to come and see you. He said that you might be able to help me."

"What do you want?"

"A way to be with my Korean brothers in Manchuria, fighting against the Japanese occupiers."

Sung Wha's words have shaken Lim. The innkeeper casts a wary eye at the sleeping traveler. His left eye twitches. He signals Sung Wha to the back, and in a kitchen effuse with the buttery smells of steamed rice, he scowls at the youth, scolding him in a low voice. "Are you a fool?! You don't say things like that! Mouthing off like an ignorant country bumpkin that you are!"

"I'm sorry, I—"

"You can be sorry only once. Fool!"

"I'm sorry."

"Fool! We're surrounded by a sea of spies. Japanese agents are everywhere."

"I'm sorry." Sung Wha backs toward the door.

"And now where are you going?"

He can't answer. Can't think. Can't feel nor sing. Can't even see.

Lim points to a spot on the straw-covered floor and motions Sung Wha to sit down. The *ondul* floor is warm and soothing, heated by the settled coals of the large cooking hearth.

"Look," he whispers, peeking in on the guest through the doorway, "that trader out there could be a spy. He's snoring now, but who's to say that he isn't trying to fool us? He could be awake and listening and pretending to make those sounds of sleep."

"I'm sorry."

The innkeeper probes Sung Wha's face. "What do you want of me?"

There's no answer. The youth doesn't move.

"You need a place to sleep?"

Sung Wha nods.

"How do you know Mr. Choe?"

"My cousin and I came upon Mr. Choe's farm by accident. We fled our village a few days ago when Japanese soldiers were sent to capture us for our part in our village's rebellion. We escaped into the forest for three days. When we finally left the forest, we came upon Mr. Choe's farm."

"And where's your cousin?"

"Ho, dat Lim! Dat sonavabitch grill me like one cheese sandwich! But I tell you, from da start can trust him."

"Do you know who the patriots are?"

Sung Wha shook his head.

"Hmm . . . so you don't even know who you're copying. I bet you don't even know what they're fighting for."

"They're fighting for Korea. That's what they're fighting for."

The innkeeper chuckled. "So, you think you're a man? Let me tell you something. There's more to it than just empty talk."

But there's hunger on the youth's face. Lim read it well: the eyes searching for the source of steamed rice; the nostrils widening at the garlicky, fiery hints of *kochu-jang*. He removed the wooden cover of a blackened rice pot, releasing a hiss and a mushroom of steam. With a bamboo paddle he turned over the rice several times, then served a mound in a bowl. Setting the bowl and small dishes of kimchee and salted sardines on a low lacquer table in front of Sung Wha, he sat down against a wall, lit his Western-style pipe, and watched the boy. "Go ahead," he grunted. "Eat."

The picture on top of the table, which was chipped and water-stained from hard use, stopped Sung Wha for a brief moment. It was a strong likeness of a tiger, its mother-of-pearl eyes radiating a frigid, frightening fire.

"Eat."

Sung Wha bowed to thank the innkeeper, then dipped his chopsticks into the food. He nudged the dish of kimchee over the tiger's head to hide its eyes.

Lim relit the pipe, puffing on it until the tobacco became a glowing orange. "How old are you, did you say?"

Sung Wha looked up, averting his eyes. "I'll be sixteen soon," he mumbled.

A child, yet with the impatience to become a man. "So tell me, what makes you want to go to Manchuria? It's a far journey, many *li*, and you have to cross the mighty Yalu River. And what makes you think I can help you get there?"

"General Yi Tong-hwi is a hero in my village, and we have heard many stories about the bravery of Koreans in Manchuria who are training to free Korea so that our country will be for Koreans again."

The innkeeper choked on his laughter. "And who taught you to say these things, in such a religious kind of way?"

Embarrassed, Sung Wha stopped eating.

"Go ahead and eat. Don't mind me. I am just entertained by your presence. Don't mind me. I have no manners. Yes, General Yi Tong-hwi. But what did this farmer Choe tell you about me?"

"He told me—my cousin and me—that you'd help me get to Manchuria."

"Ha! You expect me to believe your story? You are a funny boy. And what makes you think what that farmer Choe said is true about me?"

Sung Wha could not answer. *What am I doing here? I want to go home.*

A poor peasant. Look at the way he eats every grain of rice. Downtrodden. And young. And ignorant. He has no future to look forward to. What future? He's going to end up like his father and his father's father, and so on. Nameless, unfortunate, ignorant. Look at his hands. Large for his age. But thin arms. Another overworked youth. Family must be very poor. The clothes he wears. Those cast-off straw sandals even a beggar in the city would refuse. Pitiful.

But why pitiful? Why do I say that? I have pity on the poor.

That's not how I should think, should I? What do I really think . . .
that I'm better than these peasants? That my education and social
class are higher than theirs?

"You know a lot for a country boy," he said, grinning, "but,"
he leaned toward Sung Wha and continued in a lowered voice,
"there's a lot more you don't know."

A blank look on the boy.

"You don't know what I'm talking about, huh? Ignorance
breeds deception. Being deceived means living a life filled with
lies."

"People from my village can't read or write." Sung Wha set
down the near-empty bowl. *Is he saying that my parents are*
stupid? "But it's not hard to figure out who the enemy is. We
are not stupid." A sudden look of defiance. Challenging the
innkeeper's eyes.

"I didn't mean it that way," Lim interjected with an abrupt
softness. He deflected his eyes from the boy's. Reaching over
and taking Sung Wha's bowl, he filled it with more rice, but
Sung Wha refused it.

"Eat it, there's more." *He's hungry. He's a hardhead.*

Sung Wha remained firm.

The innkeeper settled back in his place and took a couple of
quick puffs. "I didn't mean it that way. That is not what I had
in mind. What I mean is that a lot of people don't know who
the real enemy is. Some of our own people are traitors. They call
themselves Koreans, but they're really enemies of the Korean
people."

Sung Wha nodded his head, though not sure what the innkeeper was saying. *Why does he talk in riddles?*

The boy is thinking. He doesn't understand what I said, but he's
thinking. A good sign . . . a very good sign.

Lim cleaned out his pipe, then repacked and lit it. Sung
Wha's eyes followed the first puffs of smoke to the ceiling: *this*
smoke is like that man's thoughts, harsh and airy.

"This tobacco," Lim started, "is from the United States of

America, which exports it to Japan. The Japanese, in turn, export it to Korea, where we pay an outrageous price for it. Do you know what I mean by 'exported'? Almost all our manufactured goods in Korea are from Japan. This"—sighing—"is a weakness of mine, an expensive weakness." He drew on the pipe a couple of times. "The Japanese take our surplus rice in taxes and expect us to pay an exorbitant price for this tobacco. And they make us speak and write Japanese. We have to learn the Japanese culture. Korean culture is outlawed in Korea! If we let this practice continue, one day we'll be Koreans in face only, maybe not even that. And those Japanese dogs take our women for their abusive pleasure!

"We're a colony of Japan, do you understand that? We Koreans still have our faces and our souls now, but soon, if this is to continue, we'll be Koreans in face only. Our insides will be Japanese. Then, instead of rebelling against the Japanese, our insides will rebel against our outside. We'll be rebelling against ourselves. Do you understand what I'm saying? And for some Koreans that's what's happening right now!"

What does this all have to do with tobacco?

"No, you don't understand." He shakes his head. *Ignorant peasant.* "But that's all right. You will. You're young, you have many years ahead of you, many roads to tread on. Life's toiling but enlightening and intricate journey is starting for you. That's good. I was once young, too, like you. You'll understand what I am saying, later when you're older. As long as there are young people like you who are confused at what is going on but desire understanding, I can see only a bright future for Korea.

"But you must understand the danger of going north to Manchuria. There are Japanese spies and soldiers everywhere. Why, even this afternoon, we had an unexpected visit from the district magistrate. They searched everyone, every home. They beat up several people in the village. It's frustrating to see all of this and not be able to do anything. That's why almost entire villages are migrating north across the Yalu."

"I saw them on the road today."

"Saw who . . . the magistrate and his soldiers? Mean, evil dogs, aren't they?"

"Yes."

"They came here and said they were looking for two young criminals, escapees from their prison in Seoul, who had been terrorizing the countryside in the south, robbing people, beating old women and children and raping daughters. They killed one soldier."

"And they're on the loose here?"

"Bah! But never trust what Japanese soldiers tell you. They always lie. They want Koreans to fight Koreans. They want to divide us. That's what it is. They think we're stupid, that we'd stab our own backs. They say that Koreans were bred to be colonized. That is why, they say, Koreans have such an easy time learning other languages, since they've always had to learn the language of a superior, dominant culture. Bah!"

"Where were these robbers from?"

"They said they were from P'ih-yon, that they drifted to the south, where they were caught. . . . " Lim gave Sung Wha a steady, suspicious eye. "And where did you say you're from?"

Silence.

Lim laughed. "So they were looking for you! But you don't look like a robber, but a poor farmer's son. Ha! No need to feel bad about it. I'm no agent. All right . . . but where is your companion? Didn't you say you were traveling with someone? Did they catch him?"

Calm yourself, heart. Don't leap so high. The heavens can wait. But from the blue rock watch the stars above and their shapes.

"Yes, that's right, you told me all of this already. I have a bad memory. Too many sleepless nights. So, tell me, of course there's no truth to these rumors? Are you truly a murderer and rapist?" He laughs.

Shaking his head, Sung Wha tells his story.

They talk long into the night. And the innkeeper, a former schoolteacher, a storehouse of knowledge, recounts tirelessly for Sung Wha's now eager ears the history of Korea's struggle against Japan.

"Ah! That night was too short! How my mind was suspended in fascination as I listened to his stories: Admiral Yi leading the Korean navy against Hideyoshi's invasion, implementing the world's first squadron of ironclad battleships, thoroughly routing Japan's massive fleet of samurai. . . ."

The lone visitor in the front stirred. Lim raised a finger of silence to his lips. They listened. And when the visitor began to snore again, they moved to the storeroom behind the kitchen. Someone was sleeping on the floor in one corner, wrapped in a thick blanket. "Never mind her. She's my daughter. She's very tired. She can sleep through anything. We won't bother her." And Lim began where they had left off.

It was early morning: the sun had not risen nor had the rooster cried for heaven's forgiveness. And Sung Wha did not want Lim to stop, but the innkeeper declared with a long yawn that he was obliged to open his inn in a few hours, that he'd need at least a few hours of sleep. Sung Wha curled up in a corner away from the snorer, who wasn't snoring now but murmuring and grinding his teeth. But Sung Wha could not sleep, his mind wandering through the stories again, listening to another telling of them in his mind. He squeezed his eyes tightly and told himself, *you must wake up early and be on your way, the Japanese will be back looking for you.* And then he heard a fading voice chant as his body diffused into slumber, *if only you can stay here and listen and sleep, and listen and sleep, and listen and listen and . . .*

Sleep was not long, a mere thread between darkness and light.

Waking up to noisy, discordant voices, he sat up and drew a straw blanket over his cold body: *where am I?* Oh . . . yes. The peddler was gone. He peeked through the crack of the double doors. The sky was overcast, and a crowd of about fifty farmers—disgruntled men with straggly beards and weather-bronzed faces; women with worries lining their foreheads and infants bound to bent backs—were gathered tightly together, the cold air making their breathing visible. In the middle of the crowd was the innkeeper, towering above them, his Adam's apple bobbing as he talked and pounded a fist into an open hand. Then he began listening.

"Those dogs! They're always robbing us!" said one farmer. "How can I pay their taxes and feed my family? What can I do? We'll starve this winter!"

"Yes, they're dogs. And now listen to my case," said another. "Because I couldn't pay all the taxes they said that I owed them, they've confiscated part of my land. What is a farmer without his land?"

"Those *yangban!* They're all in it together," one woman fired. "They're getting their cut from the thief's booty. And never in their wretched lives have they ever dirtied their hands in honest work!"

The rest of the crowd murmured in angry agreement.

"We must all go down to the police station and demand our rights! We must stick together on this."

"Silly! Don't you remember what they did to the rice farmers in Taegu?" one woman heaved. "The farmers went to the police station, demanding their independence. The police chief told them they were right and urged them to wait for a while until the officials returned from a meeting. Then, according to the police chief, they, the farmers, could present their case to willing ears. So, like trusting fools, the farmers waited. But half an hour later, Japanese troops surrounded the station and massacred them all."

"*Aigoo!*"

"We must go to the American church and pray."

"Yes, let's go there."

"They care."

"Why would they care?"

"They'll help."

"Help . . . how?"

A small fraction of the crowd, their pouting faces given up to unending poverty, began to break away. Others turned to watch; some, after hesitating, joined the spreading disquietude.

Lim raised his hand like a magician, stopping the crowd from breaking, cuffing its deepening murmurs, drawing them back to the center.

> *We sing from the gray sides of Our Mountains,*
> *And from the green fields of Our Ancestors.*
> *Our Voices send the darkest clouds away!*
> *Victory thunders throughout Our Land!*

He speaks in a clear, high-pitched voice that is typically not his, using a vocabulary that is in large part foreign to the farmers. But they listen. They may not understand Lim's peculiar city speech, but the brazenness of the language is empowering. Praying isn't the answer, he declares, the armed struggle is. And understanding who the enemy is. We must join fully with the patriotism and determination of our army training in the north who are readying themselves for a long, protracted war. We must be patient, for the time is not ripe yet for revolution. But there will be a time when the army will finally unfurl its power like a wild tiger released from its cage, and it will lash out and destroy the Japanese Imperial Army once and for all!

The farmers are motionless, speechless. Some shake their heads, while others nod with deliberation, their eyes drooping to the ground. And there are others who look beyond the speaker toward Kumgangsan, their eyes searching the slate-colored slopes and craggy peaks for any indication of a storm that will help alleviate their situation.

"I nevah seen him shoot one rifle. He always talk about revolution dis, revolution dat, but he no even pull one trigger. But his words was bullets, da kine dat crisscross you in and out. Invisible bullets. I no can forget how he take control dat crowd."

Sung Wha shuddered while Lim spoke, for he remembered what the innkeeper had told him the night before about how dangerous it was to talk openly about things of this nature. Sung Wha searched the fields beyond the compound and down the dirt road, looking for the spies supposedly surrounding the inn. He couldn't find any. *But who knows who might be hiding behind that tree over there?*

A dismal sky of gray clouds hung oppressively low.

Debate continued among the farmers, finally breaking up when the threat of heavy rain sprinkled down on them.

Lim entered the inn, his face long and worn from lack of sleep. "Those farmers . . . their suffering is great," he said, addressing no one. He turned to regard through the doorway the farmers' melancholy plodding down the road, then sat next to a low table and leaned his head back against the wall, closing his eyes. "This winter might be the last for many of their children." Opened his eyes. "They know that. There will be much suicide going on throughout the countryside. Young mothers will be throwing their crying, sick babies into freezing rivers, then themselves. In the mornings, we fish them out and bury them, the mothers we try to identify, the babies with no names. These farmers come here looking for answers. They're confused. They're angry. They feel helpless and hopeless. And all I can give them is a watery hope. Perhaps they're better off going to a *mudang.*"

He stared at the wall across the room for a long while. An embroidered painting of a dancing woman, a *kisang,* hung on the right side of the wall. Lim sighed. "As if I can give them hope. Maybe they're better off at the Christian church. Hope . . . much of the time now I don't know what that word means, but that is all that I can give them. Or try to give. Sometimes I can't even give them that."

"Father, we will need more wood before the night comes."

Lim acknowledged his daughter's comment with a grunt, not really hearing what was being said by this girl of perhaps fourteen with thick black hair coiled back in a bun like a

Madonna, whose dark brown eyes and pleasingly smooth, clear complexion fresh like new fallen snow startled Sung Wha, who gave Sung Wha a shy, cursory look, then disappeared back into the kitchen.

"I tell you, Yong Gil, was da first time I wen really see one wahine. In fact, I nevah even wen look at her, jus' one fast one. 'As how pretty yo' auntie was. She shake me up all inside, da way she look at me. She so pretty, pretty-pretty. I dunno. Jus' something wen make me all funny kine inside. I seen girls befo' in my village and even outside in da ada villages, too. But her, ho! I no seen one girl so pretty like dat befo'. Maybe if I spock In Ja Kang when she one young girl, maybe I feel da same way. But no can, of course. But her, yo' future auntie, my future wife, I wen get all da jittahs. Yeah, das him, da jittahs. I break out cold sweat, I think my heart was going bus' up inside, was beating so hard. And all 'cause I jus' look one time at her, from one glance. I look away quick, but my eyes still see her, j'like my skin is eyes and dem making me see her picture still yet.

"And when I look up again, she gone. I think maybe I stay *moe,* I stay dreaming. I think to myself, I wish dis no dream, but den I think again, I hope dis is one dream 'cause den I no get jittahs again next time I see her. But den I tell myself, you can hear her talk and now you hear her work in da kitchen. She cooking or maybe washing dishes, I dunno. But I too scared find out or really think about it."

Her name was Hae Soon. Sung Wha discovered her name a beautiful name *oh the sound of her name makes me think of bright sunshine beaming down from the heavens* when Lim called her (he and Sung Wha were out in the back chopping and stacking wood) Hae Soon my daughter bring us men some tea we are working hard come on we are thirsty and bring some of those rice cakes she cooks as good as her mother yes and Sung Wha had been dying to find out her name but he didn't have the courage to ask Lim but now her name was sung to him by tiny brass bells dangling in the back doorway *oh for another look at her lovely face to hear her breathe a word or two* you better watch it or you'll cut your leg off! and when she served them outside they were resting under a large oak tree and flies were buzzing all over them and Lim was swatting them with a switch Hae Soon offered Sung Wha a cup of tea and rice cakes and Sung Wha clumsy buffoon spilled the cup of barley tea on the ground and Lim laughed does she scare you? ha ha ha and Sung Wha of course felt desperately foolish. Every day Lim kept him busy with chores around the inn; he told Sung Wha, if you want to go north you'll need money and if you work for me for a week I'll give you enough money for that trip. Later early in the evening, as they sat cross-legged in the back common room, Sung Wha asked him, but what if the Japanese come here again and find me? And Lim: then let them find you you are not Kim Sung Wha anymore you are Lim Nam Soo, you are my son who has just come home from school in Seoul. And Sung Wha: but I know nothing of school I don't even know how to read or write. And Lim: then I'll teach you how to read and write. And promptly Lim opened a desk drawer and out came a writing tablet and a brush and ink block, and after dipping the tip in a small well of water and lathering up some ink, he constructed a table of the Korean alphabet. Sung Wha watched the characters flow from the brush's tip in smooth, precise strokes. Finished, Lim gave the table to Sung Wha and instructed him to practice copying the *hanggul* every day. Go ahead and practice now. So Sung Wha took the brush, holding it as if it were a chopstick, then dipped it into the ink, but too much ink ruined the first page of the tablet. . . . He is more cautious the next time: his characters are not as heroic as Lim's, for the tip does not respond effortlessly for him, but his attempt draws admiration and praise from teacher. And Lim: yes with practice you'll be able to copy these with no effort, and Sung Wha continues this lesson until the oil lamp burns down to a bud of light. Then he uses the light of the moon, until rude clouds cover it for good.

In sleep he practices his *hanggul,* and his brush strokes are achievements of mind over matter. In sleep the brush strokes, curls and stems of black ink, flow on and on, on a great roll of ricepaper that vanishes into a distant, unfolding storm. Then he wakes to a fresh clear spirit of morning, a beginning with no end.

And in the days following, a euphoria holds him: he is lifted above the clouds to the top of Kumgangsan, and now he's beholding a look-see of the world for miles and miles around; and he feels that he has been away from home for years and years instead of the few days.

One night, under a scratchy straw mat and with the cold air of the mountains whistling through cracks in the roof, he tries to picture that very recent point in time when the faces of family and friends were fleshy and real and marked with joy and anguish, when cheeks were rouged from winter's frigid winds or browned by summer's harvest sun. Then he tries to touch the smell of wrestling, sweating bodies; the odor of the outhouse that entered their home when the wind blew wrongly; the heaviness of pollinated air of deep summer that teased their eyes and noses when at play or work near the entrance of Great Tiger's forest. But there is always a blurry film between himself and the images, dulling the details, the images always shadowed or unfocused: *is this Mother? Father? Older brother? Sister? Younger brother? Where are the deep lines on* Halmuni *'s face? Why can't I see her tigress eyes?* And in the morning, awakened by a rooster's crowing and his own pangs of hunger, he tries to stop the diaphanous images from dissolving into air, and fails.

"Let me tell you about her," Lim says. Resting against the kitchen wall, he smokes his pipe, his heavy-lidded eyes watching the smoke rise to the rafters.

The smoke of the tobacco is robust and bitter, watering Sung Wha's eyes. Lim continues puffing at the pipe, oblivious to Sung Wha's discomfort.

"She was a good woman," he goes on, using the stem of his

pipe to point at the daguerreotype in Sung Wha's hand. "Don't be fooled by the picture. It was taken long ago, when she was fifteen."

Hae Soon. Hair. Eyes. Nose. Does she like flowers, too?

"She was a good woman." Lim leans forward and cleans the pipe over a brass ashtray, his eyes and his voice softening. "She was a good woman."

In the back, the sound of a heavy box sliding across the room.

Hae Soon.

"Yes, she was a good woman. Let me tell you her story."

"Where is your husband and child?"

O *Omoni*, I call for you now. Where have you been? Where are you now? All these years of suffering and now you have peace. *Omoni?*

"Where is your husband? Tell me!"

Can you tell me that story again, of *Halmuni* as a little girl climbing the mountain slopes to pick *doragi* and finding my grandfather next to his dead mother, a hunter's arrow through her heart? Please tell me that story again.

"For the last time! Where is your husband and child?"

He strikes her across the face with a cane, knocking her to the floor.

Her coat was stained with blood. You could tell that it was once a brilliant, full coat. A proud coat. And your grandfather just clung to her. I was afraid that he was going to attack me. But he didn't. In fact, he didn't even see me. He was crying a weakened cry of a cry that had long gone. He had no voice or tears. He seemed to know not what to do. So I approached him, very carefully at first, of course, and when he saw me, he became very frightened. He jumped over the large body of his mother and tried to hide behind it, but he was already too big to hide in the folds of her great coat. And I felt very sad for him. He looked so weak and lost. I came closer to the tigress and now I could smell her. I had never taken the scent of a tiger before. It was a strange smell, I can't describe it, a raw, musty smell, a smell of stale flesh. And this smell suddenly gave me a picture of a dark, warm cave and a dizzy feeling of being lifted off my feet. And from this cave came a sweet aroma of roasting pine nuts.

And when I saw his greenish eyes again, regarding me fearfully over the frayed coat of his dead mother, I already knew, even as young as I was, that he was to be my husband.

"Yes, she was that brave. I can't sleep at nights, thinking about what they did to her. Not one word from her bleeding lips that would betray me and our daughter."

"Take her away!" he commands with a jerk of his arm in the direction of the door, and the cane flies out of his hand, ricocheting off the wall.

"Away with her! Garlic-eating whore!"

The weeks went by fast, turning into a month, and the month became two, then three, until the fall harvest was nearly completed. He was Lim's son, Hae Soon's brother. And it was hard but necessary for him to lead these roles in the eyes of the farming people and the guests of the inn.

And: he felt becoming jealousy now when Hae Soon served the visitors; *why do they talk to her so long and what do they talk about and why does she talk with them?*

And: *why do I feel this way?*

One night—one of the few nights the innkeeper remained home—Lim took Sung Wha to the room where he and his daughter slept. Buried under burlap sacks and boxes of miscellany were several wooden crates, each filled with books, from which Lim selected several volumes: here's one about Japanese feudal literature and this one's about the American Civil War and this is about how Admiral Yi defeated the Japanese shogun

Hideyoshi with the world's first armor-clad battleship, and this one's . . .

Sung Wha's eyes were dazed; it was unbelievable to see so many books all in one place. And: but what language is this? I cannot read it. And Lim: it's Japanese, most of these books were printed in Japan. And Sung Wha: but I cannot read Japanese, I am barely able to read *hanggul*. And Lim: then I will also teach you *hiragana* and *kanji*. And Sung Wha: but it's too hard. And he: no it isn't. And he: I have a hard time with *hanggul*. And he: so what? So Lim began to teach him Japanese.

And what developed between him and Hae Soon was an amicable, though lukewarm, sister-brother relationship. At nights when Lim was away, Hae Soon helped him in his learning, teaching him new characters and correcting his crude brush work. And she loved to flaunt her superior intelligence, to demonstrate her superiority over a frustrated Sung Wha. But stubborn Sung Wha: like an ox, he remained bent over his work, biting his upper lip, the light of the lamp deepening the darkness of night.

And there were times when father and daughter argued feverishly about money and politics (Hae Soon: "Those stupid peasants! Can't they see that the only way is to fight back?" Lim: "Don't call them that!" "Then why are they not rebelling?" "It takes time. But they are! They are! Impatient!" "But you too have called them stupid!"). These were times when Sung Wha, sometimes caught in the middle, felt like scolding Hae Soon or slapping her across the face for not acting the way an honorable daughter should. Instead, he would rush out to the back of the inn and hike up the hill and sit under a tall, wheezing pine overlooking the inn's roof and the surrounding rice paddies, the murmurs of the forest breathing down but not deafening him from the contentious voices of father and daughter.

He took her aside one day, denouncing her inappropriate behavior.

"My father trains me to be a fighter for truth," Hae Soon stormed back, her arms akimbo and brown eyes hardened like

amber. "It is to his honor, and especially the honor of my
mother, that I act the way I do. My father himself has said that
the place of a woman is not in the home and kitchen, but to be
alongside man so we can change the world together with our
ideas and actions."

Sung Wha was dumbfounded. He had never heard this
before. What did she say? Was Lim really responsible for his own
daughter turning against him? Was Hae Soon making this all
up? If true, then what kind of devil had taken possession of
Lim's mind? Of Hae Soon's mind?

That night he waited up for Lim. When the proprietor
entered at his usual late hour, tired-eyed and carrying an arm-
load of printed flyers, Sung Wha rushed at him with the matter.

"So!" the innkeeper exclaimed with a burst of startling
enthusiasm. "You are finally awakening to the changing real
world!" Lim covered his mouth with a hand, suddenly aware of
two snoring guests.

And that was all Lim said.

Perplexed, Sung Wha retreated to his bedding. He fell in and
out of sleep that night. And in the morning he challenged Hae
Soon again: "But it is written that a woman's place is to be at
the side of her husband, to raise children, to make a home for
her family!"

"And where is this written?"

"It is written!"

"Hmph! And how do you know that? I thought you couldn't
read! You sure didn't read the Bible here!"

"Yes—no! It was told to me!"

"Then you were told lies."

Sung Wha held back a violent urge: *is she accusing my mother
of being a liar? But anyway, how can I hit her? She's a girl. And
besides, her father . . .*

Embarrassed that he had thought of striking her, he said,
"It's not a lie. It's the truth."

"Where did you find your 'truth,' in the Bible? Are you Con-
fucian?"

"No . . . but there is a God."

"There's no such a thing as a 'God.'"

"But yes! There is!"

"Many men wrote the Bible. It's a book about man's own lies to himself."

"Well, what about Confucius?"

"What about Confucius? He is a man, no doubt."

"But he wrote that a woman's role is to serve her husband. And this has been going on for a thousand years."

"Ha! And who is this Confucius but a madman spewing out poisonous lies to justify an unjust society!"

"That is not so! We must live with rules!"

"Well, I suppose you enjoy living under rules. Are we not living under rules right now? I see you are very content to live under the boot heels of the Japanese Imperial government!"

"I am not!"

"But you said you enjoyed living with—"

"No, I said I—"

"How do you know Confucius is so good? Have you read his books? Have you studied his ugly thoughts? I thought you couldn't read?"

"I—I was told so."

"You were told so. Oh, I see now. Like a chicken told to sleep in a tiger's den."

"But—it's true . . . all of this."

"Whoever told you all of this told you lies."

Again he suppressed the urge to strike her. He balled his fists, but kept them trembling at his sides.

He could not contend with her; he could not continue the debate. Hae Soon's tongue was sharper, much quicker than his. She had more education and was deft at dodging any reasonable argument thrown at her. In frustration, Sung Wha threw his hands in the air and stormed out in a fiery silence to the woodpile, where he mercilessly attacked the firewood with axe and curses.

And now Sung Wha was more aware of Lim's political parlance that his ears found difficult to understand: the class struggle, anarchism, Communism, democracy, fascism, the fight to conquer all forms of oppression, down with Japanese imperialism. *What were all of these? What did they all mean?* Sung Wha felt stupid, utterly stupid, and as he watched the attentive dark eyes of Hae Soon absorb every inscrutable bit of this rhetoric, he could not but think himself as dumb as a water buffalo.

"No, you are quiet and strong as a water buffalo," Lim corrected. He had overheard Sung Wha talking aloud as the boy was weeding the vegetable garden in the backyard. "You have much to learn. That is evident. But you are not stupid, you are not dumb. You are just uninformed. Knowledge has been kept away from you and others like you by the *yangban* and the Japanese Imperial government. They've kept knowledge from you and your kind to keep you ignorant of truth."

"But what do you mean by this?"

"You must understand this, and you must understand this well. This is the truth I'm saying. You are like a water buffalo because a water buffalo is quiet and absorbing and strong, and when the time comes, when you and others like yourself are conscious of your power, a tremendous united force like the mighty sweeping winds from Kumgangsan will sweep down and drive away all of our enemies."

He talks in riddles again. Riddles. Why does he talk this way?

One late afternoon, with the sun swelling on the horizon and ripening the cloudless sky to a dark, lush orange, Hae Soon called a sweating and panting Sung Wha, his axe perched high and then driven into a section of pine. He picked up the split wood and tossed them on a pile, then turned toward the blinding sunset, squinting at Hae Soon's dark form coming into focus. Did you hear me the first time, she asked. And he: what first time? What are you talking about? He shaded his eyes from the sun, then watched the swallows arguing above in the tree.

What does she want from me?

Impatiently: "It's a social club. We meet once a month. Do you want to come?"

What do you mean?

"Do you want to come?"

"Come to where?"

A sigh. Fresh resins of pine flushed against her nostrils. "To our social club. What do you think I've been talking to you about? Have you been listening to me?"

Words that bite. *Why does she talk like that? I could slap her across the face.*

"Well?"

He turned back to his work, spitting in his hands. "I won't know anyone there." He gripped the axe.

"It's all right. Everyone there knows you."

The sun in his eyes again. Hand shielding against its harsh rays. Axe settling to his side.

"Knows me? What do you mean?"

"Never mind. You'll see." And she left him before he could respond.

Night hid their way down the dirt road to the village. At the door of the small meeting hall stood two peasant youths, their thin faces bleak and attentive. They smiled at Sung Wha and Hae Soon, but returned to their firm stare into autumn's cold darkness. Inside, a circle of farmers' daughters and sons sat on the cold *ondul* floor, a flickering oil lamp in the center providing poor lighting for the bare interior. Hae Soon introduced Sung Wha to the circle, and the young people greeted him with smiles, some shaking Sung Wha's hand and giving him their names, others remaining silent. Hae Soon unwrapped a bundle she had brought along, unloading a small pile of books and pamphlets in the middle of the circle. The small room now filled with excited whispers as she passed out the literature, one by one, to eager hands.

With three others, Sung Wha shared a book written in Japanese. He could not read it even with what he had learned from

Lim, but holding the book gave him a shiver: there was knowledge, a power that would be gotten by just understanding what the characters mean.

Then Hae Soon spoke, and the sons and daughters of farmers listened, three or four of them looking up from each book. She lectured on China's ancient history and the people's heroic fight against a two-headed monster ("the Japanese imperialists and the Chinese comprador bourgeoisie"); and about the revolution as benefiting everyone in the world, especially Koreans ("we must fight the imperialists on all fronts, and once the Chinese Communists are successful, the Japanese imperialists will be weakened and Koreans will be able to defeat them once and for all").

The meeting ventured late into the night. Many wanted to continue on, willing to sacrifice sleep for knowledge. But all had to wake early in the morning to help their families finish the harvesting. Thus the meeting ended. Wary that the village hall could be under surveillance, one youth suggested an abandoned Buddhist temple near a waterfall as the next meeting place. It was agreed upon. The group disbanded, two at a time squeezing through the sticky sliding doors, with Hae Soon and Sung Wha the last to leave.

Back at the inn, Sung Wha was uneasy about telling Hae Soon that, though he was fascinated by what was discussed, he did not want to go to another meeting, for he could not fully understand Japanese.

"Maybe now is a good time for you to learn a bit more," she said. "Though we hate the Japanese, a good many things come from Japan that are helping our movement." She showed him several well-read, dog-eared volumes from one of her father's book crates. "Look at these. These books are important. They are written by the great Russian revolutionaries. Until the time comes when they can be translated into Korean, we'll have to read these Japanese translations."

"But why can't your father translate them into Korean? Then I'll be able to read them."

"My father is too busy. Anyway, he says that translating is a job for eggshells."

"Eggshells?"

"Yes, eggshells. The intellectuals. Their will is so easily crushed, like that of eggshells."

"But isn't your father an intellectual?"

There was no answer.

One night he dreamt that he and Hae Soon were on a grassy foothill covered with blooming *doragi*. Hae Soon was picking the orange-yellow flowers at the edge of a forest, holding a full cluster in hand. Then, deep in the forest, shrieking animals were heard. Sung Wha saw thick smoke rolling fast toward Hae Soon; red flames were leaping angrily above the tops of trees. "Hae Soon! Quickly!" Dropping the flowers, she ran toward him, but the smoke engulfed her. His eyes stinging, Sung Wha ran in, shouting Hae Soon's name, but his arms grabbed nothing but smoke.

He was yanked out of the nightmare. Lim's tormented face was over him. "Get up! Get up!"

"Da first thing I remembah was dis thick-thick smoke all 'round me and den seeing da whole friggin' roof above me, one huge red flame. I nevah was so scared in my life. All of a sudden dis terrific wind come right into da room, like one huge roaring typhoon. And all dat smoke blow up into da roof. I was so scared and was so hot, I think my heart wen cook. I thought, *I dead! I dead!* I thought I wen *maké*-die-dead in my sleep and waking up in one Christian hell."

"Get up! Get up! Quick! Go! Hae Soon! Go! Hurry! The back way!"

Sung Wha followed a coughing Hae Soon, and they escaped through the back door, but not before a shower of fire and cinder fell on them. Running and brushing off the heat from their bodies. Cracks of gunfire. A cry.

"Your future wife's father?"

Through the garden trampling on ripening vegetables and into the chilling fresh air of night. Whinnying of horses. More gunshots. More cries. Angry men shouting. Frantic men shouting. Frenziedly running up trail to forest. Stopping halfway, breathing hard, looking back. The raging fire and a garrison of soldiers rounding up farmers, lining them up before the burning structure, their shadows in terrible flight but feet nailed to ground. The farmers with hands on head. Cries and screams of children. Then: the executions. *Prak! Prak! Prak!* Hae Soon's perspiring, silent face, smudged with soot, the licks of fire dancing off her features. Tears streaming down her cheeks.

Lim is dead?

Soldiers fire into dying flames. Horsemen ride in shadowy circles, and the conflagration sends a final eruption of sparks and ash into heaven's dark. When the horsemen ride off, their flashing swords laughing, and foot soldiers march away, guns cooled by the gloom of night, Hae Soon turns from the destruction and climbs up again the mountain trail, with Sung Wha following behind, a silence between them congealed by the chill of the air, their faces, though, still warm from the fire.

"You know, I dunno what going on my mind den. Maybe I was thinking what going on hers. Everything she had, gone. Now she no mo' family. She lost her mama and now her papa. But I think I was mo' sad dan her. She . . . even when she know her father wen *maké*, only tears in her eyes, nothing else. If somebody else, dem fall apart, go crazy. Not her, but. Her was strong inside, real strong, maybe even mo' strong dan me dose days. Me, I still one kid, youknowwhatImean? Jus' one kid. And her, she mo' young dan me, but still yet, she act mo' grownup already."

"And this girl, this woman . . . she became your wife?"

"Yes. Remember that I had never seen a woman before.

What I really mean is, rather, that the opposite sex had never interested me before. Not until my eyes met hers." He laughs.

"May I ask, why are you laughing, Mr. Kim?" The minister grins uncomfortably at Sung Wha's sudden amusement.

"Don't take this personally, Reverend. I was just thinking how naive I was back then. If I just knew then what I know now!"

The minister pours more tea in his cup. Sung Wha waves his hand in token refusal, which the minister disregards. The tea is good. Sung Wha has never had tea as good as this before. It is an unusual type of tea, bitter yet soothing . . . is it from America?

"Mr. Kim, you were telling me how both of you escaped the fire. Then . . . the fire was caused by the Japanese gendarmes?"

Sung Wha nods his head. "And even if it wasn't, I would still blame them."

"So . . . how did you finally end up in Hawai'i?"

"That's another long story. I'm getting there, I'm getting there."

The stars were out that night. Perhaps the stars were reflecting traces of the fire that leveled the inn.

They continued up the trail until they came to a clearing overlooking the dark, wind-rustled and roving forest of the valley below. The scent of pollen and pine was strong. Rushing air chilled their sweaty bodies, and the starry panorama of night's sky charged Sung Wha to a dizziness.

"Do you know where we're going?" Sung Wha asked, a dryness in his mouth.

There was no answer.

He waited. He cleared his throat, about to repeat the question when she spoke.

"I'm going to Kumgangsan. From there to Manchuria. If you wish, you may come with me."

"But what about your house, your things, your...father?"

"You can see for yourself, the fire has left me with nothing."

He did not know what to say. Yes, he does want to go with

her, and no, he does not like being made fun of. And yes, she must be full of grief. How can she not be?

"My father prepared me for a time like this," she said finally. Sung Wha felt the blisters on her words.

"My father has many friends between here and Manchuria. First, we'll go to his very close friend who lives at the foot of Kumgangsan. A woodcutter. If we continue our present pace, we'll get there by daybreak." Then she set off.

The trail now descended and meandered into the rich earth-scented darkness. Sung Wha followed without hesitation. Where else can he go? And what else can he do?

They could not see the stars now, the tall pine pushing back sky and light, waving off any heaventouch with wild rages of wind and roar.

All of heaven's dust are repelled by this roar, this wind! *Yes, Hae Soon, take me through this darkness! Hae Soon! I follow you past these murmurs, these threatening gossips of animals and spirits that surround us, that I cannot see.*

Hae Soon pressed on, driven by instinct, using feeling and scent, while Sung Wha shook at each stirring behind him, to the side of him. They stopped to drink at a brook, but they stopped for nothing else in that night that was as cold as mountain water. Pushing on, they crossed a wide valley, and before day-break they came upon a small clearing and a squat hut made of mud walls and topped with a conical thatched roof, a brown mushroom dwarfed by ancient trees.

A smallish man sat cross-legged next to a fire, sharpening an axe and smoking a pipe. He was humming a song that Sung Wha moments before took as the running of water.

"Uncle," Hae Soon had whispered to Sung Wha when they first smelled smoke and saw tiny flickers of fire through breaks in the brush. And Sung Wha thought, *now her voice hints of emotion.* Sung Wha tripped over a stone and fell into Hae Soon, knocking her into a bush. He apologized quickly, and was surprised how fragile her body was.

"She smelled like—AH!—one mountain flower!"

They pushed through a final bush. "Uncle?"

The woodcutter stopped his song and searched into the darkness, a hand cupped over squinting eyes. Dropping his hand, he smiled, recognition flashing on his face. He stood up, her name rolling off his tongue, and spread his arms wide to receive. Hae Soon ran into his embrace. "Not a surprise! My lovely daughter! Not a surprise!"

He was shorter than she and built low and powerfully wide. His narrowed eyes glistened as he rocked her and patted her shoulder, and his long, ragged hair and beard were a dark rust color, streaked with white.

"The hint of your coming in the early morning air was such a joyful awakening," the woodcutter said. "But at first I didn't know who it was exactly. The smell was so familiar but so diffused. Ah! Such is old age! It gets us all. I can't smell as well as before. And my memory is not as good, too. But this is a nice surprise. And who is your friend?"

"His name is Kim Sung Wha, a friend of Father. He's one of Father's political friends."

"Ah! So you're one of those!" The woodcutter laughed, prancing a couple of steps toward Sung Wha. Then, eyes withdrawn and turning to Hae Soon: "There's something wrong. Your father?" Hae Soon bowed her head and instantly released her grief to him.

The woodcutter cradled Hae Soon's head on his shoulder. He led her into the cottage.

Sung Wha sat next to the fire and warmed himself, watching the fire burn to embers and then soft ash. His stomach rolled with hunger, but his eyes softened, and soon he was in a dream of stars calling his name and dogs chasing pregnant sows.

The sun had risen when he awoke. Squatting next to a rebuilt fire was the woodcutter, stirring a steaming pot. The aroma of rice gruel weakened Sung Wha's stomach.

"Boy, go inside," the woodcutter said, his eyes steady on the pot.

His eyes lingering on the swirling rice *chuk*, Sung Wha stood up and staggered into the woodcutter's house, where he found Hae Soon asleep on a bed of straw. He collapsed in one corner on the cold dirt floor.

He dreamed again, this time of food: mounds of rice and millet and oily fish on white platters, and persimmons and powdered ricecakes with a tin of honey for dipping, all on a long linen-covered table. It must be the spring festival, he thinks. And there is no one around. So he grabs for the food and stuffs himself, and strangely he cannot fill the emptiness of his stomach.

And now he's at the foot of a bleak, icy peak.

"Sung Wha!"

Then an echo.

Balancing dangerously on a narrow ledge halfway up a face of granite and ice, Sung Wha's tigress grandmother is waving for help. "Sung Wha!"

"Grandmother!"

He scrambles over rock and ice, then scales the wall, but when he nears the ledge, the footing under him crumbles, and he falls backward through thick clouds, Grandmother screaming his name.

The chop of wood.

Where am I?

Hae Soon's swollen reddish eyes were on him. She had been crying. She dabbed the moisture from her eyes. "Were you having a nightmare?" she asked. "You were yelling in your sleep."

He was embarrassed. He apologized. He scanned the unfamiliar surroundings and then remembered the burning of the inn, their escape into darkness and mountain, and the arrival at the woodcutter's cottage.

"That's all right," she said. "Come. Uncle has summoned us to eat."

Uncle?

Stiffly, Sung Wha followed her out to a strong resinous scent of freshly cut wood. The woodcutter was chopping and singing another song, a song of winter, his low voice edged with mourning:

> *Ah, low are the clouds, Kumgangsan cries,*
> *And high is the sun that brings us warmth.*
> *The deer lives on regurgitated fern shoots,*
> *And I on dreams of yesterday's spring.*

He stopped singing when he saw them. He pointed with the axe at the pot of rice chuk. "Eat," he said, then he returned to his song and work.

In earthen bowls Hae Soon served the *chuk:* chopped mushrooms and fern shoots suspended in a soup of burst grains of brown rice. A bland but sweet aroma. Sung Wha ate the *chuk,* and the *chuk* awakens his mouth, puckering his lips, and he stops to wonder about the *chuk,* but he's hungry and continues eating. And besides, the *chuk* is giving him a warm, pleasant calmness. He looks up from his bowl and watches the bearded woodcutter, swinging his axe in time with his singing, and for a moment Sung Wha wants to ask him about the unusual taste of the *chuk.* But he is too afraid to do so. Nonetheless, he finishes the bowl and asks himself if the feeling he is experiencing is the same as being drunk on rice wine.

His body has become heavy, and strangely his mind is able to touch the sounds around him. He regards the woodcutter again, and he admires the methodical rhythm of his tightly compact body, and he wonders if his eyes are being tricked as the fall of axe seems now to fall sluggishly in time. Sung Wha closes his eyes, and it's a long time and a gripping effort before he's able to open them again. And when he does, he discovers now a pond a short distance away, a white crane's flapping leap away; and the pond's metallic surface and the surrounding branches of trees and the clouds in the sky shaped like grotesque fungi all are framing a distant snow-capped mountain.

His eyes move down the slopes to green foothills, then back to Kumgangsan itself, and then to the white clouds that hide the mountain's many peaks.

Time does not dawn here. It never did. Today is yesterday is tomorrow is today . . . and there are no such things as villages or towns or societies. There is peace in nature, and nature is everything. There is no anger or sadness or happiness. There is no frustration or loneliness. And all is forgotten but the journey of the moment.

A sapling in a forest of giant trees.

"Are you all right?" she asks.

The white light has disappeared.

He nods. "Yes . . . maybe a little tired. But I feel fine."

She leaves him for the cottage.

Where has she gone?

Returning, she finds him in that trance still.

"Let's go down to the pond and wash up," she says.

He is an obedient, trusting child. They go to the pond and wash their hands and faces.

"It is beautiful . . . here," Sung Wha remarks softly. A bead of water rolls to his chin. Falls. The moment felt.

"I will miss her," she says.

"Her?"

"Korea."

A smile. "Then why leave?"

A hard, perplexed look. "Have you forgotten already? Aren't you going to Manchuria? Don't you want to be a patriot?"

"No . . . yes."

"Is that an answer?" she demands.

"Yes."

"We'll have to cross that mountain before winter buries the roads," she says matter-of-factly, looking toward Kumgangsan.

"The mountain is beautiful," he reflects.

She douses her face with the cold water, pretending not to hear him.

"Did the *chuk* taste . . . "

"What is it?"

"Your woodcutter friend . . . he's very kind."

She nods her head, wiping her face on her skirt. "Uncle told me that we may stay here as long as we wish. I told him that we need money. He told me that if we help him gather wood, he'd sell it to the nearby villages and share the money with us."

"The *chuk* . . . did it taste funny to you?"

"Uncle Bhak is a man of these mountains," she says.

"Uncle Bhak?"

"He sees things we can never see."

"What do you mean by that? Like what?"

"The air."

"What?"

"Just what I said."

"You talk in riddles."

She stares at distant Kumgangsan. "People say he is a tiger."

"Wh-what are talking about? But the *chuk* . . ."

"A tigerman," she says.

"A riddle again."

"A tigerman."

"A tigerman." *A tigerman. What is she talking about? Am I hearing right? Something strange about the* chuk. He laughs. He hears right.

She is joking me. She's trying to make me feel like a fool again. Or perhaps all this strangeness around us has got to her. And that odd-tasting chuk *. . . it must have magic in it, it makes me hear things and makes her say strange things. Will it make me see strange things, too? This is all getting too much for me. Sometimes I don't know when she's serious or just trying to play a joke on me. A strange girl, full of surprises. Uncle Bhak . . . a tigerman? What is a tigerman? Why is she saying this to me? Is she trying to scare me? I don't scare easily. No, I don't.*

"You have never heard of stories of men who are part beast? My grandfather used to tell me legends of woodsmen living around

Kumgangsan who have the uncanny ability to change themselves into tigers or deer, or into whatever animal form they choose."

This man of a Christian god is talking about the strange and supernatural?

"I'm surprised that you have never heard of stories concerning this aspect of nature, you being from the countryside where the storytelling is richly flavored with these tales. Korea folklore is full of stories like these."

This man of god has not heard me right. But that's okay. But instead of preaching all the time, he ought to learn to listen, open his ears and listen to others. I never said that I had never heard a story like this. I never said that. I was just acting out my surprise at that particular moment. That's all. Is my storytelling that persuasive? Is this man of god this much of a fool to be fooled so easily? I doubt it. Yet, here he talks to me as if I'm the fool.

"You know, Uncle, what you're telling me makes sense. The Hawaiians, too, believe get some people can turn themselves into different forms, like sharks, lizards, even stone. You remember my friend Solomon, the one who used to come around the house after I came back from the war? The one we used to call Blackie? He told me his ancestors were sharks. Yeah. That's why he never ate fishcake, because the Japanese used to make fishcake outta shark meat."

"Dere you go. Now you talking sense. You know what you talking 'bout. Dis *moksa*, but, I dunno dis buggah how—what —he thinking about, youknowwhatImean? He think all dis things I telling him jus' stories I wen make up, youknowwhatImean? Jus' like I telling him one bunch lies. I catch dat from him.

"You know, you can read one person fast if you know how. I wen read dis buggah. Always befo', I think *moksa*s, dey suppose to read us, da people, and go tell us what is right or wrong. But I know right off da bat dat him, him so thickheaded, him, he cannot see what I trying say to him 'cause his thick glasses, he get his own way looking at things. He think I jus' talking stories to him, faking it, making up stories, but I nevah. I talking what I wen see, experience, what I feel at da time. Das all.

"At first, I nevah like believe what yo' auntie talking 'bout, too. Me, back den, I think all dis kine stuff is all bullshit stories. Kids' stuff. Nonsense. But da voice she talking to me in, ho, so diff'rent dan her ada talking voice . . . scary, was. She so serious, nevah seem same-same her own voice. So when I listen to her, ho, I jus' had to believe. YouknowwhatImean?"

"My father calls Uncle Bhak the Tigerman." She looked toward Kumgangsan. "He was born there, in a cave."

"Many tigers live there."

"Father told me about Uncle's story."

There once was a Buddhist monk who lived in an isolated monastery in Kumgangsan. One day, in late autumn, he wandered deep into the mountain in meditation when suddenly a flash flood caught him off guard and swept him into a raging river. He lost consciousness. Later, he woke up and found himself in a lair of a giant tigress. The tigress had saved him from a sure death by drowning, but now he believed himself a meal for the beast. The monk accepted his fate. But fortunately the tigress was not interested in eating him. She began to talk to him, to his astonishment.

"Don't you remember the tiger cub you saved from freezing in a winter's storm many years ago?" The monk vaguely remembered the incident. "Well," the tigress continued, "that was I whom you saved. As you can see, I have grown. I have waited all this time to return the favor."

"But how can you remember me? I was young then, just a child. How could you remember?"

"Each human has a distinct scent. I have always remembered yours."

So the tigress nursed the monk to health, warming him with her furry body during the frigid nights. They became intimately close. They became lovers. The cold winter months passed by nearly unnoticed by the monk as he and the tigress became engrossed in a consummate passion.

Then spring came. The monk felt obligated to return to his monastery. With great sadness, they parted. He promised to return, but she forbade it, saying it was not in the gods' eyes that they see each other again. As a token of her affection, the tigress gave him a lock of her hair, and the monk shaved off all the hair that had grown on his head those past months and gave it to her.

Time passed. The long summer held many fond memories for the monk. At first, it was hard for him to readjust to an ascetic, celibate life after such an inflaming experience, but hard work in the fields left him with no time and energy to think about his tigress lover. Slowly, he settled back to a mundane existence.

Then winter came. It was a harsh winter. A terrible storm piled a mountain of snow on the monastery. But the order had stored more than enough food and fuel for the winter. Often, however, at nights, the monk would worry about his tigress lover: he worried that perhaps she was starving and shivering in her cave. Every morning when he awoke and every night before he slept he prayed for her safety.

Finally spring came, and though snow still covered the ground, the sun was bright and warm in its offering. And in a few weeks, the remains of the bitter winter melted away.

A report reached the monastery that a large tiger had attacked several distant villages and each time had taken a human as its kill. Funny, the monk thought, that with the monastery so much closer to the land of the tigers, the man-eater chose to travel many more *li* for food. Hunting parties were organized and dispersed to find the man-eater. After much effort, they finally trapped and wounded the tiger, only to see it escape.

One night the monk had a dream. It was the tigress calling him. She was crying, and her tears were blood. He awoke in the middle of the night, shaking all over and feeling a terrible premonition. Early the next morning he climbed the mountain and came upon a trail of dried blood. He followed it with alarm to the tigress' lair, where, to his intense grief, he found her stiff corpse blocking the cave's entrance. He broke into tears, his suspicions now grounded. It was the tigress who had raided the villages below but had avoided his order. The winter had been hard on her: she was emaciated, and her fur was worn thin. If only she had come to me, he thought, then I would have given her food and all of this would not have happened. He flooded her battered coat with his salty tears.

A tiny cry came from the back of the cave. The monk raised his head from the tigress' corpse, his face alert. Was it a cry . . . of a human baby? Searching the cave, he found on a cold ledge lined with lichen and human hair a starving infant. The baby was covered with a soft yellowish fuzz, a black stripe running up its back. Gently he touched the baby, who was immediately pacified. And the monk cried more, knowing this baby had resulted from the uncommon union of the tigress and himself.

He returned to his dead lover and buried her properly on the mountainside above the cave. Then he wrapped the baby in the folds of his heavy robe and carried it out. As he descended the mountain, the animated murmurings of the baby slowly transformed the heavy gloom in his heart to joy.

Shortly afterward the monk left the religious order to raise his tiger son. They settled in a small cottage at the base of the mountain, where, sometimes deep in the night both father and son conversed with the wind that carried the watchful spirit of the tigress.

Silence. Finally: "That was an interesting fairy tale."

"It isn't a lie," Hae Soon said. "It's the truth."

"Then I believe you. But . . . how did you know so much of the story?"

"My father and Uncle Bhak are very close. They're family. They're . . . brothers."

"What is this?" Sung Wha's eyes were wide with disbelief.

"They have the same father."

"But your father's name is Lim and your uncle's name is Bhak."

"My father and Uncle Bhak are half-brothers. My father's name is also Bhak. But he had to change his name because the police were after us. It was the only way we could get safely out of Seoul."

"Yo' auntie nevah tol' me lies. Sometimes, but, da kine stories she tol' me was kinda hard to believe, outta dis world. But if you evah meet her, you know right off da bat how . . . how honest she is. She no tell lies, she no try fool you like is practice nowadays, how every Tom, Dick, and Harry do. Yo' auntie, she something else. Even to dis day. And I nevah see her fo' ovah fifty-something years. But I still can see her picture in my head, real clear. She jus' like me, she no can marry again. Das how much we love each ada.

"I dunno why I always think about In Ja, but. She no can match up wit' yo' auntie. But maybe 'cause I nevah see yo' auntie fo' so many years, I get lonely sometimes. So many years wen go by, so many lonely years. As they say, so much water pass under da bridge. I think das why."

"Mr. Kim, why did you come to Hawai'i when your wife and child are in Manchuria?"

"Dat man of god, he getting to me, he beginning to bug me. Maybe it my fault telling him all dese stories. I dunno. But him, he getting too *nīele*. But he look da honest kine, I no think he da kine try cheat you or lie to you. Him da kine, little bit patronize-you type. But I think dat time I nevah really trust him. I nevah know if him okay or not, if him one agent or what. Later on I find out he okay. But dat time I nevah tol' him why I come Hawai'i. Why I tell him? Maybe he one *sung-guhm*, how

I know? Da goddamn *sung-guhm* on my trail. Da dicks from plantations, dey trying find me so dem can bus' my head open. I no like be same-same Lee Chi Ha."

I watched his long face get longer. Then I said, "I never asked you this before, Uncle, but how come you came Hawai'i and left Auntie and your children back Korea?"

For a long, stifling moment, Uncle gave me a real stink eye. I looked away. Then he grinned, only to be seized by another fit of coughs. His face turned purple. He wiped the saliva from his lower lip and rolled to his side, coughing hard and trying to clear the congestion, the phlegm that clung to his throat like stubborn water leeches (that's how he once described the feeling to me). His face was turning a deeper purple. After a minute Uncle won the bout, temporarily. And for the next few after that he gazed at the flat white ceiling, his hazel eyes watering. I noticed the intricate network of blood vessels on the yellowish whites of his eyes, the vessels a bright red, about the only part of Uncle that was visibly living. I turned away from his wasting body.

"I guess can tell you, Yong Gil," he said in a gravelly voice, his breathing forced. "You family. I guess nobody going hunt down one wanted man now, anyway, since I all broken up. No?"

He looked into my eyes and saw how his last comment had saddened me. He chuckled as if to ameliorate my pain, his pain. I reached for his hand and squeezed it, and he squeezed back.

"But I no going tell you now. Come later in da story. I evah tell you how yo' auntie and me get married? Yo' auntie and me no get married on pepah. But inside, our hearts marry each other. Da feeling mo' strong, dis way. Mo' important, dis way. Dis mo' strong dan da kine marriage you get nowadays, da kine ridiculous quick shebang dey get nowadays at da church li'dat. YouknowwhatImean?"

Sung Wha's last comment left her blushing, her eyes shying away. He felt an immediate discomfort. All he had said, while sitting next to her and admiring the reflection of Kumgangsan on the pond, was that the beauty and peacefulness of the mountain reminded him of her. It was an honest opinion. That was how he was brought up at home, to be up front about his thoughts. But now he knew he shouldn't have said that. Embarrassed, he got up without a word and went over to the woodcutter.

"What's the matter, boy?" the woodcutter asked, driving his axe into a block of wood. He wiped the perspiration on his face with a rag. There was no answer from Sung Wha. "Did Hae Soon tell you she wants to stay here awhile? That way you can help me cut and sell wood and make some money for your journey to Manchuria. But your strong back must carry the brunt of the work. I'm still strong, but I'm not a young man anymore."

While the woodsman was looking away, Sung Wha studied his profile. Bushy eyebrows. A dark-reddish beard. *Is he really a tigerman? Does he have black stripes on his back?*

"Ah, you're afraid of the Japanese," Bhak laughed. "Well, don't worry about them. The Japanese are too afraid to come up here. They're afraid of the many tigers that live in these mountains. And that's a good reason." The old woodcutter winked at Sung Wha.

Now Sung Wha noticed that the woodcutter's eyes were green, not black or brown. Alarmed, he looked away. But laughter began rolling off the woodman's furry coat and infecting Sung Wha. One moment Sung Wha was in fear; the next, he was laughing. And shortly afterward he found himself a helper to Bhak, stacking the wood that the woodsman was chopping to size.

They worked at the woodpile for the rest of the day, into the early evening. Hae Soon had quietly disappeared into the forest, emerging later with an armful of greens. Smoke soon curled out of the hut, and then the liquid, sweet aroma of rice cooking traveled through the resinous air to Sung Wha's empty stomach. The old woodsman quickened his pace, as if in a race with the setting sun, and they did not stop working until two large A-shaped pack frames were stacked high with wood.

They washed at the pond, dipping hands in the tepid water and rubbing off dust and dirt from faces and arms. Then they entered the warmth of the cottage, where they ate a *chuk* made with sliced vegetables and mushrooms. And again the food relaxed Sung Wha, and he lay back against a wall and watched Bhak sit cross-legged in one corner, smoking a pipe of herbs, his sparkling eyes affixed to the fire.

They stayed for two more weeks. While Hae Soon stayed home to collect and cook the food, the men climbed deep in the forest to work. Though Bhak claimed old age, Sung Wha found it difficult to keep up with the wiry woodsman, whose legs were hard timbers of muscle. Once, out of fun, they tracked the trail of a young buck, and Bhak ran up the trail like a tiger stalking its prey: head lowered, body tensed and hunched forward, an arm trailing stiffly behind like a curling tail. The old man crept toward the drinking, unsuspecting animal, then leaped out from behind a bush and landed on its back, riding the terrified creature until it finally threw the old man to the ground, then laughing and rolling to and fro on a bed of pine needles.

Sung Wha had never seen anything like this before. *Truly, he must be a tigerman,* he thought, and the idea scared him. But as the days of their stay quickly came to an end, Sung Wha began to understand the wild but benign ways of the woodsman. Bhak was living his life in close harmony with the natural world; he was independent of family and friends; he never hungered for food since food was all around for the taking; and there was never any worry of the Japanese bothering him, the Japanese army being miles away from this tiger-infested territory, though it was strange that during their stay Sung Wha never saw even a trace of the animal.

Sung Wha developed a quick and complete liking for the woodsman and his lifestyle. He remembered what his grandmother had said about the blood of the tiger running in their family's veins. *Perhaps I can stay here and learn from this man. Perhaps I can be like Bhak. He never angers. He never is saddened. He laughs and smiles, but never gets carried away. He feels so confident, so certain, about the way he lives.*

But Hae Soon, who was learning to read Sung Wha's mind better with each nightfall, worried how the sojourn might be infecting Sung Wha. She pounced on him any chance she had.

"You've been telling me a bunch of lies," Hae Soon said one morning, when Bhak had gone off by himself.

"About what?" Sung Wha asked.

"About wanting to go to Manchuria and joining with the revolution."

"Why am I a liar?"

"Because you say one thing and now you want to do something else!"

Though he realized that Hae Soon was right, Sung Wha was too proud to concede, and they argued for most of the morning.

"It's no easy task," philosophized the woodsman about their journey. They were sitting outside around a fire. The night was still; the only sounds besides their talking was the occasional crackling of the burning wood. Bhak was smoking his pipe, his eyes glimmering in the flickering blades of fire. "Having courage is important, but don't misuse it."

"That's why we're going to Manchuria," Sung Wha said. "We need to learn how to fight."

"Uncle, would you like to come with us?" Hae Soon offered.

Bhak gave a smoky smile. "No," he answered. He raised his eyes to a groan in the pine above them; a wind had come to listen. "I know my place," he continued, still looking into the treetops. "And no one bothers me here, this place where I belong."

"But it's important to fight against the injustices that plague our land."

"I've fought my battles already, Hae Soon," the woodsman

said, sighing. "I'm an old man. My tail is long gone. Impatience leads me nowhere now." Slowly he drew from the pipe. "And besides," he said, smoke leaving the sides of his mouth, "the enemy now is different."

"What do you mean, Uncle?"

Bhak studied Hae Soon's young, impetuous face, then turned to the fire. "Never mind. I can't go with you. I've won and lost my battles already. Now it's your turn."

And later in the evening, Hae Soon: "Uncle has changed much."

Bhak was snoring loudly in the corner.

"What do you mean?" Sung Wha asked.

"He has given up. Now he wishes to live a meaningless life in the forest."

"I don't see anything wrong with that."

"My father told me that he once led a pack of tigers in these mountains against a Japanese regiment. They devoured every single soldier. It's a well-known story in these parts, and that is why the Japanese stopped sending their troops into the mountains, for fear of Uncle Bhak and his mythical army. But now, he's changed. When one grows old, that doesn't mean one must prepare for one's burial."

They had earned several hundred yen—not an enormous amount, but enough to start them on their journey.

It was a long, hard road ahead: they would have to trek through the mighty Kumgangsan; then follow a trail north across great forests; and finally, after all those trees and lakes and villages, they'd have to cross the mighty Yalu. They'd need to hire a boat to take them to the Manchurian side, where the base camps of the liberation army were hidden well in the folds of worn, tree-covered mountains. It would be very difficult to contact the army, but they were determined to do so.

This was the simple scenario that Hae Soon told repeatedly to Sung Wha for the last three nights of their stay. There was not much detail to her plan, yet Sung Wha's mind was taken by its plain images, and Bhak's lifestyle became less and less attractive. He'd dream about that journey: taking giant leaps, he and Hae Soon would span mountains and valleys and plains and mighty rivers and villages and finally land among a welcoming band of broad-faced patriots.

Then came the morning of departure: a chilly morning with thick clouds hiding Kumgangsan completely. They had readied themselves for the journey the night before, packing bundles of food and extra clothing on small A-frames that Bhak had made especially for their trip. And though they spoke calmly to Bhak, both were anxious and worried. Bhak wished them well. He gave them a little extra money. They embraced. They were off.

"After dat, we wen go straight to Kumgangsan. Da English name is da Diamond Mountains. Ho! Is so beautiful up dere, jus' like heaven. Get all da mountain water running down, everywhere all green, so many trees, da mountains so beautiful. Yong Gil, you no seen nothing like dis in yo' life. So beautiful. So me and yo' auntie, we follow dis narrow road up to da mountain. I tell you, all Koreans, dey all make one pledge to demselves dat befo' dey die dey gotta go see da Diamond Mountains, Kumgangsan. If dey no go, den dey going *maké* not satisfied wit' dere life, youknowwhatImean? At least I can say I wen see da place. I live dere fo' little while. At least now if I *maké* I no have to worry 'bout dat.

"But, you know, something 'bout da mountains give me dis funny kine feeling inside. Da mountains so big and you so small, you nothing to it. You feel so small. Das why all da monks, you know, da Buddhist monks li'dat, dey all go up dere and meditate. You live up dere and aftah 'while you feel you no mo' one self inside you anymo'. You understand what I trying tell you? J'like somebody come and go wash all yo' inside out. You no mo' nothing inside. You one blank person. You not even one person. You still remembah yo' name, but funny kine feeling, like you no really care if you get one name or not. Da beauty of da mountains jus' take everything away from you . . . you understand what I saying? You no mo' hate aftah dat, you no can have hate inside you, 'cause all you can think 'bout is love and watching all da beauty around you. But da only thing—if you was hungry like how we was, we nevah eat fo' three days, something li'dat—I no care if get so much beautiful things 'round you it blind you, you still going feel hungry inside.

"Was three days—I dunno, maybe was mo' den dat or maybe less, but wen feel like one long time—but was 'bout three days when we get to da place where yo' auntie said we suppose to go. And on da way, shit! Wen rain so hard, all da rivers swell up so high almost take us down wit' 'im. But finally, Yong Gil, we finally get ovah dere, to dis Buddhist monastery. Yo' auntie said she know one of her father's old friends was staying ovah there. He was one Buddhist monk, but befo', he one classmate of her father. Dey grow up together, or something li'dat.

"So we go up there, we go inside. I feel kinda funny kine wen I see da place. Had one big compound and da walls was made of rock, and I remembah da rock was all sparkling, like had small-small-kine broken glass inside da rock. Inside, right next to da wooden gate, was dis big-big old bell, I think was made of bronze, but was real big kine and had dis kine inscription all over. I forget da name of dis place. Sheee . . . what da name of da place? I forget, was so long ago. How I can forget da name of dis place?!"

"So my wife-to-be and I entered the compound of the monastery. Talk about strange, eh? Nobody was inside. There was just the bare ground of the compound and a tall rock wall surrounding it all. The rocks were strange looking. They had a sparkle to them, as if bits of glass or diamonds were embedded. I have never seen anything like that before. I remember thinking at the time that that's why they must call it Kumgangsan.

"Later, Hae Soon told me that they called this monastery 'Kumgangsan,' like the mountain, and that her father had a very good friend who was studying there. She told me that though he was a Buddhist, he really wasn't. She told me that many

160

patriots had gone there in disguise to escape the Japanese but also to study philosophy, not just Buddhism. Of course, at the time I didn't know what she was talking about. In fact, I was beginning to resent her. I remember thinking, *How can a woman know more than a man?* And she was still a young girl at that! I would burn with jealousy. I thought that it was a shame for a man to be with a woman who was smarter than him. I told myself I must put a stop to all of this, I must assert my superiority over her, a woman. Ha!

"Those days, when my thinking was so backward, are times of embarrassment for me. How could I have believed in such a feudal tenet like the superiority of one sex over the other! Fortunately, I kept my mouth shut at the time.

"Now, as we entered the enclosed compound, I experienced a very intense feeling. I just can't explain it. I don't want to say that it was a spiritual experience, but I can't find the right word to describe this feeling. It couldn't have been a religious feeling because already at the time I was not religious, or at least believing less and less in the existence of a god or gods or whatnot. Do you know what I'm trying to say?"

"Yes, I do," the minister acknowledged with a nod of his head. "God comes to his children in many different ways. God is all around us."

"No. You don't know what I mean. Forget what I said. Anyway, have you ever studied the writings of Hegel or Fuerbach? And can you believe that these were the kinds of philosophy the monks at this monastery were studying?"

"We'll be able to stay here for awhile," Hae Soon said. "The people are nice. They are not your typical Buddhist monks."

"What do you mean?"

"You'll see what I mean."

They walked across the gravel-covered compound to an enormous, weather-beaten wooden door. With effort, Hae Soon unlatched the iron bolt and led Sung Wha into a cavernous, dim chamber that held the pungent scent of incense.

Set in perches cut into the granite, hundreds of puddling candles covered one lengthy wall. At the far end was a huge statue of Buddha, the top of its head melding into the high, dark ceiling, the rounded, gilded features highlighted by the candles. Several men with shaven heads and thick robes were before the statue, bowing and mumbling prayers.

"Have you been here before?" Sung Wha whispered.

"No, this is the first time for me. Don't be afraid."

"I'm not afraid. But I don't like it here. Let's leave."

"Don't be silly. There isn't another monastery around for many *li*."

"But didn't you say there are many monasteries in Kumgangsan?"

"Kumgangsan is very large. We're a bird's dropping in a forest."

"I don't like it here," Sung Wha mumbled.

"Don't be silly," Hae Soon said. "Come." And she took Sung Wha's hand and led him to a monk lighting a new candle.

"Ho! Yong Gil! No can tell you how good feeling I had, her hand holding mine. My heart jumping like crazy inside! I was in heaven!" Uncle smiles. Then another fit of coughs breaks out of a collapsing body.

A short, thin man turned toward Hae Soon's touch. He bowed, then asked them of their need.

"Is there someone here by the name of Rhuh Han Woo?" Hae Soon asked. The monk nodded his head. "Can you tell me where I can find him?"

The monk bowed again and motioned for them to follow him. He led them through a narrow passage chiseled into the side of the chamber opposite the wall of candles, to a brightly lit room filled with scrolls, manuscripts, and books organized in long racks and shelves. The monk pointed to a man slouched over a manuscript in one corner, then bowed and left them.

"Uncle Han Woo," Hae Soon whispered, touching the man

on the shoulder. She could not feel him under the heavy robe. The monk turned, his eyes crossed behind thick glasses. Then a smile flourished on his taut, angular face.

"You . . . you are Hae Soon," the monk said, his words barely audible. Then he grasped her hands vigorously. "You are a grown woman now. How beautiful. I've been waiting for you and your friend for a while. It is so good to see you."

They embraced, and Hae Soon introduced Sung Wha.

"Why did it take you so long to reach here?"

"How did you know we were coming?"

"When you live in these isolated reaches of the world, your mind becomes attuned to many strange and wonderful things. I had a dream of you and your friend recently. And I am sad-dened . . . by the loss of your father, my comrade in arms. But tell me, how have you been otherwise? And where have you come from? Where do you intend to go from here?"

Hae Soon held back her tears. "The Japanese destroyed my father's inn. My friend and I are on our way to Manchuria. Can we stay here and rest for a few days?"

"You may stay here for as long as you wish, my daughter. You know this. Come. Both of you must be hungry. I will give you some food."

They ate bowls of barley soup and pickled vegetables and drank a dark, bitter tea brewed from mushrooms and tree bark. Then Han Woo led them to their sleeping quarters, a narrow corridor lined with straw mats. Later that night, as they gathered around his bedding, Han Woo told them his story.

"What you see here is not really what you see," he said, a trickster's glint in his eyes. "Many of us are patriots, like myself. One day I will return to the struggle, perhaps venture off to Manchuria and then on to China. Many of us have come here to study ideas that are shaping the minds of men throughout the world. We have Hegelians and Marxists and Buddhists all mingling together here. The anarchists and Communists all have long left us. Maybe one day I will turn into one of them and also leave this windy place. But for now, it's a haven for my old yet still eager and hungry mind. Every man needs a philosophy, don't you think so?"

Han Woo looked at Sung Wha, who shrugged his shoulders. The monk laughed.

"Yes, it is true," Han Woo said. "We all live by one philosophy or another. The Japanese invasion into Korea is a good thing. It's making all Koreans question their existence in this world and seek what is right or wrong. To study philosophy. That is a good thing."

"But why do you hole yourself up in this mountain retreat, away from everything that's happening?" Hae Soon asked. "Aren't you being an escapist? This"—circling the air with a sweep of her hand—"is hardly the real world."

"Yes. And no. I am escaping nothing. If there is something to escape from, that is ignorance. And to overcome ignorance, one must struggle in the abstract realm of ideas. We monks have come here to gain knowledge so that we may later play a role in the liberation of Korea."

"I'm sorry to argue against you, Uncle, but the struggle needs people now. Not later. We might not have any opportunities then."

"Should we go blindly into a deep cave? Or should we wait to light our candle?"

"We should understand what has to be done—then do it!"

"Aha! Hae Soon!" Han Woo laughed. "You sound like an impatient anarchist."

"But Uncle, patience is a luxury in these times."

"Your father has denied you the life of a normal childhood."

"My father taught me to love freedom."

"Yes, you are your own person. And so young. Several young people have come here to study, but left shortly to join the anarchists or Communists. I believe they were rash in their judgment. But perhaps they have found a practical means to the solution. I'm not like that. I'm an old man. My decisions are not made in haste like they once were. I learned lessons from

errors committed when I was young. Now I must weigh everything many times over before a decision is made. Well . . . you
are young, you and your friend here—Kim Sung Wha is your
name?—so it is your prerogative to act the way you feel best."

"I sitting there, jus' listening dem talk. I no can understand
what da hell dey talking 'bout. Too much big words, no can
understand. Aftah little while, I not listening to dem. I looking
at yo' auntie, at her profile, da light from da lamp on her face.
Ho! She so pretty. I tell myself she da prettiest woman in da
world. Den I start thinking 'bout dis one time we was at Bhak's
house, you know, da woodcutter. I was looking at her and getting dis kine . . . rascal-kine ideas. And I nevah know dose days
what sex was. I jus' know when I get hard, it feel good. Lucky
thing yo' wife not here, Yong Gil. I no like talk dis kine in front
of her. Even da minister, even though I no believe in his god li'-
dat, still at least I get some respect fo' him, I never talk dis kine
in front him. But anyway, I going tell you one story."

A sparkle in Uncle's eyes, like the eyes of a *kolohe* child.

"One morning me and Uncle Bhak wen *hele* up da mountain. We was going back where we cut down dis big tree da day
befo'. We going cut 'em up fo' firewood fo' sell down da village
marketplace. Den Uncle tell me go back down to da house and
get da axe or something he forget, I no remember what. So I
wen *hele* back. I go inside da house, but Hae Soon, yo' auntie,
she not there. I figgah she in da woods picking mushrooms or
something. So anyway I find dis thing—one sharpening stone,
now I remember. So I pick up da stone, but I thirsty since I run
all da way down from da mountain. So I run down to da pond
fo' drink water. I just put my head down fo' drink when I hear
Hae Soon singing one song. Coming right behind da bush next
to me. So I get up, I jus' going say hello, when I see her right
through da bushes—and she no mo' clothes on! She no can
hear me or see me 'cause I behind da bush.

"Ho! I nevah see anything like dis befo'! She so beautiful!
But I so embarrassed, I like run away, but my eyes stay stuck on

her. So I jus' watch little while, and I feel I getting hard, real hard. Ho! So hard I in pain. I get so embarrass, I think maybe she going find me. So I turn 'round and run away fast. I dunno if she hear me or not, but I *hele* back to Bhak like one scared rabbit. All da way back up da trail.

"Uncle Bhak look at me in one funny-kine way. He tell me, 'Eh, something wrong?' But I tell him, 'Nah, nothing wrong.' But I know he know something wrong so I tell him I wen see one tiger and run away. And he ask me how 'bout Hae Soon, and I tell him, 'No-no, I see da tiger when I coming up da trail, far away from da house, so Hae Soon okay.' And he tell me, 'No mo' tigers 'round here.' And I tell him, 'Yeah-yeah, maybe something else,' and den he ask me where da stone, and I tell him what stone, and he say da stone fo' sharpen axe, and den I feel so stupid 'cause I forget da stone by da pond. Ho! He wen give me one nada funny-kine look.

"So I *hele* back down again, but dis time I make plenny noise so Hae Soon, yo' auntie, know I coming even though I no like her see me 'cause I was all hard again thinking about her when I was coming down.

"So anyway, back at da monastery, while yo' auntie and da monk was talking dey stories and I thinking 'bout dis, I get hard again. I no can look her in her face. I all embarrass inside. So I lie down on da floor, on my stomach, I trying pretend *moe*. But den I wen *moe*, I so goddamn tired."

During night cold winds beat against jagged mountain. Monastery surrounded by wild chorus: shrieks and moans and roars.

That night Sung Wha dreamt of the small monk leading him to a millet field and suddenly transforming into a gigantic tiger. And the tiger grew and grew, as large as a small mountain. It stood on its hind legs and beat thunder from its chest and roared so loud that the clouds and sky exploded away, exposing a dark heaven of dazzling stars. The tiger seized Sung Wha and flung him at the stars, and Sung Wha grabbed one star, but it was too cold or too hot—he could not tell. Letting go, he began falling, screaming, his body twisting and the stars spinning around him. And when he awoke—his shuddering and sweating body poked all over by loose straw—the stars were above him, glittering hot and cold like fiery emerald eyes of a thousand-eyed demon. He flung his arms out to brace for the crash, and then the light from an unchanging candle at the entrance of the room told him where he was.

They remained longer than the few days they intended to. A heavy autumn rain rushed over the mountain region, making the trails dangerous. The rains changed the soft-flowing streams into death rapids. The mountain groaned against the heavy shoves of the northern winds.

But it was an opportunity for Sung Wha and Hae Soon to make use of the monastery's great library. Han Woo had taken them back there the morning following their arrival and welcomed them to use it at any time. Hae Soon generously took his offer and began by studying a volume written by V. I. Lenin, printed in Japanese. Sung Wha rekindled his interest in reading, pulling out a dusty book from a lower shelf. But he could not read it as it was published in a foreign language, perhaps English, he really did not know.

"You are daring, aren't you, Sung Wha?" Hae Soon remarked, rubbing the mold off the title on the book's spine. "I didn't know you were gifted in reading German—and Hegel for that matter!"

Sung Wha felt like a fool, again. He became angry at himself and at Hae Soon for her biting comment. He slammed the book shut, stirring a decade of dust on the reading desk, jarring the concentration of a dozen or so monks. He stormed out of the library with his pride and burdensome ignorance on hold, vowing never to return.

But he broke his promise a short while later. Returning to the same spot at the table, he gathered the book quietly and slipped it back in its place on the shelf, then searched for another one, this time written in *hanggul*. Hae Soon turned to him, her brown eyes trying to touch his. He turned away. "I'm sorry about what I said."

He was surprised to hear her apology. He was stunned. But he accepted it and returned to his study of the difficult characters in front of him.

In the short time he had studied with her father, he had learned enough to be able to read rudimentary *hanggul,* though many complex characters still baffled him, holding back his probing mind. Swallowing his pride, he turned to Hae Soon and in a low voice asked for her help. She responded amicably, a sure change in her attitude.

What first turned out to be a near fiasco now metamorphosed into an engaging and productive relationship between student and teacher. Han Woo often joined them and vigorously professed his advanced knowledge, at which times, Sung Wha noted, Hae Soon seemed to defer to the monk's more complex reflections.

Sung Wha had never seen so many books and scrolls before —there were at least a hundredfold more books than Lim had owned—and never had he seen so many people engaged in study and debates among themselves. He was at first shaken; the facade of this tranquil, meditative setting was being quickly blown away. And the monks seemed to talk little of eternity and the other rubbish of religion; rather, their passionate debates were marked almost entirely with complex political terminology and ideas that confused Sung Wha. Now he thought himself dumber than a water buffalo. And though the monks discussed their thoughts with heated intensity—oftentimes their discussions turning into loud name calling and swearing, so very unbecoming of monks—he also noted how fast they calmed down once an argument had been decided or determined irresolvable. The monks would retreat back to books or behind curvatures of old scrolls, and more oil would be burned to illuminate The Way through the darkened gates of knowledge for more plodding and prodding, more tireless and unceasing mental peregrinations, this thirsting for knowledge giving an infectious, lively ambiance to the otherwise stuffy, airless gloom of library perusals and ideological reformations and . . .

Swayed by the monastery's vigorous intellectual activity and Han Woo's plea for them to stay through the fast-approaching winter, they decided to remain until spring. They would help the monastery with the gathering of food and wood in preparation for the cold months, and any free time they had would be used to study the many books of the monks' library at Kumgangsan.

The leaves of oak and maple and other trees yellowed and fluttered to the ground, leaving the spruce as a solitary reminder of life in the mountain. Autumn swiftly passed, and the winter storms began to cover the mountain with layer upon thick, impervious layer of snow, scaling off the area from the outside world.

But inside the frozen mountain, beneath granite ceilings of cavernous rooms, there erupted the fiery tosses and pitches of knowledge grappled with, grasped, and challenged. Sung Wha was amazed how a cold mountain could contain such fire. Rubbing his hands for warmth and huddling under thick robes and straw blankets, he listened to the others test their relative truths and pored over ancient tablets and modern-bound books, absorbing as much knowledge as his young, unsaturated mind could. He was unable as yet to dabble in philosophical ramblings—he did not as yet behold a concrete, definitive interpretation of the world, if it could be described in such a way—but nonetheless, he was developing his own outlook of the world, though quietly.

With the weeks flowing into the long current of winter months, Hae Soon became more skilled in her debates with Han Woo and the other monks. But there were still times when the arguments ceased, when Han Woo or the other more politically deft monks posed her a question or challenged her to elaborate on a position, to which she could not respond. In these times, her muted passion fired her cheeks, and her words became volcanic and reckless.

Of course, Sung Wha sided more and more with Hae Soon. Her arguments were sounder and truer to his developing viewpoint. Almost everything she said made more sense than what the others were contending, though he also formed a habit of blocking out anything the others were saying no matter how solid their arguments were. Perhaps it was because he was madly in love with Hae Soon; it did show in the hungry fire that possessed his heart and mind. Whenever she entered a lengthy rebuttal, it was a good excuse for him to look at her, to study the soft tones of her face, the clean and desirable lines of her mouth, eyes, and nose. How the sheen of her black hair sent shivers to his groin! Oftentimes he'd nod his head to give the impression he was following her wisdom of the political, though he would have no idea what the exact points of the debate were. He wanted to impress her by challenging the other monks, but he held back, of course, thinking that any of his offerings would be a fool's offering.

"You know, dose days, no can go meet anybody and jus' go in da bushes and—and—you know, get laid. Dose days when you go wit' somebody, you go fo' long time, you try know da ada person, youknowwhatImean? Das why nowadays everybody getting divorce right and left. I nevah see my wife fo' ovah forty years, ovah forty years! But still I love her. When you get same-same like me, you understand what love suppose to be. Love is not go poking yo' prick someplace, anyplace, anywhere you like. Das not love. Das stupid-way-think love. Da kine guys think li'-dat, dey unhappy, I no shit you. Dey dunno what is live one good life. But dey get nothin' fo' believe, fo' believe in. Dey think all life is 'bout is one good fuck and das it, but in da end dey da ones get fuck. Dey da kine like take advantage, you-knowwhatImean? Dey brag how many times dey do 'em wit' plenny wahines all ovah da creation.

"I tell you, Yong Gil, das not one man. One man, him no act

like one ignorant, like one dumb animal, youknowwhatImean? One real man, he dream, he dream da kine big dream—and I not talking 'bout making plenny money li'dat, das da kine *manini* kine dream. I talking 'bout wen you dream da kine *big* dreams, da kine when you start thinking about da whole world and not da weeds growing in yo' backyard. Das da kine dream I stay talking about. If you jus' think 'bout yo' prick and how yo' prick going feel or how yo' prick wen feel couple days ago or three years ago, or how you like yo' prick feel, you acting jus' like one animal. Sure, feel good, but feel mo' bettah good if you do it wit' somebody you love, not da kine afternoon love, or dis kine love or dat kine love, da kine love dey play in da radios all day long.

171

"Yo' auntie and me, us nevah touch each ada all dis time we travel in Kumgangsan. Da love wen grow . . . naturally. She make me proud of her, da way she think, da way she talk, da way she stand up fo' her rights and ada people's rights. But I still remembah da time when I see her by da pond, ho! She so beautiful. But dat one special time."

By the middle of winter, Hae Soon was tiring of the futile arguments. "These monks—they're all philistines! These monks are ignorant. They're not in touch with reality. All they do is study and study and study that's all! They have so many books here but are afraid to put these books down and turn these ideas into practice. All they like to do is play these intellectual games—all the while Korea is being raped!"

They prepared their leave weeks before the first sign of spring. And on a cold, sunny spring day, they left the monastery. The monks were generous, giving them warm clothes and food that would last them for a few days.

"Do you know where we're going?" Sung Wha asked, as they left the monastery's compound and stared down the path still covered with snow. He had been asking variations of this question for a couple of days.

"Yes."

"Then where are we going?"

"To Manchuria, silly!"

"But do you know how to get there from here? Do you know the roads? Isn't it far to Manchuria?"

"Yes, yes, yes! And that is why we are traveling by railroad. We have enough money from Uncle Bhak to travel by rail to Andung, which is at the mouth of the Yalu River. From there we travel by ferry across the river. Then we'll be in Manchuria. Is this all right with you?"

By railroad? Sung Wha had never seen a train before. Eung Whan's brother had told them stories from his experiences in the big city, about a giant metal beast that was as strong as a thousand water oxen and that deafened the skies with a loud blast of air almost as mighty as the Great Tiger of . . . but why didn't they take the train in the first place rather than stay the winter at the? . . .

"But why didn't we go by train instead of staying at the monastery?"

"Because there was no railroad when we came here. My father's friends blew it up a few days before he was killed by the Japanese. The railroad tracks should be repaired by now. It was an important line for the occupiers. It was the only way they could carry supplies and troops to the northern regions."

"But what if the anarchists decide to blow it up again?"

"It's a chance we'll have to take," Hae Soon said.

It took a day and a night of walking through the snow and slush to get down from Kumgangsan and another two days and nights to reach the train station, where they slept uncovered on the cold floor. And in the morning they were brother and sister, returning home to Antung after finishing school in Seoul. And what is your address in Antung? the Japanese gendarme at the station asked. Hae Soon gave him an address without hesitation. And what does your family do? They own an inn for traveling merchants and traders. And what is the name of their inn? The Inn of Returning Happiness. That is an unusual name, isn't it? I don't think so; it's a good name, and our parents will be happy to see their children returning from school. And you say that you are students in Seoul? What is the name of your school? Sung Wha's heart fell to the bottom of his gut: *how long will this go on?* But Hae Soon had a ready answer. Then an official with a thin moustache regarded them with beady ratlike eyes: for poor innkeepers, your parents must be quite well-to-do to send both of you away to such a fine school. And Hae Soon: my— our uncle is the principal there, and we are grateful that he has allowed us to live in his home. All right, go on.

They boarded the train, a large monolithic black mass of metal and steam that hoarded a slew of dark faces looking out of windows; even the Koreans wore looks of betrayal. Hae Soon confided to Sung Wha, I think I hate more Koreans who are working for the Japanese than the Japanese themselves. . . . Those Koreans are despicable!

They found an empty cabin and settled into it. Sung Wha snuggled up to the fingerprint-smudged window and looked out. In the distance he saw the snow-capped peaks of Kumgangsan. He thought: *and we spent the winter in those mountains, I don't believe it.* And: *how long has it been since leaving the village?*

A young, decorous man of Japanese nationality entered the cabin, asking in a deep voice, in Korean, if it was at all possible for him to sit with them. Hae Soon and Sung Wha nodded their heads solemnly, then looked away. The man was tall and thin and wore a dark suit and black fedora, and smelled faintly of mothballs. He carried a bulky leather bag with a shank of bamboo tied to it, the leaves having turned brown. Offering a tentative smile, a rare sight at the train station, he found no reciprocation from the two young Koreans. He stored his luggage above in the hold and settled in a corner, pulling out from his coat pocket a thin book, which he began to read from where a marker was placed. Smiling, he glanced at Hae Soon and Sung Wha, who were looking out the window, then moved his attention back to the book.

The train began to jerk forward. Nervously, Sung Wha

gripped the edge of the seat, silently wishing he was on solid ground. There was a queasiness in his gut. His eyes wandered about the room, his heart beating fast. The young Japanese national looked up from his book and smiled again. Sung Wha looked away.

"Is this your first train ride?" the man asked.

Sung Wha nodded his head. "Yes . . . my first time."

"Well, it's my first trip to Korea. I guess we share something alike." The young man waited for a response but, afraid that the introduction might be lost, promptly added, "I'm a school-teacher. My government is sending me to a teaching post in Manchuria. I have never been there. Are you familiar with those parts?"

Sung Wha nodded his head.

"Your country is beautiful. I have never seen such beautiful landscape before. I just wish"—lowering his voice and giving the closed door a cautious look—"that my country would leave your country alone. I have many Korean friends in Japan. You Koreans are a very gentle, industrious people, a very intelligent people. I'm not very supportive of what my country is doing here."

Sung Wha turned to Hae Soon, who had a watchful look in her eyes.

"I can see in yo' auntie's eyes what she thinking 'bout. Dis Japanee man, he trying fool us or what? Maybe he one spy da authorities wen send fo' find us. I still can see yo' auntie, how she nevah trust da buggah fo' nothing. But you know, inside I think how dis well-dressed man, dis schoolteacher, somehow he look all right, da way he come off, youknowwhatImean? Sometimes, eh, Yong Gil, you can figgah out one person even befo' you know da buggah. Can tell if da guy, him honest or not, if da guy like rip you off or making one front to you. But dis guy, dis schoolteacher—I think his name Wata-something, Wata-nabe, or something li'dat, I forget—but anyway, dis schoolteacher, somehow I feel he okay. He no look like dose ada Japanees who like beat you up, treat you bad, da kine dey had all ovah Korea. Later on, on da plantation, I meet plenny Japanee, but almost everyone, dey jus' come from Japan: dey young, dey really no like what dey government doing in Korea. But was real strange find one guy like da schoolteacher dat time 'cause I thinking all Japanee, no matter what, dey all da same, dey all lousy and all like boss you 'round, steal yo' things."

The schoolteacher slipped his hand into his coat pocket and retrieved a photograph of a beautiful young woman, standing in front of a rock garden covered with snow.

"She is my fiancée. She's a Korean national. We met while both of us attended Waseda University in Japan. When I got this job in Manchuria, we were heartbroken. But I had to take this job. There are no jobs in Japan. The economy is very bad. She wanted to follow me to Manchuria, but I told her it was very unsafe, that after I fulfill my contract of two years, I'll return and we'll get married. I know she'll wait for me. But it'll be a long two years."

It is winter. The snow is falling silently in fat clusters like feathery rice puffs. There is one more exposure in my friend's German camera. I am very glad he has lent it to me. I must take a good picture of my love. I will not see her for a long time. But I also have a strong feeling, which I must keep to myself, that I might never see her again. There's a revolutionary war going on in Manchuko, and I will be right in the middle of it. I think she understands the risks, but she is holding it all in, for my sake. She does not show me her grief and anxiety. I love her so much. She is a very strong person. She'll weather all the odds, and because of that, I will, too. Anyway, I told her just the other night of my acceptance of the position. "It's the only offer I'll ever have," I said, "and we need the money." I told her how I needed the teaching experience, that I'd never find a job right out of college with my record, and that it'd also be an opportunity to be on the front lines of the revolution and extend our internationalism to our comrades there.

When I come back, I'll be abreast of the struggle there, I told her. And also, of course, when I come back, we'll be married at last. We'll finally be together, and we'll never part again.

No one will ever see the tears my love sheds the moment after I snap that photograph, how her delicate, delightful, yet sad smile fades like a sun suddenly covered by a cloud. Everything now has become gray.

We walk back to my cold room above that ramshackle inn of drunk fishermen and cooing bar women, and we hold each other in a warming embrace. Though our stomachs are burning with hunger, we love and comfort and tease each other long after the fishermen's last song, until filaments of morning light slither in with the frigid air through the cracks in the wall. And then we sleep.

As the journey continued, Sung Wha and the schoolteacher— his name was Wakatani—began to talk more. And though Hae Soon, too, began to converse with the foreigner, suspicion still prevented her from doing so freely. Wakatani bought them warm rice cakes from a hunchbacked, buttery-voiced peddlar soliciting down the train's corridors. And he also shared his books with them, two books of poetry: one by a Japanese writer and the other, a translation, by a Lebanese.

"What are the books about?" Sung Wha asked.

"About love. Love for your lover. Love for your homeland. Love for yourself."

"What do you mean by 'love for yourself'?"

"What these books are saying is that you need to love yourself in order to love another person."

"I don't understand."

"It's nothing to understand," Hae Soon interjected. "Love can be written about, but it cannot be understood through books."

"These books were given to me by my fiancée. When I read them, I feel that she is reading these lines to me."

Later, after an uneasy silence, Wakatani began talking about himself.

"I come from a very respected family in Osaka. But when I went to Waseda University, I became, in my parents' eyes, very disobedient. I was . . . very bad to them. They felt that I brought the family dishonor. My mother would weep uncontrollably and my father condemned me, so I never went home after awhile. When I told them of this job, they became at the same time angry and worried for my safety. But they gave me a small sum of money, most of which I gave to my love and some to my unfortunate friends. My parents do not know of Soon Hee. They . . . they are very prejudiced against Koreans."

The schoolteacher was silent for a moment, looking out the window at the passing barren fields that perhaps would hold wheat and millet, perhaps patches of sorghum. "Please pardon me for asking, but where are your travels taking you?"

Sung Wha glanced at Hae Soon. "We have just finished our schooling in Seoul and are returning home now," he said.

"And where is your home?

"Antung."

"That is where I am going. I must catch a ferry there that crosses the Yalu River and then catch the northern train to Harbin."

"Harbin?"

"Yes, Harbin. That's where I'll be teaching. Are there any good inns in Antung?"

"Our parents—"

"Yes," interrupted Hae Soon. "There are many good inns in Antung, and very cheap ones, too. Many travelers come and go through Antung."

"Yes . . . that's what I've been told," Wakatani said with deliberation. I am too forward. I am asking too many questions.

"You know, I wasn't here at da time, but one time yo' papa tell me one story 'bout da time after Japan annex Korea. They annex Korea in 1910, I think. Was real tense time. Every time any news come from Korea, da Koreans on da plantations get all fired up 'cause was nada terrible story 'bout da Japanee crooking da Koreans.

"But one story wen really blow everybody's stack. Da story was 'bout how da Japanee soldiers wen go line up all da menfolks in one village and cut off dey left ear. Dey wen make one big mountain of ears, da Japanee soldiers wen do, right in da middle of da village square.

"All da Koreans in da plantation wen get all worked up dey hear dis. Dey break dey hoe handles and attack da Japanee workers. Was one big, big fight. Koreans . . . dey nevah like da Japanee, even dey come same-same boat ovah heah.

"But dis schoolteacher, he da first Japanee I meet who was nice. Him, he no like da adas. Him something else. Him go buy us food, go let us read his books. He even give us couple his books. Not only dat, dis guy he help us out later on. He save our lives."

The train was stopped several times on its journey. All Koreans were searched, a few arrested. Sung Wha and Hae Soon were almost detained for lack of certain papers, but their schoolteacher friend vouched for them; yes, I know their parents well, their parents are of very good standing in Antung, here, please, this is for your wife and children, is this enough? Will this do? Please. . . . The schoolteacher and his luggage were left alone, though once when an inspector hesitated over one of his bags, Sung Wha noticed a trembling in the schoolteacher's hands.

Finally, they reached the Yalu. A frosty, bright morning. Stepping down into the warm, moist steam of the hissing train, they took in air thick with rich food smells. Vendors were cooking everywhere, each having staked out a small area outside the receiving station to set up a portable charcoal stove. Hae Soon's and Sung Wha's stomachs ached with hunger, and they did not refuse the schoolteacher's offer to buy them each a bowl of rice and a strip of barbecued dried fish. After their meal, the three walked to the docks, where empty fishing boats listed, their wait for warmer weather long; and for the first time they saw the lethargic river, chunks of ice floating here and there on the surface; and across that expansive moving water lay Antung, a cluster of white roofs at the foot of mammoth hills of blue-green.

The schoolteacher thought it odd that the town was on the other side of the Yalu; if he remembered right, the two had told him that Antung would be on the train-station side of the river. Why did they give him the wrong information? Or were they really from the town? Who were these youth? If they were not from here, what then was their reason to come to the area? He did not feel guilty for helping them pass through the interrogations, but his curiosity was now piqued. He had heard that many Korean patriots were leaving the country and entering Manchuria. But Sung Wha and Hae Soon were too young to be revolutionaries. Or were they? Children were known to be revolutionaries.

He wanted to clear the questions in his mind, but he held his tongue. If his feeling were true, it would be better if less people knew it. And, if they were really what he thought they were, they were all on the same side, and he did not want to be responsible for exposing their disguises.

Hae Soon sensed something wrong in the way Wakatani's lean, drawn face was now watching them. She did not realize that wrong information about Antung was given to him, but her feeling was strong that Wakatani knew their secret. A bright-eyed Sung Wha, on the other hand, was too captivated by the crisp Manchurian air that suggested to him the fertile seeds of adventure and freedom.

They found an old ferry, its seams held together with rust, that would take them across the river. The schoolteacher offered to pay their way, but Hae Soon warily refused his offer. Others were on the ferry with them: two loud merchants bragging about recent successful trips to Mukden; five spiritless Japanese soldiers; and a tired-eyed farmer laden with farming tools.

The schoolteacher watched a flock of sea gulls ride the air currents above them. Then he looked both of them straight in their eyes, not able to hold back any longer. "Please don't tell anyone," he began softly, "but I have a secret I must tell you." He rubbed his hands together for warmth and regarded the soldiers, who were clustered in a far corner. "Let me tell you something about myself. I'm a schoolteacher, but I'm also a teacher of another sort. At my university, I was considered a very notorious person, a ringleader of trouble. The authorities labeled me 'radical,' 'rebel,' 'anarchist,' and 'Communist,' all of which I claim is correct. I have read and studied many outlawed works of Marxism, which are very easy to obtain in Japan, even though it is an imperialist country. My luggage is filled with this literature of consciousness. If I'm caught, I'll be arrested and perhaps put to death. But I'm doing this because it is necessary.

"According to my sources, we found out that revolutionary literature is hard to come by in these parts. That is why I readily accepted the job in Harbin. My wife-to-be has translated many of these works into Korean, and our Chinese comrades living in Japan translated some into Mandarin. Why I am telling you all this . . ."

A snag in the river. The approaching banks.

Hae Soon saw that the schoolteacher's eyes had softened. His face had taken on an ashen color. He needed a shave and a clipping of the hair in his nostrils. Was there a hint of tears in his eyes?

"I'm telling you all of this," he continued, "because I have found a trust in both of you." Eyes connecting. Almost losing his hat to the wind. "I also need some help. It's very important that this literature gets into the right hands. I could be exposed, but if there are others working with me, the chances that this literature gets to its destination are greater. Do you understand what I'm saying? I'm also traveling with a locker that contains a small printing press. I would like to start up a secret press in Harbin. I need to begin my teaching assignment when I arrive there, but if I have help, the press can begin its work."

He studied their long faces. A growing panic seized him: *I have blown my cover, they're not what I thought them to be, am I in danger? Why did I say all of this? Why did I trust them?*

"I don't know what your reasons are for coming to Manchu ria, nor is it my business to know, but I'm looking for people to help me carry out this work. Can you help me?"

"I nevah know what to say. You know, all of a sudden kinda strange fo' dis man start talking li'dat to us. First off, I thought dis guy was one agent fo' da Japanee police. I nevah know what to say.

"Later on we found out what he was talking 'bout was true. But dat time, I nevah see how important what 'he was talking 'bout. Starting up one printing press? Distributing radical liter- ature? And I thought he was only one schoolteacher!

"Actually, I was kinda scared, da way he was talking, and wit' dose two Japanee soldiers right next to us. But you gotta see how him in mo' one risk dan us. Here dis schoolteacher come talk to us, who we jus' meet, and da buggah taking one big risk talking to us li'dat. You gotta remember da kine repression going 'round. And also him telling us fo' help him start up one illegal printing press in Manchuria, printing up Communist pro- paganda. I think nowadays da kids say, 'Blow my mind.'

"Well, dat nevah really 'blow my mind,' but dat thing when sink inside my head kinda slow, youknowwhatImean? I nevah see how important one printing press is and all dat business. Me . . . I thinking going up dere and just joining up wit' da ada Korean patriots wit' guns and ammo, not wit' books. Books important, I know dat. After all, I get plenny ideas from read- ing all Lim's and da books in da monastery library. But books not dat important. Books not going pull da trigger, ifyouknow- whatImean.

"But when I think back, how I thinking back den, I was wrong. I was wrong. You know books—and I mean da right kine books, da kine books tell you what is right and what is wrong, da kine books dat tell you what or how things like governments work inside and out, dat kine books—anyway, books, like I said, dey no can pull da trigger to fire da gun, da rifle, but dey can show you how point da gun in da right direction and how shoot da bullet straight. YouknowwhatImean?

"And to dis day, I glad I listen to yo' auntie. She one smart-smart woman, I tell you. I glad she speak up fo' us right den. I know at first she think da buggah is one police agent. He get da kine secret-kine tone of voice, maybe he trying fake us out, den arrest us, we dunno. But like I said, later on we found out he telling da truth."

How can I describe the beauty I'm seeing? Father, you often described your love for this country. And now I'm looking at the mountains—the green mountains!—and the Yalu River!

This land is my Father, and I'm your Daughter. I want to drink your waters, and I don't care that you taste of earth and the blood of fallen comrades, more the better. You're my Father, now.

I weep no tears for my father. He was made of flesh and blood, like everyone else, and he served you well. He was a good revolutionary. My father trained me to control my emotions in front of others. He said a good revolutionary is very emotional, very passionate, that we cry for humanity, for the liberation of mankind—but also that we understand our emotions. When we cry, my father said, we cry for the people, not for ourselves. Our only desire is to destroy all forms of oppression. This is our call of passion.

I am lying. I must be honest. Tears fall when I'm alone in the dark of night, when the others snore and cannot see my grief.

But Yalu: you are my Father now. Manchuria: you are my Mother now. You'll show me what the life of an unselfish server for my people is. And when I die, Yalu, Father, please let my blood flow into you. Then run my blood to the sea.

After landing in Antung, they agreed to go with the young schoolteacher to Harbin. Wakatani paid their train fare. The train ride was long, though not marked with the frequent stops and interrogations like the first one. In Harbin, they found a small one-room flat in the back of a tailor shop where they lived through a hungry, bitter winter. It was here that Wakatani's clandestine press was founded. And it was here that Chin An was conceived.

Word of an illegal printing press in the area spread infectiously throughout the underground; the flat soon became a harbor for revolutionaries, guerrillas, Communists, and anarchists coming and going through Harbin. Stacks of leaflets and translated pamphlets of revolutionary Russian literature were taken and disseminated and read and studied all over. The press broke down several times during that furious winter, its production clearly inferior to the demand of the revolutionary printed word. And a direct result of this working press in the region was the organized mass uprisings that erupted in early spring and continued into late summer until the Japanese authorities were able to bring in additional troops to quell temporarily the ferment in the countryside. And so feverish were the attempts of the Japanese provisional governor to trace the source of the literature, that a reward of a thousand cash was declared; it would be given to anyone with information on the whereabouts of this insurgent platform. As a precaution, Wakatani and his new comrades were forced to move in early spring, and again a month later. By the end of that insurrectional summer they had moved another three times.

New stories of revolutionary developments in Korea, China, and worldwide were brought to their ears with every group of passing revolutionaries; but generally the reports centered on the events in China received the most enthusiastic listening.

"You know, in China, the Chinese people are on the verge of making world history—on a large scale like the Russian people's revolution!"

"Yes! They'll overthrow the landlords, the Japanese imperialists—you wait and see."

"I was there! Oh! How the army crushed our strike! There was blood everywhere!"

"Down with the comprador bourgeoisie and the Japanese imperialists! Down with the old order!"

"Children, women, and old people were killed, but mainly the workers. And the government was despicable enough to blame it on the proletarians!"

"Too many people have died following the Communists. Something is wrong with the way they lead the proletariat. I don't think the leadership is personally wrong, but something is definitely foul."

"I was in Peking last spring and the students closed down the university to join with the striking city workers. Everything is in a ferment there."

"Yes, I was there, too. But there's talk now of moving the struggle to the countryside."

"That, to me, sounds ridiculous. It sounds like a cowardly retreat."

"It may sound like one, but I think we'll have to do it if the Party is to survive."

"Everywhere people are on the move. The imperialists and the Chinese bourgeoisie are going crazy."

"Just last week I was witness to the most terrible bloodbath I have ever seen! Revolutionaries and workers executed by the hundreds in the streets!"

"What happens in China will have a great effect on the rest of the world."

"Yes, I do believe in what you say."

"There are liars. And then, there are liars."

With the revolutionaries and anarchists coming in and out every day and bringing their stories of the ups and downs of the revolution but in general the inevitable rise of the common people, Sung Wha could not sit still. Hae Soon saw this anxiety in her new husband, and one night she urged him to join the guerrillas while she'd stay behind for the birth of their child. At first Sung Wha objected, but soon, with much persuasion from both Hae Soon and Wakatani, he relented.

When the child was born in the middle of the following summer, Sung Wha was carrying a Russian-manufactured carbine: he was on a march that would take him to the heart of Shanghai, where he became one of the first of many Korean volunteers to join with the Chinese Revolution.

"It was—how can you say?—illustrious? wonderful? to be in da middle of all dis history making? Yeah, it was one illustrious time fo' me. But how much I want to see Hae Soon and our baby, our child, I nevah even know if was one she or one he. It no matter to me, either one I just as happy. But no matter how much I want to be wit' dem, I no can help but feel one good feeling, being on dis march to Shanghai where da revolution picking up, even though was being led by one incorrect Party line at da time. But dose days we no can understand nothing 'bout political line or whatevahs. Either you fo' da workers or you one agent fo' da ruling class. Das how was.

"Anyways, me and my comrades, we get dis funny-kine good feeling dat we in da center of one big history event. Da feeling so gigantic! You know, da Koreans in Manchuria, dey all talking 'bout what happening in China 'cause everybody know whatevah good happen in China is good fo' Korea cause in China dey fighting da Japanee, and if China beat dem, den dem, da Japanee, dem going fo' sure lose in Korea. And everybody know aftah da Chinese army win, dey going come Korea and help Koreans fight da Japanee. And so us Koreans, we da bravest, most daredevil of all da revolutionaries, I no joke you. Us, we no hesitate. We go fo' broke. When dey tell us do something, we volunteer right away. No hol' back, us. Everybody telling us how us Koreans is da most bravest, da most strongest. We no care how bad da odds going against us—we go! We no scared die.

"Den in da fall, my friend Chang Kuo-sen, he give me one message dat my wife in Shanghai wit' da baby. Quick I *hele,* look fo' her at da address she was. And you don't know how happy I was when I see my wife and my *keiki!* Hae Soon give him da name Chin An, aftah da famous Korean anarchist. Fo' two days

I no leave da room, I jus' stay dere, love my wife, watch da baby's every move, da way he sleep, da way he eat, da way he laugh. I think I no sleep fo' two days and nights. But I had to go back. I no have too much *kālā,* but I give yo' auntie all I had, couple Chinese cash. I tell her stay here and I going come back wit' some mo' *kālā.*

"But I nevah see her and da baby again. I no can help. Dey send me and my group to Tientsin fo' do political work at one ironworks. So I borrow some *kālā* from dis comrade—I forget his name, but I heard later he *maké-*die-dead in Shanghai 'cause Chiang Kai-shek was killing all da Communists, dis guy was one good union organizer—but anyway I give da *kālā* to dis friend of mine; I tell him go give 'em to my wife and baby. To dis day I dunno if he wen give her da *kālā.* I no see her and da baby since den. But I know Hae Soon wen leave after 'while 'cause I wen go back dere after I come back from Tientsin and she and da baby was gone.

"Den my nada friend tell me he see her catch one train, but he dunno where it going. Da government was coming down on da Communists, and even if nobody know she one revolutionary herself, if I know Hae Soon, she no take one chance, she wit' da baby. So I think she wen get outta dere fast as she can.

"Den I get one letter from her several months after. She wen go back to da schoolteacher's place and she tell me she pregnant again. When I read dat, I just break down and cry. I feel so happy but sad at da same time. I just hope da baby come out okay. I always think 'bout dat. Sometimes I feel so bad, how lousy one father me, I no can even raise my own children. Most times I blame da imperialists fo' all dat. But sometimes, when I feel 'im da most is when I lonely and I thinking 'bout dat. Das when I can only blame myself."

"Two years later, I got arrested, my second time. The Japanese occupation forces had been staking out this small storeroom behind a bookstore, which we used as a meeting place. They must have watched it for awhile; we didn't know they were watching, they were so secretive about it. Later we found out that one of the members of our cell was an informer—that dog! To make things worse, he was a trusted leading member of the cell.

"Anyway, one day we were set to meet at this so-called secret meeting place. This despicable lackey and several Japanese soldiers had gotten there earlier and were waiting for us. I was one of the first to get there, and they arrested me. They waited for another comrade, a young woman named Li, and she and I were quickly taken out and placed into a detaining wagon and then expedited to their headquarters for questioning. Well, she was from a prominent Shanghai family and soon her father came in, grumbling and cursing but with enough money to bribe the officials. I remember that she tried to get me out, too, saying that I was innocent, that I had just gone in the wrong door of the bookshop, but they wouldn't buy it. They had a file on me already, and later that renegade came in and identified me again. Of course, I denied everything.

"Then they found out that I was Korean. They tried all kinds of torture on me: pouring water down my nostrils, choking my lungs; beating me all over with a wooden bludgeon; striking my shins with bats. I was a terrible wreck, to say the least. But somehow—I don't know how—I resisted their cowardly attempts to extract information from me. They weren't going to get anything from me. So then they decided to deport me to Korea.

"But funny thing, you know. They made some kind of mistake. A big, stupid mistake. I was taken to Tientsin by rail and then to Dairen by boat. There I was supposed to board the South Manchuria Railway to Antung. But there was a complication. I ended up on a boat to Japan!"

"This is some story!" the *moksa* gasped. "Had you ever been to Japan?"

Sung Wha shook his head. "Never." He sipped the lukewarm tea, took a bite of a rice cake. "At first I thought we were going to Pusan by boat. It was a long boat ride. In fact, we did port in Korea, in Taegu, but only for the time it took to fill the holds of the ship with Korean rice. Then we continued on. I really didn't know what was happening. The officer escorting me was a rather strict person, someone who went by the rules of the book. But his orders, I presumed, instructed him to take me to Japan." Sung Wha laughed. "It wasn't until later, when we had entered Japan at Yokohama, that I found out why there was so much of a mix-up.

"What had happened was that while in Harbin, before leaving to join the guerrilla movement, the schoolteacher had given me a forged copy of his passport to use in case I needed another identity. Though they had prosecuted me as a Korean national and a Communist in China, somehow another official had discovered the passport, read it, and thought I was Wakatani. So they sent me to Japan instead."

"Why didn't you tell them of this mistake?"

"Why should I have? That would've been stupid to do. Besides, at the time, I didn't know what was happening."

"That's right. I'm sorry."

"If I did, that would've been stupid. If you're a Korean 'criminal' in the hands of the Japanese police, you're almost as good as dead."

"So what happened to you?"

"They took me to Osaka."

"And?"

"I was placed in this jail for Japanese political prisoners. There were mostly Communists and anarchists. They were very good people. I couldn't talk to them much, as I didn't speak Japanese too well, but we did talk. All the time during the trip to Japan I was very quiet, afraid that the police would detect my accent and realize that I was really a Korean. The Japanese Communists in the prison advised me to continue my silence.

"There were even handfuls of revolutionary Korean and Chinese students in the prison, but segregated from us. They were awaiting deportation."

"And what happened next?"

"Someone once said that even nature has her quirks and ways to rectify human wrongs. Well, I was transferred to another prison near Tokyo when something happened that absolutely changed everything. It was fortuitous at first, but that quickly turned into a nightmare, especially for Koreans."

"I don't understand."

"Well, first of all, you have to understand that Japan was in a deep economic depression, a very bad one. That was why she had to go into Korea and China to plunder the people there and to open up new markets for her commodities. One day this huge earthquake suddenly occurred, devastating Tokyo, crumbling the prison walls. Actually, it wasn't really a prison. It didn't have those huge, thick walls like a real penitentiary. It was converted from an old Buddhist monastery. Anyway, many people died, though some of us escaped. But what happened next was a nightmarish pogrom of Koreans.

"The Imperial government, afraid of looting and the rise of a domestic revolutionary workers' movement, spread all kinds of lies that Koreans in Japan were responsible for the economy being so bad, that Koreans were inherently a troublesome people infecting Japan. One rather stupid theory had it that an evil Korean scientist had started the earthquake! Imagine that!"

"I remember hearing about this, not about the story of the scientist, but about the pogrom. Many people died, isn't that right?"

"Thousands. Koreans were massacred in the streets. Daughters were raped, then murdered. Koreans were tossed off speeding trains. The lies of the Imperial government and the reactionaries took their toll on thousands of Korean lives."

"But you were considered a Japanese. They spared your life because of that."

"The officials had the passport that said I was Japanese, so that didn't help me at all. And to the Japanese people, I looked Korean. And if I looked like one, then I was one."

"But obviously you escaped."

Sung Wha reflected for a moment. "I'm thankful that I'm

here talking with you because of a friend I met while in that monastery prison. He was an anarchist. He didn't believe in any form of government and was a fervent supporter of overthrowing the rule of the emperor and of liberating Korea. He was a good friend of the famous Korean terrorist, Pak Chin An, I found out. They had gone to school together in Japan. I forget the name of that school. He told me that he was on his way to Korea to engage in anarchistic activities when he was discovered with a forged passport and arrested.

"But anyway, because of this friend—his name was Yamamura—I'm alive today. He hid me in the homes of his anarchist friends. I was underground for a month or so when he came to me with money and a fake passport and a steamboat ticket to Hawai'i. I didn't know how long this pogrom was going to last, and my friend said he could not see an end in sight, so he advised me to leave Japan and go to Hawai'i, where I could seek asylum or at least make some money, then return when things had calmed down.

"I never had time to think about it. I just took the money and the new clothes and the new identity that my friend Yamamura had given me, and with his blessing and protection, I boarded the ship that brought me to Hawai'i."

Of Madmen
Leading
the Blind

Sung Wha hobbled off the bus at the corner of King and University. He had never visited this side of town. Never. Often, after the war, he had ridden the bus through the area without getting off—back in those days it was called the trolley—all the way to Kokohead, where Eung Whan had a small truck farm. To get off in the university area was new to him. He gazed dryly into the intersection at the flashy cars whizzing by, driven by young people in a rush to go somewhere. Horns blasting, cars cutting in front of each other with disregard, angry voices swearing: he had never seen so much inconsideration in all his life . . . and all in one intersection. But where was he besides being next to this mad crossroads?

They gave him instructions to get off the bus at King and University. Yes, so that's what he did. And they told him to catch the University bus that went up Mānoa Valley, and to get off at St. Clair's library, or something like that. Scanning the sidewalk, he found a street sign, "University of Hawaii at Manoa," with an arrow pointing up toward the valley.

He looked at the valley, his heart now thumping with anticipation. He had never been to the university. But he had been to that great university in Peking. There had been a big demonstration of students against the Japanese occupation forces, and he and several other cadres had entered the university and agitated for the students to join in with the factory workers who were on strike. Some of the students were armed with sticks and clubs and rocks, ready for insurrection, and the debates and struggling went on late into the night—What is to be done?—but by early morning masses of students spilled out of the school's marbled walls and took to the rain-swept streets to join with the strikers. It was a time he could not forget. What followed, when the rains stopped, was the largest demonstration the old city had ever seen. And bloodshed. Then, as if on cue, the rains started again, and by the rise of the next morning's sun the streets were washed of any trace of the massacre.

But now, looking around, all he sees is this mad rush of cars, storefronts with glaring glass windows and garish signs gushing *Sale! Sale! Sale!* everywhere. A small crowd of students gathers at the corner, waiting for the traffic lights to change. One of them, with hair greased and standing up like a pineapple crown, impatiently steps down the curbing, readying himself to run out and dodge bumpers. Sung Wha notices a tall, tan girl standing next to him, long black hair teased by a weak breeze, with wires plugged into her ears and her head nodding as if she is keeping time with music: *why she doing dis? She mentally ill?* And she wears shorts so small and so tight that cheeks ooze out in creamy, muscular wads. Sung Wha gasps. He can see her *'ōkole! Dis one student?!*

The girl glances at Sung Wha—dirty old man, I know what you're thinking, fuck off—disregards him, adjusts the earphones.

Sung Wha curses the air, then leaves the corner.

Supposed to catch a bus near here . . . there, that must be it, the bus stop where all those people carrying books are standing. Supposed to catch a bus at the stop and get off in front of the big library . . . St. Clair's library? Anyway, the library. Ask the bus driver and he'll tell you where to get off, the cheery female voice on the phone had instructed him. When you get off, someone will be waiting for you. We'll take you to the class from there.

Okay. Okay.

But he doesn't feel like taking the bus, doesn't feel like waiting with all these people who make him feel uncomfortable, who make him feel like an outcast, make him feel invisible. He doesn't like that invisible feeling.

I walk it up, is not dat far, anyway I need da exercise.

So he starts up the avenue toward the valley.

And under an overpass. The freeway is above; he can hear the rush of cars, the rumble of a trailer truck. And on the wide, gray concrete walls that support the freeway he notices spray-painted graffiti and radical flyers plastered all over, some torn at the corners by dissenting passersby. The work of revolutionaries? Are there revolutionaries at this university? But where are they? He was surely fooled by the appearances of those students down at the intersection. Of course, all universities must have their radicals and, of course, they wouldn't be out in the open, in broad daylight. That teacher who invited him to his class was a radical. Why, there must be others. . . .

"Okay folks. We have a guest speaker today, someone who is part of the living history of labor in Hawai'i. I want you to welcome Mr. Sung Wha Kim." Kind applause. "Originally an immigrant from Korea, Mr. Kim has worked on sugar and pineapple plantations, and as a stevedore on the Honolulu docks, he was a leader in numerous ILWU-led strikes. Most recently, after his retirement as a controversial shop steward, he has become one of the leaders of a group of angry tenants at the Kekaulike Hotel in Chinatown, a struggle against eviction that we talked about last week. Mr. Kim himself resides in the hotel. This eviction struggle has been fundamental in bringing to public light the need for low-cost housing for low-income and retired members of our working-class community. So without further delay, I want to turn the class over to Mr. Kim. Mr. Kim . . ."

The teaching assistant, a sansei who has been spending his afternoons for the past several months helping the hotel residents dispense their anti-eviction leaflets and do other organizing work, sits to the side of the class. Nervously, Sung Wha offers an anxious smile to the young, clear-eyed faces of the students. He notices three haole students spread out among the forty or more local students, predominately Orientals, a few pockets of Hawaiians and part-Hawaiians. A silence exudes from their emotionless faces. Sung Wha looks down at his hands clasped together, then about the room—warm afternoon light sifting through a wall of metal louvers—and at the teaching assistant, Troy Nishimura, then back uneasily at his sweating hands.

Nishimura breaks the silence: "Well, class, do we have any questions for Mr. Kim?"

There is only a small stirring. Someone accidentally drops a book that lands flatly on the floor.

"Mr. Kim," the teaching assistant begins, irritated at the unresponsiveness of the class, "how old were you when you first came to Hawai'i?"

Sung Wha crosses the main avenue by the library and waits at a bus stop, sitting at the end of a bench. The class hadn't gone well; the students seemed bored at whatever he said—why the hell was he invited to speak at the class in the first place?

Above Mānoa, dark clouds threaten rain.

Then the sky is full of people, falling and screaming. Sung Wha trembles. His eyes dart between earth and sky. A confusion of words dribble from his mouth. Students around him scramble away, afraid that the madman might hurt them or infect them with a harmful, communicable disease.

He boarded the bus downtown; got off at Beretania Street near Maunakea; meandered past stores wedged with shoppers squawking in Cantonese and with big Chinese characters painted in gold above doorways; paused at a fragrant lei stand—*pua kenikeni,* tuberose, plumeria; plodded past XXX movie theaters smelling of piss and vomit; and stopped in front of a greasy chop suey house, his hands in pockets. He had a few dollars on him.

Money was hard to come by these days; that damn pension check was not enough to support himself even though his rent was only $130 a month for a small room. He shared the bathroom and a kitchenette with a dozen other retired workers, single men. And a handful of *mahus*. That was why they were fighting, dammit, to keep that miserable shelter as a home. The landlord wanted to evict them, demolish the ancient structure, then raise a tower of glass and concrete and steel. And where the hell were they to go if they got evicted? Across Beretania to the high-rise condos where the rent was at least a thousand a month? Well, that was what Troy Nishimura said at a rally down city hall a few weeks ago. But he was right. There were only expensive places to rent nowadays. You couldn't find a place for $130 a month, even though the place was fit enough for only rats and pigs and society's riffraff. What the hell . . . at least it was home for them; they could call this dump home. What the hell. Home. It was home.

Well, he had a few dollars in pocket, and he felt like splurging, go buy himself a large, steaming bowl of wonton mein. It would be his lunch and dinner at a little past four-thirty in the afternoon. His mouth began to water as he imagined his teeth biting into the mashed pork of a soft dumpling.

He sat down in a booth nearest to the door of the chop suey house and opened the worn red menu stained with oyster and black bean sauces and shoyu. It was nice to do that: open a menu and order. It wasn't very often he could afford the luxury of eating in a restaurant. At least now, at this time of the day, there weren't too many drunks and transvestites hanging about, those *mahus* probably still nursing dreams of the lascivious night before. . . . Wonder how many sailor boys they fooled this time? *Ah, no need to worry 'bout da* mahu*s, he thought as he mixed the watered-down mustard with shoyu in the chipped sauce dish. Da* mahu*s no bothah you, in fact some of dem yo' good friends, not dat kine friends, but jus' friends. Benito wen live at Kekaulike Hotel how long already, almost long as me. He one good Joe, and only at night he become Benita. But da buggah can cook good-kine*

Filipino food and da buggah, he no selfish—he always share his
kaukau fo' everybody eat. Yeah, at least no mo' da drunks in here,
at least da young ones not in here like at nighttime, dey da ones
make all da pilikia. *Da old ones, all dey like is dey bottle and das*
it, dey suck 'em up until dey pass out, dey no harm nobody. Is da
young punk ones, dey da ones make all da pilikia. *Even dese old*
drunks, dey get dey own dignity, dem own kine pride; dey no bothah
nobody, dem jus' mind dem own business, an' when dey ready dey
lay dey head down fo' rest someplace, anyplace. And look . . .

In the far corner booth, a middle-aged haole couple sat eating away. A camera was strapped across the man's chest, and his
fat legs, bulging out of green and yellow aloha-print shorts,
were translucent and rosy from the sun.

Chee, dese tourists, dey even hanging out where all da locals eat.

The waitress served him his wonton mein. He ate it slowly,
savoring every bite, his teeth breaking the *pi* and his tongue
prodding the soft stuffing, the taste of pork with a hint of green
onion. The next wonton he dipped in the mustard sauce, and
the fiery and slippery dumpling melted in his mouth.

He paid the bill, left a quarter on the table for a tip, then
went outside and leaned on an expired parking meter while
picking his teeth and swallowing what the toothpick had loosened. His eyes searched the empty lot across the street where
several months' back had stood the Aloha Maunakea Hotel;
they found a broken drainage pipe standing upright in the
ground, the only remnant now of that legendary place. How
could he forget that place. His good friend Sammy had lived
there. After they had evicted all the residents, but only after a
big fight, Sammy went to live with his niece in Nānākuli, far
away from here. Far, far away. And he had never heard from
Sammy since the day he was forced to move. Sammy hadn't
wanted to leave: he was more at home with the rest of the boys
in the heart of town where he had grown up. In the old days he
dived in the harbor for coins tossed by tourists from the Lurline
("Look, Mabel! Those brown boys swimming like seals!");
later, he ran the numbers games in Chinatown. He was inde-

pendent, always speaking his mind. *Yeah, da buggah one real outspoken person; he go straight up da governor's office one day and go shout and swear at da governor, but too bad da governor wasn't dere, or das what da governor's aides wen tell us. But I know fo' one fact dey was lyin', we all know dey was lyin', dem always lyin', dose sonavabitches. Dat frickin' governor was probably inside his koa wood castle office all scared and shaking, he no like see da people; but funny, yeah, how his campaign slogan say he da candidate wit' da mandate of da people, whatevah dat means. What people he talking 'bout? I wondah if he even know what he talking 'bout himself? And den wartime, dis place was one popular place wit' da service guys. Downstairs had one room dey all wait, dey all wait fo' dey favorite girl; da local boys can go, too, but dey gotta go da back way. Crazy dose days. Da girls from dey own neighborhood dey grow up wit', and dey gotta go da back door and da haoles, dey can go through da front door and dey get to pick whoevah dey like. Well, I nevah really like dat place. I remembah da first thing dat come into my mind when I see dis place: what Hae Soon going say? First of all, I think she go shoot all da servicemen: no good imperialist dogs! Das what she say. Ho boy! And I remembah dat night I wen get drunk like shit—da last time fo' me—and I jus' pass out and da next thing I remembah dey stay carrying me out wit' my zippah down. I dunno what wen happen, really. Sammy Boy, he tell me good fun, no? and I tell him shaddup! I was so shame, so shame, I nevah like think what wen happen, but every time I say to myself I no like think 'bout dis, it always come back, it always do. Hae Soon, I still love you, even aftah all da years, I cannot blame da booze, can only blame myself, my weakness; I no see you fo' so long time, all dis time I been lonely, I one lonely man. And I no had one nada woman evah since den.*

Sung Wha dropped the broken toothpick into the gutter and shuffled down the cracked pavement to Kekaulike Street, to Kekaulike Hotel. The guest of honor must rest his weary head for his afternoon nap. *Maybe Yong Gil came today brought me some food. I must be old, I get tired even thinking 'bout dis kine things.*

A large white banner, which was two bed sheets sewn together, was stretched across the upper half of the weather-beaten facade of Kekaulike Hotel. Slogans were lettered unevenly on the banner, with bright red paint: Stop the Evictions! Fight for Decent Housing! And beneath that: Coalition Against Redevelopment and Eviction. Sung Wha's heart would lilt, *ah, at least young people doing something 'bout something . . . dey getting involved!* And he couldn't help but compare the enthusiasm of the young activists with his as a young man—but how things were so different then: it was "Land for the Peasants" and "Revolution!" Though the radical fires of the past and those now sounded similar, here in America people weren't exactly starving. Or not yet. Or perhaps they were but it wasn't so obvious. When he was young, the fire of the revolution came from the many empty stomachs, and the young radicals lived for the revolution. Revolution. The world was upside down and needed to be turned right-side up. But now, the young people seem content in this world, even the activists in a way; *dey not starving, dey no feel da whip of da landlord on dey backs . . .*

"Yong Gil, I not talking 'bout figgah of speech. I talking 'bout real whips on da backs."

. . . they're not ignorant, they can read and write, they have a million choices, and isn't one of these choices whether to be a radical or not?

"My days no can choose dis or dat. You either fight da landlord or *maké*-die-dead 'cause dem. If I nevah leave my village, I be dead now, 'cause da landlord make me starve and die, he eat all my food, dat big fat pig landlord.

"But at least dese young people today, at least dey getting involved. At least dey doing dat, and not jus' driving 'round and 'round in dey car like chicken wit' no heads, like if had no mo' one tomorrow, wit' dey ears all plug up wit' da kine nonsense music."

One day a group of revolutionaries came to an organizing meeting at the hotel. The organizers of the meeting—an eclectic group of activists from the university, old ILWU organizers, reform-minded CP members, and other interested uncommitted personages from the community—wouldn't allow them to speak. A shouting match ensued. Finally, one of the revolutionaries was allowed to speak, but only for a couple of minutes. Blurring some of her words out of nervousness, she spoke of the need for revolution in the U.S. of A. and about the revolutionary struggle in Iran and elsewhere in the world, that the struggle here was tied in with the struggles of the international working class, that the main enemies of the peoples of the world were both U.S. imperialism and U.S.S.R. social-imperialism.

Sung Wha thought: *Dis girl, she confusing herself, cannot understand what she talking 'bout, her words no make sense, she no explain herself good.*

The organizers demanded answers from her: how is this relevant to what is going on right now? You guys come here and talk about these things that don't even relate to what's going on in Hawai'i. And Sung Wha had sympathy for the young revolutionary, who reminded him of how difficult it had been when he as a young man had had to explain to others the truth in his heart. He interrupted the organizers, persuading them to give her a chance: what she saying is all right, she get one right to say what she saying. And the organizers looked at him with numb faces. Of course, they could not overrule him, the leader of the Kekaulike residents. So the revolutionary continued to talk, but in that same difficult and confusing manner, using hyperbolic language that perhaps even she didn't understand. Sung Wha was amused, touched: *at least some people trying be revolutionaries. But I wonder if dey even know how shoot one gun?*

"You remembah dat story 'bout dat wahine who wave da Korean flag in front of da Japanee soldiers and wen get her arms cut off and everybody 'round her jus' stood dere looking? Eh . . . how can people be so cruel?"

She tried shifting gears, using some blemished pidgin as an attempt to give her ideas mass appeal, but the ears of the residents and activists were still turned away, except for Sung Wha's. *But at least she trying,* Sung Wha said to himself, *at least she trying.* And after the meeting the revolutionary went up to Sung Wha and introduced herself as Naomi Kang.

"'Naomi Kang?' Das da first thing wen come in my head. But I wen look at her and I no can see In Ja in her face. Maybe one of her granddaughters. Maybe. But you know, also get plenty Kangs ovah heah."

Others from Naomi Kang's group approached Sung Wha and began talking to him about revolution. What you know of revolution? Sung Wha asked. Talking 'bout revolution is serious business. First, she explained the significance of the Russian Revolution, the Chinese Revolu—But what you really know 'bout revolution? You think we can make revolution ovah here? And: we have to prepare for revolution now; right now the conditions aren't ripe, we have to create public opinion to seize power. And: seize power, create public opinion, . . . and what dese words mean? Softly, Sung Wha repeated the slogan.

How she know how make revolution? What she read in books? He held back his contentious tongue and instead smiled: but we on da same side, no? He saw himself in her again, then silently chided himself for thinking his experiences as capital. *Let me listen what she get to say.*

The young Communists began frequenting the community meetings, selling their Party's newspaper and other revolutionary literature. They visited Kekaulike Hotel every day with their propaganda teams. They began stepping on the toes of the coalition members. The coalition began to wage a backstage war of sorts against them, using friendships and favors to construct a barrier between the residents of the hotel and the revolutionaries.

Sung Wha was not offended by the presence of the revolutionaries; in fact, he desired their presence.

Dey like one breath fresh air, he told the other residents. Dem still a little bit stale wit' da words, but other den dat, dey diff'rent and good, dey going against da tide and das good.

But Sung Wha couldn't go against the majority of the residents who were swayed by the reformists to oppose the Communists. His fellow residents pleaded with him: Sung Wha, why you listen to dem guys, dem Communists? All dey going do is hurt us wit' all dey revolution talk; how we going talk to da governor or da mayor when dese buggahs no even respect da authorities and when all dey talking about is ada places in da world and not 'bout us? And Sung Wha: what den we asking fo'? And they: bettah housing, of course! What you think we been fighting all dese frickin' months fo' anyway? How we can live wit' da kine *manini* pension check we get every month? Go live in one expensive place? We gotta think 'bout if our stomach is full or not, what going on in our own backyard—not somebody else's backyard! And fo' Chrissakes! We no mo' even get one backyard! And dese Communists, all dey talking 'bout is what going on in da rest of da world and not about us; we no care what going on someplace else, da rest of da world no care 'bout us, so why we gotta care 'bout dem? You try explain dat to us, Sung Wha; we interested only what happening right here, right now! And Sung Wha: but try listen what dey talking about; what happening around da world—*it* is concerned wit' us, you no understand what I saying? And they: you *lōlō*, Sung Wha, of course we dunno what you saying, what you saying is fo' da birds, Sung Wha; how da hell we can think fo' somebody else when dat somebody not thinking 'bout us, 'bout how we suffah every day—and besides, some of us no can even think fo' ourselves!

And so on.

Though he liked the young Communists, Sung Wha's heart was with his fellow residents at the hotel. They—including himself—were old and retired and in need of a place to lay their heads at night. *I can understand dem guys, dem old futs . . . even me, I gotta have one nice pillow under my head nowadays and no get hit wit' big rent and den starve.*

But Sung Wha, what about your internationalism, your concern for the masses and the class struggle worldwide and the . . .

Well, da way I see it, 'bout time dese young people dey come forward and start doing something 'bout all dis, is dey turn now; I one old fut now my legs like give up already my eyes seeing double my mind sometimes she wandering all ovah town cannot think straight sometimes.

Wearily, feeling like a tired old goat, he climbed the creaking wooden stairs to the second floor. At the top of the staircase was a community kitchenette. A well-worn, formica-top table. Rusty folding chairs. Sung Wha hesitated. *Maybe 1 drink one cup coffee, but no, dat going keep me awake, I like go sleep, go moe, no like stay up.* He ambled through the kitchenette and on to his room at the end of an airless, narrow hall. The stale smell of his bachelorhood greeted him when he opened the termite-ridden door and entered. He stood for a few moments in front of his bureau with its large mirror. He hadn't really looked into the mirror in years; he used it as a display for his many time-faded, black-and-white snapshots, the pictures he wedged securely between mirror and wood molding. . . . When Sung Wha combed his hair in the morning he only looked at his hair, not his face. . . . When he wanted to see his face he would seek the handsome smile in one of the several photos of himself in the prime of his youth: there was one with a group of young Korean men in front of the Korean church in Wahiawā (yes, that's the one, the one where he organized and trained a group of impulsive, heroic-minded Koreans in guerrilla warfare, and yes, the same church where Lee Chi Ha was murdered and hanged like a Jesus, how could he forget all of that); and look at his face, so youthful, so primed with life, so vigorous, at the time Sung Wha thought he would always stay like that, he believed he'd never grow old, a youthful-feeling and -thinking heart keeps one young, he always used to say. . . . And even now, 1979, though at the awakening of every day he must contend with the aches and pains of a deteriorating body, he ends each day, before falling asleep, with his mind in a dreamy wondrous wandering, fond memories brought to him by these fading pictures: how defiant it felt to run free and wild and tirelessly along unknown paths; how unconquerable the feeling to have mind strong and body tempered like steel yet limber like bamboo. And there was another picture, attached to the lower left-hand corner, of him and an old friend, now deceased, Li Il-han was his name: here they are in swimming togs smiling and holding each other buddy-buddy, arms wrapped around shoulders on the gleaming sand of some beach. . . . *Where was dis? Waikīkī? No can be, dey no allow immigrants dere contaminate da sand wit' dey thousand and one diseases, only haole tourists and movie stars and Hawaiian beach boys strumming dey* 'ukulele*s under da palm trees swaying . . . but maybe 'Ewa beach, yeah, das where was . . .* but how could he remember exactly, it was so long ago. And there were other photos: Yong Gil and Mary; Yong Gil's three daughters—the first one must be in college by now; his other nieces and nephews and their children. He took from his back pants pocket a fat black wallet with *puka*s worn in the corners; not much money in it, but a treasury of fragmented and creased memories: yellowed newspaper clippings; expired faded coupons; bits of paper with ancient five- and six-digit territorial telephone numbers (they had converted to seven digits for fifteen years now?); and a water-stained business card, with the name and number of that well-known Hawaiian labor lawyer, the one who had defended and compromised Sung Wha and several others in the infamous anti-Communist trial in the 1950s, damn McCarthy period. And yes, of course, he had a few dollars, too, in the wallet, and one silver certificate that he kept for good luck: Sammy had advised him, why you no cash 'um in, Sung Wha? Can get good money fo' 'um, and he, nah, das fo' my good luck, and Sammy, what kine good luck? And Sammy laughed. Sung Wha undid the belt that held up his loosely fit-ting pants, stripped it from the pants, and coiled it on top of his bureau, a snake too tired to strike.

Taking off his shoes, he lowered himself into the metal-frame bed—you know the type, old with arches made of thick brown pipe at the head and foot that are supported by thin vertical bars like that of a prison cell: you become a prisoner of sleep when you sleep—and lay his head on a flat, stale-smelling pillow. With his eyes focusing in and out at a ceiling fringed with spiderwebs and ringed with water stains from the third floor's leaky plumbing, he shaped that taupe-colored, amorphous mass of dust and stagnant air and cobwebs and petrified bugs caught in spiders' webs, and with those lingering, silvery images from the bureau's photos . . . and he and he and and and they swirled and tangled and he formed he and and into and sucked into by blue passage blue the passage of with of dreams of dreams of of of dreams. . . .

Sung Wha climbs the highest mountains and floats on the lightest of clouds. And he sails over the stormiest sea. And when sea calms, he dips his powerful wings into a slowly rolling, massive blue shoulder and floats on this shoulder while drinking and drinking, his gut swelling oppressively. And now he must wait, he must urinate on and on and on, before he can go farther in his chase on the path of the sun.

This is his castle away from it all. He can hear the harrowing sounds of Eddie the blind man in the next room over, interminably clearing his throat. And there is the warbling and complaining of John-John: *maybe he should take his medicine, what kine medicine da buggah taking now? Thorazine da doctor geev him? A house of broken people wit' broken hearts and broken minds, but no mo' wit' broken spirits. No?*

Sung Wha never knew anyone from this house who had died in the twenty-odd years he has been living here, an uncanny statistic since this "hotel" is all filled up with retirees from jobs and retirees from life. An unbelievable stat.

But maybe he'll be the first to go among his friends. Many of his friends from earlier times and places are dead. And he was only seventeen years old when for the first time he saw a man die in Shanghai. Sung Wha's unit was attacking the police headquarters, and next to him the young comrade, whom he didn't even know, was shot in the head, blood, brains, and bone spraying all over Sung Wha; the comrade fell right at Sung Wha's feet without a gasp or cry, as if biting his tongue so as not to utter a sound informing the enemy of their position. What a valorous and glorious sacrifice: to think about the others, to serve the people. And that was only the beginning. He saw more deaths, including his own.

He had been wounded severely in another attack and was captured, and he remembered the vision he had had while they were transporting him to the jail: Kumgangsan is hidden behind a mist of light rain and strange, dark clouds shaped like a forest of shiitake. A couple of peaks are faintly visible, and then Hae Soon emerges from the clouds with a baby in her arms and a child next to her. Solemn, distant looks are on their faces, and Hae Soon's eyes, stern and scolding, say: you don't even know your children, Sung Wha, why have you chosen this life that takes you away from us? Will we ever live as a family together under one roof? Do you know their names?

The wound in the lower right side of his chest was bleeding profusely; he had lost consciousness several times since the beginning of his captivity and had to be revived each time. And he remembered: the bright light swinging above him, the military police striking his swollen, numb face. He heard them say, he is as good as dead, let this worthless Communist dog die a coward's death, take him back to this cell.

Coward's death?! No, they won't rob me of this life.

So by some inscrutable resuscitating power in his gut, he rises from his pool of blood and piss, staggers, and throws himself into the chair, while the stunned interrogators watch, their eyes flashing spots of fear and denial: no words or thoughts can accurately describe the experience of witnessing a corpse revive itself. They can ask no more questions, and the chief of the military police finally orders his minions to take the prisoner back. And Sung Wha survives the rest of his internment: more tortures, more beatings, the slime they call food, the incapacitating cold of the stone walls and concrete floor stained with blood and excrement. And during a deep winter storm he is one of three fortunates out of twenty-seven who survive a bloody prison escape, but is captured again a few months later and sent erroneously to that Buddhist prison outside of Osaka.

He has seen so much of death and dying in these beautiful days of his youth; so many unjust deaths; so many young people with lofty dreams and futures undermined—killed—murdered—their smelling, bloated bodies lining the roadside like diseased discarded animal carcasses. But they died for their dreams, did they not? Isn't it a worthwhile cause to die for the future?

But now, how everything is different, everything is changed, now that he and his friends are old and feeble in mind and brittle in body. Now: where is the death that should talk to them in alluring tones and embrace them with promises of release from the omnipresent discomforts and miseries of this life, this penalty of old age? Why do people ready for death live forever? Why hasn't death come to those who are ready for it to those who wait with pain—and burn them to unthinking dust? Why must we wait so long when there is nothing more to live for? And why does it come down like a merciless vulture attacking, only the flesh is not carrion but young and so vigorous and alive and furious with the warmest, brightest blood?

For three hours, Sung Wha sleeps a dreamless sleep. He is awakened by a soft knocking on the hollow door. The door squeaks as it inches open, finally exposing the naked light bulb of the hallway, which blinds him for a moment.

"Uncle! Uncle! You sleeping?" It's Yong Gil's voice, whispering.

Sung Wha turns from the light and sighs. Farts.

"Uncle . . . sorry I wake you up. I brought you some food."

Dropping his legs over the side of the bed, Sung Wha sits up and acknowledges his nephew with a yawning nod. He scratches his head and chest. "Come inside," he says, languidly waving in Yong Gil.

Yong Gil takes a tentative step into the room. "You want me shut the door?"

Sung Wha shakes his head. He watches Yong Gil's dark, bent figure with his offering of food.

"This time, I went down to the park, but the boys, yo' friends, they say they never see you the whole day. I thought . . ."

What you thought? Dat I wen maké*-die-dead? No be scared, Yong Gil, say it. Say you thought I wen* maké*. Why you scared say dat? Bettah if I was* maké *already. Bettah fo' me. Bettah fo' you.*

"Here. I brought you some *kaukau*. Mary made plenty *kaukau* so I gave some to your friends."

Sung Wha motions his nephew to set the food on the bureau. He yawns again.

Yong Gil sits on a stool at the foot of the bed. Silence. Then a door opens down the hall: a flip-flopping to the bathroom. The bathroom door closes, is latched.

Then: "Uncle, I know you no like hear what I have to say."

"Den no say it."

Uneasily, Yong Gil draws in a breath, releases. "I know I brought this up how many times already, but I gotta bring it up again. Mary and me . . . we want you come live with us. I know I brought this up time and time again, but we're worried about your welfare, your health. We like you move in with us. Think about it, Uncle. You not getting any younger."

"You know my answer already," he says. He clears his throat.

"I know, I know," Yong Gil rattles off.

"Den das dat."

The plumbing in the wall whines. The bathroom door unlatches, and the user returns to his room. It's John-John: Sung Wha can tell by his dragging left foot.

"But I like you think about it," Yong Gil says. "And there's something else."

"What?"

"Uncle Sung Wha . . . I don't think you should get so involved with all this business, all this radical stuff, making all this trouble with the landlord."

The words stab Sung Wha. A sharp look at his nephew. "Trouble? What you calling 'trouble'?"

"I know not my business, but all this is making you more sick. Uncle, you one old man already. You cannot keep going on like this. It's bad for your heart. And the landlord, this is his place, he can do what he wants with it. The way you guys act, just like he owes you something. He doesn't owe you nothing."

"Who 'you guys'?"

Yong Gil sighs.

"Every time you come here, you tell me same-same story. You tell me what to do. You no mo' respect fo' yo' elders or what? If you going come here every time and tell me dis same-same thing, no come. I get my own life live. I not asking fo' special-kine treatment. I not asking fo' handouts. Das why I no like live wit' you folks. If I live wit' you folks, I not going live da way I like live."

A twisted look on Yong Gil's face. Like a scolded child's.

"No get me wrong, Yong Gil. I love you and Mary. I 'preciate what you folks trying do, thinking 'bout me, bringing me food. But you gotta understand me. No can teach dis old dog new tricks."

"Uncle, we just thinking about you," Yong Gil offers.

"I know, I know. But . . ."

"Uncle, go eat the food before it comes cold." Yong Gil gets up to bring Sung Wha the food, but the old man holds him back. "Uncle, I just want you to think about it . . . okay? If you ever need one place to stay, you always have a room with us."

What kine fool you, Sung Wha? Anybody in dis damn hotel would grab da chance right away. You crazy, lōlō. *Yo' own nephew, yo' own flesh and blood, asking you come live wit' him. You going get one nice bed sleep, good food eat, one TV watch, somebody always going be around you anytime you like somebody around. And yo' clothes going get wash fo' you. Sung Wha, you going live like one king! So den . . . how come you no like go? No tell me 'cause your 'independence'! Das bullshit. You know dat. I know dat. Everybody know dat. Tell dem da reason is you no like take advantage. But dis da real reason?*

Eh, Sung Wha, everybody know you old man, so no lie. You like take advantage, no? Everything in you all dried up. You no young guy wit' one hard body and one mind can think straight anymo'. Why you like maké *by yo'self, wit' nobody care fo' you? You know you no like* maké *by yo'self but here you go, torturing yo'self. Dis mo' worse dan you* maké *wit' no mo' face.*

"Come," Sung Wha says. "Yong Gil, come. We go take one walk."

Slowly and carefully, Sung Wha puts the parts of himself together: his wallet, his belt, his . . . they leave the room and step into a back alley of the cooling late afternoon, a gritty but pleasant breeze bringing them the smell of an oily ocean. They walk along a quiet waterfront and sit at the end of an old wharf where mingling smells of diesel fuel and dried aku blood are pungent but resurrecting. They can see only a couple of stars in this stagnant night, probably bright planets, the edge of sky a dying indigo, a fleeing hint of a going day.

"You know, Yong Gil, in da old days, dis time of da day da best. Da plantation workers jus' coming home. Was hard work, dose days. Everybody really work fo' dey money. Now at least I can kick back and relax and watch da sunset. But I no regret all dose hard working days, Yong Gil. I no regret dem days. Da stuff I experience, you can fill one book wit' 'em. Da only thing I regret . . . my wife not here wit' me." He gazes across the harbor at the city's lights—there's no reflection off the water—then out to the hiding horizon. "And I nevah really see and bring up my children. Das my main regret, Yong Gil. Das da main regret in my life. Maybe by now . . . maybe by now, I one grandfather already."

They listen to the wind and the water lapping on the pillars of the ailing wharf.

"How is the sunset in Korea?" asks Yong Gil.

"Beautiful. Mo' beautiful dan Hawai'i. You like see one beautiful sunset, you go Korea. You nevah go Korea, eh, Yong Gil? You evah go?"

"No. When I was small kid I went, but I don't remember."

"Den you gotta go. Every Korean gotta go back Korea and see one sunset. You know, dey say Korea is da Land of da Morning, yeah?"

"Land of the Morning Calm."

"Yeah-yeah. Da morning beautiful, but da sunset even mo' beautiful. Da day all *pau,* everybody tired from *hanahana* so much. And when da sunset come, it telling you da end of one nada pau workday. You go—hah!—and now you can go home and wash up and *kaukau* and den play wit' yo' *keiki,* make love wit' da wife. Da sunset is da bes' part of da day."

"I like the morning the best, early in the morning when everything's still and everybody's sleeping. The darkness not awake yet. You get up early and drink one nice, hot cup coffee and it tastes good."

"Da sunset da bes' 'cause you know da day you wen wake up to is *pau,* is ovah. You wen live 'um already. You know how wen go already. Is hist'ry already. But da sunset make you think of da next day. . . . What going happen tomorrow? How da weather going be like? Things going work out right? What you wen plant today, going grow tomorrow? How going be tomorrow or da next day, or da next? YouknowwhatImean?"

Yong Gil nods his head. They watch a trace of deep purple in the far sky fade.

"I want to go Korea and see that sunset," Yong Gil says. "If you say the one in Korea is more beautiful than this one—and this one is beautiful—then I gotta see the one in Korea."

Sung Wha smiles at his nephew and pats him on the back.

The night has darkened, and the stars suddenly appear across the expansive sky like blossoming wild *doragi* after a warm summer rain.

They stay for another hour. Then Yong Gil escorts his uncle back to his room. The wonton mein is still heavy in Sung Wha's stomach, so he puts the food Yong Gil brought in the refrigerator. He will eat it tomorrow. Tomorrow. For breakfast.

Glazed eyes are lost among fabricated stars. At midnight, blues and blacks swirl and meld. The stars become crystals of a slowly turning chandelier.

Sung Wha fights the insomnia that drags him through the night. How can he sleep when the stars of night seep into his mind, blocking his dreams?

Each star reminds him of a promise broken. And: will he ever see Korea again? Will he ever see his wife and children? Can he ask Yong Gil for some money for a plane ticket back home where he can die in peace?

Sung Wha sighs, then forces out a breath, hoping it will disperse the stars.

But how can I complain 'bout dem damn politicians when what dey want is what I want. My head too tired stay straight up, I need one comfortable place put it down. My young days all pau *already, I cannot be da radical I was befo'. Da young ones now, dey gotta take up da slack, not me. Me . . . I one old horse now, jus' put me in da pasture. But funny, yeah, dey no mo' one pasture fo' me ovah here. My pasture in Korea, not here, even though I live most my life ovah here. Chee, but I still no feel I belong. I wondah if evah going feel I belong. I wen go everywhere, everywhere: China, Manchuria, Japan, Hawai'i, even da mainland fo' few weeks. Dat was something . . . da mainland.*

Instead going ovah dere mo' bettah I go home, but wasn't my money, was dat damn moksa*'s money. Mo' bettah I tell him I go back da homeland and fight dere, mo' bettah fo' da struggle.*

Instead he tell me mo' bettah I go San Fran, go talk to da Christians ovah dere und ask fo' help da cause, ask fo' money. He said dey give plenny support and money. Dey rich up dere, da minister said. Yeah, sure, dey plenny rich. And das why dey give us only nuff kālā fo' cover our fare back Hawai'i.

"Mr. Kim, your story is very . . . significant, to me. Never have I talked to anyone who was directly connected with the liberation of our Motherland. I will pray to God for you and your family and friends and for the other patriots back home. I have heard that Korean Christians are being slaughtered by the Japanese gendarmes like lambs in a flock. But I have heard, too, that they are abiding with the Word of God and diligently and patiently practicing the doctrine of passive civil disobedience."

"They are brave," Sung Wha said colorlessly, "but they are very stupid people."

"And why is that?" the minister asked, mildly shaken, adjusting his pince-nez.

"If you keep on praying to your make-believe god to help you with your problems, the Japanese police will have an easy time shooting you down."

The man of God straightened up, disturbed by the coarse statement about the Almighty Father: how can a mortal say a disrespectful thing like that in the house of the Lord!

"Mr. Kim, I do respect highly your patriotic zeal, but please refrain from saying the Lord's name in vain, especially in His house." The young minister searched Sung Wha's face for an apology; instead, he found conceit.

"Well, sir, I must leave now," Sung Wha said. He stood up, looking over the *moksa*. "I must go on and finish my work today. Thank you for the tea and your hospitality."

"You are welcome. It was an—an interesting discussion we had. Please pardon me for asking, but what kind of work do you do?"

Sung Wha peered above into the unpainted rafters of the church, then puffed his chest out. "Sir," he said, "I'm building an airplane. I will scale the heights of heaven, and once there, I will spit in the eyes of my enemies."

The minister's face paled, his lips pursed. A concern came to Sung Wha for the health of the minister, as he seemed to be choking. Then Sung Wha read the message on his face, that he, Kim Sung Wha, was not wanted in the house of God. Sung Wha got up, thanked the silent, seething minister for the tea and his hospitality again, then left.

"Da way he look at me—ho! I thought he was going burn in hell. I nevah see one guy so mad in my life. But I should be mo' considerate. Dose days I was *lōlō*, I say anything on my mind, nothing going stop me. 'Specially in one church. How I used to hate da church dose days! Dey wen lead plenny Koreans like sheep to da Japanee slaughterhouse.

"I dunno why I go into da church in da first place, aftah da minister invite me in. I think maybe was da guy's face. Honest looking. Maybe he look like my friend at home, maybe one of my fallen comrades. Maybe I think da comrade wen come back alive and was standing right in front of me, making me like talk to him."

I wonder if I should tell Uncle now that I have a plane ticket to Korea in my pocket? I know Uncle has so much pride, so much of it that it's killing him. But maybe if I give him this ticket, it'll make him feel better. If he will take it. The doctor said he doesn't have that long to live, a few more months if he's lucky. Is he able to take a trip? The cancer is just eating away inside. But with this ticket, he can go back and die in Korea. I know that's what he wants. I know.

But if he gets there, where will he go? He can't go to the north, the border is all closed up. He doesn't even know if his wife is alive or not, or where she or the children might be living. I don't know any of our relatives there who could take care of him. And I don't think even he, too, remembers any of the family. He's never had any contact with them for all this time.

So what should I do? Give him this ticket and a false dream? On the other hand, he might not even take the ticket. Maybe he'll get mad at me for intruding, which might worsen his condition. I never know what the hell he's going to do next. I have never known a more hardheaded Yobo than him. This Yobo . . . he has too much pride, I think.

I don't know why he wants to go back to Korea, but he's always talking about it. He's lived here for at least fifty years, and still he talks as if Korea is his home. And how many times already since I've been visiting him at the hospital have I heard his story of that ricepaper airplane. Sometimes the way he tells the story it's as if he's building it right in front of me. I must know this story by heart now.

And he doesn't even know what happened to his family over there. But he has family here . . . us. And he has lived here most of his life. He is more from here than there. And all his friends are locals. I don't think he even has a Korean friend right now, a friend from the old days. They're either dead or avoiding him because of all those radical things he used to do. He was always known for the strong way he talked. A lot of his friends have changed, too, becoming more middle class through the success of their children, and they just don't want to be associated with him anymore. People can be cruel.

Maybe I'll give him a subtle hint about the plane ticket. I'll just mention that Mary and I came into some extra money recently. No, I'd say that everyone in the family chipped in so he won't think that Mary and I were put out by it. This uncle . . . hard to understand him sometimes—most of the time— though he's always telling us that his life is like an open book. What kind of open book I really don't know.

"Yong Gil, I tired now. Go . . . go home. Come back tomorrow. I going *moe*."

"You know, I nevah see da *moksa* fo' months aftah dat. One day I see him on da main street, Wahiawā town, but he no look at me; jus' like I not dere. I like go up to him, even if he da way he is, and tell him thank you, *moksa,* fo' da tea and *tuk.* But I keep away from him.

"Den aftah 'bout one year, maybe two years aftah dat, da *moksa,* he change overnight. I dunno what wen happen. Somebody tol' me his family in Korea was arrested and either executed or put in prison, somet'ing li'dat. Maybe das what change him. Da people in his congregation start getting all bothered by da kine things he start saying in his sermons, like how one good Korean Christian is one who not scared fo' die fo' da righteous cause and how he fight in da name of God 'gainst all injustices. Hard to believe all dat coming from da *moksa*'s mouth, youknowwhatImean?

"At first I nevah believe all dis. Dis minister saying all dat? No can be. But one day I tell myself, maybe I jus' drop in and find out myself. So I go da church wit' my excuse jus' say thank you fo' da hospitality. I go inside and I see da *moksa* sweeping up in one corner, and when he see me—ho! He so happy see me. At first I little bit scared. I thinking he mad at me fo' something I dunno what I do. He run up to me, ask me all kine questions: what I been doing? Where I was all dis time? Why I nevah come around? Heh, heh. He thought I was mad at him.

"But funny. I thinking jus' da opposite, dat he mad at me. Funny, yeah? Den he tell me he giving up da church and going back Korea. He say he still believe in God, but he tell me how God talk to him one night and tell him go Korea and do His work ovah dere and not jus' stay here where everything safe.

"Anyway, das da time he ask me go mainland wit' him. He like go see some friends, some rich friends he go college wit', befo' his theology school days. He like me come wit' him and talk wit' dem. He said maybe his friends can arrange us go all 'round and talk and ask fo' donations fo' da Korean cause.

"I nevah know what to say. All of a sudden dis man of God change like dat and start talking all dese things dat befo' he nevah talk about. Throw me off little bit. So I tell him I think about it, cannot decide right now. And plus dat, I tell him, I almost *pau* wit' my ricepepah airplane. When I *pau* I going fly back Korea, I tol' him. But he beg me fo' wait 'til he can make some money so when we go back we can have nuff *kālā* fo' da Korean cause, so we can buy supplies and all da ada stuff like dat . . . like guns and bullets! I nevah believe what I hearing!

"So I think real hard fo' couple days, den I decide he right.

"Chee, thinking back, wit' da money he spend fo' my boat fare to da States, I can go Korea wit' dat. But like I said, dis not my money. So we go mainland, fo' five weeks, and den we come back, broke as evah."

"I don't have the training, but you do. Didn't you say you were trained as a guerrilla in Manchuria?"

Sung Wha nodded his head uneasily. *What is this man of God thinking about now? I don't have time to listen and consider his dreams. I have my own dreams to pursue, my airplane to build . . . and I'm almost finished. And then I'll be able to go back to Korea. And if this minister, this mixed-up shaman in white man's robes, who cursed me when I first told him I was building my airplane to scale the heavens, if he ever asks me if there is room on my—*

"We can turn this church into a training center. You could teach Koreans on the plantations how to fight so that when they get back home, they can immediately join with the cause. They can start fighting right away."

Sung Wha regarded the minister with caution, as if the *moksa* had lost his marbles. It was all right for him, Sung Wha, or his other radical friends, to talk about things of this nature . . . but this man of God?

"But we will need guns, bullets, knapsacks," Sung Wha said, his feet involuntarily fusing with the ground. "And many more things. And with what money to buy these things?"

"We can use wooden rifles in place of real ones. They are not the real things, but they will have to do. They are better than nothing."

This moksa, *he's really something. The first time I talked to him he is a do-nothing pacifist. Maybe there was a possibility for him to work up to a passive dissenter. But now he seems more revolutionary than me. Is this the way God works?*

"Most of the Koreans here don't have the time to train," Sung Wha said. "They must work twelve to sixteen hours a day, six days a week. When will they have time to train? And besides, after a long sixteen-hour day, they will be too tired to do anything else."

"I have already talked to several members of my congregation, and they've expressed their willingness to start training right now. They don't see much future in working for the American boss here. As it is already, they hardly see or know who he is; the boss deals with them through his cruel-hearted *lunas*. They were given an armful of promises, and not one has been fulfilled. They feel cheated, lied to. One of them told me he doesn't see any difference between the American and the Japanese way of enslavement. They would rather go back home and fight for freedom. They all pine for the day of return. They all pledge their lives in the name of God to free Korea from this distempering tyranny."

"I ask him, what you mean by one 'distempering tyranny'? He talk to me in dis educated Korean dat I nevah know what da hell he talking about."

"All this is going to take more than a belief in your God."

The *moksa* pretended not to be offended by Sung Wha's comment.

"But all of this takes a lot of time," Sung Wha continued, shaking his head. "I don't know if I have the time to do this. I have my own work to do. I must finish my airplane, soon, before winter brings the rains."

"Dat *moksa* . . . I gotta give da buggah some credit. I dunno where he learn how manipulate somebody's brain. Maybe das why he one minister, one man of God wit' His word. They train to manipulate. They call dat 'faith.' He sure know how make you feel guilty or how twist yo' arm. He do it wit' one smile, wit' kindness in his voice, wit' dis honest-honest look on his face. You no can say no. If you say no, he make you think you doing one big injustice to da world. I think if he evah tried, I think he convince me can sit two man in da one-man seat in my airplane."

Sung Wha slept fitfully that night of swirling stars above his head, if you could call it sleeping. That night he was never sure if he was dreaming or not, his body perhaps floating among clouds and stars, or was it these images entering and leaving his mind on a will not his own. Moments after slumbering into that state of fragmented images, the beginnings of dreams, he would be wide awake, his eyelids unraveled from the sapping dope of sleep. No, he could not sleep: the best he could do was doze. And he tossed about unendingly, his old body creaking more than the floorboards under his bed. Before he knew it, the razor-sharp chill of early morning crept into his room through the crack in the window. Sung Wha turned to his side and watched through dirty glass panes a haloed moon.

He could never sleep now.

His body had felt the morning. The sun was but an hour or two away. He could not sleep now because his body was on automatic wake up. It was not the first time he went to sleep and didn't sleep, his body leaden and aching for rest, his mind drifting off like a languid, pointless cloud.

The dry timbers of the hotel settled, the floorboards sagging from the same burdensome weight of yesterday, and the still air of the hallway held its place against a cacophony of overly rehearsed snores. The daily morning rituals, the unending quarrels between tenants and ancient plumbing, had not begun yet. And there were no tired shuffles on the grooved floorboards, no cars rushing down downtown streets against thick predawn air.

His eyes opening to the dark freshness of morning, Sung Wha visualized fishermen on the docks unloading their catch, hundreds of pounds of *aku, ʻōpakapaka, ʻahi,* and other fish that were getting smaller and smaller by the year, caught in the overly fished, defiled Hawaiian waters. He could hear the fish auctioneer calling out for bids, see a buyer's keen blade slice slivers from tail sections of yellowfins: smelling the flesh, fingering it, tasting it for texture and flavor.

A cup of coffee was what he needed. Stomach growled, concurring. Slowly he stretched, throwing his hands back through the metal bars of the bed frame and touching the dusty wall. He got out of bed and thawed his chilled leg joints and arm muscles by rubbing them, dressed himself, and lumbered out of his room and down the dark hall to the kitchenette. He yanked on the pull-string of the naked light bulb that swung from a ceiling of cobwebs, and with a beaten Brillo pad, soap, and water, he cleaned and rinsed the dimpled aluminum pot of the mess left by the night roaches. He filled the pot halfway with water and set it on the gas stove, lighting the burner with a match. A blue flame jumped up, its warmth and gassy smell puffing into his face. Sitting on a metal folding chair, he tried to recount the last five times he had awakened like this. But he couldn't. He had done this so many times, too many times. This morning was like the last time, and the last time was like the last. So many times. Too many times.

He looked up at the big wall clock that had been salvaged from a condemned school cafeteria. The hour hand had fallen off a while back, and no one had made the effort to fix the clock or take it down. "Let it alone" was the general consensus of the tenants. "It not bothering nobody so nobody bother it." So the minute hand spun round and round and nobody could tell what hour it was. Time told only by the minute.

Time is a liar. It repeats itself so often. Time has become so standoffish and nonexistent.

And then . . . when you look at yourself in the mirror, there's one more line on your face. Or a line has deepened. You can't remember how that happened or when that happened, but there it is. And there's that patch of thin white hair, and those knobs you call ears have become more spread apart, and around all of that float these fading, black and white photos of the past: fuzzy, indifferent faces, some with depthless, taunting smiles that suddenly jump out at you and make you feel old and useless, or remind you of memories of what used to be: *try go back, Sung Wha, try go back relive da past when you was young and hard and strong roving 'round wit' no mo' cares and when nobody and nothing really scared you, Sung Wha, everything was in your reach, Sung Wha, you could fly to da moon and stars if you like, Sung Wha, you can run across da biggest continent in da world and make revolution and you was happy even wit' all dat hardship, and you had love, Sung Wha—yes! love!—and you had dis love at yo' fingertips, you cradled it in yo' long, lean arms, warming it in da coldest winters, you remembah all dat . . . yes? . . . Come on, Sung Wha, try go back to when was . . . try. . . .*

But then you tell yourself: *no can, you sonavabitch you, you know you cannot, not in all yo' dreams, nevah in your life, you one old man, Sung Wha, ready to* maké, *your dreams have come and gone already, you no can dream no mo', you old man! All the energy fo' make yo' dreams, dey all gone, and only thing left is fo' you think about yo' dreams, live in da dreams of yo' dreams past, and das all. And all you can do now is wait fo' dat frickin' blue flame warm up yo' frickin' water so you can make yo' frickin' coffee so you can wake up to one nada frickin' day, jus' one nada frickin' day. Frick.*

Sung Wha opened the cupboard and took out a small jar of instant coffee, the generic brand, of course, with its label nibbled around the edges by glue-craving roaches. And he dipped his spoon in the jar and withdrew a dose of brittle brown stars, stirred them into the boiled water in his white mug, and watched the black liquid swirl and swirl like a muddied galaxy. Then he sat down, lit a cigarette, and waited until the coffee became cold.

221

Troy Nishimura scampered up the stairs of Kekaulike Hotel. Under his arm was a stack of printed leaflets, placed sloppily back into the paper's original wrapping. His steps up the stairs were fast and light. He was happy, maybe even overjoyed. And he was impatient to get where he was going. The disappointing twists and turns of the eviction struggle were far behind in his sprightly wake. No hassles clouded his mind. Like the problem of a budget-critical university trying to cut back on the ethnic studies program. Or the hassles with those deceitful, incompetent legislators who expertly manipulated and invalidated the already senseless public hearings, once again trying to pull the wool over the eyes of the common people. Or the confrontations with those damn Communists who wanted to take over the eviction struggle for their own "revolutionary" interest: they'd rather talk about revolutionary violence than struggle for concrete results such as better housing and decent wages for the working people.

Late that morning, he had received an acceptance letter from the Hastings School of Law. He had been on the waiting list. Days before, he had almost committed himself to the local law school, but now he had been given the opportunity to study at a first-rate institution, to become a first-rate people's lawyer. Yes, to be a people's lawyer. Or perhaps he could be a people's doctor, or a people's social worker, or a people's something. Yes, anything with "people" as a qualifier. In America, if people wanted to help others, people could become a "people" something, not just an anonymous nothing, an egoless nonentity like a priest or a revolutionary, occupations that were required in poor, undeveloped countries dominated by dictators, but not in a country like America, where if you tried hard in the system you could fight for your rights and win. Lucky you live America! Lucky you live Hawai'i!

Troy Nishimura found Mo and Eddie the blind man at the kitchenette table. Where's Mr. Kim? he asked. They shrugged their rounded old shoulders. Maybe he stay in da park, Mo said, I think he stay ovah dere, you know him, he like go play checkers wit' da old Filipinos. Right, Troy Nishimura said. He pulled out a thin stack of flyers and placed it on the table for the men and the other residents to read and distribute. Mo nodded his head in acknowledgment, though making no effort to read the leaflet. He and Shelley, the other organizer, should have shown the draft of the leaflet to the residents before printing it, but they were in a rush to get to the print shop before closing time. And anyway, in the past, whenever they had shown a draft, the residents never read it and were always in complete agreement with almost everything they did or said . . . well, except Sung Wha. Sometimes he disagreed with a few points, but he was always compromising.

"It's about the hearing that's coming up," Troy Nishimura said.

Seeing that they weren't going to take the leaflet, Troy handed one to Mo and even one to Eddie. Eddie didn't want to be rude, so he took it when he felt it touching his arm and smiled in the direction of Troy's voice. Troy reminded them: the hearing is next Wednesday; we've arranged for a small van to pick all of you up at nine sharp in the morning; the hearing is at ten; the night before we'll come down with paint and cardboard and sheets to make our picket signs and banners.

The two old men thanked him and smiled. Dis boy, he one good boy, their smiles seemed to say. How fortunate, us guys, fo' dis boy from da university come down and help us out.

Troy Nishimura trundled down the stairs, leaving them with his smile.

Sung Wha was not at the park; the men playing checkers hadn't seen him for the entire day. But Troy found him on the bridge over the canal, looking down into the opaque, scummy water.

"Mr. Kim!"

Sung Wha turned to watch the boy's approach. A particle of dust slipped under the boy's contact lens, stabbing his eye, half of his face twisting in small pain.

"Mr. Kim," Troy said, carefully wiping away the tears. "We

printed the leaflets for next week's hearing. I left some copies back at the hotel. Here . . . maybe you can hand these out now." Troy held out a few leaflets for Sung Wha to take.

Sung Wha refused them with a wave of a hand. Troy dabbed the corner of his eye with the neck of his T-shirt. It felt like a pin was still pricking his eye.

"I no need dem anymo'," Sung Wha sighed.

Damn stuff in my eye . . . what did he say? Troy rubbed the eyelid in an attempt to dislodge that pesky mote of dust from under his lens. No luck. His eye watering profusely, he regarded Sung Wha, one side of Sung Wha's image blurred.

"What was that again, Mr. Kim?"

"I said I no need dem."

"These are the new leaflets. You have to read one."

"I know what it is. You tol' me 'bout 'em already. Yesterday, I think."

"But . . . you could pass the leaflets out to your friends in the park."

Sung Wha shook his head. "No, boy, I no like pass anymo' leaflets around no mo'." Sung Wha spat into the water. A school of tilapia moved sluggishly along the litter-lined edge of the canal.

"Is there something wrong with the leaflets? We should have let you read the draft, but the print shop was closing. We had to get them printed for today."

Sung Wha shook his head again, grinning. "No, boy, nothing to do wit' da leaflet." His eyes returned to the murky canal. A small *'a'ama* crab was crawling up the side. A bloated dead rat floated a few feet away from it. He turned to the boy. "I no like be part of da eviction struggle no mo'. You understand? I no care if da leaflet is good or no good, or whatevah. I jus' no like be involve no mo'. You understand? You *sabe?*"

Troy rubbed the corner of his eye again. *There. All right. Shit.* "No, I don't understand," he said.

A Styrofoam cup was being dragged down to the harbor by a weak current.

"Is there something wrong? Is there something wrong with the way things are going?"

"No . . . no. Is all good. I feel good you young guys doing something 'bout something. What you guys doing is all good. Is all good. But . . ."

"Yes?"

Sung Wha shook his head and swallowed his half-formed words.

"What's wrong?" Troy Nishimura pressed.

Sung Wha turned his back to the youth and started to walk away.

"Wait, Mr. Kim. You can't give up. We have a hearing coming up. This is an important battle."

Sung Wha stopped and faced the boy. "You call dis one battle? One battle? Dis no battle. You wanna know what one real battle is? You wanna know? Do you? Do—" He shook his head, opened his mouth to finish, but again swallowed his words.

"But . . . this hearing is important. If we can get others from the community in addition to our own numbers to attend that hearing on Wednesday, we'll show a powerful force. The zoning commission will have to consider us. We'll have a good chance to stop the evictions."

Sung Wha laughed at the canal. "You know, Troy, I going tell you something. Even if we get da majority of people on O'ahu come to dis hearing fo' support us, dat not going change da way dose politicians and 'specially dose landlords going think. Maybe dey give us some crumbs. But later on, when we not looking, dey going pull da stops, do some undah-da counter tricks on us, and like every time, dey going get dey way."

A lost look came to Troy's face. "Then what do you think we should do? If we lose the struggle, where are you going to live? And how about the others? Mo, Eddie—he's blind—and the others . . . who's going to take care of them?"

"Dey can take care demselves. Eddie take care himself all dese years already. You know what he used to be befo' he get blind?"

"No."

"Da buggah used to be da best *aku* spotter in da islands. He can spot da school of fish from so far away, dey nickname him 'Radar Eyes.' And was all 'cause his eyes. He can see da water changing on da surface. He even tol' me one time he can even smell da fish. Unreal, eh? And if he can do dat, he can take care himself. Anyway, he get free fish anytime he go down da pier. All he gotta do is show his face and all da *aku* boats, dey give him all da fresh fish he like, mo' den he can evah *kaukau*. To dis day all da boats he wen *hanahana* still 'preciate him. Dey take care him. And he can take care himself. He no complain. No mo' *pilikia*, him. Every morning I hear him making all kine noise jus' like he ready fo' *maké*. But all he doing is clearing his throat fo' da new day. Da buggah going live longer dan me, he eat fish every day. Da buggah love his fish."

"But how about the others? Who's going to be their spokeperson? Who's going to explain to them what is happening and what can be done?"

"You. Das yo' job. You smart boy, go university. You doing one good job already. You can explain everything to dem. You explain plenny to me, things I nevah know, things I no can understand. Anyway, dose guys in Kekaulike, dey no babies, you know. Dey can take care demselvess. Dey look cripple and maybe dey little bit slow in da head. When you get old you get slow, you know. But dem not cripple, and when dey blood start moving, dey can think pretty good. I live wit' dem, so I know. But you can help dem what dey no *sabe*, right?"

Sung Wha waits patiently for an answer that never comes. The boy has no tongue. This boy can talk but doesn't talk now.

"You can be spokesman now. Das what you doing anyway right now, if you know it or not. Me . . . right now I jus' like move down dis road here," he says, pointing with the motion of his head. "I thinking too much nowadays. Time fo' me no think too much, jus' walk down dis road and think of nothing.

Okay? I know you going do one good job. I jus' like rest nowadays. I too tired."

Sung Wha leaves the speechless young man holding the ream of flyers close to his chest. Funny how Sung Wha's body and mind feel lighter now after saying what he has said. Like an unfulfilled spirit whose chain to time is broken, he is free, his covenant with the world now completed. He has led a selfless life, and now he needs to find himself in the dust and fragments of memories that surround him before he, too, becomes insensate dust. Now perhaps he can be truly free. Now perhaps he can fly.

"Uncle Sung Wha, can I hold the kite?"

Sung Wha holds the spindle, releasing yards and yards of line. The kite is flying higher and higher, shaking in the wind that is challenging it at every angle.

"No, Yong Gil. The wind is too angry at me. The wind will sweep away your small body!"

"Can I, Uncle Sung Wha, can I?"

"No, Yong Nam."

"Uncle, how come you can fly a kite so well?"

"Uncle is the champion kite flier in our village. Didn't your papa tell you this?"

"Uncle, when are you going to finish your airplane?"

"Soon, Yong Gil. Soon."

Sung Wha takes a pocket knife from his pants pocket and, while holding the tugging spindle under his arm, unfolds the blade.

"What are you going to do, Uncle Sung Wha?"

Sung Wha severs the taut line.

"Why did you cut the string, Uncle Sung Wha? Why?"

"The kite wants to fly home."

"But why?"

They watch the kite for a long while fly higher and higher in the sky until it vanishes into the clouds.

Now he can fly. He can fly on the wings of the birds he often dreams about: birds with magic feathers that glitter in daylight, with sharp beaks that point decisively in direction of sun; birds with eyes eager and glowing with hints of premonition: they see and understand everything, and yet they choose only to see one thing, and that is the glorious sunset ahead of them, that glorious ball of fire now retiring for the day . . . to hide itself behind that massive, squarish concrete wall in front of him, only to emerge once again, triumphantly, mere moments later, behind Sung Wha's sagging shoulders.

He passed through the park, waving at his friends huddled around the tables: Filipino old men sapped of youth by the haole power order, left alone to mark time with plastic Woolworth checker sets.

Dey really no want to play checkers. Dey just trying buy or borrow mo' time, das all. Dey all like go home to one family, wife and children and now should be grandchildren. Dey like one place dey can call "home." Dey retired, but now what else is dere in life fo' dem do but play checkers? Dey get nothing but da clothes on dey backs, one change nice clothes in dey small lonely room, and dat checkerboard and checkers. How many times dey gotta buy one new set? Dey get nothing else, like me, not one thing from nobody. What little dey get dey had to work fo'—and hanahana hard. Nobody give 'way nothing to nobody dese days.

Da only ones giving anything away is da ones who get nothing in da first place. Sounds stupid but is true. Dey get da biggest hearts, dey da biggest givers of dem all: da ones who get nothing to give always get da most to give. And da ones who get everything, dey stingy, dey keep everything to demselves. Ask me how much it cost fo' one ounce of love to give to one friend, to one neighbor, and I tell you, you no can buy it.

I tired play checkers. Played too much checkers: moving forward, moving backward, end of game start one nada one, end dat one start one nada one, losing and winning, buying new playing boards aftah da old board all worn-out cardboard, we talking da same thing day in, day out, every day da same thing ovah and ovah again. We cursed: we gotta play checkers 'til da day we maké-*die-dead, 'til da day we no can walk out our rooms and gotta stay dere and rot in our beds by our own lonely selfs until we breathe one last time, "Dahil Saiyo."*

Why old men like me no can maké *wit' dignity, wit' pride? Da only dignity we get is when we lie in dat hole in da ground, our faces cold and no mo' color; das da only dignity we going get in our whole friggin' life. And even den, maybe dey move our graves, make way fo' one nada big development.*

But why are you thinking like this, Sung Wha? Is all of this finally getting to you? After all these years, is your conscience bothering you, grabbing you by your low-hanging balls: how did your life turn so sour? Why did it turn this way?

I'm giving up on you, Sung Wha. Yes, you're an old man now, but you're supposed to be wiser, stronger in the mind. Your will is supposed to get stronger as your body weakens. It's a give and take. But instead you're betraying yourself. You're starting to feel sorry for yourself. That's not right, Sung Wha, that's not right. No matter how much you don't like what has happened, you just can't change things. That's a universal law, and that's called time. It's impossible. It has happened already and you can't do anything about it. Do you understand? What is done is done. And that's that. So stop this foolish talk, Sung Wha. Stop feeling so sorry for yourself. You're only making yourself feel a lot worse than you should be. It was your choice to live this life, Sung Wha. It was your choice.

But all I asking fo' is one soft place rest my head 'til I maké-*die-dead. And all I askin' fo' is when I die dey no dig up my bones and move 'em someplace else. But if dey dig up my bones, maybe dey going put my bones all in one garbage can and haul 'em away so no bother nobody. People no like look at one dead man's bones. Den maybe dey going build something on top where I used to stay buried. Shit, dey do anything dey like nowadays. Sometimes I no understand how dem guys think. It strange to me, like dey from one nada planet. But we suppose to be all human beings, we suppose to live like human beings. So how come man is cruel to one nada man?*

All I askin' fo' is dey let me see wit' my own eyes, wit' dese eyes of a man. And all I askin' fo' is dey leave me alone wit' my dreams.

Sung Wha wants to cross the busy boulevard separating the downtown from the waterfront. But it's rush hour. Going-home time. He waits for a long time before the cars begin to slow down and stop, backed up by a set of malfunctioning traffic lights ahead. He steps down the curb and weaves between the hot, shiny bumpers, stops on the median strip to wipe the perspiration from his forehead, then continues across the other lanes to the sidewalk. He leans over a concrete guardrail and coughs up the phlegm loosened by the gritty car exhaust. He's breathing hard, he's suffocating, the noxious fumes of the cars clogging up his lungs. He coughs more. When the coughing stops, his face a ragged purple, he takes a cigarette from his pocket, lights it, and smokes while watching the foamy waters from the bowels of a prostituted city purge into an indifferent harbor.

And why da stream so dirty and stink like shit? One stream from da mountains not suppose to be like dis. It suppose to be clean and cold and rushing and full wit' life. It suppose to be living, one beautiful sight fo' one pair tired eyes fo' look at.

Speaking Words,
Speaking Eyes

You can really tell a story, eh, Sung Wha? All you need is an open ear, like this minister's, and there you go: over Kumgangsan, down to the gray raging seas, then up to the clouds that know no time, on and on and on.

Sung Wha smiles to himself. Yes, he likes to tell stories about his life's experiences. Maybe at times he stretches them a bit. But just a little. He'll never stretch facts, those facts he knows that took history a long and arduous struggle to produce. Why would he deny the truth? History is made by the heroic work of the working people.

He patiently guides the stumbling mule up the dirt trail toward Eung Whan's homestead. He had enjoyed himself at the *moksa*'s church, though he is no closer to becoming a believer of the white man's god, or any other deity for that matter. But the *moksa* was a good listener; his narrowed eyes behind those thick glasses tried to penetrate Sung Wha's soul—Sung Wha saw the minister's black eyes rove over his face in search of a portal. No, those eyes of the *moksa* seemed too innocent of the world; Sung Wha's stories were being absorbed without question.

Then there was a point in the conversation when he had angered the minister; Sung Wha had simply stated a fact about the futility of the Judeo-Christian god. He was simply being truthful: only man has the stupidity to invent something called "God." And turning the other cheek to a foreign invader while he confiscates your land and robs you of your valuables and rapes your wife and daughter—what can be more ridiculous or stupid or cowardly?

But why can't life be as free as birds in flight, soaring high with the begging wind, gracefully touching the belly of an opal sky, and gliding into spacious blue canyons of airy white mountains made of rain?

The airplane will make him free. It must be built strong and light. It will make him free. Free from gravity, enslaving grace that it is. He'll travel the length of the world in a breath. Drinking of the clouds their nectar, he will be free. He'll breathe in the sweet, cool air and extract nourishment for his spirit: the redolence of mountain flowers and the rush of rivers. Perhaps he might fly to the sun and be warmed everlastingly and never come back. Perhaps he might discover the heaven the *moksa* will spend his entire life preaching about but will never see.

No, fool. Only a son of a mule would leave this world of beautiful mountains like Kumgangsan. A stupid fool.

It was dark when he reached the homestead at the top of the ridge. A kerosene lantern was burning faintly in the window. He parked the wagon and unhitched the mule, then led the animal to its food and shelter. Tired and with the minister's food still in his stomach, he entered the shed and lay on his cot, falling fast asleep.

A nightmare wakes him in the early morning, a nightmare that has visited him before. He is flying in his airplane when from out of nowhere come scores of seabirds surrounding him with their squawks and pecking holes in the wings of the aircraft. He fights back, swinging wildly, and catches only air. Then his airplane spins out of control, and now he's plunging toward a jeering dark sea.

A nightmare within a nightmare: can he wake up before crashing?

And, as always, in the cool morning darkness, counting down a racked heart, he asks himself: what happens if I don't wake up in time?

He shudders from that fading white image of birds attacking him, an image that floats brazenly above him, moving in and out of a shaft of moonlight that slips through the partly opened doorway, dividing the internal darkness. Before it vanishes completely, he turns to his side.

He thinks of Hae Soon.

She is at the pond washing herself. He is watching through a bush, her body glowing from the moonlight.

But this time he goes through the bush. Hae Soon's eyes widen in surprise. A shudder and a tiny gasp. A whispered protest. She blushes, or perhaps the moon has waned, her arms her hands covering clutching her secret skin. Sung Wha moves closer; eyes are talking in the language of moonlight: I love you, Hae Soon, I will never leave you, I love you. And he touches her shoulder, and her flesh is warm and soft, quivering, and she lowers one arm, the other . . . and her eyes are dark and draw in his: one.

The movement in his groin has grown, that repressed appendage of his body becoming large and firm, pulsating. He unbuttons his pants and slips a sweating hand into that warm mesh of hair and throbbing flesh. And he holds it, rubs it, then kneads it, tenderly at first, then hard and violently until an abundant jism bursts out and spills over his hand, soaking his pants and the hairs of his groin.

Withdrawing his hand, he wipes it on the leg of his pants. Now there's that smell, that smell of his loneliness.

The smell is warm and homey. Daybreak is soon, though they have not slept, sleep being impossible—no time for that with the baby crying for Mother's milk and months, perhaps years, of love being compressed into two days and two nights. And

Hae Soon: Sung Wha when do you have to go back? Love me again. And Sung Wha: this is a fortuitous moment for mankind we are on the verge of a great historic event Hae Soon stay here with the baby. And Hae Soon: but it is too dangerous they are murdering Communists this reactionary government I'll have to go back Wakatani said he will help us yes Watanabe how is he?

And the moon is full of premonition, glowing through the paper window; through a tear, they watch its movement across the sky while lying on their bedding and . . .

And full moon.

He wiped himself with a dirty rag, then buttoned up his pants. He lay back down, his body aglow, feeling satisfaction and guilt at the same time. The wetness became more uncomfortable. He got up and changed his pants, then returned to the cot.

Why do you have those nightmares of birds, Sung Wha? Why does that nightmare repeat itself, haunting you over and over again? Are you telling yourself right from the start that your airplane will fail? What are you telling yourself?

I'm ashamed of you, Sung Wha, for thinking such foolish thoughts. Of course you'll build that airplane. Of course you'll fly to the heavens. You'll travel over the vast Pacific Ocean and land your aircraft in Korea, triumphant and proud. And then you'll find your wife and your grown son—my! How big he has grown and how he looks so much like you!—and the newborn baby who is not a newborn anymore—but how old is the baby now? How long have you been away, Sung Wha? And is the baby a girl? Another boy?

He sat on the edge of the cot. He couldn't sleep anymore. Taking a bag of Bull Durham from his shirt pocket, he rolled a cigarette and lit it. *Today I begin piecing together my airplane. Today. Today it will come alive. Today it will come true. Today my dream becomes reality. Today it will come true.*

This is Sung Wha's plan: construct a large wing out of bamboo and ricepaper, similar in structure to his champion kites. Join the wing to a bicycle. Affix a propeller to the front of the airplane and then attach it to the bicycle's pedals by means of a bamboo shaft. Finally, connect straps to the wing so that he can secure his arms to it.

When he pedals, the propeller will spin and thrust the airplane forward, and when the airplane has worked up enough speed, it will lift off the ground. And he'll be flying. Simple enough, isn't it?

He rises before the summer sun. When he hears his cousin and his cousin's wife readying themselves for work, Sung Wha is already hard at work, cutting and splitting the bamboo and shaving off thin, curly slivers. He rests and smokes a cigarette, greeting his cousin and wife and watching them plod to the fields in the quiet semi-darkness, she with sleeping baby bound snugly to back. And when Eung Whan and Ok Soon and baby return in the late afternoon—another long day passing, their eyes reddened from sun and dust, their swollen feet caked with red dirt of field, and with the orange sun in the near distance nesting atop a forest of giant *kukui* trees—Sung Wha is still at it, back bent into the twisting and shaping and tying of bamboo slats. And husband and wife stoop and marvel and praise in dry tones this man so enamored of his work: it is difficult for them to smile, their lips sun-blistered and wind-dried. How can he keep on working, they think, with this much energy when the day is nearly dead, he working as if there is no tomorrow? Eung Whan grunts, perhaps a touch of envy in his drooping eyes: *we share the same aches and pains from hard work, but Sung Wha's work is his and his alone to keep.*

The baby begins to cry; it craves its mama's swollen breasts. Ok Soon adjusts the sling securing the baby to her back so that the baby is now cradled below an exposed teat. The baby grapples with it, finally surrounds the large, purplish nipple with puckered lips, whimpers, then closes its eyes and sucks. Ok Soon leaves them for the house.

"It looks good," Eung Whan offers. "What is it?"

"This," Sung Wha replies, lifting a partly finished frame off the ground, "is the wing that will share the wind and take me back home."

Sung Wha rolls two cigarettes and gives one to Eung Whan. He lights them and flicks the smoking matchstick toward a small pile of bamboo shavings.

"In a week, perhaps, it will be ready to be covered with rice-paper," says Sung Wha. "Then it will look like a real airplane. Like the white man's one. And like his, it'll fly and disappear into the clouds."

"You're not afraid of . . . flying?"

"No. Does the tiger not scale Kumgangsan? Does the turtle not swim the four seas?"

Eung Whan breaks into a rare, after-work smile; he finds pleasure in the defiance and confidence of his cousin. *He's going to build an airplane after all,* Eung Whan thinks, *but I still doubt he will leave the ground. Only so much man can do, and Sung Wha is trying for the impossible. Ha! But maybe Sung Wha won't be the dreamer anymore.*

"Like the white man's one," Eung Whan murmurs, his glazed eyes turning inward as he visualizes the image in the moving pictures of the smiling *miguk* pilot right before he takes his plane to the sky.

"But this is a Korean airplane, made by a Korean with Korean ideas. Look at it. Feel it. It's strong and tough. Like a Korean."

Eung Whan runs a calloused hand over the smooth bamboo. "And you'll flap your arms like a bird?" There's a joking in his question. There's mockery in his question.

Sung Wha points to the rusty bicycle. "Birds use their feathers. Men use machines."

"Hmm."

"You'll watch me when I fly?"

Surrounded by tendrils of harsh tobacco smoke, Eung Whan nods. "Yes, I will watch you fly." *Yes, I will watch you. And when you fall from the clouds, I'll be there, my ox-headed cousin, to witness your failure. And, if I know you, you'll make another attempt at failure right after that.*

Later, the men wash up and eat dinner: beef bone soup with watercress, rice, and kimchee. And afterward they tell stories, drink swipe, and sing folk songs in the exaggerated style of a *pansori*, while the children listen and fall asleep, one by one.

Nine days later, over an outside fire, Sung Wha boils a handful of raw rice into a sticky, translucent adhesive. He lays out lengthwise the sheets of ricepaper and glues the ends together to form one continuous roll. He smokes a couple of cigarettes, waiting for the seams to dry, then gets ready for the next step, retrieving the fifteen-foot bamboo wing frame from the side of the shed. He stirs the pot of warm glue. Then, section by section, he applies a thin coat of glue to each bamboo split and stretches the ricepaper over the frame, gently massaging the paper into place. Sometimes a wind plays with him, sending the paper flapping; and Sung Wha, calling the wind a bastard pig or whoring dog, must carefully lift the paper off the grabbing bamboo and start the section again. But it soon goes right. With a sharp knife, he trims off the overhang except for three to four inches, which he folds and glues to the underside of the wing. It takes him nearly an entire day to finish the job, but finally he's able to light a cigarette and sit back in weary silence and satisfaction.

In the early evening, Eung Whan's two eldest sons came to him. On Yong Suk's shoulder rested a .22 rifle. Behind Yong Suk was Yong Gil, the younger and skinnier of the two, cradling a small box of ammunition.

"*Ajisi*, let's go hunting while the sun is watching us," Yong Suk said, his voice hinting of coming manhood.

"Hunting? For what?" Sung Wha sat up and took the rifle from Yong Suk. He rubbed the oiled wooden stock, then peered down the sights, aiming the rifle toward the red sunset.

"For doves."

"For doves? And where are the bullets?"

Yong Gil offered the box to Sung Wha.

"I bought it today on the way home from school," Yong Suk said.

Sung Wha opened the box of shells and held one up to the late afternoon light. "Did your papa ever tell you about our rifle back in the village?"

The boys shook their heads.

"Ah . . . that's a long story. Sit down. I'll tell you the story."

"But we should go and hunt while there's still light," Yong Suk said.

"Ah! There's a lot of sunlight. Too much, in fact. And there's a pesky wind, too. And what did you say you're hunting for?"

"Doves. In the *kukui* trees."

"Behind here?" Sung Wha pointed behind the shed. "Doves . . . they're so stupid. They're going nowhere. They'll wait for us. Sit down. Let me tell you this story."

"*Ajisi,* do you know how to shoot a rifle?" Yong Gil asked.

Yong Suk led them through a thicket of *kiawe* trees and across a fenced cow pasture, then into a wood of *kukui* and mango: the damp smells of oily nuts and overripe fruit. The sun had set an hour before, and they used a flashlight to guide them through the moonless night. Yong Suk shone the light up one tree and discovered a flock of doves sleeping on the higher branches, warbling and cooing in sleep. "There! Up there!" he whispered.

Sung Wha studied them coolly. *Birds can't stay in the air all the time. They must come down and sleep in the darkness of trees. I can easily take a rock, aim and throw it at their heads, crushing them, and they'd fall like fat mangoes to the ground.*

Yong Suk ordered Yong Gil to shine the flashlight at the doves while he kneeled behind his younger brother and propped the barrel of the rifle on Yong Gil's shoulder.

"Point the flashlight at that fat one there! Be steady! No, that one. Yes, that one!"

Yong Suk aimed, fired, and missed. He reloaded and fired, and again he missed, and he repeated until all the doves had scattered. They went to another tree, and again Yong Suk failed to bring down a bird. At the next tree Sung Wha took the rifle and fired a dozen shots, sending several fluttering, helpless doves to the ground. Yong Gil pounced on the dying birds and tossed them in a burlap sack. They went to another tree, and Sung Wha killed more. And this continued until the sack was filled.

They dragged the bloody sack to the house, and in the back of the shed they cleaned the birds, plucking feathers and shucking out guts with bloody hands. And in a big black skillet smoking with hot animal fat, Mama fried the birds to a golden crispness, filling the house with a sweet, greasy aroma. No one talked during the meal; no one argued and fought with another for another piece of meat, as there was more than enough for this large family to eat.

After the meal the family sat on the porch, under the stars, and Papa told his ghost stories. The children crept closer and closer, eyes widened to Papa's enlarged voice as his stories darkened the already dark night. And slowly, though fighting the urge, each child nodded off to sleep.

"Yo' Papa was da best storyteller I evah know. And he learned how tell story from his father—my uncle—who was da best storyteller in da village. Ghost stories? Ho! Nobody can tell 'em like yo' papa or yo' papa's papa, yo' *harabagi.* Yo' papa's stories even make my skin all chicken-skin like when I listen to him. Ghosts? Of course, nobody in dey right mind going believe in ghosts.

"But ghosts is fo' real. But da ghost not going harm you if you no harm dem, das what I say, das what people tell me when I was one small kid growin' up.

"But I tell you, Yong Gil, nobody can tell one story like da people from our village. And das one truth. Yo' *harabagi*—my uncle, my *ajisi*– he da spokeperson fo' da entire village. Da Japanee come into da village and yo' *harabagi* go make da kine fantastic-kine stories, he tell dem. And dem Japanee believe! Dem believe everything what yo' *harabagi* tell dem, no matter how fantastic da story.

"I think was his eyes was da t'ing. Most times, you can look somebody's eyes and can tell right off da bat what dis guy like. Yo' *harabagi*'s eyes get one real honest-honest kine look. He can fool anybody. If he living today, dey call him one good actor. Like Gary Cooper. Or Charlie Chaplin. Maybe even mo' bettah dan dem. Only thing, no have cameras in Korea dose days. So no mattah how good one actor you, you no can be one actor."

So that's it. That's how I'll do it: attach this propeller to one end of a bamboo shaft. Connect the other end to a gear. Mesh the teeth of the gear with the teeth of the back wheel sprocket. When I pedal the bicycle, the propeller turns, which thrusts the airplane forward. Then my airplane accelerates down the slope. The rushing air lifts my wings and the airplane rises off the ground. I'm flying into the sky. Like a bird.

And I'd better wear warm clothing. Freezing cold high up in the sky. That's how it is up in the mountains. And I'd better fatten myself up. I don't know if I will ever have a chance to eat, flying up there. How long will it take to fly from Hawai'i to Korea? A few days? A week? A month?

And how's my old friend Yamamura, that anarchist? One of a few Japanese whom I trust. I owe my life to him. Don't have the money to pay him back, but I'll give it back later. That's a promise. I will. He understands. He knows we revolutionaries are poor. But yes, I should stop in Japan, where my good friend will welcome and feed me. He'll make a bed for me. And then off I'll go, flying to Korea.

But how long will it take me to fly that long distance? If birds can fly faster than my walk or a horse's trot, and given that I am larger than them, with my airplane I should get to Japan in a week. And if the air currents are helpful, maybe even less.

*But I'll have to toughen my body for this journey. Condition it
by carrying large rocks up and down this hill. Train more rigor-
ously than we did for that march to Shanghai—and that was a
rough assignment, fighting the enemy on all fronts. Empty bellies
grumbling constantly. Feet and ears bitten by numbing cold. Manchurian winds running right through us like sharp knives. But we
had that warm glow in our hearts, didn't we? Yes, makers of history we were. And I don't think I was even seventeen at the time.*

*There . . . that's me! With the wind blowing in my face! I'm
smiling . . . how happy I look! The clouds are so far away, all clustered like giant white mushrooms. In a forest of blue. Bird sounds.
Branches snapping. A distant rumble: the mountain tiger moving, moaning, padding over lichen-covered rocks and pine cones.
And the warm sun . . . how good it feels. But there are no birds.
Have I finally beaten them? Maybe the birds have given up, maybe
they won't fight me for the sky again. The sky is too vast for them to
claim it all. And besides, the sky is here for humans as well!*

*Ahh . . . the ocean looks so beautiful, so serene. Gladness. A good
time of year to return home. No storms to threaten my journey. The
air so sweet smelling. The season of flavorful breezes.*

He thought he had conquered the birds.

Over the next three nights he dreamed the same bad dream
of birds attacking him and his airplane. They pecked his face and
hands and feet. But somehow he always managed to wake himself before crashing into the ocean.

Except on the fourth night.

He plunged into a frigid sea still strapped to his airplane, sea-
water forced into nostrils and lungs.

With arms flailing, he finally awoke, gasping for air, his
clothes and bedding soaked with rain leaking through a hole in
the corrugated-iron roof. He fell from his cot. Outside, thunder and lightning ricocheted off the heavens. And when he
finally realized the workings of the storm, when he could finally
rescue his thinned, fragmented soul from the swamp of a bad

dream, he sat at the edge of the cot, shivering, oblivious to the clock-like drip of rain on shoulder. For him, the nightmare was real: his mouth burned with brine, and his gut undulated restlessly with the surging of the sea.

He went cold and sleepless the rest of the night, flashes of a swallowing ocean from time to time wrenching open his eyes. And during the day he could not keep his mind on work.

Instead of arguing with himself on ways to construct that elusive airplane, he retreated to a far corner of the shed and rolled cigarette after cigarette, smoking until his lungs begged for air. And he began to cough and spit out dark, burning phlegm. Later, when his lungs again begged for more tobacco, he rolled the last of his Bull Durham, finished that cigarette, then gathered the butts scattered over the ground and from them rolled four more cigarettes. And when they were gone, he went to the back of the shed and plucked dried grass, and shredded and rolled that into a cigarette and smoked it, but that was going a bit too far, the taste bitter and harsher than anything he had ever smoked.

What is the matter with you, Sung Wha? Are you afraid of a bad dream? Of a few insignificant birds? Are you a man or a minnow dancing between the hungry mouths of fear? If you let this thing control you, you'll never build your airplane, you'll never fly to Korea. You would let yourself be frightened by a harmless dream?

Sung Wha walking down the main street, Wahiawā town, feeling hungry and wishing he weren't so penniless. Oh, good food smells surrounding him. Cho running from behind him and tapping him on the shoulder. Happy to see each other. They embrace.

"Sung Wha, you've lost a lot of weight. You must be working hard."

Sung Wha laughs.

"You know, right after you left the barracks, the plantation dicks came again with the police and they tore up the place looking for you, but nobody said a word. You were lucky to get away safely. You remember what happened to Lee Chi Ha, right?"

"Yes."

"Look . . . I've been trying to find you, Sung Wha. We can't talk out here in the open too long before they start to suspect."

"Suspect what?"

"Listen. I spoke to that Korean minister at the church. He's willing to let us use the church to meet and conduct guerrilla training. We've already recruited a dozen men. There are perhaps a dozen more who have shown interest. The minister said he's already talked to you and that you've agreed to instruct the recruits."

"I told him I was building my airplane."

"Your airplane? What's that? Another of your dreams, Sung Wha? Listen. You're the best, Sung Wha. We all know that. You've been to China, to Manchuria. You have a lot of experience. It's for the liberation of our Motherland."

Sung Wha: *of course I'm for the liberation of the Motherland. And that's why I'm building my ricepaper airplane.* And Cho: *this Sung Wha...he has changed, I can see it in his eyes; they don't shine anymore, I wonder what's going on in his head? Why does he hesitate to volunteer?* And Sung Wha: *but if he doesn't believe that I can build an airplane, how can I have him believe of my intent to join with the revolution? Look at the way he looks at me with those eyes not meeting mine, as if I'm crazy, as if my head is not screwed on right.*

"We need your help." Cho clutches Sung Wha's arm, then releases it. "Koreans are disgusted with the way things are in Hawai'i. The Americans have lied to us. They're just as bad as the Japanese. Their promises are worth shit. And whenever one hears bad news from home, it's hard to keep calm and not run off to the next field and knock a few Japanese heads. There are even traitors among us. Imagine selling out your own kind! Did you hear what happened to Kim Kae Song?"

"Kae Sul's brother?"

"Yes. The one with the two-toed foot. He was stabbed in Honolulu for giving information to the Japanese embassy."

"But he's an honest person. I know his family well."

"Someone saw him talking to a Japanese agent in Chinatown. Some Koreans approached him later down the street, and when he refused to answer their questions one of them knifed him."

"A mistake—"

"No mistake. They found an envelope of money on him. A large sum. And a note."

There's a sepia tint to this scene: downtown Honolulu, on the outskirts of Chinatown. Wooden storefronts. This street is empty, though several streets over crowds bustle on this hot, market day Sunday, midafternoon. A man in baggy earth-colored clothes meanders down the sidewalk, his back to the POV. His name is called. He hesitates, and one of his shoes scuffs the pavement, but he doesn't look back and continues on, quickening his pace. Again: "Kae Song!" He is almost to the corner when three men dressed like him stop him from behind.

"Kae Song! You heard us call you. Where are you going so fast?"

"Going home. Time to go home."

"Made a lot of money, eh? How much did you make today?"

"And who were you talking to a little while ago?"

"It's—"

"Got a good tip to tell us?"

"Ha! Ha! Can't talk!"

"It's none of your business!"

"Ha! Ha! None of my business! Aren't you a funny man!"

"And why is your pants pocket so heavy? Eh, you must have struck it lucky today, no? C'mon, Kae Song, let's see how much you won today."

"Stop it! Get away from me! I'll call the police!"

"Call the police, eh?"

"Get away from me! Get away—"

"He barely escaped being cut to pieces. He was saved by two Hawaiian police officers who heard the traitor's cry for help."

"Then someone must go and finish him."

"Look, Sung Wha. Will you train us or not?"

No answer.

"Sung Wha . . ."

"No . . . I'm too busy."

"But what is more important than fighting for a Korea for Koreans? What has happened to you, Sung Wha?"

"I'm too busy."

Once upon a time, there lived in the forest at the bottom of Kumgangsan a poor woodcutter and his aged mother. The woodcutter enjoyed his work, which was providing fuel for the scattered villages in the area. At times he would spend days by himself deep in the forest, felling trees and chopping them to size and singing away the lonely time, but most of the time he admired the beauty of the mountain and the trees that surrounded him. Once his work was finished in the forest, he'd pile a mountain of cut wood on his A-shaped pack frame and begin his long way down to his modest hut and later to the villages where he bartered his wood with farmers for their rice and vegetables. And while he hiked slowly and carefully down from the mountains, he would wish away his loneliness and fantasize that he was coming home to a wife and a house full of children. But this was all a hopeless dream, for he was a poor man and a not so good-looking one at that; no woman would ever give him a second look.

One day, while the woodcutter worked near the roar of a waterfall, a deer came running into him. The deer was trembling terribly, for a hunter was fast on its trail.

"Please, sir," the deer pleaded, "can you hide me from this hunter who's chasing after me?"

The woodcutter, being a kindly man, quickly hid the deer behind a nearby bush. When the hunter came by with his fearless dark eyes looking every which way, the woodcutter directed him deep into the forest.

For this, the deer was very grateful.

"I must repay you for saving my life," the deer said. "Ask me for anything and I will give it to you."

The woodcutter thought and thought, and finally he decided that it would be very nice if he had a wife. With his head bowed in embarrassment, he told the deer of his loneliness.

"So you're a lonely man," the deer said. "Very well. Come with me and I'll make you lonely no more."

The deer took him a distance above the waterfall to a peaceful, misty pond, and warned him to be quiet. Nodding its head in the direction of a bush, the deer instructed the woodcutter to look through. The woodcutter carefully spread apart the leafy branches and saw, bathing in the pond, a group of angels. The woodcutter gasped, as he had never seen so many beautiful women in his life. He was so numbed by his astonishment that he fell into the bush.

"Be quiet! Be careful!" the deer chided. "You almost gave yourself away."

The woodcutter felt so foolish about his clumsiness.

"Take one of their robes hanging on the bush over there," the deer directed. "Then one of them won't be able to go back to the heavens. Take her home and she will become your wife. An angel will make a good wife and mother, but you must remember this: hide the robe well and don't let her see it until she has given you four children. She will always ask about the robe, but you must never show it to her until she has given birth to four children."

The woodcutter thanked the deer. Then quietly, with the foliage surrounding the pond hiding him, he sneaked to where the vaporlike garments were tossed over a flowering magnolia shrub. He took one and, though he could hardly feel it, folded and hid it under his shirt.

When it was time for the angels to return, all found their

robes but one. The angels searched frantically for the missing robe but could not find it. Sadly, the angels flew back to the heavens, leaving their weeping sister behind.

The woodcutter came out of hiding, the angel's gossamer garment tucked under his clothing, and took the angel home with him. Shortly after, they were married. And they were a happy couple, though often the angel asked about her robe, which the woodcutter would refuse to discuss. But the angel soon stopped talking about the robe when the couple's first baby was born. And shortly after another baby came. And later, yet another. The woodcutter's small cottage was now filled with the pitter-patter of tiny feet and the joyous laughter and cries of three small children.

One day, after a long, hard day working in the forest, the woodcutter came home and began to relax with some rice wine. One earthen cup led to many more, and soon he was very drunk. His wife suddenly brought up the subject of her missing robe.

"My! How long it has been since I've seen my robe," she lamented. "I wish it would be possible for me to see and hold it for just one last time."

The woodcutter, being in a very sentimental mood, agreed to show it to her. So he lumbered outside behind the cottage to a small shed where he stored his tools, and from under a pile of cut wood he retrieved a small chest that he had made for one purpose. From this chest, he removed the robe.

Blowing gently to rid the robe of sawdust, he presented it to his wife. She became elated. And upon touching the robe, fond memories of her wondrous life as an angel filled her with yearning. Without a word, she donned her robe and summoned her children, propping one on her back and gathering one in each arm.

"What are you doing? Where are you going?" the woodcutter asked with alarm, his mind desperately trying to clear the drunkenness.

"I'm going back to my sisters," she said softly. "They've been waiting for me for a long time. You've been very kind to me. I've been very fortunate to be with you, but I must go back now."

"But you belong here!"

"I've been very happy with you, husband, but my real home is in the heavens."

Then she carried the children outside, spread her wings, and flew into the sky.

The woodcutter was crushed. He didn't know what else to do but drink more rice wine and become more drunk and weep about his great loss and how stupid he had been.

Fortunately, one day, he ran across the deer while collecting wood. The deer scolded him after hearing his sad story.

"I told you never to show her the robe until she bore you four children. Then she never could have returned to the heavens. A mother will never leave a child behind."

"But what can I do?" the woodcutter cried.

The deer saw how miserable he was and decided to help him. The deer thought for a while, then came up with a plan. He told the woodcutter that since the incident of the stolen robe, the angels had become afraid of bathing in the pond. Now, instead of coming down to bathe, they lowered a bucket from the heavens and hoisted the water up. The deer instructed the woodcutter to wait in hiding at the pond, and when the bucket came down, to get into it.

So he waited anxiously, and when the bucket did indeed lower from the clouds and dip into the pond, he jumped out of hiding, emptied it of water, and got in. And that was how he got himself to the heavens.

With much joy, he found his beautiful wife and children, who had grown so big since the last time he saw them; and they, too, were very happy to see him. And again his life was filled with happiness.

But later, he began to worry about his mother, whom he had left to live alone. His wife felt his sadness and concern, and told him that it was possible for him to visit his mother only if he went down on a special horse. But she warned him that if he was ever to dismount and touch the ground, he would never be able to return.

Overjoyed, he took the first opportunity for a visit. He mounted the large horse, which glided down from the heavens on its wide, strong wings.

His mother was surprised and filled with pride to see her son mounted so handsomely on a beautiful horse.

"Come in!" she cried. "I've missed you so much!"

"No, mother," the woodcutter said, "I cannot stay long. And I must stay on this horse if I'm to return to my wife and children."

"But you must have at least some of your favorite pumpkin soup, which I've just made. I'll get you a bowl right now."

He smacked his lips. He had not eaten his favorite soup in a long time, since his stay in the heavens. Quickly his mother brought him a large, steaming bowl. In his hungry haste, he accidentally spilled some of the hot soup on the horse. The horse reared in pain, throwing off the clumsy woodcutter, then dashed off riderless into the clouds.

In desperation, the woodcutter sought the deer from one end of the great forest to the other but was unable to find his friend. So he spent the rest of his days weeping, his nights wasting in a drunken stupor. And whenever a new day's sun rose to remind him of his sorrows, he'd turn his head toward the heavens, crying out for his family and wishing that perhaps one day he might rejoin them. And, after a long period of time, he turned into a rooster, his dismal cries now crows to remind us all of his terrible mistakes.

There were long nights when Sung Wha could not sleep, turning from side to side on his cot, the silence of the trees and the still air outside discomforting to his ears, and the darkness becoming a stagnating, haunting medium for his thoughts to ramble in and feed on each other and himself. In the daytime, when he was more confident, he worked hard on his airplane dream, sweating out the flesh-pecking ghosts of the night before, speechless feathered ghosts whose red eyes taunted him about the nothingness of truth and dreams. And during those interminable nights when these ghosts came to life, when mild insomnia became fodder for his doubts, expanding them to monstrous proportions, he'd lose any small confidence he had accumulated from the previous day. In the morning he'd sit on his cot, thinking that perhaps dreams should remain dreams, untouchable and undisturbed. The birds had to be a bad omen. He tried to figure out how his grandmother would interpret his dreams; he could not even make a good guess.

At times Sung Wha thought himself a hapless rooster, with eyes straining at an ungiving sky in a frantic belief that perhaps the heavens might hear him and open up, and he'd be lifted to the stars where a godly messenger would grant him a dream fulfilled.

Perhaps the others were right. Perhaps he was a foolish dreamer.

Maybe it's the early morning sun that terribly blinds our eyes, wiping away instantaneously the memories. Or perhaps the jolt of waking up does it. Whatever the reason, most of the time we wake up not remembering what we dreamed; we might conclude that our sleep was unremarkable, dreamless.

But listen to this: we are always dreaming when we sleep. There's no one who doesn't. And it's not our fault if we don't remember what we've dreamed.

Question: isn't it true that all great thinkers and makers of world history were compulsive dreamers who actively applied their visions to change the world and, as a result, contributed— whether consciously or not—to the advancement of world history?

Late one night, when Sung Wha returned to the rooming house, Kekaulike Hotel (yes, that was its name and still is, THE Kekaulike Hotel, that classy hotel of long ago that had the reputation of outrageous hospitality

You haven't live in pros-pe-rity
Til you try our hospi-ta-lity
At The Kekaulike Ho-tel!

and the best Hawaiian music and *lūʻau*s. . . . The old-timers reminisced how lines of buses and taxis filled with tourists would come from Waikīkī just so the malihini could hear the fabulous *ʻukulele* players and the balmy sounds of the steel guitarists

And here he is, folks, the man you've been waiting for all evening, fresh from the taro patches of Kaha-LOO-ee, Maui, the Valley Isle's one and only Jimmy Barboza and his Uku String Band!

and be part of a traditional Hawaiian feast [with milk and sugar in the poi], all of which was made world famous by a Hollywood mongrel who had filmed a grand *lūʻau* there, a box office hit. . . . Back in those days the hotel had huge grounds, but now all the land had been divvied up by downtown developments, the only remnant being a three-story wooden structure, formerly the living quarters for the hotel workers, which was now the home of Sung Wha Kim et al.), he found blind man Eddie leaning against the wall next to his door, his chin sagging to his chest as if in sleep.

"Eddie, what you doing here dis late?"

Eddie perked up from his slumber. "Sung Wha? Is you?"

"Yeah. Is me."

"Eh, da university boy—whas his name? Troy?"

Eddie took off his dark glasses and rubbed his cloudy eyes, then directed them toward Sung Wha. Sung Wha looked away.

"Yeah-yeah, Troy."

"Da boy . . . da boy, he telling me, you not in wit' us. Eh, das not true, eh, Sung Wha?"

The still air between them informed Eddie of what he was afraid to find out.

"Sung Wha, tell me is not true."

"Eddie, you know me from way back. I live here how long.

And you know I da way I am, since . . . I cannot remembah when. YouknowwhatImean? But I kine of tired, Eddie. I one old man. I getting tired wit' no mo' one place fo' put my head down. YouknowwhatImean?"

"But whas dis, Sung Wha? What you call dis? You no call dis home? Eh, dis is yo' home and my home, too. No?"

Sung Wha nodded his head. "Yeah-yeah, dis my home, but you dunno what I mean."

"Yeah, das right. I dunno what you mean. If dis yo' home, den why?"

"Den why what?"

"Den why all dis humbug? Why you not staying in wit' us? You know we put plenny years inside dis place. Yo' life, my life, everybody's life, is in da wood of dis building, you know what I mean? We all going *maké* here, das one fact. You know dat. And all dis time we fightin' against dat damn friggin' *Pakē* fo' us stay here and now da boy say you like get out. Sung Wha, no leave us like dat. Dis is where yo' heart stay. Where my heart stay. Where everybody heart stay. You our spokesman. You know dat."

"Eddie, I old now. I tired."

"And what you think me? One young spring chicken? And I get ten years on you, fo' Chrissakes! You talk like you da oldest old fut around. How about me? I get ten years on you. And first of all, you da one was pushing us do something 'bout dis."

"I know, Eddie, I know."

"And now you like split. Not right, Sung Wha, not right. Yo' place is here wit' us."

"Eddie, is late now. Past midnight." Sung Wha glanced at his watch. It was eleven-thirteen.

"Sung Wha, no bull-lie to me. Jus' cause my eyes no work, no mean I cannot see time."

"I tired, Eddie."

"I know you tired. And I tired, too. But I cannot rest until I know where yo' head at. You no give me one solid an'sah yet. I like hear yo' an'sah."

"I tell you my an'sah in da morning."

"No. I like hear da an'sah now."

"Why?"

" 'Cause I like know if you going give up like one dirty old rat or what."

"And what if I not going give you my an'sah?" Sung Wha said.

"Den I going call you one *pilau* name I know you no deserve."

"You sonavabitch, Eddie. You one sonavabitch."

"I know. But you, too, if you one real rat. I tol' da boy dat no sound like Sung Wha he go desert us. Da buggah get mo' class den dat. Das what I tol' da boy. I wen stand up fo' you. So no make me look like one old, good-fo'-nothin' damn fool, Sung Wha."

"You sonavabitch old *kanaka*."

"Eh, no call me dat if you know whas good fo' you. You dirty Yobo, you, I kick you in yo' fuckin' *ʻōkole*."

Stern faces, turning to old-time smiles. Then laughter.

"So, you sonavabitch Yobo, whas yo' an'sah befo' I break yo' *ʻōkole*?"

"You sonavabitch, you nevah no can fight."

"I wen break yo' nose in da Y gym in '36. You no remembah dat?"

"How can I forget? Das da time I wen give you chance."

"Chance my eye."

They broke into ribbing again.

"How can I forget you, Eddie. You *pilau* buggah, my good friend. Okay . . . okay. If make you feel good I tell you my an'sah right now. I jus' was dreaming when I talking to da university boy. Da boy no can figgah out what real and what dream. How can I leave my home, eh? You tell me how?"

"Now-w-w you talking, now."

"Get outta my way so I can *moe* befo' I give you one right."

Eddie hunched down into a stiff boxing stance, feigning a right, then a left.

"Goodnight, Eddie."

Eddie dropped his arms and reached for Sung Wha's hand. They shook hands, Eddie patting Sung Wha on the back.

"I see you in da morning, Yobo. You can go *moe* now."

Eddie shuffled down the hall to the next room. Sung Wha went inside his, shut the door behind him, and began to cry silently for the first time since the last time, which he could not remember.

That night he had this dream: he is flying and the air is cold, spiked with ice, but his arms, strapped to the bamboo and ricepaper airplane, flap effortlessly, and he flies into a cloud, through it, and then out into the clear blue sky.

And there are no birds. Only he and clouds and wind and sun.

Below, the ocean is a dark, metallic blue.

And there is no fear in his heart, and his wings are strong and flexing as a heavy wind fills them. And he soars higher and higher and higher.

And he sings:

I have traveled the world on the winds
And climbed the highest mountains,
And I'm the happiest when I float on clouds
For these clouds will take me home,
They will take me home.

And I've seen many things in my life,
And now my eyes are tired and dry,
And still I fly on these clouds to home,
on these clouds to home.
For my heart has wandered enough,
And now it's time for home.

And when I'm home I'll tell my story
Of swimming the four seas and flying the seven heavens.
I have gone on many roads taken only by the tortoise,

And I've fought my battles like a tiger,
And ran on the wind like the deer.
But I've loved and cried as only a man.

Wind will take me home where I'll tell my story,
That if you dare to grab the star then nothing is hard.
But the path is rocky and painful; there is no other way.
And now I want to go home,
And now I want to go home.
And this wind will take me home,
This wind will take me home.

Troy Nishimura pulled Sung Wha over to the side. They were in the hallway outside a legislative conference room. The committee had taken a caucus.

"Mr. Kim, I think we're going to win."

"You think so?"

The organizer smiled confidently, nodding his head. "Yes. A friend of mine who works for Representative Yamada—"

"You mean 'bulldog face'?"

"Yes. Anyway, my friend told me that the committee was up all night last night. He said the committee is real worried. He thinks they're going to vote the landlord's request down. Election time is too near for them to vote against something so controversial. They know we have some support from their constituency."

"So we got one good chance?"

"Yes. We got a good chance. I'm optimistic. We're going to win."

"Das good. Now, aftah we win, we gotta make da landlord fix up da place. New plumbing. New paint. Patch up da roof."

"Well, I think we should wait a little while."

"What you mean?"

"I mean, I don't think we can push so hard all at one time. We can do only so much at a time."

"What you mean? I nevah stick wit' dis fight jus' fo' buy

some time. If we going win, we gotta go all out. Go all da way."
The boy regarded Sung Wha coolly. "I think we should do
things one at a time. Otherwise, they might take it all back and
we'll end up with nothing."

"What you mean? We get nothing already. And da reason dey
give in to us so far is not 'cause dey care 'bout us. Is 'cause we
wen fight fo' it. Right?"

"Yes . . . but we can't just take anything that we feel is ours.
The landlord does own the land, the building. What we have to
do is open up more channels for negotiations with him."

"Negotiations? You sound like . . . like . . . " Sung Wha
dropped it. He had nothing else to say. *So . . . da true colors of
dis boy come out. Dis college boy, he only talking fo' da landlord.
Thought I know dis boy. He talking in one nada language but
same-same translation. Should have seen him in his eyes. His eyes.
Should have seen him.*

The people standing in the hall began filing into the hearing
room.

"Let's get back in," Troy said. "They're reconvening."

Sung Wha remained unmoving. He shook his head, waving
the boy to go on without him. "You go. I no like listen bastards
talking dey two-face language anymo'."

Troy Nishimura nodded and went in.

Sung Wha leaned back against the wall, closing his eyes for a
few moments. When he opened his eyes, he saw blind man
Eddie standing next to him.

"Eddie, da boy said we going win."

"What boy?"

"Da university boy. Troy."

"Oh . . . him."

"But I dunno if what he said means we going win."

"What you mean?"

"Dey going vote down da rezoning, but still we gotta fight
da landlord no raise da rent again and fo' him fix up da place."

"So das not winning."

"Das what I tol' him."

Eddie straightened up. "You know," he said, adjusting his dark glasses, "I thought dis thing was going be one nada way. I nevah think we had to come down here every day and listen to dese damn crooked politicians give all dey stink lip. You know what I mean?"

"Yeah-yeah."

They were silent.

"What you think we should do, Sung Wha?" Eddie asked.

"You like know what I think we should do?" Sung Wha grinned. "Okay. Den I tell you what I think we should do. We should grab some guns and take over dis friggin' place."

Eddie chuckled. "Eh, Sung Wha, you always was one funny man. And how one blind man can shoot one gun. . . wit' his ear?"

"If can."

Eddie laughed.

"Eh, Eddie, you know me. I no think like one old man suppose to think. But you wen ask me."

"You make me laugh."

"But you know what I really like do?"

"What dat?"

"I like fly one airplane go back Korea."

"Ho! Going cost plenty *kālā*."

"No-no. I not going fly da kine airplane-airplane."

"Den what kine airplane you talking 'bout? Da kine model-kine kit?" Eddie laughed. "Cheap, dat kine. Cost only dala ninety-five. I buy 'em fo' you, and you can be yo' own airplane company president." He reached into his pants pocket and pulled it inside-out, showing it empty, then chuckled.

"I going fly my own airplane."

"Yo' own airplane?" Eddie roared with laughter. "I tell you, I nevah meet anybody as crazy as you, Sung Wha."

"I serious, Eddie. I serious. I nevah tol' you da story of my airplane befo'?"

Eddie laughed until tears streamed from his useless eyes.

"Tell me, Yong Gil, honest kine, if you think I crazy, thinking da way I think."

Why is Uncle asking me this? Once he was a proud and confident man. He went against everything, even the law and God. And now all he is . . . is a shriveled body. I never agreed with his politics, but I always respected him a lot. Maybe too much. I don't know why. He was always a man of action. Maybe that's why. When Uncle talked, people would listen.

I study Uncle's face. His eyes are closed; I don't think his eyes have been opened for the past two or three days. But his lips are always opened, just like he's ready to tell another unending story.

I wait. I listen.

There he goes, there he goes with another of his stories. But his voice is so soft now, he can only whisper, he's losing his strength. I have to put my ear close to him, almost touching his mouth. And sometimes I can't even make sense of his stories.

And now . . . there . . . he's murmuring again. He's asking me if I think he's crazy or not. No, Uncle, you're not crazy. Only crazy people think other people are crazy.

"Den, if I not crazy, den I selfish," he says. "Here I talking to you 'bout my dreams and stories, like dat, and I no let you talk. Yong Gil. I like hear yo' stories. Go . . . go tell me one good story."

But I cannot . . . my mind is empty, Uncle, I can't tell a story. That's what I tell him, and his face wrinkles at my response. He doesn't agree. I no can tell stories, Uncle, I tell him again. I only like listen to your story. A smile comes to his face.

"Yong Gil, tell me one story. I talking alla time. You know if you give me chance, I talk yo' ear off."

I agree, and add, but it's all right with me. In fact, I enjoy listening to you, Uncle; you make me feel young again, you make me live in another world, your world. It feels good listening to you because when I listen to you, I'm not sitting on this metal chair in this hospital any more, but I'm over there. Over where? he asks. Over there, I say, in the clouds, climbing Kumgangsan, punching out the *luna* on the plantation. I even have a very clear picture of how the *moksa* and his church look. I even have a few bruises from your fights.

Uncle smiles. There's pain on his tongue but he doesn't express it. He can smile with pain. He opens his mouth to say something. I wait. I wait. The next thing I hear is the sound of Uncle's heavy, slow, and irregular breathing. He's fallen asleep.

Every day his body looks worse and worse. I sit back and remember how he looked when he first entered the hospital. His hair was thicker and combed, face fuller; he could sit up on the bed. I look at this old weathered face, eyelids twitching. He's in his dream world now.

And I wish I were there, too.

With brush held firmly in hand, Sung Wha ponders for a moment over the clean, stretched-out ricepaper. He practices his calligraphy in the dusty air of the shed. Then, dipping the brush in water, he draws ink from a turtle-shaped ink stone, lathering the ink with the tip of the brush into a fine blue-blackness. He takes a deep breath, studies the surface of the ricepaper wing, brushes off a strand of hair with his free hand, then makes bold, unrelenting strokes: slashes and stems of the bamboo, curls of feisty rolling breakers, magnetic circles of sun and moon. He steps back, admires his work, then lays down another set of characters on the other end of the wing. And when he is finished, he scrutinizes his entire offering to the spirits and becomes satisfied, a smile erupting on his broad, sun-touched cheeks; he aspirates sharply, then rolls himself a cigarette. Lighting it and tossing the match away, he beams over the characters Good Luck and Long Life. Another cigarette later, when the ink has dried, he carries the wing out of the shed, where it becomes ablaze with the fire of sunset. After another cigarette, he returns it.

Tomorrow, Sunday, he'll fly the airplane. Eung Whan and Ok Soon and the entire family will be home. He'll launch the airplane after eating a large breakfast. Tonight, he'll fill bamboo tubes with water and make balls of rice for his journey home. In the morning, he'll position the airplane in front of the house where everyone can see, where the airplane can start its roll down the long hill and pick up speed, then lift off the ground and begin its heaven quest.

Outside, the sun is like a stealthy, closing eye.

He kneads the muscles of his legs. They are hard like rock, from climbing Eung Whan's hill every day and taking those long walks to Wahiawā or Waipahu at least twice a week. They are ready to work hard tomorrow, to pedal and turn the propeller that will give the airplane the needed push and lift before reaching the bottom of the slope, where the ground falls into a ravine. And his arms are strong: he flexes his biceps — left arm, right arm—they are marbled balls of power.

He boasts to the setting sun of his fine physical shape. He breathes the thinning, cooling air, his lungs expanding and releasing: *ahhh!* He walks down the hill to the edge overlooking the ravine, that treacherous drop into sharp crags and clawing *kiawe*. But he won't fall in there: the airplane will fly; it will rise above all those grabbing shadowy demons, and their outstretched hands will not touch him, and he'll be off toward the wilderness of the clouds, leaving their snarls behind, his wings filling with the auspicious spirits of the sweet wind. On his way home, Korea. *Hangguk kamnida.*

But now he notices the birds: flying low, dipping in formation into the ravine, then spiraling up over him. His heart stops. They circle above, and he can hear their laughter: they are mocking me! One bird releases a spurt of shit, which just misses Sung Wha, splattering on a rock next to him. Raised fists: "Damn birds! I'll kill you!" Then he stops himself. Isn't this an omen of good luck? He regards the birds again, now riding a brisk current higher in the sky. They seem to be staying in place.

Then they fall, one by one, and continue on their usual course, across the ravine and over and beyond the ridge, Eung Whan's field of pineapples.

A scream from the house.

Sung Wha turning. Yong Gil running down the slope toward him. *What? What is it? What——?*

"A fire! Uncle! Your airplane! A fire!"

Sung Wha dashing up to the smoking shed. The wing in flames. Fire bursting against the walls, lifting the corrugated-iron roof.

Bucket after bucket of water.

Finally, fire out. Smoke thick, suffocating. Airplane . . .

The rusty frame of the bicycle stands against the wall, untouched by the fire. Sung Wha kneels at the charred remains of the airplane, the smell of soggy charcoal.

"Tomorrow . . . tomorrow . . ."

"What did you say, Uncle?"

No answer.

"Are you going to build another airplane, Uncle Sung Wha?"

He thinks he sees Good Luck and scrambles through the warm, wet debris, but it is nothing but a spiraling thread of smoke. He orders Yong Gil out of the shed.

How did this fire start?

My cigarettes.

Damn fool!

Sung Wha grabs for the pouch of tobacco from his shirt pocket, catching the pocket and tearing it from shirt, throwing the tobacco to the ground and stomping on it. He is about to break down, his eyes moistening, when Yong Gil says, "You can always build another one, Uncle Sung Wha."

Sung Wha rubs the smoke and moisture from his eyes. "No, not like this one," he says, his head hanging. "No more dreams." Lifting his head. The clouds are motionless. The trees still, listening. Then: "You're right, Yong Gil. You're right."

"I know your airplane was going to work, Uncle Sung Wha.
I know."

"You knew it would fly, eh?" A thin smile.

Sung Wha turns and walks away. His eyes are tearing, and he
does not want the boy to see him cry.

And now everyone will laugh at me, Kim Sung Wha, the fool-
ish dreamer who thought he was going to build an airplane to scale
the heavens. I built an airplane, and I was going to have the last
say. But what can I show them now? How do I face them?

He walks down the hill, not knowing where he is going. He
just wants to get away, to be by himself. He sifts through his
pockets and finds some loose change, enough for some cheap
wine. He'll go to town and buy some wine and bring it back to
the house. He'll drink it with Eung Whan tonight. They'll trade
stories tonight—yes—of dreams, of wishes, forget the failures.
And perhaps the night will fall over him like a consoling dark
blanket, hiding grief until the night gives in to the morning sun.
And perhaps, in the morning, he'll have lost some of his gloom
to the wine, and to the stars. He'll drink whatever is left in the
bottle—if there's any—and then he'll go outside and give a
long, hard look at the bright, laughing sky.

Will the sun laugh at him? Can he forgive the sun?

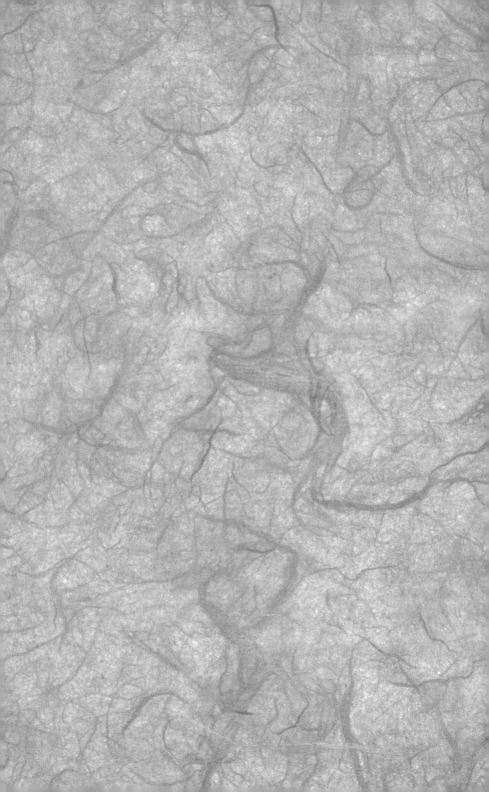

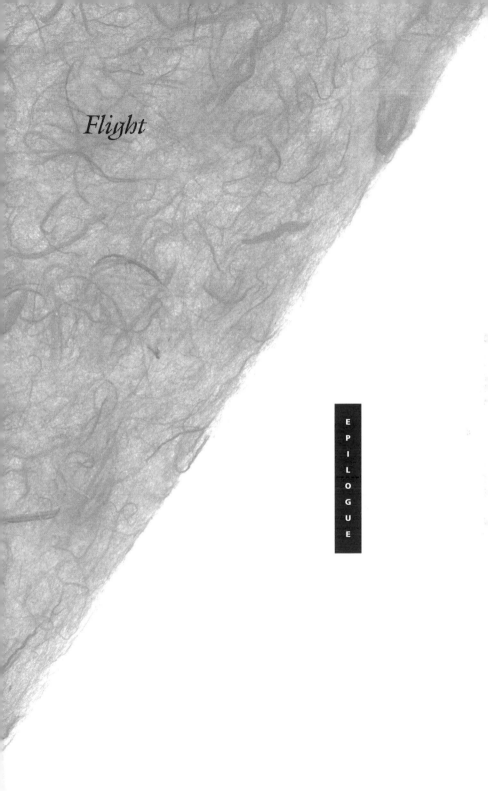

Flight

E P I L O G U E

Uncle died this afternoon. With the setting sun.

I was sitting next to him in my usual seat, and he was in the middle of another story about his life. A misfortune. A dream. One of his broken dreams. I'm not sure which one. Then there was silence. I waited, at first thinking that he was sorting out his thoughts. But he never said anything else. I waited for him to continue, for the twitching of his eyes. I watched him; his forehead was motionless and his mouth still the gray color of dying life.

Then I realized. Then I cried.

Then I cried.

That night, I flew the kite that I had made weeks before out of ricepaper and ribs of bamboo and mashed rice for paste, just the way Uncle had taught me, in preparation for this time. On the kite I drew a tiger, the one I saw entering and leaving my mind those times of story. I went to a park on top of dark Tantalus and let the kite feed off the rising wind, and I let yards and yards of line spool off the spindle, the one Uncle had made for me years and years ago. And when I could not see by the city's lights the white kite against the night anymore, because of distance and blurriness from tears, when I could not hold on to this dream anymore, I took out my pocketknife and released it to its windy journey.

And I prayed.

And I prayed.

It is so beautiful here. Cold air.
These mountains of bare rock, cold and hard rock.
And blue sky that goes on forever.
Blue sky that goes on forever.
So beautiful here. Frigid air.
Mountains of bare rock, cold and hard rock.
Clear sky that goes on forever.
Clear, wondrous sky that goes on forever.

5005